Dear Ike,

By Wendell C. Phillippi
Major General, AUS, Ret.

Published by Two-Star Press,
P.O. Box 817
Nashville, In.
47448

Dear Ike,

Copyright © 1988 by Wendell C. Phillippi

All Rights Reserved

No part of this publication created by the author may be reproduced, stored in a retrieval system, or transmitted, in any form, by any means, electronic, mechanical, photocopying, recording or otherwise, without the prior permission of the author.

ISBN 0-9630859-0-5

Library of Congress TXU 321 577

Mailing address:
Two-Star Press
P.O. Box 817
Nashville, In.
47448

FIRST EDITION
Printed in the United States, 1991.
Graphics LTD,
Indianapolis, In.

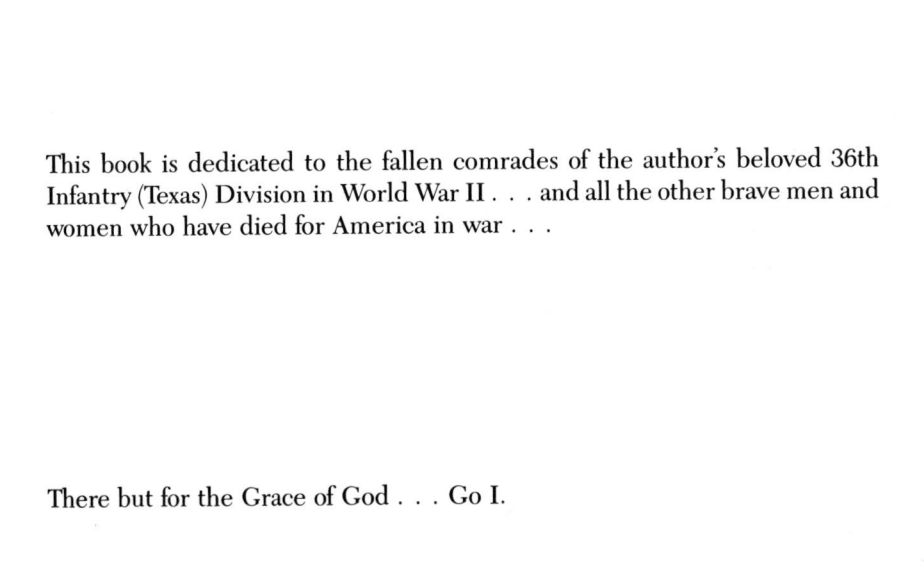

This book is dedicated to the fallen comrades of the author's beloved 36th Infantry (Texas) Division in World War II . . . and all the other brave men and women who have died for America in war . . .

There but for the Grace of God . . . Go I.

Howitzer Year Book, West Point Military Academy.

All of the Eisenhower brothers were called Ike. There was "Little Ike," "Big Ike," but usually just all called Ike. It was short reference to last name. U.S. Army photo.

CONTENTS

Foreword by Robert H. Ferrell

Prologue

Cast of Characters (Battle Order)

Dear Ike letters with the general's replies
1. George C. Marshall 1
2. George S. Patton, Jr. 19
3. Erwin Rommel 35
4. Kay Summersby 41
5. Charles de Gaulle 57
6. Franklin D. Roosevelt 65
7. Harry S. Truman 75
8. Winston S. Churchill 83
9. Douglas A. MacArthur 113
10. Omar N. Bradley 125
11. Bernard Law Montgomery 137
12. Harold Alexander 153
13. William H. Simpson 163
14. Mark Wayne Clark 173
15. Courtney H. Hodges 193
16. Jacob L. Devers 201
17. Alexander M. Patch 209

Epilogue (Quiet Resolve) 221

Notes: They include several detailed reports to enhance the
historical information involved in certain letters. 233

Addenda:
A. Original questionnaires answered by some of Ike's
commanders to the author. 249
B. Article: Why Ike Didn't Take Berlin? 255
C. Draftee to Stars 261

Credits 265

Bibliography 267

Index 271

Photographs and Illustrations

Eisenhower v
Ike, Kay, Bradley 44
Clark, Kay, Ike 47
Kay's family manor, County Cork, Ireland 54
Eisenhower Command 66
Ike, NATO Cammander 116
Command Structure, Italian Campaign 156
Bill Mauldin Cartoon (autographed) 182
Ike and Kay, N. Africa 207
President Eisenhower 219

Abbreviations on Pictures
AP — Associated Press
UPI — United Press International

Maps

North Africa Invasion 3
Sicily Invasion 20
Saar-Palatinate Triangle 62
Germany, Redoubt Area 80
Tunisia, The Final Battle 129
D-Day, Normandy, France 130
Italy 155
Germany, Pushes from East and West 169
Salerno, Italy - Invasion 179
Battle of the Bulge 195
French Riviera Invasion 213

FOREWORD

By Robert H. Ferrell, Author and Distinguished Professor of History, Indiana University.

Wendell Phillippi looks at World War II with a remarkable perspective, and this is the value of his book. He began as a private and ended as a major. He was an officer in the 2d Battalion, 143d Infantry, 36th Division, and outlasted all the other officers in the battalion. He fought in Italy, France and Germany. In this respect, then, he saw the war "as it was," not from the point of observation of service troops or rear-echelon headquarters but out in the open where people were shooting other people. He participated in two especially dangerous actions at Salerno and on the Rapido. He was nearly captured at Salerno when an incompetent corps commander exposed his battalion.

Before and after the war, Phillippi was a newspaperman, but after the experience in World War II, he found himself fascinated by military affairs. Memories would not let go, and he virtually devoted his non-working hours to the military, rising in the Indiana National Guard to the rank of major general, in command of the 38th (National Guard) Division. All the while he read the books that drew the war's strategy as well as tactics and sought to understand what had happened — what the cataclysmic forces had been that disrupted his young life and those of millions of other young men not merely in the United States. The tragedy of those awful years, 1939-1945, was ever with him; he could not forget it.

And so from experience, and from postwar participation including a reading of the memoirs and biographies and histories, he has written the pages that follow.

The accounting is in part fictitious. The letters are only literary devices to carry the feelings and actions of wartime leaders, military and civil. The purpose is to surmount the detail, the diplomatic explanations, the half-truths that marked the literary explanations. Consider, for example, the papers of Dwight D. Eisenhower, now being published; they comprise hundreds of memos and letters, and only a specialist can hope to go through them. Perhaps a dozen books have appeared on George S. Patton. As for the statesmen, Winston Churchill became a book machine in the years of his retirement, and produced his books with the aid of several machinists — more books than the average person can read. His official biographers are bringing out perhaps ten more books. Wendell Phillippi has gathered all this random production, and focused it.

In the business of divining what the high command was up to, General Phillippi has had the advantage of a long-lasting friendship with the late General Mark W. Clark. The erstwhile officer enjoyed correspondence and conversations with his erstwhile commander in Italy. The result is apparent in some of the sketches below.

Two generations, almost, have come to manhood, and womanhood, since the times about which Phillippi writes, and our generation is itself coming to an end — not all of "the boys" are around today, and the survivors are beginning to move off the scene with appalling rapidity. In our youth, we occasionally saw Civil War veterans, who indeed were relics, perhaps sitting in an open car during parades, wearing their little smashed-down (they seemed) hats, sightless eyes staring proudly ahead. We beheld the Spanish-American War veterans, survivors of a three-month frolic in Cuba, Puerto Rico, and the Philippines, middle-aged men whose martial exploits meant nothing to us. The individuals with whom we were, to be sure, much closer were our fathers, veterans of World War I, who sometimes sought to explain their experiences but only confused us with the jungle of battlefield names, all in French. The time then came for our experiences, far more serious and long-lasting. And now the later generations are forgetting them, just as we did; young eyes glaze over as we seek to recite what war was like two generations ago.

Our era nonetheless has much to relate to our children and grandchildren, and this is the burden of Phillippi's fine book.

September, 1991.

Dear Ike,

Prologue

This is a book of fiction based on historical facts. It is a commentary on the "greats" and "near greats" of World War II in the European theater as a green, mostly civilian Army with many inexperienced leaders invaded North Africa, Sicily, Italy and finally catapulted into the main effort at Normandy in France for the biggest invasion of all time.

Most of the troops were under the leadership of Gen. Dwight David Eisenhower, supreme commander of the forces of the nations which fought in the crusade for freedom, from 1942 until V-E Victory in Europe Day in May, 1945.

This book includes comments on World War II, remarks that emerge from my participation in the war as a junior infantry officer and my 22 active and reserve years in the Army from a private to major general. It includes my 40 years of reflection and inquiry on the conflict and a study of the massive struggle. The book incorporates my personal experiences and observations as well as my research. I have chosen what I think is important, interesting and curious.

The volume contains imaginary letters, based on historic facts, addressed to "Dear Ike,". The letters express thoughts which the commanders might have had voicing their successes, complaints, fears, admiration, and military strategy.

In turn, Ike replies with comments suitable to a command conference or a maneuver critique. It also will cover letters from other leaders who were allied with Ike during his tenure as boss.

Interwoven in this report are a series of items regarding Ike's close relationship with the English lass, Kay Summersby, who performed the roles of driver, secretary, aide, confidante, and bridge partner. By the nature of her job she became a constant companion. Circumspectly, most of Ike's inner circle of associates have denied an intimate relationship between Ike and Kay, but other private comments are included here.

How close did Ike come to leaving Mamie and marrying Kay? The reader may make a judgment after reading the many references to Ike and Kay in the book and from a summary of the letters Ike wrote Mamie during the war — her bitterness shows. Actually the family publication of the letters was almost counter productive.

Countless generals, presidents, and other dignitaries have enjoyed the company of women other than their wives. After the war, one of Ike's aides, with a twinkle in his eye, bragged to this writer that Ike was pursued by many of the glamorous movie stars who entertained the troops overseas.

Ike enjoyed the intelligence and wit of Prime Minister Winston Churchill, of England, probably the greatest leader of the first half of the 20th century. Winnie was a great strategist (even they make mistakes) and idea man.

Churchill reciprocated Ike's respect and was eager to share the renowned Ultra Intelligence information the British provided about secret German plans. Such intelligence was often hard to obtain and it certainly failed at Kasserine Pass, the British airborne failure at Arnhem, and the Battle of the Bulge.

Several times Ike was on the brink of resignation. British Field Marshal Montgomery was a frustrating figure, implying that his military strategy was beyond criticism. He held many press conferences, indicating that he was running and winning the war single-handedly.

Ike mingled with the high and mighty. Besides Churchill, his own commander-in-chief, President Roosevelt, valued his ability sufficiently to name him the leader of the troops into Normandy. Gen. Marshall, his immediate superior, concurred in the decision. Gen. Charles de Gaulle, of France, had great respect for Ike, as did Gen. George Patton (the man with the salty language) and Gen. Omar Bradley, often called the soldier's soldier. British Field Marshal Montgomery, who in Ike's opinion was self-aggrandizing, frequently did not perform up to Ike's expectations. Other associates were Gen. Courtney Hodges, quiet and able, colorful Gen. Jacob Devers, who could work with the British and French better than most American generals, Gen. Alexander Patch, who escaped from Gen. Douglas MacArthur's command in the Pacific to lead an army in southern France, Gen. William Simpson, who was often on loan to and even got along with the crusty, martinet Montgomery, Gen. Mark Clark, who told Marshall Ike was No. 1, and likeable, capable British Gen. Harold Alexander.

The book does not attempt to cover the great efforts of the other military services and the supporting help, including workers in the defense plants who made the weapons and ammo, or the farmers who fed the soldiers along with so many valiant and sacrificing deeds of other people in all walks of American life in World War II.

Likewise there is no effort to cover the Pacific war but the role of Gen. Douglas MacArthur is covered as it relates to Ike and other persons who are writing the letters.

This Army book then is a capsule of some of the big and little events in World War II in Europe as they involved "Dear Ike,".

WENDELL C. PHILLIPPI

Battle Order

Here is the cast of characters in **Dear Ike,**

Two United States Presidents, Franklin D. Roosevelt and Harry S. Truman, were the commanders in chief of American forces during World War II.

Winston Spencer Churchill was prime minister of Great Britain. His Chief of Staff was Sir Alan Brooke.

German Gen. Erwin Rommel commanded the Afrika Korps in the defeat of the British in North Africa. He went from personal bodyguard of Adolf Hitler, German war dicator, to one of his country's most famous Blitzkrieg generals with the tag Desert Fox. Rommel later commanded the German defense forces when the Allies invaded France at Normandy.

French General Charles de Gaulle was a French colonel when the Germans overran France in 1940. He became the leader of the Free French in exile in England and then in North Africa and France. He was President of France twice.

Gen. George Marshall was Army Chief of Staff and gave the military direction to Gen. Dwight D. Eisenhower, Supreme Allied Commander in Europe.

Ike's team included:

Gen. George S. Patton, Jr., landed at Casblanca, later commanded II Corps at Kasserine Pass, then Seventh Army in Sicily and Third Army in France and Germany.

Gen. Omar N. Bradley replaced Patton in North Africa and led American forces in the liberation of Tunisia. He served under Patton in Sicily and then was named top commander of U.S. forces for the invasion of Normandy. He later became 12th Army Group commander with the First, Third, Ninth armies.

Gen. Mark Wayne Clark was deputy to Eisenhower in North Africa and then became commander of the Fifth Army in the invasion of Italy and later 15th Army Group commander in charge of all Allied ground forces in Italy.

Kay Summersby, an English citizen, became the driver for Eisenhower when he went to England and stayed with him as chauffeur, secretary who could not type, receptionist and constant companion. She got a commission in the American Army during the war and later her U.S. citizenship under Ike's sponsorship.

Gen. Harold Alexander was in charge of British Forces in North Africa when Field Marshall Bernard Law Montgomery struck west at El Alamein to put the Germans under Rommel to flight. He controlled the invasion of Sicily and then commanded all British and U.S. troops in Italy when Eisenhower went to London to plan the Normandy invasion. Montgomery after the conquest of North Africa alongside French and American troops took the British 8th Army into Sicily. He crossed the straits of Messina into the toe and heel of Italy. He took command of all invasion forces at Normandy and then control of only British and Canadian forces when Ike assumed ground command in France.

Gen. Courtney Hodges was deputy to Bradley at Normandy, then First Army commander when Bradley became a group commander.

Gen. William H. Simpson commanded the Ninth Army which invested the Brittany peninsula and then fought under Montgomery in northern France reverting to Bradley's control near the end of the war.

Gen. Jacob L. Devers had a variety of command assignments in London and North Africa including support of the Italian operation. After the invasion of southern France he took control of the American Seventh Army (Gen. Alexander Patch in command) and the Free French Forces as 6th Army Group Commander.

Gen. Douglas MacArthur was Army commander in the Southwest Pacific whom Eisenhower had served under in Washington when he was Chief of Staff and in the Philippines before World War II.

Letter 1

George C. Marshall.
U.S. Army photo.

IKE VS. MARSHALL

Over the years since World War II historians have debated the relationship between George C. Marshall, Army Chief of Staff and former Secretary of State, and his protege, General Dwight D. Eisenhower, Supreme Allied Commander in Europe, and 34th President of the United States.

A personal associate of Eisenhower talked with the author about the relationship in an interview in February, 1987. Ann Whitman, secretary to the President in the White House years, said that Gen. Marshall was the man that Ike respected the most of all the leaders he knew or had worked with. She added that Marshall was held in great admiration and reverence by Eisenhower. She never heard him called anything but "General" in all of the years she knew and worked for him.

With that insight here follows the Marshall letter to Ike and his reply. Read and decide for yourself about the Ike-Marshall relationship over the years.

Marshall — FDR Said Stay

Dear Ike,

I was a general, diplomat, and duty-bound American. It was through my influence that you were named Supreme Allied Commander at Normandy, although I had always secretly hoped that I would get the assignment of leading the Allied Expeditionary Forces into Europe. Gen. John J. Pershing, hero of World War I, wanted me to do the job and have the recognition of being THE battlefield commander of World War II.

President Roosevelt and Congress, however, wanted me to stay in Washington and mastermind the entire war effort. I did not ask for the Normandy invasion command. By the time that decision was to be made, you were the number one American leader in the Mediterranean. Also you were the idol of the British, some of whom hoped that, because of rank, an Englishman might be chosen.

After I learned at the Cairo meeting in December, 1943, that you would head the invasion I was certainly disappointed. In fact I was mad. Mad enough not to come back home with FDR and the American team. Perhaps I was also mad at myself for not asking FDR for the assignment. Instead I grabbed up a couple of assistants, and we flew east to my "other war" in the Pacific. There I had a chance to confer with Gen. MacArthur and other commanders and to view first hand what was going on, learn of supply deficiencies, and find out the problems a good commander needs to know about his areas of responsibility. I arrived back in Washington with a lot of new information and with no harm done. I was ready for the drudgery that lay ahead as FDR's right-hand man. Little did I know or think of the many awesome decisions I would have to make. You can at least say that I supported you without rancor and with effectiveness and loyalty.

As I reflect on our careers, just what did we do that justified the publicity and credit for building up the nation — physically and mentally — to face the challenges of World War II? We then molded our forces into victory.

Was it my role to be the military medium for Roosevelt and Churchill?

Was it my destiny to be the leader of both the British and American chiefs of staff, to direct the war on two fronts at the same time — both separated by thousands and thousands of miles of water, enemy airplanes, physical obstacles, petty bickering and on and on?

How did I select Dwight D. Eisenhower as the star of the future? Were you destined to be President? It is true that you learned under the masters of military science on the American front — Krueger, Stilwell, Connor, MacArthur, McNair, and Pershing. And yours truly?

When the headlines in the early months after the Pearl Harbor attack read:

75,000 Graduates

A Week in OCS

How did it all happen?

How did we get from practically no army to a huge army?

(The vote to extend the draft and call-up of the National Guard and Reserves barely passed the House of Representatives, 203 to 202 in September, 1941.[1])

How did we equip and supply it?

How did we find the regimental, division, squadron, group, flag, corps, task force and army commanders worthy of the tasks ahead?

How did we overcome the political and financial bickering on the home front?

How did we build the atomic bomb in secret so quickly?

How did we rally the industrial might of America?

How did all the civilians make the sacrifices to make sure our troops were adequately supplied and fed?

Or, for that matter, how did we finally find a bazooka which would knock out an enemy tank? Or adequate anti-aircraft weapons for our sailors to defend their ships?

The material list goes on and on.

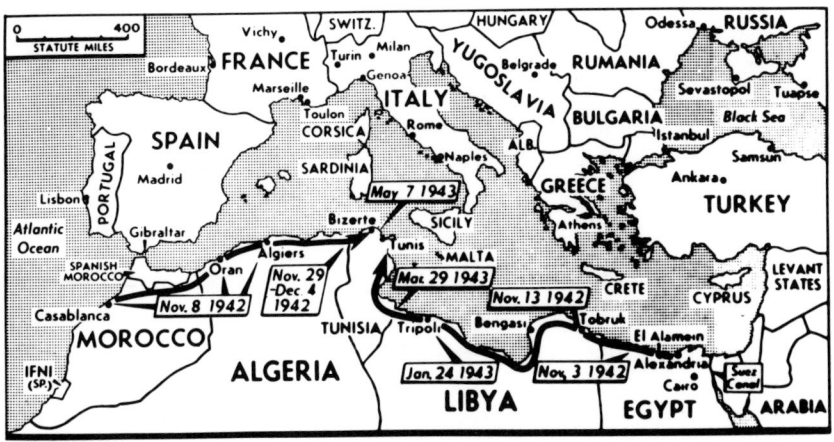

General Eisenhower became known when he led the Allied forces into North Africa. British General Montgomery started his drive to defeat Rommel October 23, 1942. AP map.

Even more important, how did we appeal to the American people to join the ranks of cadre and often lethargic forces, the Army and the Navy, to build these into fighting teams?

All of these things come to mind, but with patience, understanding and a win attitude we overcame the obstacles. The American Firsters wanted to stay home and refrain from involvement in foreign wars — but think of the hundreds of places we've been involved in ever since.

To offer a simple answer one can look at the educational and intelligence level of the American man. We started the draft just at the time the college boom was with us — mild compared to the postwar boom, but we were coming out of the depression and more people could afford a college education for their kids. Part-time jobs for college students came into being whereas, formerly, only the affluent could afford advance educational training.

All of this education paid off on the battlefields and in the sea and air. From foxholes to air attacks without adequate defense, the quality of our weapons improved and we became more mobile and resourceful in our offense and defense. The lowly G.I. was still down there fighting in the battle zone, the sailor was manning and firing from his station, the lonely pilot was dodging flack and firing at big and little targets. It is often easy for the brass to forget the work and sacrifices of that little guy out there who won the war. The rest of us were necessary but that GI really won the war going away.

I was not a West Pointer (Virginia Military Institute) as you know. But I did reach the military pinnacle despite Gen. Douglas MacArthur. As Army chief of staff, he tried to hold me to a lesser position as a National Guard instructor in Illinois. This might have been at the request of an influential Chicago banker, Charles Dawes, vice-president under President Calvin Coolidge. In World War I, I conducted the massive move of American troops to gain the final victory in the Meuse-Argonne campaign. This put "kaput" to the German Kaiser and his forces.

When I had a chance to cut MacArthur "to the quick," I did not even discredit him publicly. Actually I praised his efforts and accomplishments in the Pacific war and in Korea. But when he tried to run the Korean War and U.S. policies in the Far East without the approval of his commander in chief, President Harry Truman, his usefulness came to an end.

I spent five years as a special assistant to Gen. Pershing. I not only learned a lot but was priviledged to travel in the stratosphere of the

Army's top generals, the Presidential staff members and civilian movers. I came to know President Warren G. Harding, his Secretary of Commerce, Herbert Hoover, later President, Financier Bernard Baruch, and many others. Then it was at Ft. Benning where I refused to conform to the school solution theory that became: "Why don't you let the thing alone instead of stirring things up."[2] At Benning I found many of the future leaders of our Army in World War II. Next I had a regimental command and a stay in China. I later gained much valuable experience by directing the famous and useful Civilian Conservation Corps. This organization provided jobs and good training for many young Americans out of work and also improved the conservation efforts of our nation greatly.[3] In this capacity I became well acquainted with many civilian military leaders and people involved in government operations. They included Harry Hopkins, who, early on, had FDR's ear.[4] Afterwards I served in the War Plans Division and then deputy Chief of Staff. There was a lot of competition among the high-ranking generals, but FDR named me chief. At one time I thought I had lost the possibility of this job because of a conference with the President and some of his yes men who were discussing aircraft productions. After they agreed to FDR's idea of the Works Progress Administration building plants on Army reservations I told him I disagreed. He then agreed with me. Actually it may have impressed FDR more than I thought. On September 1, 1939, at 58 I was named Army Chief of Staff — the day that Germany invaded Poland and World War II began.

My personal life was not without tragedy. My first wife was unable to have children and my second wife's son was killed on the road to Rome in 1944. I had to tell her.

After the war I handed over the job of Army Chief of Staff and its headaches to you. A few hours later, happily anticipating retirement to my Virginia home, President Truman requested that I go to China to negotiate a peace settlement between the Nationalist and Communist forces. I said, "Yes, sir," without even consulting my wife. My devotion to duty and my country was endless.

As you know the final selection of army group, army and corps commanders was essentially mine, having observed and served with most of them for many years. I passed along some who fouled up in battle later, but most were good. When you recommended a promotion for Col. James Van Fleet I balked. My memory had him confused with another Van Vliet who was a problem drinker. You were right in changing my mind or in clarifying the situation because Col. Van Fleet became a good division and corps commander. He later headed our mission to Greece which saved that country from Communist conquest shortly after the war. He served with distinction as commander of the Eighth Army in Korea. We can all make mistakes, and we did, but we still came out on top.

My career continued many years after leaving the Army. I was Secretary of State and Secretary of Defense — both consuming jobs. At State one proud accomplishment was the Marshall plan which rehabilitated Europe. The people were fed and the economy, which we fought so hard to destroy, was revitalized. I picked up a Nobel prize for that one! I hope history records that although I didn't get command in Normandy, I always did my best for my country. You were a great leader, a diplomat to unify the Allied war effort.

You were strong enough to speak up to Churchill and other Allied leaders at the right moment and with the right decisions most of the time. You sometimes became angry but you always "played it cool" in the big decisions that had to be made. Delaying D-Day for 24 hours because of bad weather was a difficult but brilliant decision.

I overlooked the rumors and gossip pertaining to your constant companionship with Kay Summersby, the good-looking English lass, who was promoted from driver, private secretary and finally to a captain in the American WACS. Many criticized your relationship, but in my opinion she ranks in the Hall of Fame as one of those who helped you so much professionally and personally.

My only regret is that I didn't get to enjoy your company after the war for any length of time. I would like to have talked to you of your many achievements. Of course, there were some unpleasant things we could have discussed. Why, when you were a Presidential candidate, did you not defend my ability, courage and honor when Senators Joseph McCarthy and William Jenner vilified me over and over? Was it because I was Truman's man? In your desire for the Presidency, did you forget your old friend and mentor? You would have won the election without appeasing those senators.

I guess I'll never know because history doesn't . . .

George Catlett Marshall.

Author's note: Gen. Marshall once told his wife he was almost afraid to speak his opinions to President Truman because he took his recommendations so readily. He was one of those straight arrow generals and he worked for what was right rarely agreeing to a compromise. That is not to say he didn't evaluate every possibility. One of his great characteristics was that of a good listener. When he spoke it was with a decisive voice. He had a great knack of retention and will always be remembered as the commander who required that everything be reduced to one comprehensive cover page. He said if you couldn't do that you probably didn't know what you were talking about. The world leaders could well follow his example of one page nowadays so the common people would understand issues more readily. This attitude brings to mind President Kennedy, who said if you make a speech longer than 15 minutes you are likely to lose your audience and be an ineffective speaker. Politicos could follow that pattern to advantage now also.

In addition to Ike and all the famous war leaders, Marshall also left a trail of proteges who influenced the country for a long time:

Gen. Omar Bradley, first peacetime chairman of the Joint Chiefs of Staff.

Gen. Max Taylor, the general who became a close advisor to Kennedy and was an architect of the Vietnam war. (It is unlikely that Marshall would ever have sided with the warlords there who failed us so miserably.)

Airborne Gen. James Gavin, ambassador to France under Kennedy, and an expert research technology executive.

Maj. Gen. Troy Middleton, president of Louisiana State University.

Gen. J. Lawton Collins, Army Chief of Staff, and later vice-president of the Industrial Division, Pfizer Co.

Gen. Mark Clark, U.S. Far East commander and commander of the United Nations forces Korea and later president of the Citadel.

Maj. Gen. Ernest (gravel voice) Harmon, president of Norwich University.

★ ★ ★ ★ ★

"Vicious Attack"

Queen Frederika, of Greece, was a constant correspondent with Marshall. She was always seeking his advice on how to improve relations with America and seeking whatever help she could get for her country. As time went on Marshall wrote:

"Important groups of the Republican Party are extremely hostile to me in their pre-election endeavor (March, 1956) to tear down everything the Democratic Administration did, and are now attacking foreign relief assistance . . . You may not be aware of the fact that I have been more viciously attacked than any other public figure in this generation.

"In view of these conditions, I fear that my assistance . . . would concentrate a bitter and hostile press attack."[5]

The new Ike administration did seem gleeful in its exposure of the Truman era, although history has certainly reversed the trend both in respect to the man and his achievements.

Marshall, of course, never seriously considered any political boomlets. They also occurred for Clark, Bradley and MacArthur. Only MacArthur took them seriously and never lost his contacts with various congressmen or influential Americans in his political toe testing. He got 3 delegates from the Wisconsin primary in 1944 and one vote at the National Republican convention in '48. In the end he realized it was better to steer his empire in Japan and the Far East rather than get into the mainstream of the American Republic.

"Brass WACS"

Gen. Marshall never got involved very much into the Kay Summersby affair. Some historians have written about a letter allegedly received from Ike about divorcing Mamie in order to marry Kay. None of the historians have uncovered such a letter though it is referred to later in the book by Margaret Truman among others. It is interesting to note that Ike's headquarters put Kay in for the Legion of Merit (American) and it was turned down.[6] Of course this much abused and overly used award would not have been appropriate in any case. Most of the Kay involvement centered around the Army GI (personnel) and Brig. Gen. Frank McCarthy, who was on Marshall's staff and later became a famous movie producer (Patton).

However, the initial refusal of an Army commission for Kay is confusing to say the least. The first request was turned down because she was not an American citizen and a member of the U.S. Women's Army corps. She then flew to America on an Ike plane to try and get her commission and the citizenship arranged. It was not until later with the personal intervention of Ike, obviously, that she got the commission and citizenship. Marshall's office was a bit confused on this matter because he had allowed three Australian gals to become WACs in the Pacific theater earlier. It took the personal intervention of MacArthur to get the commissions.[7] According to one report one of the gals was secretary to his deputy, Gen. Sutherland, and maybe a little more. MacArthur ordered her out of his headquarters.[8] It would be interesting to find out why "yes" in one case and "no" in the other, initially. And to think that MacArthur got his request when he was way below the Marshall favorites. War is a funny game. It should also be noted that MacArthur, despite his earlier efforts to hold back on Marshall's progress on the ladder, got his five-star date of rank two days before Ike's. Marshall's was two days before MacArthur's. Of course MacArthur was a favorite of Congress also and some powerful chairman or committeeman just saw to it that the dates went in that order.

Vinegar Joe "Go"

Gen. Joseph W. Stilwell, who was in early contention for the No. 1 ground commander in Europe in World War II, ended up being shanghaied to China. But not on purpose. He led the list of top corps commanders as the day approached when American troops would land somewhere in the European area. Actually it was a proposed operation (our first) at Dakar, North Africa, the shortest distance to support on sea and in the air. It would have given America a toehold to move against Hitler and Mussolini. While the planning was going on (the operation was finally scratched), President Roosevelt and Winston Churchill conferred about the fate of China, which had been under years of attack and part occupation by the Japanese.

FDR wanted to support Chiang Kai-shek and Winnie was lukewarm. As a result Great Britain was glad to turn over China to the U.S. and continue its main interests in India, Burma, Thailand, and those areas of the Far East it had been involved with for a long time. Stilwell had done duty in China and other places in the Far East and knew the language. Henry L. Stimson, Secretary of War, and Gen. Marshall, Army chief of staff, finally assigned the China task to Vinegar Joe. He never wanted or volunteered for it but said he would go if he was ordered. He was so ordered. To send him into the turmoil and confusion of an American Chief of Staff for the Chinese army may have been a massive blunder, but Stilwell did his job as best he could. He had only American air troops and no ground forces except for the Chinese units. The air force consisted mainly of the Flying Tigers, under the command of Maj. Gen. Claire Chennault, who had become the American darling of Chiang and Madame Kai-Shek.

So Stilwell, who might have gotten the North Africa command, was left with a thankless job for most of the war with lots of special envoys, intrigue, confusion and a divided, chaotic, and corrupt China. Stilwell finally got command of the Tenth Army in June, 1945, on Okinawa when Lt. Gen. Simon B. Buckner, Jr. was killed. He was not MacArthur's choice. So with the end of the war nearing, Vinegar Joe never got to use his great tactical potential.

How did he get the name Vinegar Joe? Stilwell could be acid, and after one of his famous chewings of a student officer at Ft. Benning, Ga., the victim went back to the barracks and drew a caricature of Stilwell "with a none-too-benevolent expression rising out of a vinegar bottle with three X's on the label."[9]

The picture went on the bulletin board and became well known on the post. Stilwell heard about it and got the original to frame and made copies to send to his friends.

His vinegar emerged in China and he often referred to Chiang Kai-shek as "peanut."

Actually Stilwell never has received adequate credit for his remodeling of American battle tactics from trench, semi-static warfare to fire and movement.[10] Thus was born fire and movement in the U.S. Army, which was becoming the way of other modern armies. The Germans get credit for the switch from trench war to modern day tactics (before potential space electronic, computer warfare, that is) which included the development of airplanes and tanks for the battlefield. When the Germans were stalemated after the battles of the Somme and Verdun in 1916, the men and officers of the German Army analyzed their battle tactics and modified their basic techniques to include infiltration, surprise, massive gas and high explosive shells aimed at artillery postions. Then came the rolling artillery attacks with troops following as the fire moved forward. All of this soon included planes and tanks to speed the maneuver. It erroneously became known as the Hutier tactics for Gen. Oskar von Hutier, victor of an attack against Riga in 1917. Authorship of the new technique lay "more properly with the men and officers throughout the German Army."[11] This tactic applied to organized units on all levels and is not to be confused with guerrilla warfare, which has been employed for centuries.

Vinegar Joe left his X mark indelibly in American history.

IKE SAYS:

Dear General Marshall,

You were THE American leader — executive agent for the Allied Chiefs of Staff and unelected assistant president — as America waged a two-front global war after the Japanese struck at Pearl Harbor in 1941 until the final victory days in 1945. Almost as important, though, you became chief of Army chief of staff at the age of 58 on September 1, 1939, when Germany invaded Poland to start World War II. You had to mobilize a poorly equipped, poorly housed and poorly trained army of less than 200,000 regulars. Our nation tried, in a meager way, to provide a little more than sympathy in support of our allies who were trying to stand up, finally, to the obstreperous Germans and Japs. Your genius will be forever for future generations to study the way America makes war — out of love for peace and freedom, not for spite or revenge. It is difficult for many people in the world to understand our American attitude in waging war — to free those enslaved by tyrants as we once freed ourselves in 1776. You understood why we waged World War II. And so did I.

After your brilliant maneuvering of troops in World War I under Gen. Pershing, you came home only to see the Army demobilized, ranks reduced in the interest of economy. I had stayed home directing the tank training corps at Camp Colt in Gettysburg, Pa. It was tough for me not to get to do what I had been trained for all of my military life — lead troops in battle. So many of my fellow officers did gain battle experience.

The American army had made the difference in the War I stalemate and without our efforts the Germans might have been victorious. But victory was one thing, peace was another. People had "no stomach" for a large standing army. Your dream of a citizens army in the wings did get off the ground and you had a meager National Guard and reserve force — poorly equipped, and often without leadership, which meant inadequate training. At least the active Army was busy with these units in an advisory capacity.

Along the way you kept a little book of potential leaders. Most of us came from your ready reference.

By some miracle you overcame all the handicaps and obstacles. Having had experience in high places although MacArthur sidelined you in Illinois for a while as a National Guard advisor, you went to the top.

We all watched, unbelievingly, as Adolf Hitler, "The Horrible" dismantled the Versailles-Wilson peace treaty and overran Poland. We had no resistance offered as he gobbled up Austria, Czechoslovakia and signed the Axis pact with Italy and Mussolini, another tyrant. After he invaded France, we sat idly by in awe and disbelief as Britian stood alone. Little did we realize that soon Hitler would head for Russia.

The Nazi dictator had been allowed to expand his Germanic nation in every direction. He used the excuse that he needed more room, more resources, more men, more women, more babies, new and more arms to defend his nation. He said that many of the countries belonged to Germany. Little did the general public (and some military leaders) know or appreciate the techniques he was developing in the air, on the ground and at sea. He was enrolling a huge army and would soon again be a menace with submarines which had been so successful for his nation only a quarter century before. His new Blitzkrieg developed the employment of combined arms more effectively than mankind had ever known. He knew what he wanted and got it. But you saw the problem developing and had great influence with President Roosevelt as well as other government and civilian leaders in America. You did what you could to aid our British and French allies, which at first was not much. But preparedness was the name of the game and you were ready for mobilization — in part from your experience with the development of the Civilian Conservation Corps, the Guard and Reserve elements. Your goal was to build a team for war when it came as many of us knew it would.

With your guidance, I soon found myself at the head of the crusade from North Africa (at 52) to Normandy, to Paris, the Rhine and Elbe rivers. There we met our likewise victorious Russian ally, who defended his homeland with great sacrifice, and then drove to victory in Berlin to meet us after suffering millions of dead. Along the way the Russians inflicted two-thirds of the casualties on our common enemy, Germany.

Yours was a great talent for selecting the right men for the right tasks in most cases for planning and fighting a two-front war in the Pacific and Atlantic sides of America. You gave me a few bad generals who had the rank but not the talent to fight divisions and corps. I know you were disappointed in my defeats at Kasserine Pass and the Battle of the Bulge but I would like to point out that I had a share of victories, including:

An early peace with the French military and political leaders in North Africa after our invasions at Casablanca, Oran and Algiers. We failed to move effectively to conquer Tunisia but the reluctance by the French to surrender, British delay, and the weather combined to thwart our efforts. After we got there the Germans took advantage of our weaknesses. We suffered a setback at Kasserine Pass when our green but gallant troops had to fight the Germans with inadequate anti-tank weapons and a failure in leadership. We made sure that Spanish Morocco was neutralized so no military or civilian spies and saboteurs could use that route to disrupt our battle, occupation and training plans. These accomplishments seem to have been forgotten.

My experience as commander of combined army, naval and air forces in North Africa gave knowledge for even bigger operations.

I reduced the enemy air and naval base at Pantelleria in the Mediterranean in three weeks without losing a man on the ground. We destroyed the enemy forces with our air power, which was not always superior in the skies at the time. We captured 11,000 men. Our only casualty was a British Tommy who was bitten by a mule.

I put together a team for the conquest of Sicily that led to the downfall of Mussolini. We neutralized Sardinia and Corsica without any great loss of life thus establishing needed air bases. My Allied effort at Salerno was the best we had known to date. We held on when other less gallant forces might have surrendered or evacuated the beachhead. Many great soldiers paid the supreme price for the toehold in Italy. But it gave us a foothold on the Continent, along with combat experience and a strong ally for the future in world affairs. I saved Gen. George Patton from disgrace after the unfortunate slapping incident in Sicily. He might have suffered from the flush of victory after he beat Gen. Montgomery to our objective with his faster and superior tactics. He obviously was high on the fighters who had done well in victory and furious at anyone who appeared to be a malingerer or failed to respond when ordered into battle. He was the man to spark our entire invasion follow-up at Normandy and to sweep across France in a manner that could only have been orchestrated by a Patton. He did save my ass twice — at Kasserine Pass and again at the Battle of the Bulge. He was entitled to brag about his exploits. That doesn't mean I didn't have to restrain his aggressiveness and abrasiveness at times. His "blood and guts" theme paid off but there were a lot of men who were glad they didn't have to serve under Patton. And in his fast drive, there were many generals who had to retake ground with severe fire fights after Patton had announced their liberation to the press.

At Normandy I made sure we had the necessary strength to secure the beachhead, although the planners thought it could be done with fewer troops. When Hitler decided to repel us at Mortain and destroy the beachhead, Gen. Bradley and I were ready and repelled his forces with counter moves. Many of our troops and commanders were new to battle but most passed the test.

While some critics may disagree, my decision to destroy the German army west of the Rhine was a wise one and saved lives — accomplishing our battle objective — the defeat of Nazi Germany. My decision after the invasion at Normandy to make a second invasion in southern France, despite Churchill's objections, will go down in history as one of my best. It was successful beyond my greatest hope and gave me the mass I wanted for victory.

Your biggest help was your role in running interference with the British, and the other brass in Washington, in order to give me a free hand in my operations and make decisions only a commander on the spot can make. Likewise I in turn used the same technique with most of my subordinates. Your support in all of my major decisions not only proved we were thinking on the same wave length but also making moves that would mean defeat of the enemy — our mission. The military world was ours not the political arena.

Despite my willingness to let subordinates fight their own battles, the crusty Montgomery, at 57 in 1944 and only three years older, assumed a superiority role combined with a sort of fatherly benevolence and tolerance. He was one of my most irritating problems. The man would not give. I guess I gave in too much at the start, and finally had to say to Churchill and the Allied supreme powers that either he went or I did. By then we almost had the war won, and I could slough off his complaints, although it put great pressure on me in addition to my daily functions. It was essential to keep everyone relatively happy and make decisions without undue pressure. You never failed me when I needed you against Churchill, Alan Brooke, Montgomery or the White House. While we had naval and air control problems, my theater never suffered the dilemma you had in the Pacific with so many admirals and generals quarreling with MacArthur. I guess you could say we covered the in-fighting very well and most of us kept peace in the family for the good of our overall efforts.

I have to say my admiration for the British effort declined as I reflected. If their ground effort had matched air and naval support, victory would have come sooner. My biggest mistake was to agree with

Montgomery to undertake the air drop at Arnhem. We gave him the supplies and troops for a massive drive to the Rhine river and he failed. Our generals always thought he was never aggressive enough after El Alamein, and historical studies are proving them right. As an Amerian G.I. would say, I should have kicked him in the butt to get him going a few times.

Another of my disappointments with Montgomery was that he failed to capture the port at Antwerp to give us a bigger base to operate from near the battlefront. It would have shortened our supply lines and saved much gas, time and energy in the final drive to destroy the German army west of the Rhine. It was not that he didn't have enough incentive. Not only was the port critical to our efforts but the sooner we drive to the heart of Germany the sooner the enemy could no longer fire on England with their ground based bombs. The V1 and V2 played hell with the British morale at home. But with all of our constant harping about the British and Canadian armies' efforts it should be pointed out that they had a lot of flat terrain to fight in France and a quagmire of water obstacles in the low countries as they drove northeast after the capture of Paris. Of course they obviously didn't take advantage of a defeated German army when we had them on the run. It was another example of breaking off the pursuit east of Paris to regroup when another push might have brought victory.

I perhaps failed in not putting enough effort into our drive into southern France. We hardly considered help to the east for our faltering efforts in Italy, or rolling up the Germany army when we hit the Rhine in the south in November, 1944.

There were all kinds of possibilities to exploit that successful maneuver but with our efforts in support of Montgomery we did not have the manpower and supplies to do both at the same time. While our shipping capacity was tremendous we never had enough and felt as though the Pacific was draining off naval equipment we needed. No doubt Pacific planners and fighters thought the same thing about our drain on manpower, air, naval forces and supplies. It was hard to realize that while the American army was such an overwhelming part of World War I, it took all arms to pull off victory in World War II.

We learned to live with the British on cordial terms, and I considered Churchill a great ally but learning to tolerate Montgomery took a long time. Of course he was a hero to us, originally, and thus a little difficult to overcome when he did not find himself in command. The same situation existed with French Gen. Charles de Gaulle. We had our differences but early on I realized that he not only looked like a soldier but was genuine. Perhaps our love of tanks in warfare had something to do with our relationship. Of course he was forever irritated by the fact that America was to direct the victory team in the invasion of France and I was to be the leader. I can't blame him for wanting to be commander but you can imagine our GIs fighting under a French general? While we got along fine with the British and French, it was after all an American battle to free Europe from the West, just as it had been in World War I. The French were contrary at times. While we gave them enormous supplies and equipment, they fought only when they wanted to and like the British were always reminding us that they had to preserve their manhood and couldn't suffer the same casualties as in World War I. It was tough fighting my own government for DeGaulle's recognition but we finally got it done. France after all these years still wants to keep its distance and has not always been cooperative. It is a proud nation but, alas, was unable to recognize the enemy early enough to head off near disaster in two World Wars. Their postwar efforts to maintain the peace were confusing.

Our Soviet allies were great fighters — as tough as they come. They made our job easier. We all watched their progress with great interest as we both fought with success and then again when we seemed to be progressing only mile by mile. Their situation map was always heartening and gave hope that the Germans were not invincible, as they sometimes seemed. It is not easy for the public-at-large to realize how fiercely the Germans fought us on both fronts. It was obvious they were beat. But they never realized they were beaten despite pounding on the ground and in the air. We were never going to let up until we had unconditional surrender. They fought almost as hard at the end as the beginning. We finally overwhelmed them and paid a horrible price for victory. It is strange that a few years later as NATO commander I would come to ask German cooperation in an alliance to organize our forces against possible Russian aggression in our liberated battlefields, once the seat of Nazi terror, destruction and strong defenses.

I tried to set an example for cooperation with the Russians and developed a warm relationship with Marshal Georgi Zhukov in Berlin and in Russia. I invited him to the United States but the Communists wanted no part of that sign of mutual cooperation. I went to Moscow to tell Stalin how we fought the battle to free Germany. He regaled me with war stories that were hard to match. It seemed as if we were on the verge of friendly relations. But when the political bosses took over, the Red menace appeared as gruesome and awesome as always. We were to see the Russians set up brutal regimes all over their conquered country including Poland, which had been the first victim of Nazi aggression at the start of World War II. We had hoped for a better world on our side on the Iron Curtain which soon descended after the surrenders were signed. It turned out that my job a few years later as President would be one of slowly losing confidence in any ability to work out peaceful agreements and settlements with Russia. It had to be a very discouraging time for so many GIs who thought we were fighting World War II to end wars. We found ourselves in a nuclear arms race with many other nations. You felt I had deserted you after I became president and the press kept hammering over and over that I didn't defend you against the right wing Republicans who were calling you names. I thought I did, in a Denver press conference, but that reference is only a minor footnote in history. Perhaps I fell victim to the political spotlight. It was not that I didn't treasure the friendship, advice and counsel of the wisest man in the American army — George Marshall. You were more to me than a superior officer and leader. You made me what I was as a general and gave me the advice, experience, knowledge and help I would need, not only as supreme commander of the Allied crusade in Europe, but also two terms as President where I emulated all of the good habits you and so many others taught me along the way. Thank you teacher. Thank you, General Marshall.

D.D.E.

Author's note: It is interesting that Congress at one time wanted to promote Marshall to a higher rank to keep up with the rank-conscious British. He remarked how silly it would look to be Marshal Marshall. The ideas was dropped.

Letter 2

George S. Patton. INS-UPI photo.

PATTON — OLD BLOOD AND GUTS

Dear Ike,

I ranked you a lot but you had more smarts than I did. After all I was a battle field commander and you were the planner, diplomat and great leader. But I must say I saved your ass at Kasserine Pass when the Germans overran our forces in North Africa in February, 1943.

I was a foul mouth at times and taught my soldiers to kill the Boche so they wouldn't get killed. And I was inspiring to the GI on the battlefield. I gave him hope and success.

In Sicily I showed the slow-moving British Field Marshal Montgomery how to beat the Germans. After my slapping of two soldiers who complained of battle fatigue and were in a hospital in Sicily, you and Marshal saved my ass. I became the Normandy D-Day decoy. The Germans thought I would lead an army near Calais, France, which we never did. But when you were in trouble in Normandy because of Montgomery's snail pace in battle, I was the one who led an army in France and broke the Normandy stalemate. It gave you a great victory.

I headed east and south and poor old Monty finally headed east and north to play catch up. I should have been allowed to capture Paris but you gave the job to Gen. Courtney Hodges' First Army and the Free French. We made great progress until Hitler decided to counterattack us in December, 1944, in the Ardennes. The Battle of the Bulge was our biggest disaster in the war. Hitler really thought he could overrun our forces, recapture Paris and turn the war around. And who did you call on? Georgie boy. You were desperate but I told you and Gen. Bradley not to worry. I turned three divisions around at once and by Christmas I had reached Bastogne and we soon liberated the area. You and Bradley had spread your inexperienced men too loosely without adequate reserves on a broad front. Georgie would never have done that. My theory was to attack not defend. I saved your hide again and was glad to do it. Let me add that Gen. Alexander (Sandy) Patch and Gen. Jacob (Jakie) Devers, along with the Free French forces, took up the slack in my rear and on my right flank. Patch of course was a gallant fighter who was glad to get out of MacArthur's command in the Pacific and come to Europe where the command control was a bit more organized and had more brains. You gave Monty the First and Ninth Armies and the Limey didn't get his attack started until January. Wanted to tidy everything up, you know!

I must admit, in all humility, my battle plan at Metz was not the greatest but you were giving the ammo and supplies to the troops up north.

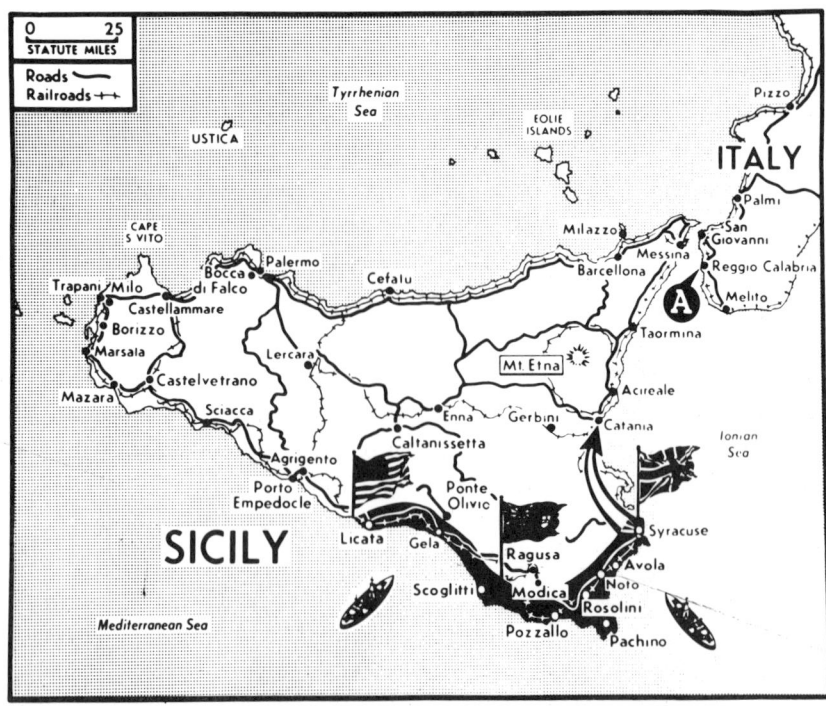

Despite a head start in the invasion of Sicily by the British, the American troops got to Messina first. Black areas show early ground held by Allies. AP map.

As a person, I gave you a hard time and not just over the slapping incident or my political comments during and after the war. I even visited some divisions stateside and alerted them for my command in North Africa when they were not even a part of my task force. In combat, I often bypassed channels and sent my needs to the headquarters I thought could do my army the most good. I kept demanding and demanding more men and supplies until I got them. I fought giving up a division in combat and it often took more than one order to pry an outfit loose from my Army.

I hear actor George Scott later told the story in the movie, Patton, about my reincarnation. And he also told of my taking over a listless and defeated II Corps at Kasserine Pass. The only trouble with the movie was that our tanks in a counterattack looked just like the tanks of the Germans. So it is on film. In battle I captured, bypassed, and outflanked the enemy in huge numbers. Defeat never came to my mind. It was always win, win, win. I went out of my way to make officers wear ties and khakis in training in hot North Africa. I wanted them to look different and stand out. When I arrived at a unit with sirens and horns, I wanted the troops to know that Georgie Patton had arrived. Because Georgie Patton inspired confidence and, man, did we need confidence! We always knew, despite our victories, we had to kill off the enemy until he was destroyed.

Yes, I was known as old blood and guts. Old I was. I outranked most of you young upstarts who were in charge. I made many statements about you, Gen. Mark Clark, and others that were ill-advised. Heaven knows, I apologized publicly for my short comings.

Speaking of Clark, he often recalled our relationship with one of his favorite stories about me. In Italy when I was in the "doughhouse" because of the famous slapping incident, Clark told me one night after a long day of inspecting front line units that he was tired and was going to bed. He reminded me to say my prayers.

I replied, "I will . . . and I pray for the same thing every night: that you will get into trouble here in Italy, be defeated, be relieved and they will put me in your place." Strangely enough, I was not kidding.

My nickname came from my repeated pep talks that the two most important elements in battle were: the need of "guts" and "the desire to spill the enemy's blood."[1] (*Author's note:* GIs often cracked, "Yeah, his guts and my blood.")

I had a set speech which I read over calmly in preparation but it was a hell raiser when I was on stage before the troops. Many of my comments have not been published. I had an overriding feeling that our soldiers and the American public needed an overnight change of their mental habits. I knew it was impossible but that was why in my bombastic fight talks I had to shock them out of their ordinary habits and thinking with the kind of language you heard in my talks. When I said "Rip your bayonets into the bloody bowels of the enemy" it was intended for shock effect. It worked.[2]

Other Patton-isms included:

"Your own fire reduces the effectiveness and the volume of the enemy's fire, while rapidity of attack shortens the time of exposure. A pint of sweat will save a gallon of blood . . . . Catch the enemy by the nose with fire and kick him in the pants through movement."[3] (Actually he often used ass or balls instead of pants.)

"We are going to kill the Boche, you kill them before they kill you and you can live to see victory. The same goes for those purple pissing Japs. They are better dead than alive.

"When you are old and gray and your grandchildren sit on your knees you can tell them I killed the bastards before they killed me. While others stayed home, you made the fight, killed the God-damn bastards and won the war.

"When asked by your grandchildren what you did during the war you can say you served in a force for victory and freedom and didn't stay home shoveling shit."[4]

"With your bonds and blood we crushed the Germans before they got here."[5]

"God damn it, if I had been a better general most of you wouldn't be here."[6]

I often have wondered what MacArthur or you would have done with me in the Pacific war? Probably nothing because of age and my reputation of being too good and too competitive. You can bet one thing for sure and that is that a change of scenery or different type of military action would never have changed my personality. I would have gone in with the leadership to win and with dedicated, fighting men at my side to make sure I did win. (Dropping of the A bomb precluded this decision.)

Of course I always wanted to fight the Russians while we were there in strength in order to defeat another enemy. Speaking of victories, I even saved the Lipizzaner horses and the famous Imperial Spanish Riding Academy when I liberated our part of Austria. Would a noncalvary man have cared if the horses fell into the hands of the Russians?

Frankly I always thought we would head for eastern Europe and Russia after we got to Austria, the Elbe River, and other places in Germany. Some Germans thought the same thing. I never got along with the post-war life. I said it was hard to tell on which side of the street the Nazis lived and when we started our nonfraternization plan and tried to prevent love and marriage, we were in a heap of trouble.

You sure tolerated me but I also fought like hell for you. I hope history recorded that I was the best battlefield commander of World War II, because I probably was. You were a dear friend and a fine leader. It takes two to know one.

I never lived to read all the plaudits and thanks from the American public, media and historians because of a lousy accident at 60.

George S. Patton

P.S. You had Kay Summersby. I also had a friend in Europe. An army commander was entitled to that pleasure also. Jean Gordon, niece of my wife, came to Europe in 1944 as a Red Cross doughnut girl. She was alert, sensitive, charming and clever. I adored her. She was about as old as my daughter and was stunning in a uniform. I didn't want her presence in London to be known but the word got around. She later was my table companion when I entertained important visitors, including lunch with Marlene Dietrich. When a prominent Ike confidante kept quizzing me, I told him she had been mine for years. When my wife, Beatrice Ayer, an heiress and horse lover also, inquired about her presence, I wrote and said the first that I knew she was overseas was when you wrote and told me.[7] My wife got mad about it later and I once wrote her not to worry because she was in the company of other Red Cross girls and I was no fool.[8] (After his fatal accident Jean returned to America and was distraught and crying. Within two weeks she killed herself.)[9]

A Tragic End

Author's note: Gen. Patton, while a rascal at times, simply knew how to cut through the battle mustard. He was a firm believer in capturing high ground, attacking the enemy on his flanks, bypassing strongholds and not just striking enemy forces head-on, unless absolutely and, finally, necessary. Many other commanders often failed to use this battle plan and suffered severe casualties which might have been avoided. It was a little hard to fight with or alongside his army because major units often moved so fast they bypassed pockets of resistance and left the cleanup jobs to other units. His troops often drove through and around enemy forces which hid in basements, foxholes, rubble, forests and other concealments only to come out and greet the cleanup troops with some first-class firepower, mine fields, roadblocks and other delaying tactics.

Patton's death at 60 was a tragedy. He was on an autobahn in Germany showing a fellow general all the rubble still remaining on the battlefields in conquered country, when his driver was fascinated enough by his conversation to take his eyes off the road for a moment and when he looked back, a big army truck was in their path. Only Patton, who died several days later, was killed in the accident. He was sitting in the back seat, was hurled forward and then back to his seat — a broken neck. He never recovered. His adoring wife, Beatrice, flew to Europe with another medical team to be at his bedside. When she came into the room, Patton said it was good she had arrived, because it might be the last time he saw her. Ten days later, December 21, 1945, he died of acute heart failure.[10] It was not the way Patton would have elected to go. If he had been killed in battle he would have been proud so to go. He probably thought, in his last moments, that he would return to fight the enemy somewhere else in his next life.

An F at Leavenworth?

For many years there was a Patton story concerning his comment about the instruction at the Command and General Staff School at Fort Leavenworth, Kansas. It is worth relating.

In late January, 1945, Patton pulled off a cross borders mass movement of troops affecting five corps and eight divisions. The weather was bitterly cold. It was snowy and wet and the changes took place on an inferior road network.

In his memoirs, *War As I Knew It*, Patton recorded: "Had any one proposed such a troop movement at Leavenworth, people would have gone crazy, but here it was being done. However the difference between this operation and a problem at Leavenworth was that here we had an old and experienced staff of extremely capable men, while at

Leavenworth one could have nothing but students more or less bemused with formulas."

At the doughfoot level, the statement came out that Patton went charging up a hill to an observation post when the attack jumped off, and shaking his finger in the air, exclaimed: "If I had done this at Leavenworth I would have got a fucking F for my grade." Actually the attack took place after the horrendous defeat in the Bulge penetration and it gave the army a new spirit all along the line. It is easy to forget that the fighting in Europe in January, February and March, 1945, was hard going. It looked like the Germans should give up their long and losing struggle against the Free World. Such fanaticism by the Nazi followers of Hitler tends to be forgotten in so many postwar writings. The great mass of his troops now including young children, old men and cripples, still believed that Hitler would produce secret weapons to win the war despite loss after loss on the ground and with virtually no protection from aerial attacks.

The Patton Stamp

The Patton Stamp was suggested by many persons but the veteran who continued pushing to get the stamp printed was Tom White, an Indianapolis printer by trade, who always claimed he was a bugler for Patton while in the tank corps in World War I. Active in the World Wars Tank Corps Association, White badgered any one who would listen to his idea for a Patton stamp. He prevailed on Hoosier congressman William G. Bray, of Martinsville, Ind., in 1951. Bray negotiated with two postmaster generals to get the stamp issued on Patton's 68th birthday anniversary, November 11, 1953, at Ft. Knox, Ky., home of Army armor and site of the Patton museum. Bray was a tank officer in World War II, who served on the House of Representatives Military Affairs Committee many years and also served (lieutenant colonel) in the 38th Division, Indiana National Guard.

IKE SAYS:

Dear Georgie,

You have become so famous in history that it is, indeed, difficult to address you with an objective outlook. So let's try the subjective.

You did save my ass at both Kasserine Pass and the Battle of the Bulge. Despite your high regard for your rank, your candid and critical opinions and flamboyant manner, you rank high in the all-time great American commanders. For that I salute you.

But before you get carried away with my praises let's look at the record. You rose fast and deserved all of your promotions. But man, did you need a throttle? Yes, you did. And I provided that. I also was the fellow who put together the plans and operations to make you look good. People are inclined to forget that aspect of military operations.

By all rights you should have been at the top of the pile of commanders, but you had a knack of alienating political leaders, fellow generals and even some of the men under you. You were fairly sure that you were right all of the time but you were not always so — which puts you in the same category as the rest of us mortals although you thought your reincarnation at times put you on an upper level.

You did bring to fruition our dreams of making tanks and the armor concept, which we learned about in World War I (you on the battlefield and me back home training tankers) a decisive force in battle. Even your uniforms made the American public realize there was something different about a tanker. Your personality pleased some and displeased others.

Let's look at your record which you are so proud of — rightly so. You had an advantage in that you were well off and your wife was rich — so that low pay was never an obstacle to your progress. You also knew some of the right people in the right places, and you used your knowledge and influence to good advantage. You were a good polo player and that was important in the era in which you grew up. It is a shame that polo is now a lost art in the Army arena.

Most important of all you had ideas and put your words and promises into action. After the usual schooling, you went overseas in World War I and made a brilliant record. We stay-at-homes (Bradley and Middleton among others) were envious of your growing reputation. To say you wanted to close and clash with the enemy would be an understatement. It was something in your blood and something you never forgot. I think you would have enjoyed dueling German General Erwin Rommel at Kasserine Pass in North Africa, rather than jockeying your troops around to defend our battlefield position as he drove holes in our defense and continued to upset the Allied world as the unsurpassed Desert Fox. When British Gen. Montgomery, with 8th Army, drove him west into our positions you, the French, and British 1st Army suffered from his rebound. After our great landings at Casablanca (your task force) Oran and Algiers, we were slow in clearing Tunisia and a stalemate developed. Critics forget the weather, distances, green troops, logistical supply and, most of all, inadequate tank and antitank weapons.

After our forces secured Morocco and Algeria we headed for Tunisia with the support finally of the Free French. Initially our green troops had difficulty with the terrain, inadequate weapons and a tough German Afrika Korps. We were lacking in leadership and when we were penetrated and defeated, I relieved our Maj. Gen. Lloyd Fredendall at British General Harold Alexander's insistence and you organized the American forces and gave them a new fighting spirit. But just to make sure, I sent Gen. Omar Bradley along as my eyes and ears. You made him your deputy and thereby gave him the experience I needed in a man to later lead my crusade through northern Europe. He, like Alexander, had some misgivings about the qualities of the green American troops, but you and I had full confidence our boys would develop into good fighters — the match of any other nation. We were not disappointed and after you, with Bradley again at your side, invaded Sicily even Alexander came around to our way of thinking. The American troops could do the job required. You made a monkey out of Montgomery, as you say, in clearing the Italians and Germans from Sicily. We were then ready to spring Gen. Mark Clark and his Fifth Army into Italy as Mussolini was overthrown and the Italians surrendered.

Because of Montgomery's delay and the slow pursuit of the retreating Germans by our combined allied Navy and Air Force units, we allowed far too many of the enemy to escape across the straits. We made the same mistake when we freed Corsica and Sardinia.

But was Sicily too much success for you? You became famous as a general in a sad and strange manner. You slapped two soldiers in a hospital. You thought they were malingerers. And perhaps they were. But you were wrong and you covered up the incident until I found out about it. You were on the hot spot because you had let your enthusiasm for victory exceed your inner strengths. You had no right to slap those men and I told you so. Everybody is not built for combat but you thought they were. Bradley and I knew better. So did our boss Gen. George Marshall back in Washington. So we let you cool it. You were shelved but not forever because all of us knew we would need you again in battle. The war went on and you fumed. Finally President Roosevelt told you that soon you would get a command. But it was not an easy road back. You still tested my patience with remarks you made in public or private about fellow generals and political issues until I considered putting you back on the shelf and giving Third Army to Gen. Courtney Hodges, whom I could trust implicitly. He was Bradley's deputy for Normandy. You again repented and after we secured a stronghold in Normandy — and no longer needing you for a decoy for a possible crossing at Calais, which had succeeded in keeping Hitler from committing his reserves at our landing beaches totally — your army was ready to become operational.

I know it was hard for you to have Bradley under your command in Sicily and then less than a year later Bradley had you under his command. At times we have all said we would serve under almost anyone for victory but in reality we all want to get to the top and stay there. You were the Sunday punch for the breakout at Normandy after Bradley's brilliant Cobra plan broke the stalemate of two months of fighting a determined German army on the beaches and in hedgerow country. All of this time it had taken Montgomery's forces a month to reach its major D-Day objective — Caen, where we needed airfields and a springboard for the advance to Paris and the Seine River.

You drove across France with a dash that made headlines back home. You were the hero Americans were looking for. Heaven knows that Bradley deserved more than he got, and I would have liked a little more credit along the way — not only in headlines but from the White House also. Gen. Marshall was warm in his thanks for all of our war efforts — in a reserved manner. Marshall also pointed out that we should be giving more credit to lower level units — corps and divisions and their commanders. This was a mistake Clark had made in Italy for far too long.

The British took care of Montgomery and the Commonwealth troops in headlines but he also took care of himself in making it look as though he was the only hero and supreme commander of all the troops. I finally had to go on the ground and assume command of all the troops to keep you, Bradley and possibly others from resigning because of the hero of El Alamein's bragging and assumption that he was winning the war — singlehandedly. In the end, history may record an accurate picture but as the years passed he emerged as more and more a hero until I told author Cornelius Ryan the facts. That statement is well recorded now, thank goodness (see Author's note in Montgomery's Letter 11).

In the Army days of yore, rank was utmost in our minds, planning, responsibility and promotion. But a lot of that hanky panky was forgotten when World War II came along and we had to use the best men for the hard jobs. There were times when even with my rank I could not get everything done that I wanted to do — control of our airpower, shipping, adequate troops, ammunition and many other things necessary for early victory.

But back to the battlefield. You wanted to capture Paris, but I let the French have the honor and, just to make sure, I gave Gen. Hodges' First Army the mission to insure that our capture was fast and complete. You kept driving east and south and soon were spread out on a broad front without the gas and ammo to drive deep into the enemy's rear. Montgomery played catch up on our north-left flank, and while we dreamed of an early capture of Antwerp, because it was a key supply point, that was not to come until many months later.

In the meantime, Gen. Jake Devers and Gen. Sandy Patch were driving up hard from the south after I pulled off a second invasion into France on the Riviera. It was a success beyond all hopes and it surprised Winston Churchill along with a lot of others. We did not get a lot of credit for it, because it came just as we had started our massive drive across the north and, while the meager force had some fierce battles, it kept driving at a raceneck speed giving us a new supply route for all the forces. We still left Clark and the Italian campaign without much support — never seriously considering a dagger into the German back in northern Italy as Mussolini had done to the French in 1940 when Hitler blitzkrieged into France.

Just as we had hoped (and some even thought) the war might be over by Christmas, the Germans reorganized before we could drive on a broad front effectively and destroy the Germany army — our No. 1 mission. Montgomery tried his ill-fated attack at Arnhem where he failed miserably although the American forces accomplished their mission. You were slowed as you approached Metz, Trier and Nancy. The Germans wanted to stop us on foreign soil. In the Alsace Lorraine areas there was still a mix of German and French allegiances. They were confused as to which side to jump to. One day the Germans were there and the next day we were in control. Because of some of the back and forth battles there was good reason for the natives not to always trust us. You would go through an area and the Germans would filter back in. The same thing happened in the Seventh Army when we withdrew in some areas to take up the slack as you attacked with a 90-degree turn at the Bulge. The Germans reoccupied the areas we gave up. Then we had to fight all over again to regain lost territory. And the war correspondents and folks back home sometimes wondered why the battles were so slow and costly. Only the G.I. at the front line knew of the real danger and frustration in battle.

The southern Army group was slowed by weather, weariness and lack of supplies although the Free French did an amazing advance with a rebuilt army — American supplied — in helping to free their homeland. You analyzed the French partisans rather well when you said, "Better than expected and less than advertised." The press and home front people just never quite realized how strongly the Germans were resisting. And then they made their last desperate gasp in the Ardennes to destroy and defeat our spread out forces on a fifty mile target — aimed at splitting our forces as they had done to France and Britain in 1940. It started on a 50-mile front and penetrated 50 miles in depth. It played hell with our dispositions, gave us heavy and unexpected casualties and demoralized a lot of our troops. While we were all wringing our hands, you anticipated a counterattack in the Bulge and, after a week of defeat, I authorized your plan to attack the south flank of the Bulge shortly after I committed my last reserve, the 101st Airborne, to occupy Bastogne as a blocking position to the Germans. It worked and you pulled off a miracle when defeatism reigned in our ranks. Because of the infiltration, I became a virtual prisoner of my own headquarters. The Germans captured so many that they could form units with American uniforms and infiltrate our positions. Their death squads wanted some top brass to show the civilian population there was still some fire left in the Nazi hordes. While we said, oh yes, let them retake Paris and we will sack them up, the truth of the matter was that we were worried at the front as well as in the rear, which extended back to Gen. Marshall in the Pentagon and the White House. We gave the American public and loved ones of our servicemen a very worrisome and troubled Christmas in 1944. It was not the kind of a Christmas gift they had desired. They wanted the boys home and the boys wanted to go home. That is something that historians keep forgetting when they write of how we should have conquered Berlin and Eastern Europe. While you were ready to fight the Russians, our civilian leaders and population, along with most military planners, wanted to get the European war won and to finish off the war in the Pacific. We left the political decisions to others. While we disagreed on the subject, we still made a better world out of it by trying to live with the Russians. We thought they would cooperate but of course they didn't. They were confronted with more enemy divisions, took the most casualties and inflicted the most casualties on the Nazi enemy.

Within four days after your attack into Bastogne you made contact with the 101st at Bastogne while Montgomery tidied up his front and refused to let Hodges, Gen. Joe Collins and Simpson counterattack in the north until he was ready for a set piece battle. You not only made the Germans realize they had lost another battle but you restored morale and a fighting spirit in the rest of the front line troops and we managed to regain the initiative all along the front. But it was weeks before we cleared the Germans out of the Bulge — just imagine how hard they were fighting to keep us off their homeland. Meanwhile, we proved that while air power was effective, when the skies were clear, the battle was won on the ground. We were always proud of our air arm and the close support and bombing raids they pulled off. But despite the massive air attacks the Germans just kept firing back at us on the ground and continued to provide ammunition, troops and supplies for their front lines.

One has to wonder what would have happened if we could have driven to the Siegfried line all along the front and then pulled off a massive airborne drop in the enemy's rear. It is easy to second guess what might have been.

Still the battle raged on the planning front as to how we could end the war. I continued the broad front strategy and Montgomery wanted a single thrust to Berlin. We all wanted more troops and supplies for the final drive to victory. Luck was with us when Hodges found a bridge at Remagen — the last one intact — across the Rhine and drove his forces across. Of course we were a little gun shy at this point and did not want the penetration to be cut off and pushed back into the Rhine. You knew the problem and sneaked across the Rhine the day before Montgomery finally made his massive drive up north with Simpson's Ninth Army under his command. The Seventh Army and French went across and now we were in a drive for final victory. How sweet it was! The glory days were ours and victory came in early May. We let the Russians have Berlin with all of its casualties, and we saved Denmark. We drove into Bavaria to see if there was a Southern Reboubt battle holdout, which we feared, and joined Clark's forces coming up from Italy. Resistance was determined but spotty. We also drove hard enough into Austria to insure that country's independence after the war. You drove deep into Germany and freed great scientists and secrets along with saving the prized Lipizzaner horses in Austria. Only a calvaryman at heart would have made this a special mission.

The Germans were too weak or too disorganized to form a stronghold in the south so we have been criticized ever since for worrying about the possibility of a stalemate in the homeland of the original Nazis. Hitler killed himself April 30, 1945. While many Germans wanted to surrender to the West and not the East, I held out for unconditional surrender and a friendly meeting with the Russians, our ally. You and a lot of Germans would have been glad to join forces and strike East. May 8 was declared Victory Day!

Since Gen. MacArthur did not want you in the Pacific, you were destined to help rehabilitate a defeated and decimated Europe. You had little sympathy for the problem and installed too many Nazis in high positions. I had to relieve you of a field command. It was a hard task to perform. You really did not believe in the nonfraternization policy and could not tell the good guys from the bad guys. I am not sure we really found much of a solution to the problem because our boys wanted to be friendly with the enemy in many areas. When the Cold War broke out we soon realized that the Russians would not cooperate and could not be trusted. We found ourselves in bed with the Germans in order to defend Europe again from an advance from the EAST. But that is all a political matter and we had been fighting a military war.

You were about ready to come home to possible retirement when you were badly injured in an automobile accident. Your internal injuries were fatal and your death watch brought you back to the headlines again. A nation prayed for its hero. You died just a few days before Christmas, 1945, and again the home front with most of its warriors back, felt a tinge of sadness to lose a great hero in such an unworthy manner. You deserved better. You would have enjoyed holding your grandkids on your knees and telling them how you really did win the war. You were just sorry you could not have gone to the Pacific to fight. History remembers you for your gallantry, and I thank you for saving my ass at Kassserine and the Bulge — as a fellow general and as a friend. Our paths crossed often in defeat and victory. We were both better off for having had one another's help.

As I salute and sign off I cannot help but think of the final remarks you made when you left the Third Army. You turned to an aide and said: "The best end for an old campaigner is a bullet at the last minute of the last battle." Eight months later you were fatally injured in the accident.

The author, Martin Blumenson put it rather well in his book, *Patton The Man*, when he wrote that you were probably more famous and a legend in your own time because of your untimely death shortly after the war in an auto accident. The war was still fresh in everyone's mind and the American people wanted to read about their heroes. As a result the death watch on you just before Christmas in 1945 was a chance to pay tribute to a great American figher and a hero to so many.

Historians have made sure that as we faded away into history we would always be remembered for what we did to win World War II.

Attack!

D.D.E.

P.S. Besides our long comradeship in life and a close wartime association we had another interest in common. You had your Jean Gordon, the niece of your wife by your side at times and I had my constant companion — Kay Summersby. Both lives had a tragic end. Your Jean apparently thought she had another possible mate after you were ready to go back to Beatrice, but it blew up and she killed herself — for two reasons? And my Kay, whom I discarded, wrote two books about our relationship, finally married and then died of cancer.

POW Killing

Author's note: Besides the slapping incident in Sicily by Patton the matter of the killing of prisoners of war also surfaced during the war. It is fairly easy to understand, because after hearing a Patton fight talk one could get the idea that killing of the Boche meant fewer casualties of our own. Of course he meant to kill them in battle not after they were captives. The reports of POW killing by war correspondents came to the attention of Bradley who told Patton, his superior at the time, that an investigation of cold-blooded killings had to be made. In the court-martial after the inquiry, two men were convicted, returned to the unit for the duration and later were killed in action. No doubt other killings took place.

Letter 3

Erwin Rommel. AP photo.

ROMMEL — TERROR OF NORTH AFRICA

Dear Ike:

I really gave you your first blood bath of World War II. I was one of the most successful commanders of German troops from the first round in 1939 — mainly because I was aggressive, fearless, and out front most of the time. I loved to ride in a tank and put my life in danger. That went on for quite a while until Adolf Hitler decided I should be dead in 1944.

But to back up. I was sent to North Africa to rescue the Italians, who were poor fighters, with my Afrika Korps. I became the reigning terror of the Allied world. Everywhere I went I was a winner. We pushed the British back to Cairo. If I had had the supplies and manpower, I could have run the Allies out of North Africa. But I didn't. Ike, your invasion of North Africa was very good in 1942. In fact it was the first American effort in the theater. You found out how good Patton, Truscott, Bradley, Harmon and scores of others were.

At Kasserine Pass I gave you a new asshole. Of course the British and French were not too helpful. Your troops were not experienced, and in a next to last move we drove hard and long into your rear. It was a severe experience for you. You almost lost.

After you relieved the inept Maj. Gen. Lloyd Fredendall (reluctantly) you sent Gen. George Patton who knew what war was all about. Patton loved battle just as I did. And he was determined to win. And he did. I got sick and went back to Germany. Gen. Von Arnim took over and did a great job of an offensive retreat in Tunisia. But you captured thousands of our best troops in a massive assault to drive the Germans to the sea. I couldn't believe those pictures of truckloads of our soldiers heading for prisoner-of-war camps.

I regained my health and was given the job of defending France against the Normandy invasion and any others you had planned. The German generals and high command were confused but when I took over we reorganized an entire new defense with obstacles, mines, anti-aircraft positions, etc., which delayed your advance for some time. We diffused our troops because of orders from higher up. We thought you would make a second landing at Calais, France, and you had a big army under Gen. Patton waiting for the hooker, but you didn't. Of course Patton delivered the big blow at Normandy and later stopped our drive in the Battle of the Bulge. You were fortunate to have Patton on your side. If you had taken him out of command, after he slapped two soldiers in a hospital in Sicily who pleaded combat fatigue, you would have delayed your eventual victory for some time.

Therefore, as the most successful German field commander in World War II, I salute you, though I'm not just sure how much credit you can take. But you got the job done.

I certainly gave you a rough time twice. I trust I will go down in history as one of the great front line generals. It will always be hard for me to understand why Hitler made me commit suicide at 52 in October, 1944. Jealousy perhaps?

Erwin Rommel

Author's note: There were so many other German generals involved it would be impossible to mention them all. Of course Gen. Von Rundstedt waged the breakthrough in the Ardennes to rip up the American forces in the Battle of the Bulge. Heinz Guderian was an outstanding commander in the opening drive of World War II into France and the Netherlands. Kesselring was in charge of the Italian and Mediterranean areas and successfully prevented the Italians from giving the Allies much help in Italy, and his masterful defense position slowed down the advance up the boot of Italy for most of the war. There were many other famous generals — Ceeb, Bock, Model, Manstein, Dollman, Kluge . . . It should also be noted that when Adolf Hitler took over the German army generals they didn't like it, but went along with his game plans. He made some brilliant decisions but more were bad than good.

IKE SAYS:

Dear General Rommel,

The very mention of your sobriquet, the Desert Fox, struck terror in the hearts of many a brave fighting man. You were so invincible for so long that the Allied world began to treat you as a hero instead of the villain you were. You commanded a German thrust into France in 1940 and dashed across the country to Cherbourg. Your reputation began to grow. Of course you had already amassed medals and a reputation from your fighting days in World War I.

Your life must have been a hell-on-earth existence. As a brilliant tactician you had sworn your loyalty to Hitler because of your love of the German nation and the army, and then you along with many others realized he was a menace. You bore a double-edged sword and paid your life at 52 in 1944 when Hitler decided you were in on the plot to kill him. If you would commit suicide, his representative said, your family would live in safety. You did, and your family was safe. After the war your son, Manford, became mayor of Stuttgart.

You went to North Africa with the Afrika Korps to rescue your Axis ally, Italy. You and the British played march and countermarch across North Africa. Twice the Axis drove 1,500 miles east into Egypt, only to have to flee 1,500 miles back west. The British army made the same movements in reverse.[1]

You came close to running the British out of North Africa, and if you had succeeded in reaching the Middle East, the results would have been disastrous for the Allies. The war would have been prolonged for a long time unless we had decided to use the atomic bomb on Germany as we finally did to bring Japan to its senses. I was against use of the A-bomb as a military weapon, incidentally, for a variety of reasons. So we are all grateful that the British held on and the Middle East oil was saved and available for our side. That is not to say we didn't suffer from losses on our supply routes.

While Hitler gave you some of his best troops, I hate to think what would have happened if Hitler had given you additional supplies and troops in North Africa. Hitler and his generals wanted to win in Russia first. You had another advantage over us, though, that is not often referred to. Your tanks were initially tops. It often meant the difference between victory and defeat. As a longtime student of tank warfare, I once wrote an article on its importance and was told by the Infantry board to cease and desist — the same thinking didn't believe in air power as an equal combat arm either for many years. I had to admire your ability to win on the battlefields, and I knew your defeat was the No. 1 goal of the Allies in 1942. Little did I realize you would be my opponent again when I directed the forces into Normandy in 1944. With your abilities you made the invasion much harder. We gave you almost two years to reorganize and multiply your defenses on the French coast line.

But back to armor in battle, for a moment. You must realize that America did not have any great research or development of tanks and anti-tank weapons between the wars. We sent them into battle without adequate weapons. To read some of the accounts written in the postwar years of how our troops fought your deadly Tiger tanks makes one cringe for the early endeavors of our green soldiers in battle. Obviously, the British developed such weapons faster. We finally were able to outproduce you, which meant we could outmaneuver you in battle, and by then also had a worthy tank destroyer. But we never had a weapon as effective as the Panzerfaust for a close-in tank killer. You also had the mighty and versatile 88-millimeter anti-tank, anti-air weapon. Its "swhish" alone telegraphed fear to the ears of our brave and green soldiers. So you had the weapons and leadership to throw the Allies off balance for far too long. But the American soldiers, with their inadequate weapons still made the difference in battle — they combined brain and brawn to overcome many of their problems. We finally developed weapons and trained men into combined arms teams equal to any in the war. The German small units were still tops. It took our mass and firepower to overcome many a roadblock, small unit defensive position, or a well-placed 20-mm weapon.

Our forces were better fed which meant less personal sacrifice compared to your ration. We even managed to provide turkey and all the trimmings to men on the front lines at Thanksgiving and Christmas. Our supply lines were excellent, except in initial battle zones when the soldier carried his ration as your troops had to do far more often.

You and your successor, Gen. Juergen von Arnim, lucked out several times in North Africa. When British General Montgomery had you on the run at El Alamein, he stopped fighting to regroup thereby enabling you to escape to fight another day. When he got to the Mareth line he did the same thing. When we were hit at Kasserine Pass, Monty in the south and British General Anderson's 1st Army likewise only leaned forward in support.

I had sent Maj. Gen. Lloyd Fredendall to join the British and French in seizure of Tunisia and the final defeat of your forces in Africa. He was not the fighter that Marshall and I had hoped and our forces were an easy target at Kasserine Pass where you defeated us piecemeal. It took my bombastic Gen. George Patton to blunt your adventures into our territory. He wanted to take you on in the worst way and obviously was spoiling for battle. For insurance, I sent Gen. Omar Bradley as his deputy to make sure of American tactical control since Patton like you was a front line soldier who wanted to close with the enemy. Coupled with our inexperience and lack of anti-tank weapons, it took a while with British and French attacks to drive you into defeat and out of North Africa. We captured some of your finest fighters. They spent a long time in prisoner-of-war camps in America. It was a beautiful sight to see those strong, lean, blond soldiers by the truckload passing through to our port areas for internment.

You became ill and had to return to Germany and Patton never got to duel you again on the battlefield. The British brigadier and historian, Desmond Young, has sized up your rise in the military: "He merely had the qualities of courage, boldness, determination and initiative in so exceptional a degree that they could not fail to attract attention. He was a Freyberg (one-legged Aussie hero of both world wars) rather than an Orde Wingate" (early jungle guerrilla fighter).[2] You knew something about waiting for promotion in the army also. It took 19 years for you to go from captain to colonel. But you were a major general at 39 — promoted partly for Hitler's safety. (I went from major to major general in 20 years at 52.)

We broke your forces in Normandy, and I doubt if any amount of defense on your part would have stopped the American boys who had little of your professional training. They wanted to win the war and go home.

D.D.E.

Letter 4

Kay Summersby. AP photo.

THE IKE-KAY AFFAIR

To set the stage for this next letter first read this excerpt from a letter to the author from Gen. Eisenhower's son, Brig. Gen. John S. D. Eisenhower, on July 25, 1985. It is probably the most revealing letter ever written about the relationship of Ike and Kay Summersby.

". . . I thought Kay (Summersby) was terrific. She may have been an opportunist, but someone in Dad's position must accept that failing in his close associates. None of us are saints. Kay held a position on the staff very much like Mary Tyler Moore in her former TV series, the girl Friday. She may have wanted to parlay that position further, but it wasn't in the cards, even though Dad probably broke down and expressed affection now and then. It is difficult to picture someone of Dad's disposition, off and alone, carrying big responsibilities, being able to resist feeling an affection for an attractive, loyal woman like Kay. She did a lot for him; to my way of thinking, she therefore made a real contribution to the war effort.

"Of course the whole business had its tragic aspects. News of it hurt Mother; and if Kay had expectations, the let-down when the two rejoined the world of reality must have been bitter. But a denouement like Butcher and Molly was not in prospect."

And from Ike's Diaries, edited by Robert H. Ferrell: "Heard today through a mutual friend that my wartime secretary (rather personal aide and receptionist) is in dire straits. A clear case of a fine person going to pieces over the death of a loved one, in this instance the man she was all set to marry. Will do what I can to help but seems hopeless. Too bad she was loyal and efficient and the favorite of everyone in the organization. Makes one wonder whether any human ever dares to become so wrapped up in another that all happiness and desire to live is determined by the actions, desires — or life — of the second. I trust she pulls herself together, but she is Irish and tragic."[1]

THE GENERAL FINDS A LADY

Dear Ike,

By the time I met you in London in 1942, I was already familiar with the military world, as the daughter of an Army colonel. We lived in Innis Beg, Ireland, while I was growing up, and my great concern was whether the rain would ruin the hunting, a tennis party or sailing. I was brought up a proper young lady, serving tea with finesse. (Innis Beg is now a somewhat run down estate on a small but lovely emerald island in County Cork.)

Since my mother spent most of her time in London, I ended up there working as a film extra. Before long I married Gordon Summersby, a young publisher. I once wrote: "Inevitably there was marriage, a dismal failure." Next came modeling and photography. With the outbreak of World War II, I soon joined the Motor Transport Corps. I learned that it was "looked upon as a sort of social sorority."[2] Then you came along and took over my life for the next three years. Soon I fell in love with Col. Richard Arnold. We planned to marry after the North African campaign.

Dick might have been my only real love. He was ranked eighth in his class at West Point, and the yearbook stated that he was a literary devotee reading everything including the comics. He had a fine sense of humor and was very handsome. He was all a woman could care for, and care for him, I did. When his life was ended in Tunisia by a lousy mine, the chain of command broke down, and it fell to you to tell me of his death. You put your arms around me as I sobbed and thereafter tried to keep my mind off my great loss.[3] There was some horseback riding, some bridge, some free time, and lots of sympathy from you and your staff. It was a difficult time. I'll never forget your help in this time of crisis and tears.

The war went on. You helped me return to reality. After that damned Tunisia battle we invaded Sicily. Gen. Mark Clark stormed ashore the Salerno coast of Italy and we held on by our fingernails for five days.

By the end of 1943, other thoughts were on your mind. You were headed back to England and the big show up north — the invasion. You took me along. I know that I was of help to you, but little did I dream that my role would be one of nearly constant companionship.

You decided to return to your inner family's hide-a-way at Telegraph Cottage, where you first located in August, 1942, when you tired of the luxury of Claridge's, the loneliness at the Dorchester, and the social pressures of London. It was a quiet, modest house in the country. After the war was over we even returned there for a final luncheon with your inner circle.

You and Capt. Harry Butcher, Navy aide, shared quarters and rent at Telegraph Cottage, a quaint house with lovely flowers and shrubs and near a golf course but very secluded. I lived nearby with five WACS. Gen. Walter Bedell Smith, your chief of staff, often joined us for a good bridge foursome. By now there was talk about our togetherness.

In Gen. Bradley's memoirs he recalls that at a victory parade after the Allies had conquered North Africa, you and I were at the Tunis airport greeting dignitaries. He later commented that when the Normandy beachhead opened up, you brought me along on your staff and that a few eyebrows were raised. We ignored it all — there was a war to be won.

In November, Sir Alan Brooke, the British counterpart of Marshall, came to Rheims with Churchill. Brooke, under the influence of Montgomery (who wanted your position), was not very affable. Years later author David Irving reported that "Brooke was not edified by the curious lunch table menage, with Kay Summersby presiding and Churchill on her right; it was not the kind of thing that could have happened in the British Army."[4] (Brooke apparently never believed that Kay fed Roosevelt and Ike a chicken lunch in North Africa in 1943.)[5]

How true, Ike, but you were different. You set your style, and it was first class. I appreciated being included.

I lived through some hectic times: Montgomery's ill-fated drop at Arnhem, the Battle of the Bulge where Montgomery had one of his divisions and two of your armies. He held a press conference and claimed victory. He gave no credit to Bradley, Hodges, Collins, Simpson, Patton, or Middleton. That was one time you nearly quit. Monty tried to apologize, and you were ready to relieve him. You probably would have, except for British pressure and public opinion

After the war when I watched you receive the Key to the City of London, an honor seldom bestowed, I was glad of your previous diplomacy. Then we went to the theater and you moved me next to you where your son was sitting. Photographers recorded that scene for history.

General Eisenhower and General Bradley at London theater after the war. Kay Summersby (center) was seated away from Ike but he insisted she move to be with him. AP photo.

Finally with your armies spread all over Germany, the Russians took Berlin which, already decided, was to be in their postwar sector with a multi-country command. When we went to Berlin you conferred with Marshal Zhukov. Such travels were an unbelievable delight for a captain in the WACS who also wanted to be an American citizen.

I admired you more than any man in the world.

I Should Have Known

There were two times I should have known that my love affair with you would not come off. After your arrival in England, I took you on a tour of London — the usual tourist attractions — but I drove by Bryanston Court where the American Mrs. Wally Simpson lived when the Prince of Wales was courting her. You shook your head and said: "A shame the King lost sight of his duty."[6]

The second time was after our two-and-one-half years together when we returned to the Riviera and then into Germany. You commented: "Whenever we're together like this it seems so right, the way things should have always been. But perhaps." In our private conversations you repeated the words, "but perhaps" more and more. You were trying to tell me something. I replied: "It's too bad we didn't meet each other years ago." You nodded. Said you thought this would never happen to you. You replied: "Sometimes in the Army, you don't discover what it's like in the world outside."[7]

You worried about your age a lot. I was 18 years younger. You said it was all right but worried about 10 years from now. Or 20. You added: "Age isn't going to change what we have."[8]

There has been a great dispute and much discussion, over the postwar years, about the possibility that you wrote Gen. Marshall requesting permission to come home and divorce Mamie. Marshall blew his stack, apparently. Did you get his reply? Author Merle Miller in *Plain Speaking* says President Truman heard of the letter and asked Marshall, before he left office, to destroy the letter. Truman, who didn't want you to get into the political arena and didn't particularly warm up to you, except as a military leader, was afraid the letter would be found and used as material against you in the future. He allegedly called Marshall, who never admitted to such a letter. (Personally, I liked Truman at Potsdam).

Lloyd Shearer in his January 2, 1977 report on you and me in *Parade Magazine* said he asked Margaret Truman Daniel, the President's daughter, if the letter episode was true. "'I think it was.'" she said. "My father wasn't the kind of man who ordered Gen. Marshall around . . . But I think he (Truman) suggested that it might be better if General Ike's letter about divorcing his wife be taken out of the file. I think that's true. I have always thought that was true."

Remembering, I think of my last visit to see you when I finally got to the States. I brought our dog, Telek, a Scottish terrier, whom we shared like two little children, to see you in the Pentagon. You enjoyed playing with Telek again. That was long after I realized our affair was over, although you blushed during my visit.[9] Telek died several years later in my arms and my thoughts were still of you.

I had always expected to return to the States and work for you, as I had for three years, then you broke the news that you were returning home without me, and I was offered a job in Berlin by one of your buddies, Gen. Lucius Clay. I still thought then, incorrectly, you would send for me from the States. I did hear you at a forum at Columbia University when you were president there. Our paths crossed on the campus and you sent an aide to take me out for a drink and to tell me it would never be the same.[10]

It is amazing that the media and officialdom overall managed to cover up our affair during its existence and ever after. The bigger the coverup the easier it is to cover, eh?

All you or anyone has to do is read my two books on our relationship and know what happened between us. To some it may make no difference. To others it will be a beautiful love story. History is now recording the deeds of many wayward Americans in a fashion never before reported. Your history does record that Jefferson, Burr, Hamilton and many others had their affairs. In the 1920s most Americans had never heard of President Harding's lover, Nan Britten, who later wrote that she bore his child. The cover-up was first-class. Franklin D. Roosevelt, your commander-in-chief during most of World War II, had a love affair with Lucy Mercer Rutherfurd that did not end until he died at Warm Springs, Ga., with her at his side. Now Americans know about the shock waves that occurred in the inner circle of the family at the White House when Eleanor learned the affair was still ripe. She thought the ardor was over long before, though both let it be known they no longer made love after the affair surfaced. FDR's mother, Sara Delano, had pleaded with him to give up Lucy. The love was too strong for him to overcome. And then people question our mutual attachment.

Then there was Gen. Patton with his love, Jean Gordon and others — all duly recorded by several historians. And Martin Blumenson, the Patton expert, writes freely of Patton's peccadillos, in his book *Patton: The Man Behind the Legend.* He often bragged about the number of condoms he took to London after the war was over.

Kay Summersby was always there. Here she rides in the back of a jeep between Generals Eisenhower and Mark Clark. Photo courtesy Dwight D. Eisenhower Library.

In later years the affairs of President John F. Kennedy and Martin Luther King became common knowledge. Their wives never suffered from such pecadillos in the American court of public opinion. Their wives were still in the upper tiers of respectability although some Americans never forgave Jackie for marrying the Greek tycoon Onassis. She knew what she wanted and got it. I knew what I wanted and didn't get it.

As a constant companion I wrote a lot of things about you that I probably should not have. But a woman scorned is a woman scorned. You might not have been elected President if you had left Mamie. Even the political camp of Sen. Robert Taft, of Ohio, looked into our possible romance for use in the Republican Presidential nomination race with you in 1952, when you upset the regulars with your extreme popularity.

I always wanted to believe that you had written a letter to Gen. Marshall saying that you wanted to divorce Mamie to marry me. The possibility of a letter became public knowledge when Merle Miller interviewed President Truman for his book, *Plain Speaking*. Alas, the letter was never found and Truman said he had it destroyed from the Marshall file. As a result most historians have doubted it ever existed. Truman's longtime aide, Maj. Gen. Harry Vaughan, told the Associated Press after the report came out that Truman sent it to the Marshall personal library after it wandered around the Pentagon files for a time.

Together, we associated with kings, prime ministers and generals all through the war but that was the end of it. I enjoyed every minute of my association with you. I just regret that after the war I became another nobody. But, as I have said before, I should have known.

Love,

Kay Summersby.

IKE HAD A CRUSH ON KAY

P.S. I am enclosing a postscript to you from Mollie Butcher which might further explain our relationship, General.

My husband, Harry Butcher, a CBS vice-president, and your naval aide, was a close associate of yours professionally and personally.

Lloyd Shearer, in writing about us in *Parade Magazine*, Jan. 2, 1977, tells the Ike-Kay story well. It was not until the end of the war that the rumors that you had fallen in love with your driver, Kay Summersby, surfaced. The rumors had floated for some time.

Another rumor, according to Shearer, was that, "Butcher has fallen in love with Mollie Ford, who ran the information desk at the Red Cross club in Algiers. The rumor had it that both men were going to divorce their wives and marry their new found lovers."

Butch did. You didn't.

Butch says that if you had really loved Kay you would have gone the divorce route. Butch always claimed he was always so close to your daily affairs that you had no time for intimacy.

I saw things differently. I could tell, as Shearer reported in my interview with him, that you were deeply in love with Kay. He wrote that I said: "Ike had a tremendous crush on Kay but Butch was always covering up for him . . . Kay was a decent, honest, forthright woman.

She was not flirtatious." I told Shearer my personal belief was that after her real beau, Col. Richard Arnold, was killed by a lousy mine in Tunisia: "She became incapable of feeling too strongly about anyone else, that her relationship was pretty much a one-sided affair . . . Ike was infatuated with her. He was really crazy about her."

After all you had Kay with you all the time — with Roosevelt, Churchill, King George and all the Allied commanders. You sent her on trips to the U.S.A., to Russia, Germany and the Middle East.

I told Shearer: "No matter what Butch says, she was more than a diversion."

Mollie Ford Butcher

IKE SAYS:

Dear Kay,

Well, . . . uh . . . that is to say . . . you've about said it all. Our relationship was genuine and wonderful. I caught you in a time of grief when your true love, Col. Richard Arnold, was killed in Tunisia at age 32 in 1943. He was a good soldier and likeable lad.

The West Point register upon his graduation in 1932 said he was "One who could at once discourse with the wisdom of a sage or contribute with relish to the most light minded topic of a bull session." He was a student of military history as I was but also liked the funny papers. You know my preference was Westerns.

When Dick was killed the chain of command forgot to tell you through channels, and it became my most unpleasant task to tell you of his death.

While you could have been with him more often, I wondered early on if you saw the opportunity of staying at my side for the fringe benefits a headquarters of my size provided, plus working for and companionship with a general on the rise?

It is strange that I was opposed to women in uniform until I came to Britain and saw you and others who were making a great contribution to the war effort. I wrote in my memoirs *Crusade in Europe:* "But in Great Britain I had seen them perform so magnificently in various positions . . . that I had been converted."[11]

As the war progressed we were seen together everywhere. Many of my fellow generals have recorded in some length about our relationship. I was being told on many sides that the relationship was not good. We forgot the side looks and snide comments. Our affair probably did have something to do with my failure to write my wife more often. I used the excuse of not enough time, nothing to say and even a lack of writing paper. It is easy to rationalize when your interests are elsewhere.

Your attention took some of the pressure off a man who had to serve so many above him, those alongside him and those below him. The pressure of knowing that men are dying and getting wounded in battles that you are directing when you are responsible for victory is tremendous.

Of course I always enjoyed having you with me when I reviewed troops. Personally I felt an age difference (18 years) and I knew that divorce was frowned upon by most in the army. People just didn't do that sort of thing in my youth, though strangely enough forty years later 50% of marriages in America ended up in divorce. In those days little was known about the affairs that generals, presidents and kings had outside the family circle.

You wrote in some detail in two books about our relationship. I can only let the record speak for itself. You had your version of our affair; others had theirs and a few have recorded them. I probably knew that it would end with the war. You didn't — at least I am sure you hoped it wouldn't. I was a good enough student of history to know that a hero in my position was on line for even greater things in life — I really didn't want to be President but then I didn't necessarily want to be supreme commander of Allied forces in Europe either. They were both thrust upon me. As I often told my aide, Col. Ernie Lee, what I really wanted was to command a division in combat as a two-star general.

You now realize that Mamie was a big help in that drive for leadership in life and my entry into the political arena which ended up in the White House — the dream of every American boy.

I was flattered by your attention. I loved to hold your hand and steal whatever intimate time we found. History will never know what happened between us. You published your version at a time of great ambition and then, without adequate funds, wrote a more intimate memoir never accepted for its authenticity. I gave you a $1,000 gift for your help along the way. I offered you the beautiful jeweled (sapphire) cigarette case that Gen. Charles de Gaulle gave to me but you wisely refused it on the basis it might offend the general. You were wiser than I was in making the offer.

While I was irritated over the years by the writing of some of my generals about personalities, I appreciate the fact that they never made any big thing out of our companionship. Gen. Mark Clark may have put it best, when he told one author that he just never asked me about my affair with you. Who could ask for better loyalty?

You were a star in my big show. You were a great help and a good companion. Remember I gave you a record of your favorite song by Noel Coward from "Bittersweet" in North Africa?

> When I'm recalling the hours we've had,
> Why will the foolish tears,
> Tremble across the years?
> Why shall I feel so sad,
> Treasuring the mem'ry of these days
> Always?
> I'll see you again
> Whenever spring breaks through again.
> Time may lie heavy between,
> But what has been
> Is past forgetting.
> This sweet memory
> Across the years will come to me;
> Tho' my world may go awry,
> In my heart will ever lie
> Just the echo of a sigh,
> Good-bye.*

   And so long, Kay, oh so long!   **D.D.E.**

Author's note: Over the years many of Ike's lieutenants (colonels and generals, that is) have written about the constant companionship of Ike and Kay in the European Theater of Operation in World War II. It is amazing that this relationship is one of the biggest romance cover-ups in history. It isn't exactly that there was anything wrong or new about such a relationship. It is amazing how so many from top to bottom have taken part in the cover-up but alluded to it in various volumes written about the war.

*"I'LL SEE YOU AGAIN"
(Noel Coward)
©1929 (Renewed) WARNER BROS. INC.
All Rights Reserved. Used By Permission.

Here are some typical reports:

By Col. Robert Allen, one of Gen. George Patton's staff officers, a longtime Washington reporter and columnist, who was known for some of his earthy diggings in the name of honest journalism: In his book *"Lucky Forward"* (the code name of Patton's headquarters) Allen writes:

"Eisenhower arrived at Lucky for an overnight stay. He rolled into the bomb battered Kaserne (barracks) from which Kraut corpses were still being exhumed, in a long, sleek limousine. At the wheel was Kay Summersby, henna-haired British driver, attired in chic slacks and battle jacket — the instantaneous popeyed focus of all Lucky gallants. By her side was the Supreme Commander's fuzzy little Scotty. Surrounding the car was a squad of hulking motorcycle MPs, flashily attired in Sam Browne belts, white leggings and other trimmings."[12]

A young, aggressive general, James Gavin, who later wrote a book *"On to Berlin"* after Ike's death, thought American forces should have been unleashed to capture Berlin, commented about Kay: (After a review of the 82d Airborne Division in England in August 11, 1944.) "General Eisenhower stopped at General Ridgway's home . . . for tea. Some of the staff were surprised when his chauffeur, Kay Summersby, joined us. Chauffeurs do not normally join their generals for tea. She was an attractive woman, and she seemed to be a very nice person." Gavin goes on: "There was considerable gossip about Kay Summersby. It must have been troublesome to General Eisenhower — if he was aware of it. I once asked John (Beaver) Thompson of the Chicago Tribune if it wasn't just gossip." Thompson replied: "Well, I have never before seen a chauffeur get out of a car and kiss the General good morning when he comes from his office."

Gavin goes on to say that in reading Kay's book, *PF*, "I was startled to learn that after General Eisenhower's visit to the airborne troops, before they took off for Normandy on the night of June 5, he chose to spend the night in a caravan with Miss Summersby."[13]

Maj. Gen. Everett Hughes was an old friend of the Eisenhowers who served as his "eyes and ears" on various assignments. He also kept a diary and also kept his girl friend in his entourage during the war (known as J.P.) Hughes wrote that Ike wanted to hold Kay Summersby's hand, accompany her to her house. To Ike the relationship was innocent enough and lots of fun. "He deeply resented but would not comment upon the gossip."[14] The fact that his wife Mamie could see him in pictures with Kay didn't seem to bother him. She was even behind Ike in the final surrender pictures at Rheims. Col. Ernie Lee, Ike's Army aide, always contended that Ike never slept with Kay. Others disagreed. And Kay's second book put some doubt on Ike's sexual ability — both written after their separation.[15]

In his book *Combat Commander*, Maj. Gen. Ernest (Gravel Voice) Harmon, who commanded an armored division during most of the war, recalls Kay as "pretty" and relates this story. While riding with Kay Summersby at the wheel of Ike's sedan in North Africa, they passed a truck train, which was stopped by the side of the road. "The men were all out urinating against the tires of the trucks. I speculated briefly on Miss Summersby's reaction, but then she volunteered that she wasn't bothered in the slightest. She was used to seeing that sort of thing, she said."[16]

The "in" crowd in many instances listed the romance as one of Ike's failings. Others said that her relationship with Eisenhower helped him win the war — a rather glib term, used often in comments and historical reports.

Mamie Counter Productive?

Author's Note: The book, *Letters to Mamie by Dwight D. Eisenhower*, was edited by John S. D. Eisenhower, their son. His mother gave him the letters in 1972. The publication reads like an after thought to reassure the world that Ike really loved Mamie and not to continue to worry about all the gossip of his constant companionship with Kay which keeps popping up! The result is a counter productive report. Some headlines around the world said the book refutes the Ike-Kay love story. Some said the letters portray Ike as a defensive spouse. But the web is woven for better or worse, and it takes a reflective reading to understand it. Of course, the public was later exposed to a constant series of pictures showing the loving couple in public. At that time they had reunited and Kay was no longer in the picture.

Naturally, Ike wrote Mamie regularly about how much he regretted their separation. He tried to get her to fly somewhere in the Altantic for a reunion but she refused to fly. His letters indicate he often had the "red ass" over their separation. The term was used widely by GIs and other officers who were home sick and wanted to be at home in bed with their wives and lovers, among other things. Ike told Mamie: "Don't go bothering your pretty head about WACS, etc, etc. You just hold the thought that I'm not so worn out by the time this is over, and that you'll just have a wreck on your hands. . ."[17]

In Algiers, Ike ended a letter saying he was all alone and there was no more paper around to continue. Can you imagine a three-star general in the biggest headquarters in North Africa ever running out of paper? Of course GIs often wrote the same thing to their complaining wives about shortage of paper and this was often true at the front line. The mails were delayed during the war, and many a letter went down the drain by enemy action in the oceans that separated loved ones. But Mamie complained almost constantly about not receiving enough mail from him. At one point she got typewritten letters and Mamie was obviously suspicious. Kay, in her diaries, said that she had typed a letter to Mamie for the general to sign.

Kay Summersby grew up in this Irish manor house in County Cork. Ann Perry Photo.

It was a two-sided coin. Ike wrote and complained that he knew nothing of her bank account and how many war bonds she had purchased. When a visiting Senator told Ike that Mamie said he was a poor correspondent, he wrote and told her he wrote her four letters for every one he got. Another common complaint among GIs. One time Ike got a letter Mamie wrote much earlier in which "you gave me the devil for not writing and threatened to ignore me unless I did better." A short time later Mamie wrote a note saying that she had just received eight letters all at once. Again a typical happening among GI ranks.

The complaining went on and on. In October, 1945, long after the war was over, he wrote: "You complain about the dearth of news in my letters but I don't know what you'd consider as news . . . I try to tell you about some of our common friends as I encounter . . . but aside from that there seems to be little to tell. Sometimes I get discouraged trying to write — I never seem to please."[18] It is in this letter he mentions that Kay Summersby is coming back to the states with Gen. Lucius Clay to try and get her U.S. citizenship.

Young Eisenhower writes in the preface to the book: "I cannot completely ignore books such as Merle Miller's, *Plain Speaking*, and Kay Summersby Morgan's *Past Forgetting My Love Affair with Dwight D. Eisenhower.* Certain sentimentalists considered it a beautiful love story and others characterizing it as rubbish. I will not evaluate Mrs. Morgan's effort, although as a witness to many of the events she mentions I can say that her imagination played a stupendous role. No one alive can say isolated incidents . . . didn't happen." He kisses off the Miller report on the divorce letter about Mamie and Kay to Gen. Marshall as "spiteful falsehood."[19]

Letter 5

Charles de Gaulle. AP photo.

DE GAULLE — FIGHTER, SURVIVOR

Dear Ike,

I have to give you a strong and sincere vote of confidence for your appreciation of my role as the leader of the Free French in World War II. Strangely enough, Prime Minister Winston Churchill of England, and the United States President Franklin D. Roosevelt were never really on my side. I don't attribute this entirely to my ego.

You understood my problems and knew my position. My troops never failed you but there were times when we couldn't move fast enough. We started our army from scratch and had very little to scratch with. There was a lot of bickering and controversy in France after our fall. Some French troops escaped at Dunkirk after the fall of France in 1940. Others came from French colonial territories, the Middle East and some managed to escape from or via the unoccupied part of Vichy, France. It took awhile to get them retrained, equipped and organized into fighting units.

I had studied the role of armor after World War I and became, in my opinion, an authority on the conduct of future warfare, tactics, and equipment. One of the problems the Allies faced early in World War II was that the Germans were ahead of us in the use of armor, airplanes and fire and movement. This strategy was very different from World War I static trench warfare.

We did rally our forces and helped you in the thrust in North Africa, which expelled the Germans. While you were planning for the big show in Normandy we were still doing some good work in Italy. After we got stuck at the Rapido-Cassino area (the Gustav line) with all the rest of the Allies, we almost stopped fighting. Churchill's Anzio-Cassino link-up had fallen flat on its face. We had to retrain, regroup, and reorganize the entire Allied thrust. This was a three-month stalemate. Then the French, under Gen. Alphonse Juin, and alongside new American troops, stormed a mountain mass below Cassino. The British pushed forward in their usual painstaking manner. The Polish general, Wladyslaw Anders, who had been a prisoner of the war under both Hitler and Stalin, led his troops, some of whom had been returned by the Russians, to storm the bloody Cassino ridge land.[1] Historians have recorded that the Abbey at Cassino itself was unfortified (which is true), but one has only to walk a short distance to the nearby Polish cemetery and see how valiantly the Poles had fought to get there. This was one of the classic battles of World War II. The Poles accomplished a mission which the Americans, English, New Zealanders and Indians had previously failed.

Many have said that I was the greatest French general since Napoleon Bonaparte. The historians will have to decide that. But I owe much of my success to you. Over Churchill's and Roosevelt's plans, you insisted that the French and I play a major role in the war. At the time I was surprised that you were that intelligent and powerful. You also were very thoughtful to allow a French division to lead the parade through Paris after the liberation.

You almost crossed me up when you wanted me to withdraw from Strasbourg on the Rhine River. We had just captured that before the Battle of the Bulge. I know your reason was to block Hitler's second phase of the Bulge counterattack. I protested quite vigorously, saying we would fight our own Allies to keep Strasbourg.[2]

I told you to leave the specific decisions to American general Jacob Devers, who was the field commander over my forces. You did. With the brilliant help of your Seventh Army under Lt. Gen. Alexander Patch we kept Strasbourg as an anchor.

Meanwhile the British and Americans to the North had a high priority on equipment for the Rhine crossings, along with the exploitation of the surprise capture of the bridge at Remagen. But we were not to be denied. To the south we crossed the Rhine with inadequate equipment and troops. We had reached the Rhine before any other

Ally at Basel in 1944 but could not take advantage of our victory. The Germans for some reason (Hitler madness perhaps) held out in the Colmar pocket for a long time.

FDR and Winnie wouldn't have given me a part of Germany without Stalin's and your help. Stalin, the clever one, of course, made the unilateral decision that France's part would be carved out of the U.S. and British territories.

After the war, I led the French nation until the politicos came along and took over, because I had not taken time to organize my own political party. Later I became President of France from 1959 to 69.

Our common bond may have stemmed from the fact that France helped America achieve freedom in the Revolutionary war, just as America gave France freedom in World War I and II.

Charles de Gaulle

Author's note: DeGaulle was adamant in his discussions with Stalin and other Allied leaders in references to postwar occupation, separation of Germany and the partition of Berlin. This attitude spurred Stalin to remark in Moscow in 1944: "It must be very difficult to govern a country like France, where everyone is so restless." DeGaulle agreed and replied, "And I cannot imitate your example, for you are inimitable."

Stalin pursued the matter and mentioned Maurice Thorez, the French Communist leader, whom the Provisional Government had allowed to return to Paris. DeGaulle was quiet. Stalin added, "Don't take offense at my indiscretion. Let me only say that I know Thorez and that, in my opinion, he is a good Frenchman. If I were in your place I would not put him in prison." After a pause Stalin said with a smile, "At least not right away."[3]

★ ★ ★ ★ ★

Relations between Eisenhower and DeGaulle did deteriorate when the French decided they did not want the North Atlantic Treaty Organization headquarters to remain in France. They were very sensitive about target areas during the cold war era. NATO headquarters was moved to Brussels where it remains. DeGaulle was also upset when Ike recognized a new West German army. DeGaulle did relent, finally, realizing it was a wise move politically and economically. He saw the value of an armed buffer zone between France and Russia.

IKE SAYS:

My Dear General De Gaulle,

You always looked like an officer and a Frenchman. You became a symbol for Free France, her colonies and the world which even Roosevelt and Churchill could not tarnish or overcome. FDR was more anti-DeGaulle than Churchill. Through all of our differences, you emerged as the leader of your native land, although America and Britain were the principal liberators. That is not to negate your fine Army, which served us well on many fronts — especially in my favorite invasion of Southern France.

As a practical military matter to persuade the French troops to fight with the Allies instead of the Germans, I appointed Darlan as French leader of North Africa. When he was assassinated, I tried to make Gen. Henri Giraud, at FDR's insistence, the Free French leader. He did get you and Girard to stand still together long enough for a picture at our Casablanca conference, but our efforts to merge you two, in a joint adventure, never really worked. You kept emerging as the leader and Churchill gave up his objections. I had to recognize you as the civilian leader at 54 (my age also) after the invasion of France before the American government agreed. Most of us knew you were in charge all along. It is strange that you were hard to sell because we knew you as a pioneer in tank warfare and tactics, the one who didn't want to surrender to Nazi Germany after the invasion of your homeland in 1940 and of your flight to London to organize the survivors from the evacuation at Dunkirk. You were more of a hero to the average American than you were to our government, which was swayed in large part by Admiral William D. Leahy, who had been FDR's emissary to the Petain government after your country's defeat.

In short, I was in the business of forming a unity team and you were an essential part of that team as both a fighting man and a political leader who could bring order out of chaos.

To you, the American GI seemed "good-natured, bad-mannered." Londoners said, "They were overfed, oversexed, overpaid and over here."[4] Many would plead guilty on all counts.

I guess author Stephen Ambrose expressed our mutual feeling very well when he wrote: "De Gaulle admired Eisenhower for his openness and honesty; Eisenhower admired DeGaulle for his abilities and his uncompromising devotion to the cause of French sovereignty."[5]

Speaking of the American GI, I am reminded of the fact that we really never understood the French Army. You were gallant and proud fighers, but your cooperation with us was often in question. In North Africa we became allies, but your commanders in many cases made it difficult for us to carry out our mission. We had already learned the hard way. Americans always thought, from President Roosevelt on down, that your nation would cooperate with us to the fullest in our fight with the Germans. But your leaders allowed many of the big and important ships in the Mediterranean to be destroyed by the British instead of sailing into allied ports. Why couldn't we have found a solution for the problem? Even though we equipped your forces, much as you had done ours in World War I, on many levels we didn't seem to coordinate our efforts with any great unanimity. The exception to this experience, I suppose, was your First French Army's cooperation in the invasion of southern France. There the American-French team was superb. But again the American GI never really knew when the French army would attack alongside us in our continuous pressure against the defending Germans. As a result, the Colmar pocket magnet occurred when you drove brilliantly to the Rhine and our forces drove north to join the Normandy forces. But for several months during the winter campaign, we never reduced the Colmar pocket which caused a drain on our forces to the north.

On the other hand, your Gen. Alphonse Juin made one of the great attacks on the hill mass southwest of Cassino, Italy, when both the American and British forces were unable to break the stalemate into the Liri Valley and the southern advance to Rome in the bitter winter of 1943-44. And then don't forget the Polish troops who drove north of Cassino to victory. You both joined our forces as we broke out of Anzio to liberate Rome. One has to raise the question: Just what were the British doing all of this time?[6]

Of course you won the battle of Strasbourg and rightly so. In my near panic, when the Battle of the Bulge happened, I was desperate to shorten our lines and consolidate our forces on a strong defense, so that Hitler's wild resurgence of military strength could not delay our destruction of the German army west of the Rhine. It was obviously Hitler's and his generals last stand. Their gamble paid off initially. I didn't realize what the earlier capture of Strasbourg meant to the French. I was only thinking of military defense when I wanted to pull your troops out and shrink the overstretched American Seventh Army to better defense positions because our intelligence indicated a second thrust towards Bitche after the Bulge attack. Because of our movements and new defense positions, we withstood the secndary attack and, at your insistence, Strasbourg became the southern anchor of our defense. You prevailed in changing my mind about its possible abandonment on strictly military grounds. I give you an A-plus on that countermove.

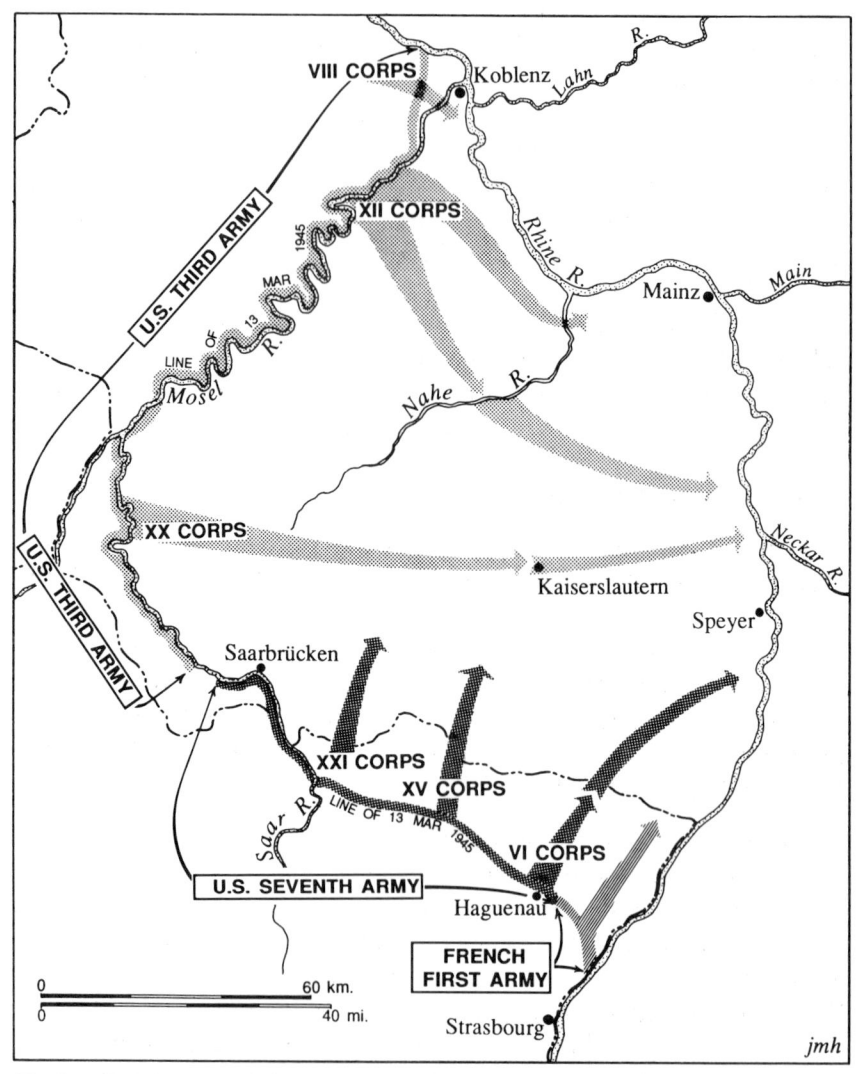

The Saar-Palatinate Triangle. 13-25 March, 1945. Here Patton and Patch penetrated the Siegfried line and closed to the Rhine River.

Again you fought your own battle in part. With fewer resources than our American troops, you crossed the Rhine and pushed into southern Germany including the famous Black Forest. So far our political leaders had not decided what territory you would occupy in the postwar arrangement, so you proceeded to stake out your own claim. You overcame us again in Stuttgart when I wanted Gen. Alexander Patch's troops in there as we headed for Bavaria, the southern Redoubt and the German nuclear development plants and secrets. Our drive was so successful that both sides had plenty of the spoils. We learned to live in peace and harmony in the occupation zone, though your troops sometimes refused to help out our supply needs when military traffic crisscrossed our occupation lines.

You continued as the President of France only to lose out in 1948 when you forgot to organize your political base. But you came back to reign for 10 years over your beloved country. We did organize the North Atlantic Treaty Alliance with headquarters outside Paris, but you kicked us out to Brussels. I convinced you that we should allow the Germans to rearm as part of your defense efforts against our former ally, the Russian bear. It was not an easy decision on your part but we soon realized that victory did not automatically secure peace. We had to stand up to Communist aggression.

Through it all we renewed the common bond between America and France which had existed more than 150 years before when the United States gained its freedom in the Revolutionary war with our British motherland. It has been a strange triangle but we did use it to our mutual advantage in our fight with Adolf Hitler in World War II.

D.D.E.

Letter 6

Franklin D. Roosevelt. AP photo.

FDR: IKE'S THE MAN

Dear Ike,

I played the waiting game with you on the selection of the American commander for the Normandy invasion. Our World War II forces, with British and French partners, and the mighty hordes of the valiant nation of Russia, brought off the greatest sea, land and airborne assault of troops ever on an enemy's territory. Nothing had matched it before and nothing may ever again. Thank God, the development of the secret atomic bomb, which I began in the underground area of the University of Chicago stadium and in New Mexico's desert lands, made it unnecessary to amass an even greater invasion force. We still had anticipated a landing on the homeland of the Japanese Rising Sun.

My choice was not easy. I had you and Gen. George C. Marshall in a neck and neck contest. I decided at Cairo, with some needling by Churchill and Stalin, that the leader of our major, mighty, and decisive thrust fron the West into the feared and hated Nazi stranglehold of Europe in 1944 would be — you Ike. And I withheld the public announcement until Xmas eve when I could inform the American public, as a military present, by naming a commander for our next major war effort designed to end the war in Europe, with help of the Russians. Just think, we had to keep the crazed Hitler wondering for another five months where we would strike. We weren't yet adequately trained nor had the forces necessary to insure success as we moved to liberate France. We were indebted to France forever for helping us gain our own freedom in the Revolutionary War. You even were so eager to find out that you reportedly queried my son, Elliott, about the choice of commander. I told Gen. Marshall, who was the expected choice by most: "I feel I could not sleep at night with you out of the country."[1]

Robert Sherwood later wrote that it was one of my hardest decisions. When I left Cairo for home on December 7, two years after Pearl Harbor, I stopped in Tunis and greeted you with a cheery: "Well, Ike, you'd better start packing."[2]

I had long tended, as an administrator, to parcel out authority among several people and "let them compete with one another."[3] I at last decided that one man, Dwight David Eisenhower, would run the European War. The boy from Kansas, who went to finishing school at West Point, who did not get into combat in World War I but still rose to the head of the leadership circle by this time, was selected as supreme commander for our crusade in Europe.

In the Pacific and Far East I even surpassed myself in this multiple role of leadership competition. "In the great arc stretching ten thousand miles from the northeast of Japan to the Southwest, Admiral Chester Nimitz commanded the northern and central Pacific, Gen. Douglas MacArthur the South West Pacific, and Gen. Joseph Stilwell and Gen. Claire Chennault in the China-Burma-India theater, and each of these pursued his own tactics and relied on his own special combination of arms and services."[4]

As you know, I learned the inner workings of the military organizations and the military mind when I served as Assistant under Secretary of the Navy in World War I. I realized that command belonged on the

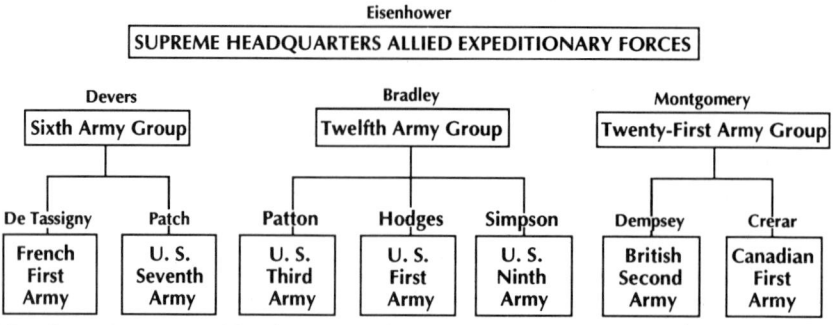

Eisenhower
SUPREME HEADQUARTERS ALLIED EXPEDITIONARY FORCES

Devers	Bradley	Montgomery
Sixth Army Group	Twelfth Army Group	Twenty-First Army Group

De Tassigny	Patch	Patton	Hodges	Simpson	Dempsey	Crerar
French First Army	U. S. Seventh Army	U. S. Third Army	U. S. First Army	U. S. Ninth Army	British Second Army	Canadian First Army

Eisenhower's command for the second front and defeat of the German army.

battle areas. Compared to Stalin in Moscow and Churchill in London, I took a philosophical attitude in the White House. I made it a point, "To look at things whole, to avoid the danger of immediacy, opportunism, expediency, piecemeal planning."[5]

Perhaps I leaned too heavily in all of this on my comrade, Admiral William D. Leahy, who worked out of the White House as my personal chief of staff. Likewise, I left a lot of the work to Harry Hopkins, statesman, my long-trusted friend, and expediter of many, many endeavors in civilian and political affairs. In war, he assumed a more important role in foreign policy, especially relations with our allies, Russia and Britain. He earned the trust of many statesmen, and arranged for you and Gen. Mark Clark to have your introduction to Churchill, who assumed he was leader of our two-man team. But he leaned on me heavily because he knew where the troops and equipment were coming from, in the main, in our joint wartime struggle with a devious and determined enemy, the born-again German military giant.

Your selection, Ike, was not an easy one. After your initial success in the invasion of North Africa, your troops and commanders got complacent and bogged down in Tunisia, but the Allied brass were convinced you were the No. 1 American to lead our forces in the "Big Show." I even dragged my feet when Marshall wanted to promote you to a four star general to keep up with those British Limeys, who kept promoting officers to constantly outrank our people at the conference table and on the fighting front. I wanted to wait until you had more fighting experience and had knocked the Germans out of Tunisia. Under pressure, I relented and never regretted my decision. It was ironic that you soon suffered the horrible loss at Kasserine Pass, but I kept my faith in you.[6] It is strange that the same thing happened when I agreed to make you a five-star general. The Germans immediately made their massive counterattack in the Ardennes and gave us a terrible licking in the costly and disheartening Battle of the Bulge. You were lucky to have Gen. Patton to pull your chestnuts out of that fire, because the British were of little or no help in our time of crisis, although they tried to take credit for the counter punch.

It was in Sicily in December, 1943, when you and Patton realized that I had supported George Patton after the slapping incident. I knew that we needed his spark and drive for a successful invasion thrust into France. After explaining to Allied military leaders of the strategy at Teheran planned with Stalin and Churchill, I turned to George and said, "General Patton, you will have an army command in the great Normandy operation."[7]

I would have to fault you for worrying more about diplomacy than battle dispositions at the Bulge. But historians will fight over these decisions as long as men study military tactics. It did help you defeat the German army west of the Rhine, as you planned, but it sure played hell with the morale of the home front, and a lot of innocent American lads lost their lives in the enemy's last lunge. I also have to give you credit for bearing the cross of French General Charles de Gaulle on your shoulders. For some reason I never could stomach the man. Some said I hated him. Others felt I was overly protective of my favorite ally, France, and perhaps inwardly that I felt his escape to London was mostly showmanship. I now realize that he had an inadequate army and that the French political leaders were not prepared to battle the Germans again, just 21 years after the end of World War I. People will never believe the inadequacy of their forces and ours in the face of a buildup of several years of German military might in the air, on the sea, and on the ground.

The truth of the matter is that I had my greatest trouble with your Army counterpart in the Pacific, Douglas MacArthur. I got rid of him as Army Chief of Staff, although he thought Washington could not function without him. It was a disappointment when I began to learn of some of his erroneous reports such as saying the Philippine Army was a trained, fighting force, or that his defense at Clark Field was adequate. I later learned that he had a meeting the day before Pearl Harbor with all of his military chiefs and told them not to worry about a surprise Japanese attack because they were incapable of same.[8]

He seemed to be carrying on a feud with the Navy constantly and didn't even get along with his own Army Air Corps. He was still running a detached command from his lofty level. And then, when the Japs did attack, he didn't know where to send his planes in retaliation. After the surprise (?) attack my only hope and position was to keep MacArthur in command for the defenses. He had a certain popularity with many Americans as a hero of World War I and to others who were not in sympathy with the bonus marchers. He had built up quite a clique of influential congressmen and businessmen during this regime as Army chief.

As we kept losing the war in the islands, I told Gen. Marshall to write up a citation for a Medal of Honor for the general. This was a morale device and also continued to give hope for the defense of the islands both at home and on the battlefront. I even made one of my gallant, inspiring fireside chats to shore up the American morale in the war effort, which was suffering badly from one Allied defeat after another. But I followed MacArthur's plight and was ". . . eager to help him."[9] I read every battle report. Immediate help for a garrison so far away was impossible. It is ironic that you were our Pacific planner at the time and could offer no quick cure for our problem.

Mac even went along with President Quezon when the Filipino leader wanted to neutralize the islands, which was really a gimmick to wake up and convince Washington of the need for more help. Secretary of War Henry Stimson and Marshall were disturbed that MacArthur did not disown the proposal.[10]

Well, Ike, you had quite a constant companion during the war in Kay Summersby. I enjoyed our picnic lunch with her in North Africa. You were not the first fellow to require the attention of more than one woman in his life. We were only two of many. I had my Lucy Mercer Rutherfurd, my wife's one-time social secretary, for 30 years. It started when I was Assistant Secretary of the Navy. The world never knew at the time but . . . our flirtation never ended. She was with me when I died at Warm Springs. When Eleanor found out about the romance, we had had five children and Lucy was a Roman Catholic. The showdown came at Hyde Park when Eleanor offered a divorce over and over again. My dowager mother begged me never to see "that woman" again. I refused the divorce and kept seeing Lucy. But I never slept with Eleanor after that. Eleanor even once said: "Sex is a thing a woman must learn to endure."

Yes, Lucy and I had our secret phone calls, secret meetings, secret picnics, and secret rides with Secret Service people everywhere. They kept a secret — Lucy's and mine. I once even stopped at her estate, and we kept a train with my private car on a siding one entire day en route to Hyde Park in the sweltering heat. The passengers never knew why the delay occurred and we even forgot one of the Secret Service lookouts when I departed.[11]

So, Ike, we both won in love and war. My love lasted but you went back to Mamie, and you and she became the ideal American couple in the White House as it turned out. You kept the peace for 8 years while I had to wage the war for more than three years after having brought the nation out of its worst depression.

Though historians and critics have tended to criticize us for concessions to the Russians, you and I both know the battle death figures of World War II:[12]

Soviet Union 7,500,000
British Commonwealth 364,775
United States 292,131
France 210,671

The Germans suffered about two-thirds of their casualties on the Russian front.

You and I know how many lives, American lives, they saved. Little wonder that the Soviets are still reminding America of their losses.

Franklin Delano Roosevelt

Love at Warm Springs

Author's note: When Eleanor learned that Lucy had been with FDR at Warm Springs in April, 1945, she was stunned. She confronted her daughter Anna with the information. She admitted that she knew about the affair. Aunt Polly (Laura Delano, cousin of FDR) had given out the secret, on the theory it would reach Eleanor sooner or later anyway. Anna admitted she had been hostess at affairs in the White House when Lucy was present. This, naturally, infuriated Eleanor also.[13]

Lucy, a society gal whose family had lost its money, became a governess to the Winthrop Rutherfurd family, eventually marrying him after his wife died. Actually FDR's polio paralysis in 1921 had made him a prisoner of his wife and mother. The world did not know how bad his paralysis was until years later. He was always in a wheel chair, except to speak, and then he was cleverly manipulated at the beginning and end so that his inability to walk was not noticed by the audience or in the thousands of pictures and film reports seen the world around.

Lucy, could not attend any of FDR's inaugurals, and his funeral, and became hysterical after FDR's death. Her recovery was slow and release of the news of their romance and FDR's paralysis even slower.

Mac Versus Navy

Of course, Roosevelt always was the mediator between the Navy with Admiral Leahy at his side in his dealings with MacArthur. As the war went on Admiral Chester Nimitz wanted to bypass the Philippines, but MacArthur had made his famous declaration, "I Shall Return," and FDR and the American public would not have stood for a bypass.

Militarily it would have been a life-saving move, in all likelihood, to forget an early return to the Philippines. Our forces would have been more effective in Okinawa and the islands closer to the final assault area on Japan.

Roosevelt even worried about MacArthur politically. He was worried about two people in 1944 — Dewey and MacArthur. An astute politician — as keen as any in the 20th Century probably — FDR said ten years before that he considered MacArthur and Huey Long, a radical and self-serving demigod from Louisiana, two of the ". . . most dangerous men in the country." He knew MacArthur was strong with many Republican leaders and that he was anti-New Deal. He could campaign against FDR and charge that America had deserted the Philippines and starved the Pacific theater in favor of the European crusade. But in a secret file he had the information that MacArthur had said "he was sure he could defend the archipelago." He claimed the enemy could not launch an air attack on the islands.

In a letter to a Nebraska congressman, MacArthur referred to the "sinister drama of our present chaos and confusion."[14] MacArthur finally lost interest in the political balloon. He even made another murmur in 1948 but decided to stay with his empire in the Far East. He made his swan song speech to the Republican convention in 1952, which nominated Dwight D. Eisenhower as its candidate. A strange happening of events and intertwining of American leaders in world affairs — FDR, Ike, MacArthur, Marshall . . . the latter being mentioned as a running mate for FDR in 1944.

IKE SAYS:

Dear Mr. President,

You were my commander in chief for the tenure of your office which was a long time. I served faithfully, almost suffering in the political limelight as head of the Allied Forces in my crusade in Europe. It has been reported that I was apolitical. I had never considered myself to have party affiliation. I have remarked that the only time I would have voted for you would have been in 1944 because a war was going on.

When the Democrats pursued me as a possible candidate after the war, I finally indicated that I really was a Republican. With that admission, my life was never the same again. Despite what I said, the politicos decided they wanted a victory at the polls, as well as on the battlefield and I was their man. By 1952, I found myself in a campaign running against the New Deal and the Fair Deal, which had lasted for twenty years.

I was known for my opinions, bluntness, barracks language and temper. When you were elected in 1932, I remarked that it was a good thing. We needed a change and someone who could get something done. But I also recalled years later to friends that while I had to help you to bed as a young officer from too much drink, they would never have to put me in bed for the same reason.[15] Even in my memoirs I would not attack you.[16] I had a hard time including you in my list of "towering governmental figures on the West" but I finally did.[17]

Historians have reported our body chemistry just didn't mix.[18] And I guess that was true. You were debonair, determined, courageous, self-assured — way above my status in life when I was leading the troops of several great nations in a massive war in Europe.[19] Besides that, I had been a planner for your strategy in the Pacific with no solution because there was none, due to our inadequate preparation following World War I.

You kept me dangling for a long time as the Allied commander and it was only after Stalin demanded to know who would lead our massive invasion of France that you selected me. And then you waited a long time to make the public announcement.[20]

I had arrived at my status as a good soldier and patriot with great faith in my country and responded to the call of duty again and again, while wondering about the sacrifices a soldier and his family have to pay — and I mean low pay, change of stations, slow promotions and family hardships to name a few hazards of my soldier occupation.

On one of my return trips to America, we discussed the future of Germany and you wanted it broken up into small states. I felt Germany should be kept intact and developed as a friendly, democratic nation. As the war progressed, I realized that while I was fighting the Germans with all the force we had, the nation would be a great buffer against the onrolling Russians from the East. After the war my disillusionment with Communist leaders surfaced. At the conference tables of both military and political leaders, I realized the love affair with the Red Army was only a temporary one. I guess history has borne me out on that one. You and President Harry Truman, felt you could deal with Stalin. While I admired the man and what he had done to repel the invading German forces, I soon learned that while my acquaintanceship with Marshal Zhukov was friendly, warm, mutual — it would not lead to peace or agreement on the many questions facing our two nations. He certainly did not remain the hero with the ruling Communists in Russia for long after reporters wrote of our mutual admiration society in headlines and stories all over the world. He was soon shelved. It took a long time to convince you that Gen. Charles de Gaulle was the real leader of the Free French. Early in North Africa, the British and I realized that DeGaulle was going to be the French leader but you, back in the remote White House, had to be dragged into recognition of that fact and recognition of DeGaulle much later. The British, who also had a bit of disdain for the general, realized much earlier that working with DeGaulle would be to the advantage of all. In fact, after we had driven across France and I needed someone to turn to for civilian takeover, I put DeGaulle in charge and the State Department finally recognized what so many of us in the field already knew.

While you bragged about your close relationship with Churchill, you also deferred to him in much of our military planning. As a result, I was in a close working relationship with Churchill and together we solved many problems and made military decisions which were necessary to ensure success on the battlefield. We needed a coordinated allied team which could use its resources, manpower and talent to mutual advantage.

I also was the man who had to say no to Churchill when it was necessary. He had a habit of over debating an issue which could not be decided in his favor. Oh, yes, I should mention that Marshall also led good interference in our constant battle with Field Marshal Alan Brooke, the British chief of staff, who never gave up trying to replace me with Montgomery as the ground commander of our forces. He wanted me to be the team cheerleader and administrator while Monty carried on the battle. How long the war would have taken if Monty had been put in charge? When the British once realized that we had the bulk of the troops involved in the conflict, they renewed their efforts to at least have the top military man in charge, in order to grab more of the headlines and glory. I doubt if I could have held the American generals if Monty had taken over the field command after the invasion.

It would have helped along the way if I could have had more praise and support from you publicly and privately during the time we were in North Africa until our entry into Germany. You never let me forget my place in the pecking order, did you? And we all failed to give our individual divisions and corps and division commanders the publicity they all deserved. Our public relations efforts were not nearly as effective as the British. You did back me up in my firm stand to make Churchill agree to carry out the invasion of southern France. He fought me to the bitter end on that one but you answered his complaints with a reply to leave the decision to the supreme commander. Such backing was great. It also is interesting to note that Gen. Marshall finally convinced Alan Brooke — with whom he did not exactly get along — that America had divisions in the U.S. which could not be landed at the Normandy ports. Southern France had the depots which could move troops into action much faster. Churchill at the last moment was still arguing that we should use Brittany ports. It would have taken much longer to get the troops to the front. Besides the transport had to be landed also and my decision for Anvil/Dragoon meant a shorter connector since we moved to link up at an early date — much earlier than many planners had hoped. We have to give the French forces and our Seventh Army credit for that speedy triumph.

You did promote me twice on Marshall's recommendation — once when our troops were slow in liberating Tunisia and again just before all hell broke loose in the Ardennes and my drive across Europe had slowed to a snail's pace. But historians and newsmen often forget how stubborn the Germans fought our advances.

D.D.E.

P.S. In Algiers we all got a good laugh when your secret service man, Mike Reilly, wouldn't let Kay Summersby, my chauffeur-aide-secretary-companion, drive your car. When you finally met her you said you had heard a bit about her. You then asked Kay why she didn't drive you from the plane. As she blushed, Kay replied, "Your Secret Service wouldn't let me."[21] Everyone laughed. Then you asked her if she'd like to drive you from then on and she was delighted. She also appreciated the affection you showed for Telek, the famous Scottie I gave her. Likewise, when you invited her to have lunch with a "dull old man."[22]

Letter 7

Harry Truman. UPI photo.

TRUMAN VERSUS IKE

Author's note: When FDR died, Harry S. Truman in 1945 at 61 became the 33d President of the United States. This was the eve of victory in Europe. A big surprise for the end of the war in the Pacific was in the offing, through the soon-to-be perfected atomic bomb. Here is the commentary Truman might have written now to Ike concerning his relations with Ike as commander in chief of America's military might and later when Ike succeeded Truman as President.

Dear Ike,

Our lives criss-crossed in a crazy, mixed up pattern. History may eventually say that we ended up as enemies. Why I'm not sure. Actually we should have been close friends, cooperative in our work against the Communist world and the forces of tyranny. But we weren't. I may have been a stubborn Missouri mule but you were a country boy from Kansas who went to the top with a lot of help. You seemed to want to maintain an aloofness and independence that I found abrasive at times. I was never sure of your cooperation except when you rallied around the flag with me to head the North Atlantic Treaty Organization forces on January 1, 1951, which established the military defense of Europe as the Russians started to rattle their sabers against us. You left that assignment to conduct a vicious campaign against my Presidency in 1952, when we should have continued our efforts to consolidate our stubborn Allies and prepare the nation for another era of peaceful greatness. I guess you could say I did it my way as President and you did it your way when you succeeded me.

I never really believed in your Presidency and never thought generals should go into public life. You quoted me in *Crusade in Europe* as telling you there was nothing I wouldn't do for you including the Presidency in 1948.[1] Frankly, I never believed in professional soldiers running for President — guess the memory of Grant's two terms partly colored my thoughts. But then I never let anyone forget that I had commanded Battery D of the 129th Field Artillery in World War I in France, as a National Guardsman from Missouri.

Well, I would like to share my thoughts about three of your Army comrades — Marshall, MacArthur and Bradley.

I stole Gen. Bradley from you after the war to run the Veterans Administration. He was another "good ole" Missouri boy. In fact after you picked him for your No. 1 American ground commander in Europe for the Normandy invasion, you sort of forgot his greatness at your worst battle, the Bulge in the Ardennes. You took his First Army and gave it to that questionable British General, Montgomery. I later was referring to him and an American General (Maj. Gen. Ernest J. Dawley, who was relieved) when I talked about squirrelhead generals at Salerno. I didn't mean Mark Clark, either, because I called when the story hit the papers and told him personally I was not referring to him.[2]

Montgomery didn't do anything with his troops until after Patton drove from the south to the Bulge flank to entrap and rout the Nazis. You know my knowledge of history has always been pretty good, both as a boy and as a man.

We both admired Gen. Marshall very much. He was one of my most trusted servants after I became President. He made you what you were and then you turned on him. You even refused to defend him against that slimy Joe McCarthy and witch-hunter Bill Jenner. (Both senators, McCarthy from Wisconsin and Jenner from Indiana waged vigorous campaigns of name calling — Communist frontmen as they referred to men like Marshall.)[3] You ran a dirty camapign against my administration in 1952 and that guy for Vice-President, Richard Nixon, spread the manure-smelling untruths in a vicious and disruptive campaign. He even accused me of being soft on communism, crime and corruption. Why, I fought against those three evils all of my life and my record shows it. Gen. Marshall was a faithful citizen and served his country more gallantly than any other person I know. I even said during World War II that Marshall was the greatest living American, this when FDR was living at 1600 Pennsylvania Avenue. His patriotism wsa unquestionable, but you chose not to defend it adequately. You kept referring to remarks you made in his defense at a Denver press conference. Why couldn't you have defended him in Wisconsin or anywhere and often? Did you ever call on him for advice and help during your administration?

During World War II, Marshall had to stay in Washington because President Roosevelt and the Congress could not get along without him. He would have made a great battlefield tactician as he had proved in World War I.

My relationship with MacArthur has been detailed in many volumes. As you know, I finally found out about MacArthur's character and ambitions just as you learned much earlier in your association with him in the 1930s. After he continued to try and make foreign policy in the Far East and disrupt our United Nations peace effort in Korea, I had no choice but to relieve him of his duties. I even flew to Wake Island during the war to meet MacArthur to detail our policy, to better coordinate our public remarks on our efforts to restore peace and to keep the conflict from spreading into World War III and the annihilation of mankind. Mac never thought in those terms — only of himself and victory at any price. Thank heavens, you also kept the peace for the eight years you were President. I think I realized during your terms that history was going to be more kind to you as President than I ever expected.

After you were elected, I offered my entire staff and facilities for your use, but you chose to go your own way. You only allowed me one audience. You and MacArthur tried to run the Korean War before I left the Presidency, but I blew the whistle. When I learned that MacArthur was giving you his attack-peace plan while I was still commander in chief, I blew my stack. I reminded the General that I was still his boss. His plan was to bomb a fair amount of the world in Asia and drive back to the Yalu River where he had failed so terribly in 1950, after he had assured me the Chinese would not intervene in the war. His plan wasn't anything new to me, despite Mark Clark's agreement. As you wisely decided, it wouldn't have worked without causing World War III in all probability.

We met again at the funeral of President John F. Kennedy, your successor as President. What we said and chatted about in the car we shared, going to the funeral, and later at Blair House has never been recorded at any length. History will never know if we did anything except exchange pleasantries.[4]

Harry S. Truman

P.S. I forgot to mention the gals in our lives. Mine were all legitimate. I got my comeuppance from wife, Bess, regularly and worried about my mother and her mother. I stewed over our daughter, Margaret, no end and was never madder than when a review of her vocal concert, by Paul Hume, appeared in the Washington Post. As a piano player of some note (even Stalin liked my Chopin rendition as Potsdam), I let the no good critic know what I thought of him.

Well, while the war was going on we enjoyed hearing the rumors about your constant companion, Kay Summersby. Even Roosevelt had lunch with you two in North Africa. There was a great deal written about a letter you sent to Marshall wanting to divorce Mamie and marry Kay after the war. Marshall let you have it, and I destroyed the letter you wrote before I left the White House. Historians have never been able to uncover any real evidence of the existence of this letter. Perhaps it was yet another part of the big coverup.

Of course, FDR had his girl friend, Lucy Mercer Rutherfurd, who was with him when he died at Warm Springs, but that affair which lasted for nearly thirty years was really covered up outside the family and inner circle.

Unquestionably his wife Eleanor made him pay for his misdeeds. There have always been rumors about Presidents and generals and their romances. Why, President Harding is supposed to have slipped his girlfriend, Nan Britten, into the White House for rendezvous. As the press later became more open about these affairs, the exploits of President Jack Kennedy practically became household conversation.

Did Truman Offer???

Author's note: Did Truman offer Ike his support if he wanted to be President of the United States? This question has been debated ever since the Potsdam Conference in Germany in July, 1945. As the years went on, Truman, almost grew bitter toward Ike, and not without reason, went out of his way to say that he never had endorsed Ike during his Presidency. He did admit he was exuberant in his remarks to Ike when he met him in 1945. "I told him how grateful the American people were for the job he'd done . . . he said that under no circumstances was he going to get into politics . . . He said I said it (support for President), but I didn't . . ."⁵ On the other hand, Ike recorded, the President turned to him and said, "General, there is nothing that you may want that I won't try to help you get. That definitely and specifically includes the Presidency in 1948."⁶ In his second book, Bradley repeats the Ike quote and says, "I kept a poker face" when the remark was made.⁷

Years later in the April 1, 1991 issue of the New Yorker magazine, Clark Clifford, Truman loyalist and confidante, said his boss (Truman) "would have been delighted" if Ike had run for President as a Democrat.

Clay Blair was coauthor of the second Bradley book and one wonders if Blair and Bradley's second wife, Kitty, wrote more of the book than the general. While Truman fell out with Ike, he never quit praising his fellow Missourian, Bradley, whom he selected for the massive task of returning millions of soldiers home and handling their various needs as director of the Veterans Administration. Then he named him Army Chief of Staff and later chairman of the Joint Chiefs during the Korean War.

Truman's relations with his top generals are always fascinating reading. After the capture of the Philippines and the return of President Sergio Osmena, Truman did not follow MacArthur's advice and named Paul V. McNutt, former Indiana governor, his high commissioner. McNutt had served there with MacArthur from 1937 to 1939 and was a match for the American generalissimo with his Filipino uniforms, pay and pompous operation. It was McNutt not MacArthur who rehabilitated the Islands for independence. Meanwhile MacArthur sat on his Japanese throne running the military and the government. When Independence Day came for the Philippines in 1946, McNutt ran the show and MacArthur came down for the ceremony. McNutt never gloated over his authority but reinstituted a civilian government as best he could, and introduced the Islanders to competitive commerce and development. While the Communists tried to take over, McNutt gave his all to make the Philippines a successful nation.⁸

IKE SAYS:

Dear President Truman,

I was your obedient servant as an Army officer while you were in the White House. We grew up in the Great Midwest of America, but while our paths crossed over the years our thinking almost never came together.

You hailed me as a hero when we met in Europe after the war and offered me support for anything I wanted including the Presidency but you later changed your mind. And once I was out of uniform I admitted that I had thought for some time that our brains were not on the same wave length ever since the end of World War II.

Our common interests included admiration for Generals George Marshall, Douglas MacArthur and Omar Bradley. We also agreed on the importance of the unification of the military after the war and the creation and continuation of the North Atlantic Treaty organization for the Free World's defense in Europe.

Beyond those objectives our thinking went in different directions for many years to come. It was not until our attendance at the untimely death and funeral of President John F. Kennedy that we sat down and talked in friendly terms as long-time comrades. We probably should have long before.

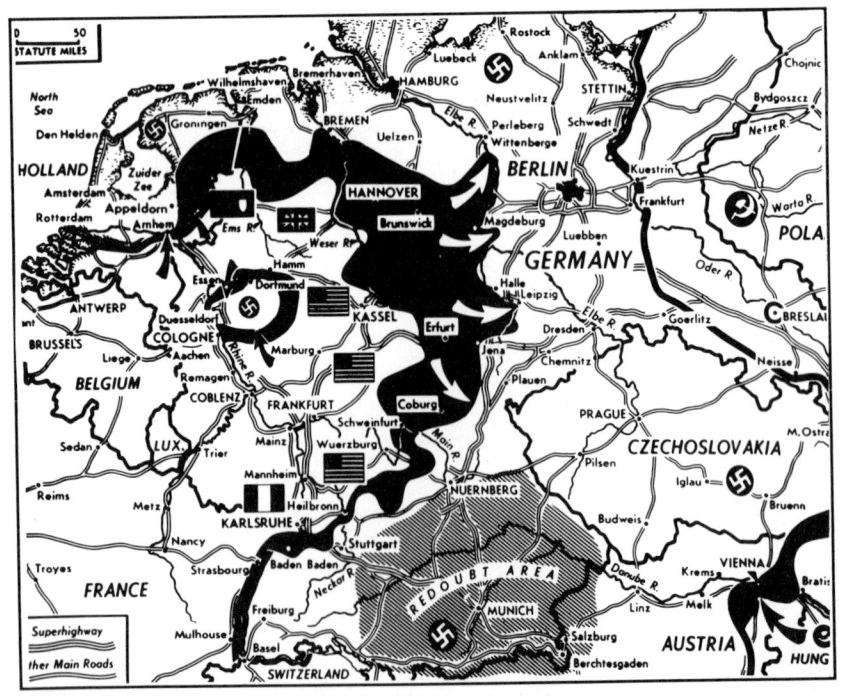

The battle lines in Germany on April 13, 1945. The shaded Redoubt area was a suspected last stand area for the Nazis. AP map.

I was an irritant to you in many ways. When we went together for a reunion of the 35th Division, after the war, I was the center of attention. I caught the headlines. Throughout your Presidency, my name shone a bit brighter, perhaps, than yours in the eyes of veterans, politicians and the voters. My name surfaced as possible opposition in the Presidential race of 1948 but I declined, stayed in uniform and left them guessing about my political dreams. At the time I didn't want to be President but it must be admitted that I had growing pressures from many directions for me to take off my uniform and become an active political leader in America. You beat Tom Dewey in an upset in 1948 and you made the most of it. You re-established an independent political base and while many did not realize your greatness, you have emerged as both a hero and a very capable President who guided America through a difficult era. You, after all, had always been interested in the Army since your days in combat in World War I with the Missouri National Guard, and as an overseer of military spending and contracting while you were a senator. Your leadership in this effort obviously put you in good standing patriotically and politically with FDR when he accepted you for Vice-President on his ticket in 1944 at age 60.

As Army chief of staff after the war, I was in a good position to advise you on many matters, but while you took Gen. Marshall into your confidence and had compete faith in him, you ignored me in such decisions as the Truman doctrine for deterring the Russians, aid to Greece, the Russian blockade of Berlin and other matters being orchestrated in part by the Army and my associates in the great crusade in Europe during the war.[9]

After I left the Army and became president of Columbia University, you turned to me for help to put on my uniform and come back as commander of NATO which was floundering without leadership and almost without troops. I answered your call to duty as all good soldiers should, when asked, and put up our defenses and the free world's in Europe. I even urged the Germans to form an army in mutual defense only five years after we had defeated them totally on the battlefield, with the help of our good Ally, Soviet Russia. The Soviets had turned on us and were busy gobbling up territory around the world and encouraging aggression by North Korea into South Korea.

It wasn't a political trick, but during my campaign against your leadership and administration in 1952, I promised to go to Korea and end the war at the 38th parallel. On that point, I would say we were in agreement that our real goal was to re-establish the 38th parallel as the boundary between North Korea and South Korea, which the peace table conferees had agreed upon in 1945. It is strange that one of our negotiators just drew a mark on the map dividing the country, and there was the 38th parallel in history once and for all.

But let's get back to the Presidency. Your tenure was a turbulent time and your decisions look better now in many directions than they did at the time. Politicians and people seemed to want better government than they were getting after years of the New Deal and your Fair Deal. I always thought my brother, Milton, was more qualified for the presidency than myself but the politicos put the pressure on me. I finally succumbed and that started the duel between your side and my side. I ran against your record and won a smashing victory. My running mate was Richard Nixon who waged an ever harder — and perhaps — vicious campaign against you and your administration. Along the way I gave only token acknowledgement of our mutual hero, Gen. Marshall, while some of my party leaders, mainly Senators McCarthy and Jenner, vilified the war and postwar leader with undeserved criticism and questions about his loyalty to the American cause. Such below-the-belt comments were not in the American tradition of fairness, and while I defended Marshall in a Denver press conference, it got little notice. My omission of his defense in Wisconsin with McCarthy on stage has been criticized ever since. Both senators took every opportunity to shake my hand and jump in my campaign bandwagon.

While you offered your staff for briefings after my election, I took a cool and distant attitude and decided to do it on my own — much in the manner you treated me while you were President and I was Army chief of staff.

Despite your political remarks my feeling was: "Don't see, don't feel, don't admit, and don't answer; just ignore your attacker and keep smiling."[10]

D.D.E.

Letter 8

Winston Churchill. AP photo.

ARCHITECT FOR VICTORY

Dear Ike,

We both believed in victory in battle and in politics. My symbol was a 'V' for Victory made by holding up my index and middle fingers. Your crusaders marched across North Africa and Europe to free the continent from fascism with the help of the mighty Russian army.

Later in victory, you ran for President and improved upon my sign by throwing your arms in a 'V.' You won in your campaigns and the people and the world voted: "I like Ike" — your trademark.

Your entire body seemed to cry out for victory.

I liked Ike long before your political campaign. Our paths crossed so often and intertwined so much in World War II, it is sometimes hard to recall what you did and what I did in our dealings with so many allies, great leaders and associates including some stubborn ones. But overcome we did.

You were just a colonel in the American Army at Ft. Lewis when I started fighting the War, which I had been predicting so long before its actual outbreak in 1939. The devious Nazis invaded the small, poverty-ridden, impoverished country of Pulaski's native land of Poland on September 1. France and Britain declared war on Germany two days later. The Polish Army was so out of date it still relied on horse-drawn artillery and antiquated weapons. Their only hope was VALOR. They loved their native land and are still fighting for it. I would have to say that one of my major disappointments in World War II was the failure to establish a free and independent Poland after our victory on the battlefield. They gave us so many men to help in the fight and we failed in the overall mission to liberate the Poles. We let Stalin and the Russians trick us into a coup that meant more years of poverty, impoverishment, domination.

But we didn't lose them all. In fact, our road to victory came from mutual cooperation, and hard fighting. The war began at a time when the world little realized the horrible tricks that monster Hitler had played upon mankind. He cared not for Jews, women, children, soldiers, or the German nation. His heinous behavior proved that he was only concerned with Adolf Hitler and his ego. Even now it is difficult to give him credit for anything affecting human progress, such as the autobahns and the Beetle motor car. But with his charisma and evil military genius he did hold us at bay for too long. And your military forces didn't swing the balance, with adequate troops, for almost four years after the war started. He made us wonder even up until just before V-E Day — wonder how we would destroy the maniac who had held the German people since 1933. Seldom have so many fought and died for so many bad causes and for so many wrong reasons. Hitler's tenure on this earth was despicable. We had to dig out his roots and destroy him — a new German terror that raged across Europe.

Your President, Franklin Delano Roosevelt, of whom I was very fond, early on gave me you and Gen. Mark Clark to play the major roles for the American springboard based in England, which would lead the Allies to victory in North Africa, Sicily, Italy, France and Germany. His military genius, Gen. George Marshall, found you for both of us. FDR was truly a great and long-suffering American who dedicated his every word, thought, physical fiber, and superior brain power to military victory.

The moment you hit London in 1942, there was little doubt that my dream of freedom could come true again. I passed the mantle of military leadership to you, or as you would say in your language, I passed the ball to you in your court for military salvation. I told you and Clark that we had been bled dry in World War I and we could not repeat the performance 21 years later in World War II. We had simply spilled too much blood in battle.[1]

I tabbed you the "American Bulldog" and Clark the "American

Eagle" right away. I could tell you would give us the uplift of spirit to unite the Allies and lead us to victory after we had suffered so many defeats over a bloody, treacherous and discouraging three years of war. Your counsel and leadership overcame many of our faults, our doubts, our misapprehensions, and our inadequacies. Is it possible to pay a greater tribute to any wartime and peacetime leader of mankind? It is seldom one comes so close to a leader of men who can overcome so many obstacles, military reverses, petty bickering among services, nations and people. But you saw our common enemy and overcame all of these problems and obstacles. You led a crusade so free people could return to civilian life and breathe free air in so many nations, new and old, and find a better life than our forefathers enjoyed. The victory meant liberty for many but not all. We just failed in our attempt to overcome the Russian bear. He was too much for us. Of course, he was too much for Hitler also. We have to give him credit for stopping the Nazis in their drive east to conquer the No. 1 Communist country in the world and to seize the rich oil fields and other natural resources and areas we all needed so desperately just to survive, let alone win a war.

So much for philosophical thoughts.

How did we overcome our problems and win the war? Just think of the poor state of readiness in the American Army and Navy alone. Our ability to produce weapons and vehicles for war was pitifully inadequate. We weren't prepared to fight a professional army of Germans, and much of our armor was old-fashioned. But with help of the free world and our combined leadership genius — industry, farmers, manufacturers, researchers, scientists, Rosie the Riveter, the private in the rear ranks — victory became possible. It perhaps was the great American dream rekindled after your nation had bailed us out of the trenches and near defeat in 1917-18.

Needless to say, my pride swells within me when I think of my own American heritage — my mother, once an American — and the bond we shared for so many years, even though my country would have denied you your freedom if your great citizenry hadn't fought for what it believed in before, during, and after the Revolutionary War.

Coming from the ranks of British power, and after writing about and forecasting the dastardly deeds our German cousins were playing on their war trumpets, I told the House of Commons in my first statement at age 66, as Prime Minister in 1940:

"I have nothing to offer but blood, toil, tears, and sweat."

The following month, in the fight against Germany after France fell in June, 1940, I pledged:

"We shall not flag or fail. We shall fight on the seas and oceans, we shall fight with growing confidence and growing strength in the air, we shall defend our island, whatever the cost may be, we shall fight on the beaches, we shall fight on the landing grounds, we shall fight in the fields and in the streets, we shall fight in the hills; we shall never surrender."

My two messages thundered and rang around the world. I was picking up a small nation with a world-wide empire, which we were to lose in part with victory, at a time of despair and distrust. While you Americans had come to our aid with volunteers, Bundles for Britain, some ships and planes, we were still very much alone until the Japanese attacked Pearl Harbor.

The Germans would never conquer England. And perhaps history has never recognized Hitler's fear of water — so as to understand why an invasion of our tiny island was never attempted. It was a salvation for our side in a struggle that involved most of mankind.

While victory never ensures peace, at least it gave us a chance to go and mend our ways, return to being our brother's keeper, to preserve mankind in the new nuclear age that was about to descend upon us — with all of its risks, power, improvements and innovations. The A-bomb, though, made life even more worrisome, risky, frightening. Its finality certainly encouraged our youth into thoughts of revolt and shrank our world even more.

In 1941-45, we had to weld a team of fighting men. We had fought some successful set battles, staged some massive air raids, defended our territories in many areas, conducted some successful (that's what we liked to call them) retreats. We maintained a foothold which could be nutured and cultivated into enemy territory. We had to overcome countless problems and obstacles.

The American manpower ranked high on the list of requirements for victory. You soon were producing tanks, planes, anti-aircraft guns, powerful artillery weapons, new rifles and machine guns, better portable food rations, better clothing to protect our soldiers, and motors and ships that could move our soldiers from crisis to crisis as needed. This production ensured versatility in our maneuvers at a much faster rate than the enemy dreamed, although he had already seen the great advantage of mobility in modern warfare. We just outproduced him, besides outfighting him.

Once we blunted the Germans, the counter moves became a massive undertaking for Roosevelt and me (along with our military chiefs and civilian ministers, aides and deputies).

The sly Japanese bombed Pearl Harbor, which made most Americans realize this war was theirs also. While many of your civilian leaders had hesitated earlier, the day of infamy made the conversion from sympathy and covert aid and individual help to a rally around the flag. Civilian careers were forgotten to share the privations in uniform in war with their No. 1 English-speaking ally. It didn't make us happy to see the Yellow tide swirl in victory in the Far East for so long; it did unite our countries. I must admit we were inclined to leave the Far East to the American forces. We provided a worthy anchor in India, Burma and other possessions in the Pacific. But we had enough problems to solve and we left the rearming and liberation of China to your U.S. forces.

After my agreement over the Atlantic Charter with FDR the question immediately arose of how we would reenter the Continent and who would lead our endeavors. I had my British choices. But Marshall had you and many others ready to take up the crusade leadership. Little did we know that we were also creating a President when "Ike" became a household name in America and in most of the world. It was your destiny to lead us out of the wilderness of confusion, doubt, distrust, defeatism.

I had little to do with your selection, but would like a little credit for your success. Weapons and bombs and motors provide the hardware but war is won by leaders who can mold men and equipment into a successful and effective fighting team on the battlefield.

We had probed for soft spots around possible invasion areas. Marshall wanted an immediate landing on the coast of France to free our occupied ally and to confront the German war machine head-on. We held out for a different path via French North Africa and the soft underbelly of Europe. We were barely holding out in Egypt. After we had stopped the Italians, who had been running around Tunis, Libya, Ethiopia and other areas with some military wins and losses, the Germans took over when they failed and the British suffered loss after loss. Until our breakout at El Alamein in October, 1942, and your invasion of western North Africa the following month, we had never had a real victory in North Africa. After that, we never had a major reversal.

Following much haggling and negotiating, we agreed to send your forces into a semi-friendly area of western territories where the Vichy French, through an agreement with Hitler, continued to control its North African colonies. We hoped that Spain would remain neutral and it did, although we had plans to occupy Spanish Morocco.

It was necessary for us to have a locale where we could build bases for contermeasures and a battle training ground. If we had first tried to invade Dakar and environs it would have been an even longer and more difficult struggle to clutch the throat of the enemy in central Europe and to strangle him into defeat.

Roosevelt agreed to the North African invasion and we then learned by doing. Your green American troops drove east while our veterans drove west from Egypt, to join in a final victory in Tunis and to capture most of the Germans, although we drove some of them out to sea to fight another day.

Your President gave me a bad time for a long time about the role of Gen. Charles de Gaulle and his leadership of the Free French. His animosity towards DeGaulle apparently came from some bad influence on several fronts. He honestly thought America could deal with Vichy France, and thus neutralize the French Fleet and convince the fragments of the French Army scattered around the globe to join in our efforts to lift Hitler's stranglehold on Marshal Petain, hero of World War I, and his occupation government. When DeGaulle first came to Britain after France's fall in June, 1940, we British likewise suspected his plans. Egotistical actions made him hard to deal with. Roosevelt felt he was not popular enough to lead the Free French forces, when he made an attempt to capture Dakar. FDR was inclined to use Gen. Henri Giraud for French leadership and we considered him and other potential admirals and generals for leadership. After much haggling DeGaulle emerged from Algiers after our invasion there as the popular leader and while we tried Admiral Darlan initially, his assassination almost opened the role for the French martinet. Roosevelt tried to sell Giraud with a trip to America where in Detroit he praised "the magnificent achievements of the Nazis in reconstructing German society."[2] You and I learned to get along with DeGaulle shortly afterwards, as loyal Frenchmen turned to him. The bad advice probably came from Admiral William D. Leahy, who had been sent by FDR to the Vichy

French government after Hitler's conquest. Leahy served as FDR's chief military advisor in the White House throughout the war.

One of my early victories in the Mediterranean, seldom reported, was an agreement in 1941 with the Russians when we took control of the Middle East in cooperation with the French and ensured our continued sharing in the rich oil fields. It boggles the mind to think what would have happened to all of our valiant efforts if Hitler had been smart enough to fight for possession of the Middle East. And by our maneuvers with the French, we made sure of our mutual interests after the war in the forever-troubled Middle East, which continues to suffer from religious and political wars now five decades later. Our effort to neutralize the area, in the interest of world peace and self-determination, kept failing.

When we joined forces with Russia, our biggest role was to provide the supply lifelines to the Russian Bear in the Middle East. One of the best routes was through Persia. An active German mission was present in Teheran and "German prestige stood high"[3] when we agreed with the Russians to enter negotiation with the Persians on August 17, 1941.

We fixed the date for British and Russian forces to move into Persia on August 25. Four days later it was all over. The oil fields were quickly overtaken, the local generals ordered the troops back to barracks and the Shah issued a cease-fire. Our casualties were 22 killed and 42 wounded. Arrangements "with the Russians were smoothly and swiftly agreed."[4] Teheran was jointly occupied on September 17. The creation of the supply route to Russia through the Persian Gulf was now possible. While we began the project, your United States forces expanded the operation. Over a period of four and one-half years, five million tons of supplies moved over the route. Imagine that the Big Three could meet there with security and comfort two years later.[5]

Next our forces had to be prepared to defend against possible moves by the Germans through Turkey or the Caucasus, we developed strong defense positions in Palestine and Syria.[6] The French helped out in occupation of Syria. In effect, we axed Hitler's Oriental plans. Just think of the results if he had made the oil fields of the Middle East his early goal instead of the capture of Stalingrad, Leningrad and Moscow. His terror might have reigned much longer and slowed the entire war efforts of the Three Great Powers. Too often we have been inclined to forget our Soviet ally because after victory he became very defensive in relationships with the Western World; he never let us forget his severe casualties suffered in the Great Patriotic War against the Nazi terror, or the fact that we did not bring our full forces in mass to oppose the German until June, 1944, with the Normandy invasion. While our losses were great, their losses were greater.

After destroying the super Afrika Korps in North Africa, it was Sicily where more green Americans with some veterans and the British 8th Army, caused the surrender of Mussolini and the downfall of the Italian fascists, irritants for so many years. El Duce's union with Hitler did demoralize and slow our ultimate victory. The remaining defeated Italian Army and Navy were never of much help in our Allied liberation of Italy. Their divisons disintegrated before our very eyes.

The struggle in Italy followed, and what a struggle! I gave you Montgomery, who did not help Clark very much, but I did give you Alexander in the command circle and he proved to be an "English Ike" in dealings with you and the American forces. Clark and your troops, aided by a British corps, secured a beachhead at Salerno and we struggled slowly after a six-day blood bath on the beaches. We seldom had the luxury of thinking of miles of quick conquest as we were to enjoy later at Normandy and Southern France. But the Russians, whom we should never forget, were counterattacking and counting their drives in miles — and heavy casualties on both sides. In Italy we drew off German divisions from the backs of the Russians.

You and Monty came back home to England to begin the buildup for the greatest invasion of the war at Normandy. While North Africa proved the testing gound for Allied cooperation, the Sicily and Salerno operations in Italy were the proving ground. After the beachhead was secure, I wrote you: "As the Duke of Wellington said of the Battle of Waterloo, 'It was a damned close-run thing,' but your policy of running risks has been vindicated."[7]

I took over the struggle in Italy and conceived the idea of landing at Anzio combined with a drive through Cassino in the Liri Valley to join our forces in the liberation of Rome. I failed to see all the obstacles in our path! The Rapido River, which had to be crossed where the enemy held the observation advantage. We had inadequate forces, more green replacements, suffered from a lack of shipping and offshore gun fire. As a result we bloodied ourselves again at the Rapido and did not have sufficient forces to push onto the high ground at Anzio. We thereby failed to entrap the German armies on our front and established a winter-long stalemate in a campaign already bogged down with mud, low morale, superior enemy fire, poor leadership, poor coordination.

About Anzio, I said: "We hoped to land a wild cat that would tear out the bowels of the Boche. Instead we have stranded a vast whale with its tail flopping about in the water."[8]

Historians keep bringing up my failure at the Rapido with a recounting of the Battle of the Dardanelles in World War I. There at the request of the Russians we had tried to invade and conquer Turkey to get a supply line to our ally. In 1915 the British cabinet only agreed to my use of Navy troops initially and by the time we sent Army forces in it was too late. Again, like Anzio, were both forces aggressive enough? The Turks had built defenses and moved reinforcements into the areas we wanted. At a high price in casualties we lost the battle. The disaster led to my downfall as First Lord of the Admiralty. I had learned a partial lesson. At least at Anzio we made a joint, if feeble, effort with combined arms but it was insufficient. We did, however, compel Hitler to pull out more of his forces fighting the massive infantry, artillery, armor and air giants of the Red Army. By now we were even beginning to win Stalin over to our battle plans. We did finally liberate Rome just two days before you led the mighty allied forces into France.

Your Bradley and Patton were warriors the like of which is rare in history. They knew what they were doing and would not fail. Of course, they had so many great subordinates — Collins, Middleton, Hodges, Gerow, Harmon, McLain, Van Fleet — the list never seemed to end.

We found new leaders at both the top of the command ladder and in the front lines. We paraded hero after hero in the enlisted and junior officer ranks. The field graders matured and went to higher commands while only a few faltered or were found unworthy of battle. It was a great disappointment that Monty failed to rally his forces to keep up with Bradley and Patton. You even had to give him Gen. William Simpson and his brilliant Ninth Army to be more effective. But, as we told you, the British were ready for set battle and we were still worried about the preservation of British manhood. We could not lose our flower of manhood and continue to be a proud nation. Maybe that was why we also failed in Italy. Had Monty been aggressive in joining Clark's forces and had our troops driven harder below Cassino to help the valiant American forces, we might have suffered fewer casualties and ensured an earlier victory.

Your battle plan did not fail. With Marshall's help, you kept feeding more and more troops into the battle in Europe. As you broke out at Normandy, your Patton was ready to entrap and boasted that he was ready to drive Monty's slow-moving forces back into the sea where they had landed in the invasion. How you controlled all of those temperamental generals, I will never know. But you did.

My British comrades and I never gave up trying to tell you how to run the war. When your troops, with the French, captured Paris, Bradley had two armies in rapid pursuit of the enemy. We still planned, with your agreement, Monty's fiasco at Arnhem. We all wanted to cross the Rhine, and with the German army in disarray, we thought it was time for an airborne attack. We just waited too long, and while the American troops were successful, the British force failed to achieve its objectives. We were too ambitious, too distant, or we were not aggressive enough. Our press wrote about our losses, but very little about your victory, to the horror of Generals Jim Gavin and Matt Ridgway, who wrote postwar books.

Meanwhile in the south, your invasion, with French and American troops, in Southern France was successful beyond my imagination or hopes. I was never really for the idea. I suppose I have to say that I was still trying to establish British heroes. You drove north so fast that the two invasion forces were forged within thirty days. Under your command then, the Seventh Army drove to the Rhine at the Belfort gap. Again you deferred to British thinking and let Monty have supplies and forces for the airborne drop at Arnhem. I guess you are entitled to some second-guessing on this decision, to speculate on what might have happened if you had made an effort to roll up the German armies from the south, with the Rhine as a natural barrier against enemy counter moves. Some of your leaders to the south asked you to consider such an operation, but you turned them down. At the time, we did not really know of the supply capacity from the French ports on the Riviera. One could easily argue that the Germans would have moved more troops to the south to block the drive. But that might have opened new areas for combat by Patton or Hodges in the enemy's rear. You were set on destroying the Boche west of the Rhine but the one early possibility of doing so from the south hardly got a decent appraisal. Historians have never second-guessed us in that decision.[9] Perhaps, in my opposition to the invasion in southern France, I was too hopeful that our air attacks against the industrial railroads and munitions factories and communication centers of the enemy would ensure a fatal or knockout blow. Both of our countries developed air power faster than we did on the ground or at sea.

The British Royal Air Force was the single "armed service of a major European country to embrace strategic bombing between the wars, as the most appropriate way to avoid large-scale ground combat."[10]

Hitler's Luftwaffe was designed for strategic bombing. But I must give the evil, demon dictator of Germany credit for the use of close air support of his armor and infantry in the Blitzkriegs into Poland in 1939 and again into France in 1940. He always wanted to avoid attacking civilian population areas because that would give us a good excuse to retaliate. It was when his planes bombed London on August 24, 1940, that I seized the opportunity of retaliating by sending 95 RAF Bombers against our German cousins in Berlin the next night — for precision bombing of industrial targets.[11] In a strange way, this shift to the bombing of London allowed some relief for the RAF and our defense installations. The winds of war make for strange happenings.

Throughout the war we debated the use of air power. Many military leaders thought we could bomb Germany out of the war. Your American youth hoped that would be true, that the day of foot soldiers in battle was at an end. The headlines gave both your people and mine hope that the magic of air power would turn the battle tide to victory without resorting to the horrible land warfare we had experienced a quarter of a century before. Sons might not have to follow in their fathers' footsteps. Alas, that was not the case. We learned the folly of winning the war with headlines and bombers alone. That is not to take anything away from the gallant RAF night fighters or the ever-arriving support by the American bomber pilots, who preferred to fly by day. Our final armadas were massive and decisive as the ground forces occupied the various territories. One of the main problems with bombing was that the enemy had so many targets we were inclined to scatter our raids. So many times the Germans rebuilt their factories quickly and developed underground assembly lines for their armament. Or moved their production efforts and remaining facilities to other areas in record time. Our losses in the air increased so rapidly that we had to provide more fighter escorts for the bombers and that limited the range of the big ones. It was not until 1943 that we obtained parity with the enemy air power. In North Africa our forces were under constant threat of enemy airpower — only after we invaded Italy did we rule the skies in the Mediterranean. For a while troops were told to shoot at anything in the air that was firing at them. In all of the confusion some of our pilots were shot down or had to bail out. The policy did make for better map reading and dissemination of information as to location of enemy and friendly troops.

Maybe southern France would have been a preferred entry all the way, as some suggested but on the top level the idea was vetoed. Aren't you glad, though, that I did send Alexander and some of his forces from Italy to reclaim and free Greece from the Germans so the Russians would not have it in its sphere in the postwar era.

Later the horrendous Battle of the Bulge occurred in December, 1944, when it seemed, for a while, that all of our efforts were failing us. We had to start fighting the war all over again as though victory was not within our grasp. Combat replacements became critical. But many of our rear area troops proved to be good fighters as we drained what we could to reinforce the forward troops.

I hope my influence wasn't so great that I swayed you to give so many of your troops to my populist general, Montgomery, when the Germans again went through the Ardennes, as they had done against France in 1940. They of course drove the worst wedge in our forces in Europe since the invasion. You and I knew they could drive to Paris and we could sack them, but we did not like the responsibility of all of those losses on our historical record. You had decided that you could not cover the entire front in great numbers so you thinned out your lines with inadequate defense positions. With bad weather our air superiority could not help you, after the initial thrust of the Nazi killers at Bitburg, St. Vith, Malmedy and so many other places. The attackers were completely coldblooded. They lined up some American troops and shot them. They had forces out to kidnap you. You had to practically live in confinement until the peril subsided.

I never lost my faith in you but you did give Montgomery a large share of your forces to contain the northern lip under his control. He waited much too long to really help out. You know that Harold Alexander was my first choice for deputy, but Montgomery had been so successful in battle in North Africa and Sicily, in our thinking, that I had to select the hero-of-the-moment as your British deputy for the invasion and also the task of control for the landings and battle maneuvering initially. Thank goodness, you had Bradley at hand in both cases. But Bradley probably never forgave you for giving Monty so many of his troops. When Gen. Patton drove into the heart of the German spearhead in the Ardennes, I knew victory would be soon at hand. He was a great one. I am glad you and Marshall kept him after the Sicilian slapping incident.

When the Bulge finally collapsed — and it was a stubborn drive — you had your armies ready for the final thrust into Naziland, der Fuhrer's adopted country. The winter of 1944-45 was cold, bitter, wet, snowy, but our forces kept pushing against the wind, sloshing in the mud, dodging bullets, suffering from shell fire. German troops left the Ludendorff bridge at Remagen intact, and you poured troops through the gap. It was Gen. Hodges' First Army's finest hour after suffering at Normandy, Aachen, the Huertgen Forest, the Bulge. Monty again dragged his feet and only after Patton's Third Army had joined Hodges on the east bank of the river, did he make his methodical, set-piece crossing against light resistance. We British hailed our hero again and you Americans became justifiably bitter over the downplaying of Hodges and Patton.

Patton and I both enjoyed pissing into the Rhine River.

You then wisely, with the help of air power, sealed the Ruhr by closing a mass pincer around it and wisely avoided going through it, which you probably should have done at the Huertgen forest earlier. It is easy to second-guess so many of our decisions now that it is all over. Likewise people have been second-guessing us ever since the war, on many fronts, and that is the democratic way. Dictator nations even criticize success in battle — such as Stalin's status in disgrace in most of Russia but not his private Georgia. Of course, I was voted out of office right after we won the war, and that too is the democratic way.

Critics are now wondering outloud how much our experience counted in the long run. We certainly used it to a psychological advantage in our planning, training, and troops useage at the times as we moved from one campaign to the next.[12] We even promoted more rapidly to insure an upper hand.

Monty and Field Marshal Alan Brooke, my trusted Imperial chief of staff, were in disfavor with you and Marshall, so I decided we should have a new battle plan and head straight for Berlin in a single thrust with Monty in charge to liberate the Nazi capital as the war's end neared. You felt that destruction of the German army was your mission, to be followed by occupation of the territorial zones as stipulated in Allied talks in London in 1944-45. I disagreed on your plan to meet the Russians, but you won out. It was time to defy the Russians and try to move militarily onto Berlin despite the agreement reached by Roosevelt, Stalin and myself. We were not interested in a blood bath with the Russians, but Berlin was a prize we wanted. I know your concern was that the United States still had another war to win in the Far East against a stubborn enemy — the army, navy, and kamikazes of the Rising Sun. Historians have argued that you could have changed the course of history. But I suppose one has to face the facts of political life and know that Allies should live up to agreements. We found ourselves later in the position of doing most of the giving in our post war relations with Russia.[13]

I shared the Ultra secrets with you and other American leaders to give you advantage in battle against the Germans. We broke the German encoding machines with Polish cryptologists. Later the British and American code experts came into the operation. It was very valuable to have broken the code. This information was especially valuable in our war against submarines and air power. Some of Ultra's help gave us the advantage of surprise in land battles. It failed miserably when the Germans assembled its forces in mass for the Ardennes drive. It was your most disastrous battle for the entire war. There were times when Ultra was a help to you, especially in North Africa, early in Italy, and before Overlord's execution.

The air war was forever with us and forever changing. As we gained superiority in North Africa and Italy, we then faced buzz bombs — the V1 and — the V2 rockets. As our forces overcame the Zero, M-109 and other German aircraft, the enemy came up with jet airplanes to again surprise, frighten, and add to our bewilderment — always wondering what would come next. Naturally the enemy propaganda forces effectively spread the word that der Furhrer had yet another secret weapon that would deliver victory. So many people believed the Nazis would pull off victory — after all, they had kept surprising and pleasing the German populace since they came to power in 1933. Their rumor of a massive Southern Redoubt stronghold in Bavaria and the Alps failed to materialize, although again you had that possibility to consider in your final drive in April, 1945.

While my "finest hour" may have been the inspirational defense of the British Isles in 1940-41, yours came in the planning and execution of the complicated and difficult battles of North Africa and Europe. You took a green, uncoordinated military force and made it into a victory team unmatched in modern times. But you went on to another finest hour — your leadership of the American government for eight difficult years of peace, no little accomplishment for a man who had performed so brilliantly as a general of the free world. A tip of the hat to my comrade in arms, a Kansas lad who went to the top of the victory ladder on two counts, general and president. I salute you.

Winston Churchill

P.S. In all of your trials and tribulations, I was always proud that you found an English lass, Kay Summersby, for your almost constant companionship. She was a perky girl who easily caught attention. My King and Chief of Staff were not accustomed to such an open arrangement, although we all know there is nothing new about battle commanders, kings, prime ministers and presidents having a lady friend in attendance in time of stress, need or loneliness.

Author's note: Winnie Churchill, as he was affectionately called, made some excellent judgments but also made some mistakes in his career in both World War I and II. His ill-fated plans to seize the Dardanelles, in the first war and his Dieppe raid in the second, plus the ill-fated effort to capture Rome via Anzio-Rapido in 1944. In the Dardanelles operation Naval and land forces were committed piecemeal and cooperation between the services — and support from his government — failed. This operation led to his dismissal as First Lord of the Admiralty.

Dieppe was a costal raid in France, in August, 1942, to harass German defenses and to gain intelligence for a possible later invasion site. The 6,000 man strike force, mostly Canadians, was completely inadequate. Many men were shot before they landed. The director of the force was Lord Louis Mountbatten, one of Churchill's favorites. The Allies claimed we learned from the operation but history has judged it a disaster. Years later Mountbatten found out how bitter the Canadians were. They still blamed him "for having murdered the Canadians at Dieppe."[14] Troops had been sent in without an air strike, landed at known positions and ordered in even after the strike time and date had been learned by the Germans.

To a lesser degree, Churchill's military maneuvers led us into one of the worst fiascoes of World War II at Anzio and the Rapido River in Italy, in January, 1944. The idea was an end run, of a sort that had been successful in Sicily on a smaller scale by American forces under Patton. While U.S. and British forces invaded undefended beaches at Anzio and Nettuno, the other half of Fifth Army was to cross the Rapido and its lower basin, the Gorigliano, southwest of Cassino. It took place while Marshall and Eisenhower were more concerned with the planning and support for the big landing the following spring in Normandy, France. As a result, the forces under Gen. Mark Clark went in with neither adequate troops, nor weapons and with meager help from naval forces. Gen. Clark got the blame, but Alexander and Churchill were the executioners. Troops landed without opposition and, when the Germans reacted with reinforcements, the Allies could only dig in. As a result, they failed to capture the commanding high ground, giving the enemy observation hills to scan the entire landing force. Troops to the south failed to break out of the Liri Valley to form a pincer on the Germans and join the forces to the north. The British got across the Gargilano without a great deal of trouble, but also failed to gain the high ground. The American forces were massacred with withering fire from excellent defense positions and never established a bridgehead to the south of Cassino but did to the north of the Abbey. Because of boundaries, Americans could not exploit the south foothold by the British and there were no forces left to exploit the crossing to the north — both ran into mountainous obstacles since the fortified lines in the valley could not be breached. There was no junction until four months later.

Why anyone, from Churchill down, thought that forces in the south were strong enough and capable of driving so many miles north in cold, wet weather, against massive mine fields, strong machine gun and artillery fire, and all the other hazards of masterful German defense, is a question that has never been answered.

The truth is that many of the engineers ordered to build bridges across the swift and cold Rapido ran in the face of enemy fire. There were a few bridges constructed under the cover of darkness before the enemy laid down a pattern of fires in front of the worst hit two regiments, the 141st and 143d, both of the 36th Division. It was impossible to keep the engineers in the areas necessary to build and rebuild the bridges as they were shot out. The engineers often claimed they lacked adequate material and were not properly covered by friendly fire to counter the enemy rounds. Where was our air power all of this time when it was so desperately needed? The truth of the matter is that veterans of the 36th Division were almost prepared for the fiasco. The practice runs over the Volturno River before the crossings were poorly executed; they failed to create working teams of infantry and engineers. The corps commander Maj. Gen. Geoffrey Keyes, was told simply that engineer support was inadequate. There again he must have had such pressure from top-side that he had to try a half-assed plan.[15] Lack of engineer support and units that deserted under fire are seldom mentioned in published reports of the Rapido action.

Why there was hope for success in the Anzio-Rapido operation is beyond one's wildest imagination. Our leaders have never explained the fiasco, and obviously historians and military men have been reluctant to blame Churchill — he was the voice of hope.

One could almost come to the conclusion that as late as six months before Normandy, Churchill was still dragging his feet about the war. He wanted to fight in Italy and the Balkans. He apparently still hoped he could postpone Normandy — let the Russians and Germans bleed, as so many people hoped. The British-American team could reclaim the bulk of Europe later. But Marshall and Ike wanted to end the war in Europe with a massive thrust to destroy the German Army in a decisive battle. Churchill made a thrust to capture Rome, and innocently enough gave his own troops a horrible blood-letting at Anzio in the face of a better trained and equipped German force. The Allies played into the hands of the enemy, unwittingly, and while we caught them by surprise initially, we made a piecemeal effort just as Britain, under Churchill's leadership, did in the Dardanelles campaign — only a few years before.

Another Churchillian flaw was worship of air power. He was not alone in this. Many Americans had the same thoughts. Land armies were branded as outdated over and over by leaders and laymen on both sides of the big pond, as it was called in World War I.

Just look at the record. Our headlines, early in the war, kept reporting fantastic air raids with thousands of casualties, destruction of railroad marshaling yards, communication centers, defense plants and on and on.

A German author, Gregor Janssen, has described the bombing strategy, "the death dance of German towns in 1942." He adds: "For a long time, Churchill was convinced that this strategy was the weapon to beat Germany with. Yet the British air assaults on the Ruhr . . . Berlin . . . Rhine towns . . . did nothing to advance the military prosecution of the war and left the flow of arms production almost unimpaired — on the contrary, they strengthened the public's will to resist and brought blood grist to the mills of Goebbels' propaganda machine . . . it was the British strategy, in fact, that turned the cities of Germany into bastions of her industrial strength."[16]

In October, 1943, he continues, "One of the biggest air battles of the war was fought out in the sky above Schweinfurt, and American losses we're so high that the city was immune to attack for the next two months." In that period, output was restored to its previous level because production was switched to other sites.[17]

Finally, he wrote: "It was not the bombing of towns but the destruction of her transport system that broke the economic resistance of the Reich."[18] It was only when we penetrated and bombed Berlin, after London was hit, that Hitler and his supporters realized we were in the war for real and could bring destruction on the homeland. It was the first time a major assult had been made on the Nazi capital. We even thought a raid by Gen. Jimmie Doolittle's planes from a carrier off Japan would knock some sense into the Yellow race of Japan

The final destruction of Dresden, Germany, in February, 1945, is difficult to understand. One could flippantly say that we had an excess of bombs, and the Allied high command desired to dump them. At the same time, some critics say that the A-bomb was not necessary. There is a big difference. At the time of the Dresden bombing, the Allies were on the eve of final victory in Europe. When the A-bombs were dropped, the Allies were on the eve of the invasion of the Japanese mainland where casualties might have been the worst of any American fight in the entire war.

The truth is that Allied tactical and strategic commands on both ground and air operations in Europe often failed miserably.

Techniques of ground-to-air and air-to-ground operations were not perfected until near the end of the war. One strategic technique was certainly seldom effectively used. Instead of hitting towns, massive railheads, and other areas in a spray gun manner, the targets for the bombs should have been major railroads and bridges which connected big centers of communications out in the countryside. As it happened the enemy had the equipment and labor force for repairs, but if the pinpoint bombing (the most difficult type, obviously) had disrupted enemy lines of communications in the boondocks, repairs would have taken much longer.

A second basic failure of air power was the lack of support for ground operations. Late in the war, air attacks speeded the infantry in battle with the same still stubborn enemy, but they were not available or not used for fire power in many battles. Once in a while they were not used in surprise attacks.

Initially a lack of air support was notable. There were two major problem areas: Air-to-ground communications at times was almost nonexistant and mediocre at best. Most radios between ground and air units did not have common channels. In fact this was also true between infantry and artillery and between infantry and tanks. Units had to exchange radios or employ mobile radio detachments for communication. And naval gun-fire was an even greater problem. Artillery fire problems were solved early in the war, and it was the greatest weapon the ground forces had for fire support. But the little fellow on patrol, or in the foxhole, or involved in small-unit action was up the creek without a paddle (er, radio) for big fire support.

Boundaries of front-line units were often inaccurate, as relayed to higher headquarters. Or they changed too rapidly to be relayed to a firing unit. As a result, if you were bombed by your own planes you either moved the boundaries forward where fire might not be as effective or you were reluctant to call for such fires. If all of the equations mentioned were solved, after hours of coordination, you often heard the message, "No fires available." It was a discouraging procedure for front-line troops.

Back to Churchill. He was always fascinated by the tank. Because of that interest and the fact that Eisenhower had trained the American tank corps in World War I at home, the two leaders found another common interest.

Barracks chatter always gave Churchill credit for the tank's development — along with many other adventures and projects. But he only had a vision of what a tank could do. In World War I he pushed hard for its development, because he could visualize it as an armored man. After all, our forefathers wore heavy armor plate in battle. He could visualize a mobile man surrounded by armor carrying heavy weapons to inflict damage on the enemy. One of the tank's purposes in War I was a vehicle which could be used to cross trenches.

The French were quicker to advocate the new weapons after War I, but the Germans really made the tank an awesome and feared weapon on the battlefield. Once we solved the tank problem on both sides of the Atlantic (manufacturing and as a fighting weapon) it was our great weapon in the drive across Europe to destroy the Nazi Army.

Churchill also received credit for the Mulberry seaport that the English used at Normandy. An American Navy lieutenant has recalled how, "The pieces that made up the breakwater of Mulberry were barged across the channel and put in place by what were the equivalent of peace-time tugs. When in place, their buoyancy tanks were flooded and they were allowed to sink in relatively shallow water as they were for the protection of shallow draft craft (LCM, LST, LCI, etc.). While much was made of the fact that they were hulks of abandoned ships, the ones that I saw looked like they were made for that particular purpose. I believe they were loaded with stone. Obviously they projected above the surface of the water after sinking. The Mulberries were three-sided with an opening in the seaward side to permit ingress and egress. They seemed to be effective and were badly needed during a week or more of violent weather following the landings. Sea stories at that time gave Churchill complete credit."[19] The same was true in the ranks of the American Army when it happened.

Historian Max Hastings writes of Mulberry: "The Mulberry harbours, whose creation had done so much to convince doubters, such as the prime minister, that Overlord was feasible. In fact there will always be grave doubt as to whether the Mulberries justified the enormous cost and effort that was put into them." He adds that Americans unloaded "stores at a greater rate directly across the beaches." The storms of June 19-23, severely damaged the American landing supply facility and the Mulberry harbour.[20]

Churchill once said that "War is a game with a good deal of chance in it, and, from the little I have seen of it, I should say that nothing in war ever goes right except by accident . . . There is only one thing certain about war, that it is full of disappointments and also full of mistakes."

The great prime minister's voice, his courage, and his V sign for victory were all assets which helped the struggling and ill-prepared Allies mount an offensive to defeat the menace of the 20th Century — Adolf Hitler. Many Germans said they hated Hitler, but they followed their leader to the bitter end. They uprooted and killed Jews, and fought the "friendly" troops from the West as hard as they did their not-so-friendly enemy from the East.

It was not an easy victory, and Churchill set the theme and the pace for the victory crusade in Europe under Ike's direction.

IKE SAYS:

Dear Mr. Prime Minister,

To say that I had great respect and admiration for you and greatly appreciated my friendship with you would be an understatement. But to say we never disagreed or quarelled and lived in perfect harmony would be an out and out lie.

It was my job to sell myself and the American army — you English often tended to consider Americans upstarts from the brass to the privates. Just how you arrived at this aristocratic holiness has never been explained or appreciated by many Americans who came to bail you off a sinking warship without adequate finances, resources, manpower — in short a nation on its hands and knees using words and air power in hope of staying afloat instead of sinking on your island with an anchor held by Nazi Germany with Hitler as the executioner.

This feeling was not to stand between us though in all of the war years and while your brass much more than yourself looked down at the end of their noses at our arrival, you and I early on established that there would be unity and teamwork in our effort to free the world, along with our Russian ally, of the reign of terror inflicted on the world by Hitler and his people.

I had experience dealing with political leaders and brass, so the assignment as American commander in England was not a difficult task.

My only problem early in the mobilization effort was that I wanted to command a division and fight it in battle. Instead I became supreme commander of all of our forces at 53 and finally outranked all of your generals and admirals and won the heart of London and the cooperation of all of the allied fighting forces, despite my lack of combat.

And I never let success go to my head. I had a temper but I controlled it. After all I had served with MacArthur.

And while I didn't seek five stars, I never shirked from leading the largest free world army in history. I continued to speak my mind on issues with deliberation, and made sure that people liked Ike because I liked people. Again while I didn't seek it, the Presidency, the U.S. sought me out seven years after my victory in battle.

You and I were comrades to free the world. While you lost out after V-E Day at age 71 because of the homeland privations during the war you later returned to power to lead your country when others floundered. It is strange that a similar thing happened to Gen. Charles de Gaulle after we had installed him as the No. 1 Frenchman, despite Roosevelt's objection. He was so busy rebuilding his country that he forgot to build a party. He came back to rule for 10 years and help France rise to her old glory and build the basis for a vibrant nation in the post war era. The only difference was that I never lost an election. But I may have been afraid enough of losing that I said some things that hurt others and failed to defend some of my loyal friends. But speak my mind I always did with caution and wisdom.

I was the great moderator also between you and Roosevelt, between Alan Brooke, your chief of the imperial general staff and Gen. George

C. Marshall, my boss and one of the most powerful and brilliant leaders of the 20th Century.

I am sure I appeared to you on my arrival to London in early 1942 as the clean cut American from Kansas. I may have appeared naive. I was a bit in awe not only of your accomplishments, tactical knowledge, and charm but also your role as a symbol of freedom in your fight against the Nazi tyranny. Your leadership had held your country together in the ruthless Battle of Britain when you suffered from terrible aerial attacks and never knew if Hitler would send his troops across the channel in an all-out invasion.

As I said, all I wanted was a division but my superiors had decided to give me a theater command — boss of the entire operation. And my bosses had some smarts. Behind them were staff people and commanders, many of whom did have battle command in World War I, who would plan and help me in my endeavors. I had some of the best brains in the army with me such as Marshall, Clark, Gruenther, Smith, Bradley, Truscott, Devers, Patton. We were confident of victory but you and your leaders never let us forget that you had been fighting the enemy and dying since 1939.

You may have had more influence over me and my fellow officers than you should have. But we learned fast and by the end of the war many of your leaders were living on reputation not victories. Never did I go out of my way to criticize them publicly for their reluctance to close with the enemy. I can't say the same for your side. Many of your commanders, and even you, fought me to the draw on many a military decision. Our President put it very well when I wanted a second front in the south of France and he told you to leave the military decision to the leaders in the field. That was great support for me. After it was over, so many of your leaders, writers and historians rewrote World War II as they desired with little respect for the truth.

It isn't that you should have censured or throttled them in their efforts. You should have cleared the record when they made some of their incorrect charges. Such as Alan Moorehead when he wrote in 1945 that "with nice timing Alexander entered the city (Rome) on June 4th." Almost everyone knows that the entry was by American general Mark Clark.[21]

It's a free world and I spent most of my time trying to preserve unity. My naval aide, came the closest to telling the true story of our relations in *My Three Years With Eisenhower* but I even tried to restrain him. I spent many hours writing to you and others clarifying my positions on disputes and arguments in order to soothe ruffled feathers. I never received like treatment from your side and finally blew up when Cornelius Ryan interviewed me. I told him that Monty "always wanted everything and he never did anything fast in his life." Ryan went on to say that I interrupted him during the interview and said in effect that Monty said I knew nothing about war. I added: "Gadddammit I don't know what you heard in Britain . . . when the whole danged thing (WWII) was done . . . I never heard from the British any goldarn paeans of praise. And you're not going to hear it now, particularly from people like Montgomery."

I said that if he goes down as the greatest soldier in the world I didn't care. Of course I cared. At last I had said it. The comments got very little publicity as people were beginning to forget the war and its heroes.[22]

That is about as close as I ever came to the truth in our relationship. It was the bare-assed truth, which the British would not believe and few Americans have heard. So history goes.

Even after we were well on the way to victory after the capture of Paris and the second thrust into southern France, Montgomery took it upon himself to confer with General Marshall in October, 1944, about my role. He wrote of the meeting: "Our operations had, in fact, become ragged and disjointed, and we had now got outselves into a real mess." Fortunately his complaining didn't impress my boss. We went on with the war as planned despite Monty's debacle at Arnhem a few days before.[23] There was no end of Monty's bragging. After the long delay in capturing Antwerp in November he wrote to me that the free use of the port was a naval matter. Of course earlier capture would have speeded the allied victory. He never commented on such matters unless he could detect an American flaw.

You get credit for a lot of ideas and help in my crusade. Your suggestion for Operation Torch into North Africa stands near the head of the list. It was our training ground for a new and battle-worthy army. I guess Marshall, the American public and I never realized the potential slaughter of an invasion by Allied forces in France in 1942 or 1943. We were not ready for it. Your experience paid off. It paid off in blood of thousands when you sent the commando force into Dieppe in 1942 just to show how dangerous such an invasion would be. As we now know, it should have been called off because the Germans were alerted to our plans. Those forces, mainly Canadians paid a terrible price to prove your point. Some would say it was a cold blooded maneuver, others would say it saved countless casualties. But Torch was successful and your decision, in effect, made me front page news for the rest of my life. I came from nowhere to lead the Allied forces during the remainder of the war.

After the successful invasion of North Africa we had a long and depressing fight with the Germans in Tunisia, as the Afrika Korps delayed Monty in the east and slowed the Americans at Kasserine Pass. The French joined our forces for the first-three nation joint effort. Your Gen. Alexander, despite his low regard for American troops, became a trusted ally and friend for many future and successful operations though at a slower pace than the American press, the American President and the American soldier desired.

We finally defeated the Italians and Germans in Tunisia in May, 1943, and were beginning to gain some superiority in air power. With the capture at my direction of the tiny island of Pantelleria with air power we knocked out another enemy position which would insure our control of the Mediterranean. In the meantime, we had been planning for the invasion of Sicily and with more green American troops Generals Patton and Bradley outraced Montgomery to our final objective at the straits of Messina. Alexander found out American troops could fight and win battles. Monty must have been so frustrated that he again employed his slowdown tactics as he went across the straits to invade Italy. My general, Mark Clark, with an American division (36th) and two gallant British divisions, went farther north and invaded Italian below Salerno, some miles south of Naples. It was a tough fight to stay ashore but we did it.

We occupied Sardinia and Corsica for needed air bases, but allowed too many Germans to escape, as we did in North Africa and Sicily when our air and naval forces were incapable of intercepting the enemy.

After the near disaster at Anzio, and the terrible losses at the Rapido River and Cassino during the winter of 1943-44, our forces had little heart for driving up the boot to yet face one mountainous area after another, one river crossing after another, one deadly enemy defense line after another.

After the four month fight at Anzio, Gen. Clark liberated Rome by changing directions and not conquering another mountain mass.

His British colleagues criticized him for it and many of your historians have forever written that he changed his orders to be a hero and liberator of the Holy City. Then you promoted his superior, Alexander, when American forces made the victory possible. You did the same thing for Montgomery when you gave him five stars after I took over as field commander on the Continent. Bradley, Hodges and Patton had cracked the Normandy stalemate. It was hard to understand and historians are now finding it even more difficult to understand. Your forces certainly outranked ours throughout the war. We never believed that rank alone won wars. The American soldier was a great fighter and wanted to win and go home. He didn't look upon the military as a way of life. His attitude cost us casualties but his aggressiveness saved many. Your idea of committing many more troops into Italy and then the Balkans just never seemed plausible to most American generals — particularly Gen. Marshall and yours truly. Clark was the only major commander interested in a Balkan thrust. It was difficult terrain, hard to supply and failed to meet the enemy head on. While we drained off a few troops from the Russian front to Italy we would have prolonged the war if we had not gone ashore at Normandy and again at southern France to force the Germans to begin withdrawal from Russia, whose armies were ready to join the continental nutcracker on the enemy forces and to bring the war to Nazi homeland which was required to win victory.

Perhaps you never noticed but our fighting men in France had a different outlook on battle than those in Italy, where the going was tougher, enemy shelling was always with them, and the local population could do little to help our advance. Casualties had been high from the day we landed at Salerno, the weather disastrous, and the Germans maintained superior observation from mountain outposts all during the war. It was a thankless war and once we got some more experience from it the time had come to employ our troops to the greatest advantage. A long struggle into Yugoslavia, Albania, Hungary and Rumania would have been futile for us to attempt to conquer. Your efforts to save Greece were effective and our troops after the war, with the Truman doctrine, saved the country from Communist takeover. At least we created a neutral country — friendly at its convenience and hardnose in some of our postwar peace endeavors.

Author David Irving puts it fairly well: After you again pleaded for support for the Italian Campaign, to "stab through the Ljubljana gap into 'Europe's armpit' as he now termed the Balkans." He continued: "Eisenhower firmly declined. To him, Italy was a blind ally, and he wanted no more valuable forces diverted there. The episode had become a nightmare for Eisenhower."[24]

Of course Anzio was a failure because we didn't have the troops necessary, shipping was inadequate because of both the Normandy buildup and the war in the Pacific. My heart always went out to those troops stuck in the Italian mud and making progress inch by inch.

Before and after our landings at Normandy we always had a problem as you pointed out, with use of air power in a friendly country. We needed to knock out the Germans wherever possible in order to speed our advances. But pinpoint bombing was difficult and often our raids were not heavy enough to permanently damage enemy installations. You hoped for victory through air power but I knew that ground occupation and destruction of the German army were the essential elements for victory. It took a long time for me to gain control of all our air power. So many forces had operated independently for so long it was difficult to form unity teams of the various arms, even after our two nations had forged the command structure. I had to put my job on the line with an or-else posture to gain control of all of our forces. My Army and Navy feuded constantly on invasion plans and then when we put the arms of both nations along with the French forces it was a miracle of our time to gain unity and fight successfully side by side.

Our deception plan of a dummy army in England to make Hitler think we would make a second attack across the channel at Calais paid big dividends. Perhaps even more important, it kept Hitler from committing his reserves to drive us back at Normandy. One has to wonder what would have happened if Rommel and the generals could have fought that part of the war without interference. At times Hitler was clever in his battle plans but he stumbled on others including this time.

Following the breakout at Normandy, the early capture of Paris came as a pleasant bonus. We had the enemy on the run but couldn't pursue him fast enough and outdistanced our supply lines. The entry into southern France, which you resisted, helped our supply and manpower problems. But we bogged down while good weather was still with us, and the German delays made us fight through another long cold winter. But before winter came we gave Montgomery the troops and supplies for an airborne operation at Arnhem. We have fought and refought the battle at Arnhem many times. It was a mistake and a disaster. Why Monty didn't force the battle to victory I will never understand. Likewise why he was so long freeing the needed port at Antwerp. Of course all of the territory was needed to destroy the German missile bases, which were still inflicting casualties on your civilians at home plus land destruction. The individual soldier surely wanted to stop the bombings of his homeland.

Your forces likewise failed to come to our aid in any great numbers when the Germans drove into the middle of our forces in the Ardennes. They cleverly deceived us and our intelligence wasn't worth a damn. I had allowed my commanders to spread our forces too thin as I spread the maximum number over the largest area possible to speed the end of the war in a final drive. After all many thought we would win the war before Christmas, 1944. But I early realized the war could not be over until we occupied Germany, together with our Russian ally. The Americans won the Battle of the Bulge and then Montgomery came along and tried to take credit for the victory. That was another time when Bradley and Patton threatened to resign. If they had, I probably would have followed. Who can speculate on such serious matters? I suspect Brad and George would have carried through their threat. Their writings are filled with bitterness toward Monty. In fact they say some very uncomplimenterary things about me and my relationship with him.

Our forces regained their momentum when Hodges' First Army found the Ludendorff bridge over the Rhine intact at Remagen. It was another break we deserved. Staying with my mass frontal advance plan, we poured troops across to secure a bridgehead but still left men and supplies to establish other bridgeheads all along the front. Patton slipped over before Montgomery finally made his big thrust, without any severe opposition. Critics now say I should have made a bigger effort at Remagen.

On the American side we continued to think Berlin was not a military objective because it was in the Russian zone of occupation and because of the many casualties that would have been inflicted upon us in the German last stand stance. And would we have had to fight the Russians to gain Berlin also?

Gen. Bill Simpson, who got along with Montgomery in a remarkable manner, wanted to drive his Ninth Army to Berlin. He wrote of his disappointment 10 years later when historians began to write that he did not have the manpower and supplies to pull off the drive. His arguments were convincing, to say the least. I was fighting a military battle though and not a political one which was your territory. Besides we had another war to fight with Japan and there was no prospect for an early defeat of the yellow peril at that time because we didn't know about the A-bombs.

In order to insure the merger of our forces with the Russians I contacted Stalin directly on the military linkup. You objected to my prodecure but Gen. Marshall backed my decision — he too had to win in the Pacific. At the time you said to your chief Alan Brooke: "There is only one thing worse than fighting with allies — and that is fighting without them."25

Victory-in-Europe day was a great occasion. We all celebrated as the lights went on in London again. The soldiers lived it up for a while, until we started redeployment to the Pacific. We faced great problems of civilian starvation, disease and most of all the displaced persons. Along the way we tried denazification for a while but our soldiers found it difficult to distinguish between Nazis and nonNazis. Many Germans tried to win us over with a desire to join forces to fight the Russians. The anti-Nazi policy and desire to fight the Russians got Patton into hot water and I finally had to relieve him of any occupation duties. It was a sad day for a gallant soldier. He had only one desire and that was to fight again — be it the Russians or the Japanese. His death in an auto accident nine months after the war ended was a tragedy. He made us both look good several times during the war.

Perhaps some of my success helped to make the great one, Winnie Churchill, even greater. My feelings were portrayed in my tribute to you at the time of your death:

"His loss will be felt in the United States as deeply as it will be in the British Commonwealth. For Sir Winston — in time of war and in time of peace — captured the imagination of all Americans. His indomitable courage, his indestructible faith in the society of Free Nations and in the dignity of free men typified our way of life. From him, America and all free lands gained added inspiration and determination of a just and enduring peace."

D.D.E.

P.S. You were kind in your acceptance of my constant companion, Kay Summersby, all during the war. She became an important part of my life and was a good throttle on my temper, my emotions, my stress and my well being. Leave it to historians to fight over our intimacy but you knew the value of women in wartime — on many fronts. As we all know Kay became bitter over the affair but my destiny was to lead me in other directions — mainly the white House with my beloved Mamie by my side. You — like so many — looked the other way during the war because you knew that Kay was good for me at the time.

Author's note: The truth is that many American soldiers felt that the British were looking down their noses at the American conduct both on and off the battlefield during the war. In the battle zone they left the impression in many cases that we were novices and they were battle-wise and battle-worthy. The civilian influx in the green American army was no comparison to the professional of the Commonwealth forces. The British regimental system is of great tradition and there were many veterans from prior service in the same units. By comparison American units were in a constant state of change, since new units had to have cadres from older and more experienced units because of the army's rapid expansion. The attitude at rest camps was much the same. The British seemed to rest up for the next phase of whatever came along. The Americans were resting up in order to go back to their units and fight a war and go home to resume employment, family life and careers. To many Britons the army was their career. A tour in peace or war was another phase. The huge influx of Americans with their money in England for the massive buildup for Normandy possibly started the slogan, Ugly American. The two nations didn't exactly mesh. So just imagine what Eisenhower's job was at the high level of command and coordination.

A lot of Britishers were happy when D-Day came. They were happy because they always complained that the American GIs were overfed, overpaid, oversexed and over here.

Letter 9

Douglas A. MacArthur. AP photo.

MACARTHUR's EGO TRIP

Dear Ike,

Our rivalry for hero worship, showmanship, military leadership, and influence among the American populace may have been unsurpassed in the annals of the great American Republic in the first half of the 20th Century.

By the time you got to the top, I had already been there for years. I did bring you along in the shadows never thinking you would rank me, but I had you there just in case. It takes a hero to know one.

For starters I was the son of an Army hero, Maj. Gen. Arthur MacArthur, whose brigade took part in the capture of Manila in the Philippines in 1898. He was the last military governor of the Philippines. I whipped through West Point as the No. 1 cadet, became the hero of the 42nd Rainbow Division in World War I (conceived the idea of the Division being representative of many of the states), Army Chief of Staff for almost five years — the longest in history then, and retired to become field marshal in the Filipino army.

Your shadow image showed you as a good football player at West Point with a bad knee. Your marks (61st in class of 164) were not very good for a future supreme commander, let alone President of the United States, when those ratings were far more important for advancement than they are now. You ended up with the development of the tank corps in the Army and stayed in the states throughout World War I. Seemed at the time as an unlucky break but in reality it never hindered you. I found you soon afterwards.

I was so jealous of your rise that I often referred to you as "the best clerk" I ever had. Other times when I knew better, I rated you tops, potential of great command, and wrote in your efficiency report: "This officer has no superior of his time in the army."[1] You came on board before we ran the War I bonus marchers out of Washington when they protested in order to get the rest of their bonus without further waiting. It was the depression and some of them were really hard up. It was a time when the country was going isolationist.

Many citizens had never been in sympathy with our entry into World War I. I had little sympathy for the bonus marchers. You had a lot of sympathy for them. In fact, despite President Hoover's orders (twice, no less) I burned up their camp in the Anacostia Flats and the immediate problem was solved. My bonus march attitude rated this comment by you: "I just can't understand how such a damn fool could have gotten to be a general."[2] As a lieutenant colonel at 49 they said I held you back. Anyhow I had you in the Philippines with me where you were given the job of training my Filipino forces without adequate men, supplies or funds — and I took the credit — that is until they failed me when the Japanese invaded their homeland.

You finally escaped from my command and you were headed for stardom. Others in the Army high command, mainly Gen. George Marshall and Lt. Gen. Lesley J. McNair, also thought you had great potential. Under Lt. Gen. Walter Krueger (later my Eighth Army commander in the Pacific) you helped him win the Louisiana maneuvers as chief of staff of the Third Army. From then on it was all a hero's rise. You even went faster than I did. Although your long-time buddy, Gen. Mark Clark, got his star first after you both had served in the 3rd Division so capably and displayed some new tactical ideas, you soon passed him in the command chair while in your role as a War Department planner. You seemed to write me off after Pearl Harbor because (even I have to admit reluctantly) there weren't enough troops, planes or ships to save us on Corregidor and Bataan. You soon got new direction and turned your back on me and began to run the show for the buildup of our forces to attack what the politicos and Churchill and Marshall thought to be the No. 1. enemy — Germany. And to free Roosevelt's beloved France.

I watched your rise during the invasion of North Africa, Sicily, and Italy before the big Normandy expedition. After the Patton incident, I said you were washed up and that it would prevent you from being chief of staff. I added: "There was a crooked streak in Ike and George Catlett Marshall which would show up in the long war." Two months later, I hadn't changed my attitude. "Eisenhower's curve had gone down since last summer . . . not now considered the great leader he formerly was." By July, though, my Army commander, Lt. Gen. Robert Eichelberger, recorded: "There was no question in his mind (MacArthur) now that he (Ike) could have Chief of Staff if he wanted it."[3]

You were not quiet on this matter of personal opinions either. You have been quoted as saying in October, 1942, that: "I wouldn't trade one Marshall for fifty MacArthurs . . . my God, that would be a lousy deal. What would I do with fifty MacArthurs?"[4]

And so it went as we slugged at each other. You were successful in the Normandy invasion, because you learned diplomacy besides acquiring a great deal of expertise in combined arms warfare particularly as it applied to naval operations. You were for the use of tanks and air power long before I realized their potential in battle. You had to fight for control of your airpower (while I almost forgot to use mine in the Pacific at the time of Pearl Harbor) but you did what you should have done. You put your job on the line and took control of all air power in Europe as the British bickered and delayed your control as long as they could. My hat is off to you on that one. I fear history has recorded that I didn't handle my air power as well. There are conflicting reports on what happened but when the Japanese attacked Pearl Harbor and the Philippines, my planes did not get off the ground, and I suffered a tremendous loss of planes at Clark Field. I used the excuse that we didn't have a good air counterattack capability and didn't know where their bases were in nearby Formosa.[5]

I kept my promise of, "I Shall Return," and liberated my beloved islands in October, 1944. My fortune of $500,000 given to me by President Quezon had already been sent out of the Philippines for safe keeping before the surrender of Corregidor. You didn't take any money for your services. Some have said that we should have saved our forces for a bigger invasion of Okinawa in preparation for the liberation of Japan. Not the downfall of the Emperor, mind you, because I didn't want that. My knowledge of Japanese history and culture promised that the Emperor's presence could be invaluable.

You returned home a hero and I stayed to preside over my new empire in the Pacific and the Far East. You must admit that I controlled the British and Russians effectively in my postwar operation and reorganized Japan economically.

Rebuilding the Philippines held a special place in my heart. Our predecessors had worked hard to teach the Filipinos how to develop a free and independent status. Our nation's long range goal was to make the Islands less dependent on America for strength. Our liberation mission was to develop a free and independent country.

You returned to the United States an American hero, and became Chief of Staff of the Army, as I knew you would. A few years later you

General Eisenhower has just been told of General Douglas MacArthur's relief by President Truman. Ike was commander of NATO at the time. AP photo.

returned to Europe to reunite all of our Allies into a common bond for the defense of Western Europe. The Russian threat was ominous. From Tokyo I watched as the Russians built up North Korean forces. By 1950 the North Koreans were ready for war and invaded South Korea in June. The South Koreans were not prepared for an attack, for which we have to take a fair sized rap. Thus the free world forces, under the direction of the United Nations, were drawn into a conflict to defend the World War II treaty agreements and boundaries. It was a tough struggle, but we had held on in the face of superior forces.

The most brilliant maneuver in my career came in September, 1950 at age 70, when I launched the fight out of the tiny toehold we held in South Korea and landed new forces by sea at Inchon. We caught the enemy in the rear by surprise. I never really worried about my record in military history after that victory. Never mind that I failed to drive to the Yalu River on the Chinese border with a unified command and the Chinese forces counterattacked in undefended terrain between my two independent forces being controlled by me from Tokyo — miles away.[6]

Later I was relieved by President Truman for failing, he said, to follow orders, corresponding with various political leaders, and not clearing my messages to the civilian and military leaders. Also I had told him the Chinese would not interfere in North Korea. My instructions from the Joint Chiefs of Staff were so broad and general, that I thought I could initiate my own ideas and stay out of trouble. I found out differently.

You played the game and stayed the American hero in most quarters. I lost a few along the way. While I had some interest in the Presidency, dating back to the 1920s, my feelers and plans always seemed to fizzle. But you fell in with the Eastern establishment, including a former tank commander, Henry Cabot Lodge Jr., Tom Dewey, and others. Although the Democrats might have liked you also, the Republicans definitely did — and got you. You even picked up the Presidency of Columbia University along the way to the White House. The political draft caught you on the uptake and while Senator Robert A. Taft, of Ohio, had definitely been the favorite especially among the conservatives in the party, you passed him with a coalition of various elements of the party including the liberals with a swish that left the Taft forces reeling. The American people found a general of the army ready to occupy the White House. The last one had been Ulysses Simpson Grant, who was elected at age 46 in 1868 following his exploits on the Civil War battlefields.

In your campaign, you promised peace in Korea and after election you flew there to find out how. You ignored one of my successors and your former buddy, Mark Clark, who by then had refined my plan for total victory in Korea. After you got back, you listened to my plan but you were in a position to ignore me and you did. I watched your Presidency from my ivory tower in the Waldorf Astoria and really did fade away just as I promised in my farewell speech to the Congress. At least I got to address the convention that nominated you in Chicago before a group that once could have, or might have, made me the nominee if I had had your grassroots.

Historians later began to refer to me as the American Caesar because of my political-military success. The title of the American hero of World War II belonged to you. And you kept us out of war for the eight years of your Presidency. I always liked to think that I trained you right.

Douglas MacArthur

P.S. Oh, yes, Ike, I had a girl friend also. We both brought them back but I brought mine as a mistress and set her up in an apartment near the War Department.

Kay Summersby, your constant companion, came to America to live but not as your mistress.

Since my first marriage to Louise Cromwell Brooks was something less than a success, I found my satisfaction in an attractive Filipino vaudeville star, Isabel Rosario Cooper, known as both "Dimples," and Elizabeth Cooper, to the entertainment world.[7] She was of Scottish parentage and beautiful. As Chief of Staff, my duties were many, and I finally relented, allowing her to go to law school. At 54, I was losing interest and also was fed up with Drew Peason and Robert Allen, Washington columnists, who continually reminded readers of my "dictatorial leanings." I sued for libel ($1,750,000) and when they threatened to call her to the witness stand, I dropped the suit. It even cost me $15,000 to retrieve the letters which I wrote to her.[8] After my end of duty in Washington and upon my return to Manila, I found on board ship Jean Faircloth, my second wife and soulmate for the rest of my life. She was with me a lot of the time during the war and while we were seen everywhere as an ideal couple who had a son, I always signed my letters to her "Love MacArthur" in my usual formal manner.

Gen. Marshall's attitude was that, "If feminine companionship serves in any way to help MacArthur, let her stay there. MacArthur is not a young man. Maybe he needs a wife."[9]

. . . Of Tanks and Planes

Author's note: MacArthur had his quirks on the military side. After World War I he was slow to recognize the role of tanks in modern warfare and didn't begin to understand the role of airplanes in future conflicts even with their success in 1917-18. He sat on the court martial in 1925 that convicted Col. Billy Mitchell, former Chief of Pershing's Air Service, because he was too aggressive in his desire to develop air power as a mighty military weapon. In 1945, MacArthur wrote Sen. Alexander Wiley, of Wisconsin, claiming that he, "had cast the lone dissenting vote against Mitchell's conviction. He admitted, "When the verdict was reached, many believed I had betrayed my friend."[10] Obviously his long silence reinforced his desire to clear the record of any doubt about his role in the Mitchell courtmartial. Author Carol Petillo, says there was "Little evidence to support this contention" (of how he voted for Mitchell).[11] MacArthur apparently was beginning to be convinced of the importance of air power finally after the (German) Blitzkrieg blows in 1939-40.[12]

But in view of the surprise Japanese attack he didn't really become convinced of the role of air power until 1942.[13]

Of course MacArthur's hatred for the Navy was inexcusable but overlooked, in the main, by the general public. Not by the Navy, though.

One has to wonder how much faster the Pacific war could have been waged if MacArthur and the Navy had been a harmonious military team. He didn't fully understand the enemy's potential and his country's own military capability. The stars in his eyes and his ego didn't always help the struggle against the "Purple Pissing Japs" as Gen. George Patton used to call them.

Why there were no Congressional hearings to establish responsibility for our failure to protect our own forces in the Japanese assault on the Philippines remains a mystery. Failure to conduct an inquiry probably just proves what a great lobby and admiration society MacArthur had at the time.

IKE SAYS:

Dear General MacArthur,

What an opportunity to answer you after all these years of conflicts, major policy decisions and a study of two five-star generals who captured the hearts of many Americans. There were the MacArthur haters and the MacArthur lovers. I always wanted to think that my fans were Ike lovers. But I know I stepped on a lot of toes along the way especially when I eclipsed so many American generals who were senior to me as well as a few British prima donnas who thought they should have had my job as supreme commander of Allied forces in Europe.

Perhaps my learning experience under you gave me the strength and depth of character to learn to live with the British hero Montgomery who was as unpredictable and as uncooperative as you. I never made an issue out of his obstinance until long after the war was over.

Our military association in Washington and the Philippines saw some conflicts. Strangely enough our different attitudes never changed in many matters.

During my service with you in Washington when as Army Chief of Staff you ran the bonus marchers out of town with, perhaps, the agreement and urging of the Secretary of War, Patrick J. Hurley. It was against the orders of President Hoover and my thinking also. I thought the men wanting their World War I bonus had a valid protest point but you did not. In fact you felt they were of a rebellious nature trying to stir up trouble and were a part of the Red Communist influence then talked about in our country after the Bolshveiks had taken over Russia. It was typical military thinking of the time by a lot of brass.

When you took me with you to the Philippines, my job was to train troops, and while I put all of my effort in that chore, we had neither supplies, equipment nor men to build an effective army. You knew this, but I suspect we left the impression with the natives and our government in Washington that we were building an effective force. Little did we think at that time that the Japanese were capable of launching a massive air and ground attack on our forces stationed there. They fooled us all — or made fools of us — whichever way you want to look at the fiasco.

I came back to the states to start training American troops with the 3d Division and then went on maneuvers as chief of staff with Lt. Gen. Walter Krueger's Third Army. My work there got me my first star. Marshall called me to Washington five days after the Japanese attacked Pearl Harbor and I went to planning operations. I was immediately faced with finding a way to get supplies and reinforcements to you — an impossible assignment. We continued to be hopeful as you did, both on location and in your battle reports. Just why our planes at Clark Field were sitting ducks, never retaliating in time to slow down the enemy, will never be understood. Your lack of cooperation with the Navy is still a mystery. All of it hindered our fruitless efforts at defense of the Islands. You established strong ties with President Manuel Quezon and endeared yourself so much to him that he gave you half a million dollars. Officials in Washington never questioned the gift seriously, because we thought it might mean that both of you would try to hold out against the enemy for a while longer. Quezon wanted to neutralize the islands to prevent any further action, and when you seemed to agree, we were more confused than ever. The records don't show any reason for acceptance of the gift, and at that time I recorded that "In many ways MacArthur is as big a baby as ever."[14]

When Quezon wanted to reward me for my efforts, I refused the money as graciously as I could, in order not to offend our ally. I did accept the certificate of appreciation written to accompany the money. Anyone knows an army officer with my pay could have benefitted from such a gift. I gather you appreciated your gift later in life when you were ensconced in the Waldorf Astoria Towers.

All this time we were trying to find ways to help. We did start shipping supplies and men but they had to be diverted and sent to Australia for the establishment of a springboard to fight our way back in the Pacific. President Roosevelt ordered you to leave the Islands in order to lead our troops back, when we all realized that your forces could not hold out. It is strange that you saw occasion to criticize your successor, Lt. Gen. Jonathan Wainwright, when he had no choice but to surrender to superior Jap forces.[15] You apparently thought they could hold out until you organized forces to return as you pledged. You returned all right but it was 31 months later. There is some question from a military standpoint whether the Philippines should not have been bypassed in favor of major invasions closer to the enemy. It was a huge area to fight in and required several commands in various geographical locations. This, in part, came about because the Navy didn't want to fight under your command. My operations in Europe were simple compared to the complex command set up in the Pacific. One thing is certain — while I tried to pass the credit around to my commanders, you grabbed the headlines and subordinated the efforts of your army commanders and individual divisions.

Your record of military cooperation and understanding of combined arms is full of negatives. Because you were such a hero of World War I at 38, you thought your judgment should not be questioned. While I considered myself a tank expert, you never caught up with the armor concept until the Germans "blitzed" Europe with tanks and planes in support of ground troops. You sat on the courtmartial that convicted Col. Billy Mitchell of insubordination. He was accused of being too strong an advocate of air power development and its employment in war. Surely you knew the great success of the aces in your first war. Why were you so slow to change? Because of your attitude there is little mystery as to why the Navy admirals didn't like or trust you. While you were building up a lobby in Washington for the Army, you must have overlooked the fact that the Navy was doing likewise and that President Roosevelt was assistant secretary of the Navy in World War I.

Your record in Korea is also a checkerboard of black and white. You never warned us that there was real danger in Korea, only five years after the end of hostilities, if you knew about it. Our forces there were woefully weak and we had not trained the Korean army to competent combat status. A lot of people must have been loafing on the job. When you took command of the United Nations defense force, you opted to stay in Japan instead of working from a battlefield position where you would know more of the actions involved and would have been a tremendous stabilizer to our retreating forces. Individual commanders and huge reinforcements, plus a loyal South Korean ally, made the difference. A lot of brave men died there. But with our American desire for offense instead of defense, we pushed the enemy back. Your invasion at Inchon at age 70 was a classic example of brilliant planning, execution and leadership. The tidal wave Gods were with you also, or else we could have had a catastrophe on our hands.

You ended up with a succession of my brilliant leaders from the European theater — Walton Walker, Van Fleet and Matt Ridgway. They gave great leadership to the Eighth Army. You or your commander, Lt. Gen. Edward Almond, in charge of the X Corps — not under army command — proved somewhat of a disappointment and embarrassment. How? After you drove north you kept separate control of both the army and X Corps — again from Japan — and the two forces were not coordinated. As a result, in the drive to the Yalu, you left a mountain range gap in the center. The Chinese drove down the middle of your gallant fighters to overwhelm them and send them into mass retreat. It was so bad that President Truman at one time considered use of the A-bomb to prevent the annihilation of the corps, in event they could not escape or be rescued. So all of your brilliance at Inchon was lost in the exploitation of your success.

Worse, over a period of time, you ignored the President, took it upon yourself to deal with the enemy, tried to reinforce your position through congressmen, and last but not least, issued public statements not endorsed by Washington. President Truman flew out to Wake Island to clear the air. You pledged loyalty and agreement but continued to commit the same mistakes, public utterances without clearance.

It all was too much for my comrades Bradley, Marshall and the joint chiefs, and so with their agreement, Truman fired you in April, 1951. Such public clamor! One would have thought the world had come to an end. But in the end history is proving Truman right and you wrong. You came home a hero with a tremendous reception, which you deserved, and then pledged you would fade away. As you were doing so, I left my command at NATO in Europe and returned to America to run for President. After I was elected, I went to Korea to find a solution to a truce and while I ran into a lot of flack I did settle the fracas. Before doing so I gave you the courtesy of listening to your plan of ending the war by attempting another try to conquer North Korea — your military planning included inclusion of Chinese nationalist troops, carrying the fight to mainland Communist China, and employment of atomic weapons.

I knew the people wanted peace and that our objective was to restore the 38th parallel which had been agreed on in 1945 at the end of the war. We had no other territorial claims in the Far East. You didn't agree, and you lost. I won and kept the peace in the world for the next eight years, although France pleaded with me to intervene in war in Indo-China.

It is an interesting reflection to compare the loyalty of South Korea to that of the new South Vietnam, our ally a few years later in a truly winless war.

You never had a joint staff operation throughout your career such as the one we found necessary for planning and victory in Europe. No wonder we got little help from other nations in Korea.

That was MacArthurism. You were a loner. You had good war records and had made your mark in American history as a real hero. It was a shame to see it tarnished by your own doings. I learned a lot from you and over the years you have directed a fair amount of flack in my direction. I withstood it and got what you always wanted — the

Presidency of the United States. As we always said in the barracks: "Tough . . . ." Regards.

D.D.E.

P.S. You got commissions for three Aussie gals on your staff in the Women's Army Corps, long before I was able to get one for my driver, secretary-receptionist and constant companion, Kay Summersby. I assume it took your personal intervention, as I finally discovered that was what was required on my part. Our Col. Oveta Hobby didn't want to commission anyone who was not in her ranks and eligible for normal promotion.

Author's note: One has to wonder if Eisenhower got his idea for a lady friend, Kay Summersby, from MacArthur. The general fell for a Filipino chorus gal and brought her back to the states keeping her in separate quarters. They both lost their love and went their separate ways, after some hectic developments. Ike's affection for Kay cooled as the war ended, and while she said he kept telling her she would return to America to be with him, in reality he got her a job with Gen. Lucius Clay. When she attempted to make their paths cross a couple of times, after she became an American citizen, Ike was safely back in the arms of Mamie and Kay was out in the cold. Eisenhower had other plans and, obviously, anyone in public life at that time who was being pressured to run for President was not about to have a back room mistress. It had been done previously but knowledge never surfaced at the time except among a few intimates. The Ike-Kay coverup was one of the great mysteries of World War II. Most American GIs went back home, though a few strayed and probably wanted their hero to do the same. It is fascinating to think what the mood of acceptance would be in this permissive era years later.

Letter 10

Omar Bradley. UPI Photo.

BRADLEY: WHERE'S THE CREDIT?

Dear Ike,

On second thought and in my second book I have come to the conclusion that I should have been the one who got credit for directing the American armies at Normandy and the drive across France and Germany in the great war. After all I commanded more troops, more armies, and I went farther than anyone else.

You had the diplomatic role and I did the tactical work, directing armies on the battlefield chess board. My moves were mostly winners, but the mission of destroying the German army west of the Rhine was not an easy one. Thank God, you made that your battle plan, because Hitler refused to fall back to the Siegfried line where he could have delayed our advance even more than he did east of the West Wall.

The Normandy breakout was a battle classic, but at the Huertgen Forest and the Battle of the Bulge we had about all we could handle. When First Army grabbed Ludendorff bridge at Remagen on March 8, 1945, we knew the war could not last forever, as it often seemed to. We encircled the Germans at the Ruhr and with thrusts north and south out of Remagen along with Lt. Gen. Jakie Devers' 6th Army Group on our south flank. People of course forget how difficult so many of those pockets of enemy resistance were to clear. Never did we know if there was a stronghold in the Southern Redoubt or what our role would likely be in the war with Japan. At least I had by then a well-trained, experienced and victory-minded Army Group (12th) to strike the final blow, if necessary. It would have been interesting, though bloody, to see what would have happened when you and Douglas MacArthur clashed over the command structure for the Pacific theater, if it had occurred. Thank God, it didn't. Dropping the A-bombs prevented that problem as well as saving thousands of American lives. Many people, mainly the younger generation, didn't understand that the bombs accelerated the end of the war. This puzzled me until the day I died in 1981.

Well, Ike, I guess I'm entitled to some more second guessing and post mortem thinking. You know when the Battle of the Bulge came along in December, 1944, you gave my First Army, yes an entire army, and some of my best commanders, to Monty. He was still not taking orders from you. He was still smarting over the fact that you had taken charge of the ground field command of the entire operation in August instead of the September 1 prearranged date. You left me with Middleton's VIII Corps and Patton's Third Army. Your excuse was the need for decentralized communication and control due to the split in our forces. Actually you wanted Hodges to protect the north flank, because you couldn't count on Monty's help, while Patton drove from the south. Your other excuse was that I should spend all of my efforts supporting the Maj. Gen. Troy Middleton and Lt. Gen. George Patton forces. You left me nothing for maneuver. After we won the battle on the south flank and freed our encircled troops, Monty got off his duff and attacked. Some of my commanders assigned to him went ahead and attacked earlier despite his greedy hold on the reins of my troops. Then he announced his victory and explained to an unsuspecting and prejudiced British press how he won the Battle of the Bulge. Allied harmony was necessary, but you went too far on that operation. Your moves probably delayed the war finale for quite a while. Just how you could counterattack with Monty's defense plans will always remain a mystery to military history. And to think a lot of British historians yet won't admit what happened at the Bulge.

I outlived most of our victory team at Normandy, as a five star general, I must admit I enjoyed all the fussing over me at thousands of public events, and the adulation was deserved as I looked back over my accomplishments. I served in the Army all of my life except for a brief tour of heading the Veterans Administration after our victory in Europe. For a while I joined the Bulova Watch Company as an executive officer and had some other business connections.

I rose from almost nowhere but became famous on the battlefield, passing many senior officers along the way, just as you did. I was a lieutenant colonel in 1936 and had three stars in 1943. You went up even faster, but we had to catch up with all that British rank just to match their promotions and command on an equal level.

Our paths didn't cross very much in the early years. We both missed combat in World War I. Gen. George Marshall was a supporter of both of us and when you selected me to replace Gen. Patton in North Africa during the final stages of battle, it was obvious you were grooming me for a higher command. I prevented the British from splitting the American command into piecemeal detachments just as Gen. John (Black Jack) Pershing did in War I. I moved the entire Corps in a position to capture Bizerte and 40,000 prisoners and our green troops finally came through. I may have been a little over critical of the early combat days of the American soldier. But he quickly learned by experience. Americans wanted to attack and they are good at it but poor defenders as we all learned — when we received some battle bloody noses.

After the invasion of Sicily, as II Corps commander under Patton's Seventh Army, you selected me to be the senior American field commander for the Normandy invasion. There was more bristling from the old pros. Even though we both made mistakes, we succeeded.

The counterattack at Mortain, after we had firmly established the beachhead was a serious personal effort by Hitler to drive to the sea and cut off forces at the base of the Cherbourg peninsula. His ambitious but costly counterattack would then drive our forces back into the channel. We responded quickly and, while the 30th Division took the brunt of the attack, we moved our forces rapidly to defend and to attack the new Nazi move. Since the Montgomery forces were continuing at a snail's pace and had failed to capture its D-Day objective, Caen, weeks later, Hitler moved some forces from the Canadian-British forces in order to attack us. By this time Patton's Third Army was ashore and quickly took over some of the corps and division troops from my First Army. He made an effective and fast sweep around from the west and headed for the Seine. Monty finally moved but failed to reach Falaise in time to trap the German army. We had plenty of forces to trap from the south but you waited to make an orderly linkup and, as a result, too many Germans escaped to fight us another day. This fiasco can be laid squarely in Monty's lap, and Patton gets the credit for the wide sweeping envelopment. But encirclement was lost.

I felt you were rather pro-British for not encouraging our Allies to play a larger role in our attacks.[1] In fact I continued to think you were an inadequate field commander but excellent off the field as a diplomat-planner.[2]

After the Battle of the Bulge, even Kay Summersby got into the act. She was furious with Montgomery's press escapades — especially when he used American troops for victories to whom he conveniently neglected to give adequate recognition. When Monty came down to lunch she sat at another table rather than insult him. Strange commentary: Kay became more pro-American and you became more pro-British.

Earlier when the Normandy beachhead was finally opened up, you flew over to check on progress and extend congratulations. You brought Kay Summersby, raising a few eyebrows.[3] I was always a little curious about your relationship with Kay Summersby, but as others of rank, I never commented — just observed.

As early as May, 1943, after the win in North Africa, I went to Tunis for the victory parade. There you and Kay were "greeting the legions of dignitaries who were mostly British . . ."[4]

Your American commanders, except Lt. Gen. William Simpson, were getting a little mad and threatening at the Bulge time. Patton and I talked at various times about just giving up, and going home and letting the British grab the headlines. You finally wised up and almost came to the same decision. Yes, you played the role of diplomat at the expense of the army commanders. Such facts are beginning to come out now, although the British rewrite of War II history is doing its dangedest to take most of the credit. Makes one praise Lt. Gen. Mark Clark for striking out and taking Rome earlier, even though British boss Gen. Harold Alexander wanted his 8th Army to get in on the capture.

I wrote in my second book, "I . . . made one of my biggest mistakes of the war."[5] That was the time I agreed with your plan to turn over two of my armies. I failed to defend battle-weary Hodges and agreed to a new boundary. This split the Bulge in half and gave Monty so many troops while the British had offered little to help the American forces stop the counterattack in the Ardennes.

Tactically I didn't look so good before and in that battle, but the reason was that you took my troops and initiative from my control. Your new fifth star stayed pasted on just as your fourth did after Kasserine Pass.

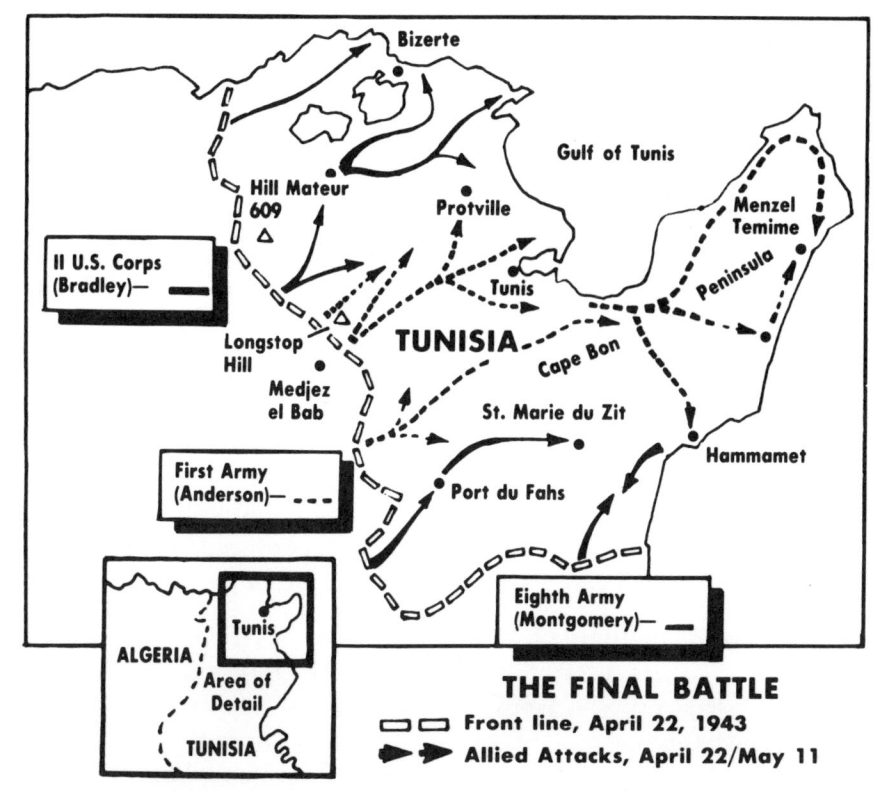

THE FINAL BATTLE
⬜⬜ Front line, April 22, 1943
▶▶ Allied Attacks, April 22/May 11

Final drive in Tunisia. Gen. Bradley kept the American forces intact with its own mission. Permission New York Times.

In my second book, written in conjunction with Clay Blair, an excellent journalist, I leave the impression that I was the guy they should have been writing about for leading the troops across Europe. When I retired from the active Army in August, 1953, at age 60, the author, John Mason Brown, wrote in the Saturday Review that he looked in vain for editorials about the general . . . "admired during World War II by millions who did not know him and worshipped by those who did, however slightly." Brown was with us in the Mediteranean and in Sicily for quite a while.

Ernie Pyle, who gave the foot soldier more accolades than he did the brass, made no bones about the fact that he was an admirer of mine. My voice, Ernie observed "was high pitched and clear but he spoke with knowledge and authority." Pyle wrote that I could be "fair, terribly firm, but never gross or rude." You and Capt. Harry Butcher, your navy aide, urged Pyle to go discover Bradley. I commented after his series was published widely in America that "Pyle had a difficult time making me 'colorful.' "[6]

Montgomery was a big problem both in working for him initially and then fighting side by side as equals during the long and grueling campaign. He considered all of us as inferiors and wanted to control my armies constantly. He ignored many of your commands and seemed to live on his reputation — which was checkered with delays and failures to exploit success. His troops often leaned forward into battle without real dedication.

I didn't even like Patton because of his many personal failings. However you let him get by with all of his publicity and fanfare. I'll have to admit he was a helluva fighter and probably deserves his high marks in history as one of our best. Poor old Lt. Gen. Courtney Hodges (First Army) was too self-effacing to even try to match Patton's charisma. And his press office didn't help much. Maybe he didn't handle the press, as an Army commander must, to tell of the exploits of his troops.

After crossing the Rhine I went to Cannes for a brief vacation. There I found you, Lt. Gen. Walter (Beetle) Smith, Kay and others from SHAEF ensconced in a fabulous seaside villa. Kay and Smith had decided that you needed relaxation after the emotional and physical stress you had endured for so long. Good thing they did. You were tired. We all got back to run the final show with a race into Germany and then V-E Day, May 8, 1945. After the VA assignment from my fellow Missourian, President Harry Truman, I became Army Chief of

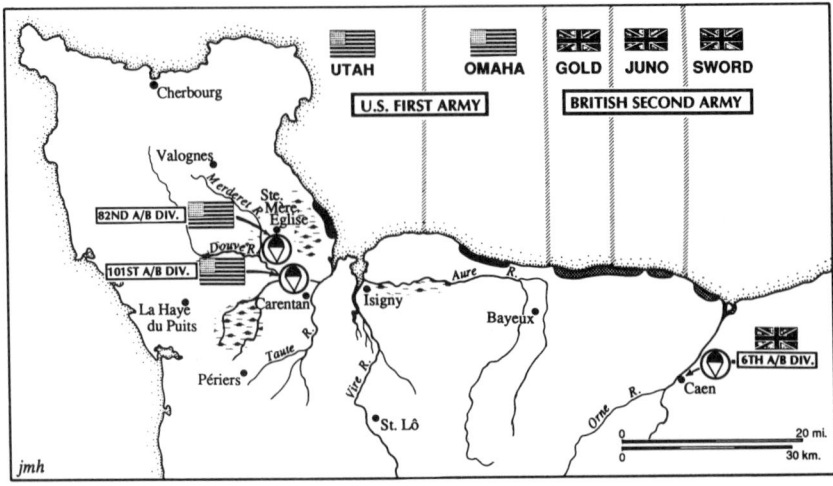

D-Day, Normandy, France, 6 June 1944. Scene of the greatest sea-air assault in history.

Staff following you. I became the first chairman of the Joint Chiefs of Staff, and during the Korean War many of my old team became a part of that major conflict. I retired in August, 1953 with Five Stars.

Happily, I married a second time — the vivacious journalist Kitty Buhler. She had written early episodes for "Dragnet" and the "Untouchables" on TV. She convinced Hollywood that a film of my experience would be profitable. It was not accomplished. After all, George Scott playing Patton would be hard to top. (I was an adviser for the Patton film.) I guess my film script is still on the shelves. My wife was a lover of horse racing, and I became interested in the windows. I related the military to horse racing in an interview with the Chicago Tribune (April 16, 1978): "The idea in an amphibious invasion is to maintain momentum.". . . "It's like the horses" . . . "It's hard to figure them when they open."

Life was very comfortable in my later years. Even in a wheelchair it was great to be honored over and over.

Ike, you assigned 1.3 million men to my army group. We won it going away, and I never forgot my army commanders: Hodges, Patton and Simpson.

Omar N. Bradley

P.S. In rereading my letter I realize that I overlooked another major disagreement about our final drive in Germany. I had Gen. Simpson poised for the drive to Berlin and Gen. Patton was headed for Prague — both deep in the planned occupation sector of the Russians, who our political leaders had agreed to anticipating a need for the Russian Army in the defeat of Japan after V-E Day. And the pesky Russians had never really committed themselves to such an effort. When I told you the final drive to Berlin might cost 100,000 casualties you reaffirmed your decision to only meet the Russians on the Elbe. Actually Gen. Hodges' First Army met the Russians first at Torgau. Patton sizzled also as we slowed him. He was ready to fight the Russians after we defeated the Germans. Bill Simpson fairly well took care of the Berlin decision in his long letter to the New York Times in 1955 about how he could have captured the Nazi capital. Historians and veterans have refought that decision ever since 1945 and probably will forever. Your critics are a little inclined to forget that we did indeed have another war to finish off successfully in the Pacific and at the time thought we needed the Russian help.

IKE SAYS:

Dear Brad,

Once I found you I knew I had a leader, a tactician, a general of wisdom, a man who could carry the ball in battle, tolerate uncooperative allied generals.

Besides, you became known as the GI general, probably the best accolade a general in the American army could have.

Your wisdom and training came to the forefront most candidly when you were faced later with our mutual adversary over the years, Gen. Douglas MacArthur (by then we were all five-star generals). When you saw his strategy and the Korean war struggle you commented that escalation of that war "Would be in the wrong war at the wrong place, at the wrong time, and with the wrong enemy." President Harry Truman said you were "absolutely right."[8]

Again I have to give Gen. George Marshall, Army chief of staff, credit for sending you to me. When the Kasserine Pass fiasco occurred in North Africa, I sent the explosive Gen. George Patton to blunt the counterattack, reorganize our forces, and renew our aggressive role against the successful and notorious German Field Marshal Erwin Rommel, who had captured center stage throughout the world as perhaps the brightest and best field general in the Nazi army.

For a throttle, I sent you along as his deputy and as my eyes and ears to monitor the battle and reorganization of our defeated and retreating forces.

Patton was 57 and very rank conscious. You were 50, younger than most of us. I was 52. But remember, everytime I got another star you got one also.

Your tactical planning and execution on the battlefield paid off. I realized then that you were probably the great potential ground leader of the American forces. Your insistence that the II Corps fight as an entity in Tunisia, and your leadership record, proved to me that you should lead the American force into Normandy. I told Gen. Marshall that because at that time he was expected to be the field commander. I would return to Washington to replace him. Fortunately I got the command because President Roosevelt wanted Marshall to stay as leader of the nation's overall operations on a two-ocean front. I must say that we both riddled the various staffs we had in North Africa and Sicily but we needed the trained commanders and staff officers to make a successful thrust in France. As we look at the overall experience and problems we encountered in the Normandy invasion we should thank Churchill and other British leaders who earlier had resisted our idea of taking the war directly to France in a cross channel push before we had gained some battle experience and developed leaders on all levels of command. Operation Torch in North Africa was a blessing for our green and untested troops and their leaders.

Your writings and memoirs on the war and our relationship are interesting and proved what I kept telling Capt. Harry Butcher, my Navy aide, and the wartime correspondents. I advised them to go down and interview you instead of concentrating so much on my operation. I was only partly successful in this endeavor. You did deserve more credit than you ever got and perhaps Clay Blair's book about you will help future historians put your role in a more favorable light.

It wasn't an easy task but you got along with Montgomery in the initial invasion at Normandy and soon had your major objectives including the capture of the Cherbourg port. Monty fiddled while Caen, one of his objectives, burned with shell fire without capture. Then came the hedgerows which bogged down your army in a most serious manner. You reorganized your forces and made massive assaults on the enemy to break the stalemate when Monty decided his British-Canadian forces would only be a hinge as we freed ourselves to make a brilliant dash across France and put the Germans to flight. We knew we deserved a break but didn't know where it would come. We could take credit for making the breakthrough with brains, brawn, desire and firepower.

And as all that happened, my plan for the invasion of southern France paid off with Generals Lucian Truscott, Sandy Patch and Jakie Devers sharing the honors. Truscott was my man and I wanted him for the Normandy invasion but he first had to capture Rome with his VI Corps in Italy. Then he made the thrust into southern France. His drive exceeded our greatest hopes. Perhaps I should have listened to him more as to how we could have rolled up the Germans from the south and gone to Gen. Mark Clark's aid on the French-Italian border. But I was determined to destroy the Wehrmacht west of the Rhine in my realization that the Nazis would not give up easily, German morale would not collapse and air power was not going to force an early surrender. History proved me correct.

It is a little late, but history now records that I did bend a little too much in Monty's direction, notably when your forces were attacked in the Ardennes where the Germans came through against France in 1940 in its famous Blitzkreig. We underestimated that possibility in 1944, and concentrated on territory where we thought we could attack to out maneuver the enemy and destroy his forces in the shortest period of time. We put up a weak defense line without adequate reserves to protect and screen an area that we thought was a fairly good defensive position. How wrong we were.

You never forgave me for giving Monty your First Army when the counterattack came after I had already given him our Ninth Army for his group command. But you still had Patton to save our war effort, which hinged upon a successful counterattack. Just think of it — Patton our only hope. We had defended him often after the Sicily slapping incident and numerous other times when he made derogatory statements within and outside our team's inner circle. He drove quickly and hard with great success. Then Monty took the credit. No wonder you and Patton were furious. It is ironical that I left you with only one army to close the Bulge. But in the face of defeat, Maj. Gen. Troy Middleton and his brilliant VIII Corps held on with great tenacity and courage unparalled in our defense history. It would have been expedient to have given you the land command but it would have destroyed our allied team spirit and unity which was so essential for victory. Many of my fellow officers and critics never realized that.

After I gave Montgomery one of your armies he went about his business of tidying up the front lines, altering positions and conducting patrols. He did little with his troops which only included one British division. After Patton turned the tide in our favor he moved.

You have stated your position on my failure to capture Berlin very well. Of course both of us would have liked to have captured Berlin but it was no longer a military objective. It never had been really. Destruction of the German army and Hitler's Nazi regime were our goals. A few years later we welcomed a new German army under the new Democratic government into the Allied fold to defend Europe against the Russians. Victories and defeats make for strange bedfellows at times.

As for the final drive for Berlin, people forget that many of our troops had been fighting in Europe since the invasion of North Africa in 1942, and were becoming weary. We were low on good company and field grade officers.

I know that you and Patton often disagreed over my handling of battle objectives and priority supply allocations, especially on the disastrous Arnhem operation, along with my deference to Montgomery from the breakout at Normandy until the end of the war. You both were ready to resign and let Monty carry the ball. Thank goodness you never made such a move. It might have led to my resignation also — who knows?

But remember your successes. Your capture of the Ludendorff bridge at Remagen in March, 1945, sealed the victory cap for our efforts. You drove deep into the heart of Germany. The bridgehead gave the entire American army a new spirit, which it needed after the Bulge. You could see it on the face of G.I.s in the line. It was like reading or hearing of another Russian breakthrough against the Nazi forces on the Eastern front. It was difficult for civilians to realize how much those Russian victories did for our morale. Many command posts kept situation maps showing the position of the Russians as well as ours in their overlays.

Your First and Ninth armies next encircled the Ruhr, the massive German industrial complex responsible for many enemy successes. It was a masterpiece of military coordination and still the Nazis refused to give up.

I gave you the most difficult jobs of the war and your success in battle was your payoff to me for my trust and confidence. You took the toughest jobs without hesitation.

While I lost you after the war because President Truman wanted you to head the Veterans Administration, I got you back to take over my job as chief of staff when I left the army to become president of Columbia University. And you performed brilliantly as chairman of the joint chiefs of staff. We defeated the Communists in Korea and reestablished the 38th parallel boundary which, after all, was the mission of the troops, despite what other generals, politicians and historians have said or written.

And in your reign we saw the end of the controversial, brilliant and sometimes questionable leadership of Gen. MacArthur. I am sure your support of President Truman in this decision was decisive and appreciated. While MacArthur was a great American hero, he had lost contact with reality and felt himself above the American government — which could not be tolerated. I learned that when I first served under him and again when I consulted him about his Korean plans after I was elected President.

History will always remember you as the G.I.'s general — who could ask for more?

D.D.E.

Author's note: I consider General Eisenhower the over-all genius behind the victory crusade in Europe in World War II. His drive, determination, enthusiasm, loyalty, and unity spirit with our allies were unsurpassed. However, a great deal of his tactical success belongs to Gen. Omar Bradley. In turn battle credit has to go all the way down from his army commanders to the squad leaders — the farther down, the harder the fight and the more casualties. Bradley's success is covered in most generous manner in the Clay Blair book in collaboration with his second wife, Kitty. Some critics have attacked the book but it gives Bradley some of the credit which he earned and historians have tended to forget or ignore. Ike used Bradley effectively in North Africa, Sicily and he was the guiding light for the Normandy invasion. His breakout of the stalemate was a credit to alltime American fighting. In the tradition of General Pershing in World War I, he made sure American troops were kept as a fighting team and not used as support and reinforcements for the British which would have been their preference. It is interesting to note that Gen. Bradley was unsure of the ability of the green American troops to fight the Germans but he was determined they would win or go down as a fighting unit, not piecemeal. When put to the test on their own under his leadership, they did not fail him and proved they were as good soldiers as those of any other nation.

Letter 11

Bernard Law Montgomery.
AP photo.

MONTY TO IKE: IF, IF, IF . . .

MINUS	PLUS
Vain	Dedicated
Braggart	Empathy for Soldier
Narrow	Admired
Rude	Thoroughgoing
Slow	Appeal

Dear Ike,

I wonder if you would give me the above accolades and criticisms now that many years have passed since our great victory over the Germans in World War II?

By the time you came aboard, I felt I had almost already won the war at El Alamein in North Africa. After all, it was the first great victory by our British Commonwealth forces since World War I. You know, when I was asked once during an interview, "Who do you think were the three greatest commanders in history?" I replied without hesitation, "The other two were Napoleon and Alexander the Great."

Being a hero and an egotist by the time I joined your command, I tried to play God most of the time while I served with you. Notice I didn't say under you. I tried to save you, save Bradley, save Patton, save

Alexander. But Patton and Bradley didn't want to be saved. They beat me in the Allied battle for Sicily and again at the Normandy beachhead. Imagine doing that to one of your own!

You see it was not difficult for me to save people. I had already saved Prime Minister Winston Churchill from possible defeat in the House of Commons with my victories in North Africa before we joined as a team of Allied cooperation. Churchill certainly needed a hero to improve his image to the British press and the British public. We had defended our rear ends all around the globe with one loss after another in the air, on the ground and on the sea. Of course, I could have ended the war if you had given me all of your men, troops, equipment, and air power. I was known as the set battle plan man, slow mover.[1] It probably would have taken me a little longer than it did you even though you had green commanders and inexperienced but energetic troops who were more skilled in attacking than defending. All along I had better plans and more vision than your American commanders. I would have been successful, but that your country was paying most of the bills and providing the bulk of the manpower.

To prove myself a hero, I directed the British Eighth Army, at 55, with the support of Churchill (and Gen. Alexander) who gave me the mission: Defeat Rommel. This was the greatest mass of troops and firepower yet seen in War II by Great Britain. We fought across North Africa in the second and final victorious march — across the mountains, sands and wadis, and heat of that desolate continent. Our earlier drive had been against the hapless Italian army whose equipment even outdated ours. Alamein came at a time when the Allied world had developed a psychosis about German General Erwin Rommel. His brilliant exploits of doing so much with so very little and displaying heroism at the front had not been seen by us since War I. He did almost run us all the way to Cairo. Just think what would have happened if Hitler had ever gotten control of the Middle East. My army saved the world from possible defeat and gave hope when darkness covered the globe. Of course, I made Alexander look good along the way but didn't offer many accolades in his direction. Others wrote that Alexander made me look good. And Churchill finally had some victories to tell Parliament about. My British press was so good and fast on reporting my exploits — I didn't discourage them — that most of the world knew what I had done almost before I did it.

Grudgingly, I give the French and Americans credit for some help in our Commonwealth capture of so many prisoners and for covering so much territory speedily in the final days of the campaign in Tunis.

Next in Sicily you were the boss over Alexander. I devised the plan that prevented a sack of the Italian and German soldiers by concentrating my forces, including Gens. George Patton's and Omar Bradley's. We failed to trap many enemy troops and I must admit Patton got to Messina before I did. The enemy retreated to Italy to fight us again.

There the going was a little tougher. I did not want to land first on the Continent but you said go ahead. I let your deputy and long-time friend, Gen. Mark Clark, with the American Fifth Army with a British Corps, do the dirty work by invading Italy in the main effort below Salerno. There they hit the Germans head-on and the remains of the Italian army disintegrated on the spot. Everyone thought my army would drive north fast to join the American-British forces on the beachhead but I fooled everybody. I just waited until I was ready to move and by then Clark had a secure beachhead. Sure taught him a lesson though, didn't it? You Americans were hardheaded at times. We went in there without enough troops, equipment, air and naval support. You American rebels always thought the idea was to attack the enemy continuously and win the war. By this time the British were getting accustomed to the fact that World War II had just become a way of life. One victory was only followed by another attack. Even though you probably didn't want me, you got me (over Alexander) at Normandy and I wangled the initial ground commander's job until you came on board several weeks later. Of course, Bradley took his objectives and saved me with the breakout at St. Lo, again with that Patton smashing east for Paris. My armies didn't exactly take their initial objectives as quickly as planned. They were weeks late, in fact, in getting to Caen. And then that Patton, with his Third Army, kept bragging about how he could cut off our breakout and he wouldn't have us in the way in his race across Europe. History has recorded him as a dashing, rough-talking fellow. He did cover a lot of ground and put the Nazis to flight. Of course, if you had given me his petrol and equipment I could have won the war in a single thrust under my control.[2] I don't know why I'm so conceited on this point, but it has always ruffled my feathers that I never got to run the "Big Show." The only times I found my plans being followed, with your concurrences, were at Arnhem and the Bulge, where both failed miserably.[3]

I wrote, pleaded, even leaked to the press my great expectations and tried again and again to convince you and the Joint Chiefs that I was the one to be ground commander — in control. Even after the Battle of the

Bulge, where I claimed victory with one British division and all of the American forces on the northern lip, you didn't cave in, ole chap. You just plodded along and even-threatened to quit if I didn't give up and start obeying orders. Bradley, likewise, offered to quit. So did Patton and I don't know how many others. But that Gen. William Simpson, with his Ninth Army, was a fine soldier. He and I got along and he often carried the battle tide for my forces. When you finally got mad enough at me you grabbed his Army away and gave it back to Bradley. I finally caved in, but by that time your armies were so far ahead I just played catch up until the war was over and never ceased second-guessing until the day I died.

I blew hot and cold on the capture of Berlin. In October, 1944, I agreed with you that Berlin was not a good objective. But as I moved forward the encirclement of the Ruhr, a major turning-point battle, was near completion by the First and Ninth American armies. Then Churchill and I saw the possibility of a single thrust to Berlin with my troops reinforced with most of your troops in the north. We weren't worried about the intelligence reports on the alleged buildup of the Werewolves (Nazi Underground Army) and fleeing troops toward a so-called Redoubt in southern Germany. I even told the British Chiefs that Berlin was my objective in late March. This notion infuriated you, because you had already told Stalin of our intentions not to drive to Berlin. He didn't believe you, anyway, and sent Marshals Giorgi K. Zhukov and I.S. Konev in competition to capture the last objective in Europe.[4]

It was rough going between us. I never gave up. Even after you became President of the U.S.A., I treated you like a colonial leader, looking over your shoulder and second-guessing a lot of the things you were doing. I finally got to visit you and told you how the Battle of Gettysburg should have been fought. I held a press conference and upstaged you by announcing in a loud voice that Generals Lee and Meade both should have been relieved of their commands because of the manner in which they fought.[5] I even invited myself to join your family Thanksgiving reunion at Augusta Golf Course.[6] I never tried to discuss Civil War gallantry, though, with any American school kids. It might have been murder in the classroom for a post-mortem subject.

Speaking of classrooms, that's where you were deficient, I guess, although the record says you were No. 1 in your class at the Command and General Staff School. Did you forget your knowledge of tactics or were you too busy trying to keep Gen. George Marshall, your boss, and

Churchill, happy? Your strategic plan to destroy the German armies west of the Rhine just never fitted into my plans, although I must admit some success after I had agreed to your directions. Your plans won the war but I never admitted it. I just kept on complaining, writing and talking of how the British really won the war and what a bad general you were. But you never gave up easily. You, the American hero, became President.

When I wanted to return to America for a second postwar visit for some more oneupmanship, you just never bothered with a direct reply to my feeler.[7] I could have again told you how to keep the peace around the world and at the same time not admit that you did win the war. Or that you settled the Korean War and maintained peace for eight years of your Presidency. But I might have mentioned that you saw the great autobahn road system in Germany's Third Reich, which plan you sold to Congress, giving you the go-ahead to start building the interstate highway network in America during your term as President. We always learn useful things in war, you know.

Well . . . back to my writing and reading of how I could have won the big one if given a chance. Those thorns don't smooth off in the clouds, any more than they did on earth, dear Ike.

Bernard Law Montgomery

Monty's Failures

Author's note: Although he never admitted them, here are Monty's battle failures:

1. No exploitation of his success at El Alamein.

2. The plan for the attack in Sicily concentrated in one direction too much to entrap the enemy, who retreated to Italy to fight again.

3. Lack of an aggressive drive into Italy to aid the American Fifth Army at Salerno.

4. Failure to capture D-Day objective of Caen, until weeks later.

5. Failure to break out at Normandy but took credit for American forces that did the job.

6. Dropping of paratroopers into middle of German army (and armor) at Arnhem.

7. Reluctance to attempt to cross the Rhine earlier. (The U.S. had two armies across by the time he started.)

8. Proposal of a single threat to Berlin instead of pursuing the Germans — who panicked and were in flight after Allied capture of Paris.

Monty's biggest mistake was failure to support Ike in the free world's crusade to liberate people and territory from North Africa to Germany who were enslaved under the Nazi heel. His constant bickering slowed the operation when Ike was seeking and getting cooperation from so many.

The British plan of attack was always difficult for Americans to understand. For many ground efforts, it consisted of sending out a platoon in the attack. If that was successful, then a company was sent to reinforce the platoon, then a battalion, etc. The process was slow and agonizing to the Americans who attacked with divisions, corps, and armies most of the time. It took a major invasion or crossing for Monty to make a massive assault after El Alamein.

Monty's stubbornness appeared most obviously in Sicily, even down to small matters. When Gen. A.G.L. McNaughton wanted to visit the Canadian forces from his home province, Monty refused the request.[8] Any wonder that if he couldn't get along with his own, he never really treated the Americans as equal? It is almost impossible to describe the man's vanity. One has to read volumes written about him to sense his love of power, his disdain for his fellow commanders.

One of Montgomery's idiosyncrasies concerned cigarettes. The first time Ike was in a map conference with him, Monty said he smelled the burning of something and would that person please put it out. The person was Eisenhower. Still, Monty used to beg Ike for additional allowances for cigarettes for his troops. In fact one historian relates that Monty was busy passing out cigs from the back of his jeep in southern Italy while his troops were resting — at the very time he should have been fighting up the Italian boot to help Gen. Mark Clark hold his beachhead at Salerno with American and British troops. Monty had landed in Italy ahead of the main invasion effort, to help trap enemy forces escaping from Sicily. He may not have realized that the Germans were going to push troops south to attempt to drive the beachhead at Salerno into the sea. He did not help Clark, only touched off bickering about the British cooperation in Italy, which never ended during the entire campaign and remains of great interest to historians.

Monty was as adept at handing out American cigarettes as criticizing American military plans.

"Nuts" Messenger Talks

The colonel who delivered the "nuts" note to the German commander who demanded surrender at Bastogne at the height of the Battle of the Bulge, Col. (later major general) Joseph (Bud) Harper, had no love for Montgomery. An early paratrooper, Harper was a regimental commander in the 101st Airborne Division when Brig. Gen. Tony McAuliffe muttered the word "nuts" when he got the German note demanding surrender. When he couldn't think of a reply it was suggested that he use his earlier word "nuts" for his reply. He did.

Harper, many years after the war, lamented the British rewriting of World War II which put the British in a good light while denigrating the Americans. Montgomery and most of his fellow British historians have reiterated that Monty won the war. Harper put it this way:

"Thank God, it was the British Airborne who dropped at Arnhem and not the Americans. He and he, alone, was responsible for the almost complete annihilation of that splendid British unit by disregarding positive intelligence reports concerning the location of German armor in that vicinity. I really felt for those poor guys . . . I commanded a Glider Regiment of the 101st Airborne in that operation. (September, 1944.) Montgomery, to me, was a greatly overrated egocentric. He was the leading British commander in Europe and was supported vigorously by their press. I suppose it was mostly because of national pride, tinged with professional jealousy of Eisenhower and our other outstanding top commanders."[9]

Ike Sizzles

When Monty's memoirs were published, Ike was furious. He suggested that U.S. and British wartime leaders have a one-on-one (man-only type) conference to discuss issues and actions alluded to by Montgomery. Of concern was Monty's statement that he always planned a breakout to the right in Normandy, not at Caen, which was closest to Paris. Lt. Gen. Omar Bradley carried the ball at Normandy. As First Army commander he drove inland and sent Maj. Gen. J. Lawton Collins and his VII Corps west to capture the port of Cherbourg. Then Bradley slipped Patton's Third army, which had been the decoy for another thrust from the Dover-to-Calais area much to the east, between Collins' forces and his own First Army, which made the breakout at St. Lo and in conjunction with Patton's forces broke the beachhead wide open.

Monty also took credit for winning the Battle of the Bulge. Ike almost quit over this outlandish braggadocio. Monty also wanted a single thrust to take Berlin, which would have ended the war sooner.[10]

In 1966 Monty repeated his original assertion about the capture of Berlin to John Eisenhower, Ike's son. In his excellent *The Bitter Woods*, young Eisenhower records that Monty said, "To take Berlin in the spring of 1945 would have been foolish." John says Monty never questioned the use of that statement.[11]

In another book, by Cornelius Ryan, a native of Ireland, who became an American citizen in 1951, recorded in *A Bridge Too Far*:

"In a taped interview, President Eisenhower almost relived for me his emotions at the time of this bitter argument with Montgomery. When I told him I had interviewed the field marshal, Eisenhower cut me short and said, 'You don't have to tell me what he told you — he said I knew nothing about war — right?

"Look, I'm interested only in getting this thing down truthfully and logically, because any historian has to make deductions . . . Personally I don't believe I would put too much weight on what generals remember, including me. Because memory is a fallible thing . . . Goddamit, I don't know what you heard in Britain, but the British have never understood the American system of command. When the whole damned thing (WW II) was done . . . I never heard from the British any goldarn paens of praise. And you're not going to hear it now particularly from people like Montgomery . . . His associates — they've said things about him that I would never dream of repeating . . . I don't care if he goes down as the greatest soldier in the world. He isn't, but if he goes down that way it's all right with me.'"[12]

Ryan notes in his book that while Monty got credit for the term "single thrust" to Berlin, he never offered such a specific idea. Ike's staff coined that phrase, apparently, after Monty had suggested throwing 40 divisions into a drive toward Berlin. He wanted those 40 divisions under his command and they would have been largely American troops.

Ridgway on Monty

The American Airborne commander of the XVIII Corps, Maj. Gen. Matthew B. Ridgway, recalled this about Arnhem:

"This Operation Market-Garden was Montgomery's ill-fated attempt to trap a German army in Holland with its back to the sea. When he found he could walk a mile and a half up a road that an advance element of the British armor was unwilling to try he concluded that stronger leadership from the top command could have brought British ground forces into contact with the 1st British Airborne Division which had been dropped beyond the Rhine."[13]

Ridgway also recalled that Field Marshal Alexander once offered to fire Montgomery, then his deputy at NATO. "The deputy being Field Marshal Montgomery and the offer being one I appreciated but of course declined."

Monty Loses an Aide

Little is known about Monty's personal relationship with women. His mother was described as "cold and loveless" in a controversial biography written by Alun Chalfont, a military specialist, who was Britain's minister of state for foreign affairs, between 1964 and 1970. His book caused an outrage in England when he reported an allegation that Monty had a homosexual relation with an aide, Capt. John Poston, who was killed in 1945.

Chalfont says Monty's physician, Dr. Bob Hunter, reported that the "young soldier's death so affected the general that for two days afterwards no one could get a decision from him."[14]

A reviewer of the Chalfont book, Ernest Volkman, wrote in *Newsday* in 1976:

"Montgomery didn't like women and seemed comfortable only in the presence of young men. This (homosexual charge) amounts to a cheap, unproven shot, and was the main cause of public fury that broke out when the book was first published in Britain. (The British have long accepted the fact that Montgomery was not nearly the great general they had thought he was in 1942.) A number of other hunches about Montgomery's psyche by Chalfont are equally questionable, and while they may be titillating barracks gossip, they hardly do much to illuminate Montgomery's role as a military commander."

Not all British historians hence have reported favorably on Monty. Besides Chalfont, the list of critics on Monty, includes Capt. Basil Liddell Hart, Corelli Barnett, J. F. C. Fuller and R. N. Thompson.

IKE SAYS:

Dear Monty,

I spent a long period in my life trying to defend your actions and our relationships throughout the war period. I wrote you letters of congratulations. I told you of the many triumphs you enjoyed. I wrote of my deep and warm feelings for you personally. I thanked you publicly and privately for your help and cooperation. I gave you more troops than I should have at times in the heat of battle. I forced Allied unity on all of my troops and our Allies. But through it all you emerged as an egotist, an eccentric, a braggart — and double-crosser in American slang.

You not only failed me in battle but long after the war when we should have forgotten and given credit where credit was due, you kept saying Monty won the war, I was a bad general who knew very little about military tactics, and generally disrupted whatever warm feelings the Americans had for their British counterparts. Unfortunately, you made the critics on my staff including some of your fellow British officers in my command look good. They criticized me for tolerating your failure to accomplish objectives in battle. You became my No. 1. critic. I really don't think I deserved that. A horde of other British writers, critics, politicians, soldiers and others started in earnest after World War II and worked overtime to rewrite history in your favor. We Americans never asked for much credit. We supplied the bulk of troops, supplies and ammunition. We had given the British nation much of the same troop support in World War I when Germany had you and the French down on your knees praying for victory. President Wilson, American commander in chief, and Gen. John J. Pershing, field commander, never asked for adulation or praise. And they never got much. But history tells the story of the gallant fight of the green, untrained and inexperienced Americans as they marched and fought across Flanders Fields, the Meuse Argonne, Marne and hundreds of other places to remove the yoke tightening as the German Kaiser and his allies conquered much land. This was beginning to bleed the manhood of France and Britain.

You joined the American slogan which we hear too often: "Get the boss." I guess your reasoning, and that of your fellow countrymen, has been that if you tell enough mistruths your printing presses and library records will overcome the great American victories on the fields of battle in North Africa, Italy, Sicily, France and Germany. This is not to say that your troop support was not appreciated or that it was not battle worthy when committed. It is saying that we gave you credit for what you did, but you and some of your countrymen have never given the American G.I. his reward for fighting and dying to free the free world when Adolf Hitler held you by the throat and was truly threatening your life.

My only hope is that the historian and student of military tactics, strategy and techniques will see through your thin veil of filibustering in the name of ego and national pride. No one, certainly not yours truly, is knocking you or your efforts. I defended you when you were wrong many times. But when it was all over you went out of your way time and time again to insult me, to debunk me and almost to prove your disloyalty. We will never know how much sooner we could have won World War II if you had just given a little more on the battlefield. If you had kept the enemy more off balance, we could have delivered the killer blow with our American and other allied forces at a faster pace, with more decisiveness for a speedier victory.

Look at the record. You were a great hero in the headlines of October, 1942 when you broke out of a stalemate at El Alamein. But in November, 1942, I led the American-British drive into Algiers, Oran and Casablanca to free the French and to insure their switch to our side in the fight for liberty.

You failed to exploit your victories. We struggled on and conquered North Africa long after fighting should have been finished. If you don't believe me, read the memoirs of Rommel, Kesselring and others.

We established Allied unity with Gen. Harold Alexander and others, despite your foot dragging. In Sicily our forces invaded with your plan and our American General George Patton and our so-called untested GIs made a monkey out of you in cleaning up on the Germans and Italians. Because of you and our air and naval forces we allowed far too many of the enemy to escape.

My long-time colleague, Gen. Mark Wayne Clark, took a brilliant British corps and one American division into Salerno for a real bloodbath and established a shaky beachhead, after which the Germans almost drove us back into the sea. The British troops — not in your command — really held off the German onslaught. Where was your famous Eighth Army? Down on the toe and heel of Italy waiting to drive north after Clark was firmly in place with his gallant troops, and then you held a press conference to tell the world you had joined forces with the American Fifth Army. What a shame! But we held our tongues.

The stalemate persisted most of the winter. It was the American effort with Alexander's help and the great French forces, which finally broke out and conquered Rome. This should have been an earlier victory. Again your Army sat on its duff during most of the winter while the Americans were fighting and bleeding on their quagmired front.

Both of us had turned to leading our forces into France at Normandy. I brought along the talented Lt. Gen. Omar Bradley, of North African and Sicily fame, who saved the invasion, while your forces formed the so-called hinge around which American troops had to fight and die for a beachhead breakout. We again had a stalemate because of lack of action on your part. I made one big mistake there and repeated it several times in the next 11 months of fighting on the continent. I failed to inspire and push you on to greater heights. I respected you too much. I thought you wanted to win the war as fast as I did. But I misread your thinking. The British under you wanted to wait and probe feebly to see how fast the Russians and Americans could drive the enemy back to his homeland for final victory. While the American attitude was to attack, attack, attack, yours was defense, defense, defense. What a great group of spectators and loyalists you could have led in the American athletic arena when your team didn't have the ball. It was the GI who carried the ball most of the time although Generals Clark, Hodges, Simpson and many others didn't complain during the war or publicly afterwards. I can't say the same thing for Generals Patton or Bradley. And danged if they haven't been proved right. 'Tis a bit embarrassing for me. Their foresight was greater.

Even my constant British companion and aide, Kay Summersby, saw right through you and became more American than British. Some of my critics in turn said that I became more British and less American as the war progressed. How's that for a switch? At least it proves that I supported your efforts and appreciated what you did in our unified command. The least you could have done would have been to provide the same treatment for me and my soldiers. But no — you spent the rest of your life belittling me, my troops, my plans and my victories. As a result, I bore the criticism from all sides. Even fellow British officers on my staff were critical of your failures. And after the war most of those working with me were relegated to oblivion, and even poverty as in the case of Lt. Gen. F.E. Morgan, who was the architect for the Normandy invasion long before we came on the scene.

But let's leave the post-mortem battle table and return to the fighting front where our troops were willing to give their all. When the Germans were in disarray after the rout at Normandy and the liberation of Paris, we could have driven them back to their homeland before they reorganized on fallback defense positions. But no — you waited to enjoy the sweets of victory. You wanted a certain number of troops, supplies, petro, time and an oversupply of ammunition before you would pursue the enemy when he was on the run.[15] You devised plan after plan to get more troops from me, to take my field commander's job away from me and to monopolize the headlines. The British press was willing to play your game. I read in vain for any praise of my efforts in North Africa, Italy, Pantelleria and other places of victory.

In desperation, I guess, we gave you all you wanted for a plan to land airborne troops in the Arnhem area in order to get quick entry to the Rhine river and to speed the capture and opening up of the needed supply port at Antwerp. There your troops were massacred. Your ground effort failed to connect with the drop that American Gen. Matt Ridgway saw no excuse for. The British press failed to report adequately on the success of the American effort under your command. Many of my fellow officers knew the game you were playing by now and severely criticized me for my failure to push for your relief or at least for a promise that in the future you would drive your troops harder and faster as we moved forward. This is not to say that your armies did not face difficult terrain and enemy strongholds but in your British rewrite of history you failed to mention that the American and French forces had the same obstacles and kept attacking them until victory came.

The clever Germans found the big hole in our lines in the Ardennes in December, 1944, where they had come through against the French in 1940 and plunged deep into our lines — some 50 or more miles in places. You talked me into giving you another American army in your sector and then sat and watched as Bradley and Patton drove into the enemy flank to stop the onslaught at Bastogne, forever the shrine of the quality and bravery of the American army. Did we ever get much credit for that from you? No, you just waited until the smoke had cleared and then went on stage to declare that your maneuvering and tactics had turned the tide, while you had hardly turned a hand. That brought absolute rebellion in my ranks. It even brought me to the point of making demands from Churchill and Marshall, which almost brought the entire command structure to a crisis. Either I was the boss, or you. We could no longer live under the allied umbrella of unity with your outspoken, incorrect and flagrant mistatements (deliberate I presume) to the troops, press and the world at large.

The joint chiefs gave me the vote of confidence. There would have been little or no unity under your control and command.

We fought on and reached the Rhine first, crossed it with two armies, and then with your set-piece battle and much fanfare you crossed, almost without opposition. Little wonder. The enemy was engaged on our front as he had been so many times before.

But were you through questioning my leadership? No, a thousand times no. You wanted my troops for the fast route to Berlin as you had been harassing me since we broke out at Normandy. Such loyalty.

I wanted to make the final drive in the war a great success. You remember that too many people — including us — thought we were on the verge of victory in the autumn of 1944 when perhaps we should have been. But we underestimated the German enemy.

After the lucky break at Remagen to cross the Rhine my own plans were in effect for a successful juncture with the Russians. I had given you Simpson's Ninth Army for too long for which I will forever be criticized on the American side of the Atlantic. As Patton, Gen. Sandy Patch and Gen. Jakie Devers and the French were pushing deep into Germany in the south, my plan was to encircle the Ruhr in the north. It was the industrial area we needed for the final German defeat. Simpson's army went to Bradley and we used your forces for his protection as he and Hodges' First Army made a classic encirclement of the Ruhr to meet at Paderhorn. I made sure of the control of American forces in our drive to the Elbe and the linkup with the Russians.

We had now decimated the German army and victory was at hand. I wanted no more misunderstandings. America still had a war to win in the Pacific. My multi-front advance insured victory although you, your colleagues and historians have never given me much credit for it.

My plans to stop short of Berlin also enabled us to conquer Denmark and make it a free country on our side of the Iron Curtain. This was a nation that really appreciated liberation. You British forget that accomplishment as directed by me — you just take credit for its capture in your zone. Many Americans have enjoyed the Danes, with their affinity for the USA.

The Russians made overtures toward Denmark, but our occupancy meant their exclusion. It is my gut feeling and always has been that the

Russians would have fought us in Berlin — ally or not — in order to keep our predetermined division of Germany. So many people forget that when we gave up that territory and others, in the Balkans for example, we were doing everything at the conference table to make sure the Russians joined us in the fight against Japan since our manpower resources were beginning to dry up. The A-bomb was not in the planning part of a field command such as ours. And I have often wondered just how much help you would have supplied in the invasion of Japan? About as much as you helped when we had to fight off the Red threat in Korea in the 1950s?

It does seem strange how well (and much heat I took) I got along with our English speaking cousins. We expected the French to be a bit difficult — and they were — but when the showdown came they showed initiative seldom displayed by some of your commanders.

Let's hope that future historians try to get all the facts straight from the British rewrite of World War II.

Your experience in part came from defense, retreat and withdrawal, the set-piece battle and waiting for the other guy to carry the burden in many battles. The American including this general was attack-minded. Defeat made us more determined to go out and strike the knockout blow, you know, ole chap.

Yours for truth will out in our endeavors in future histories.

D.D.E.

Letter 12

Harold Alexander. AP photo.

ALEX — MONTY GOT CREDIT

Dear Ike,

I was the architect who piloted the Allied war machine in North Africa, the Mediterranean and Italy. I guess, though, you could call me the guy who got stranded at first base with three power hitters on deck — you, Montgomery, and Marshall. I wanted to join the big show at Normandy but never got the chance to be your deputy.

Field Marshall Montgomery got the credit for the victory at El Alamein in North Africa, and should have, because he was the Eighth Army commander. But I had to help put the operation together and overcome the defeatist attitude the British had when they had fallen all the way back to the defense of Cairo. We were deficient in plans, equipment and men . . . I convinced the Prime Minister I could put together a winning team which could run Rommel out of North Africa. Heaven knows I wasn't his first choice. He had a succession of Middle East commanders who couldn't go forward — only backwards after the Germans moved in on the Italian army, which was rapidly falling apart.

From Alamein in October, 1942 on, it was success after success. With the French and Americans we drove the Germans out of North Africa and I later became the Earl of Tunis for the conquest.

For the drive in Tunis you gave me two great American generals, George S. Patton, Jr. and Omar N. Bradley, after I pushed you to relieve Maj. Gen. Lloyd Fredendall, who could not lead his II Corps effectively. I know it was tough for you to relieve one of Gen. George C. Marshall's proteges. But it was necessary in battle to have effective commanders. Later on in Italy I had to apply the same pressure on you to relieve Maj. Gen. E.J. Dawley, another choice from Marshall's little black book of leaders, who almost lost control of his VI Corps at Salerno.

After your troops recovered their losses and position at the Kasserine Pass fiasco Patton moved forward, although he was frustrated in his desire to take on Rommel, the German hero in North Africa, because Monty and I did not have enough confidence in the green American troops. Patton's mission was limited in an advance to the sea partly because I was not sure of the final roles my two armies, the British First and Eighth, would play in the final act. As it turned out, you and Gen. Bradley convinced me to have a separate sector in the final drive for Bizerte which was difficult but successful. Again I was still doubting the ability of the green, inadequately-trained American troops. Later on I gained respect for your troops as Patton dashed across Sicily when Monty again went about his slow, set-piece battle.

I had a variety of both good and bad military actions. As a young officer I led a brigade of German Balts to retake Latvia from the Bolsheviks and in 1935 became a hero on the northwest frontier of India. A few years later I was the rear guard commander at Dunkirk. Had we not saved our men there we would have been desperate for troop strength. Just how the British and French failed to work out adequate defenses before the Germans moved in World War II remains a mystery today as well as then. It is hard for multi-nations to cooperate in battle but look what you accomplished, Ike. You got us all on the same team pulling together and, after a series of setbacks, the Allies won the big one in France. We destroyed Hitler who had become the terror of the world generally and, specifically, in the minds of the British soldier and civilian. I also conducted the retreat of the British - Chinese army from Burma in 1942. Then we won in North Africa, conquered Sicily, and invaded Italy. This was to be a long and grueling campaign.

My forces, with Gen. Mark Clark's Army in the lead, captured Rome. I know you and Clark at times felt we were not carrying our full load in Italy and elsewhere. The British learned to stop, rest, probe, and wait another day for the set battle — which would normally be successful, because we had experienced so many operations which

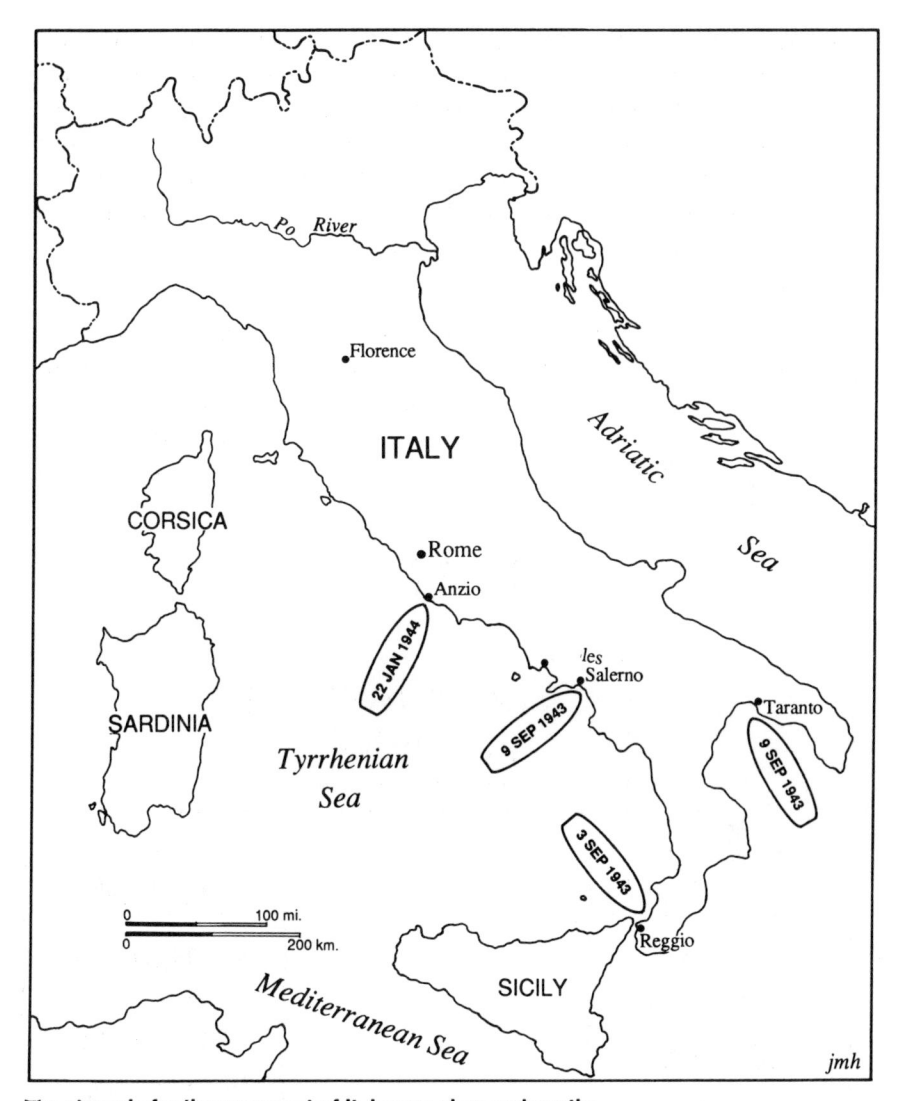

The struggle for the conquest of Italy was slow and costly.

failed or did not work out as successfully as we planned — Anzio and the Rapido River are good examples.[1]

I must confess I made a bad basic change in our invasion of Sicily. I let Montgomery convince me we should only make the invasion at one site instead of two, which would have trapped the Germans and Italians and put the squeeze play on them. As it was, Patton landed alongside Monty's west flank for the latter's protection, obviously. Well, it ended in a foot race for Messina, the northern end of Sicily, and Patton won with largely inexperienced troops which were now proving themselves to me and Bradley. I think Monty learned a lesson there from the Americans. I had done all of the work to make Monty look good, and he let me down. Likewise when he landed on the toe and heel of Italy they were feeble attacks. I finally got him into gear, but by that time, Gen. Clark had already secured his beachhead at Salerno, with the aid of a British corps in his control. From then on I ran my own show and made my own decisions.

In the meantime I had a large area to command. We did manage to move into Greece and save it for the free world. We encouraged Tito in Yugoslavia and arranged with him for the use of his territory if we drove across the Adriatic into Central Europe. Of course my leader, Churchill, wanted to fight more of the soft under belly of Europe. You and

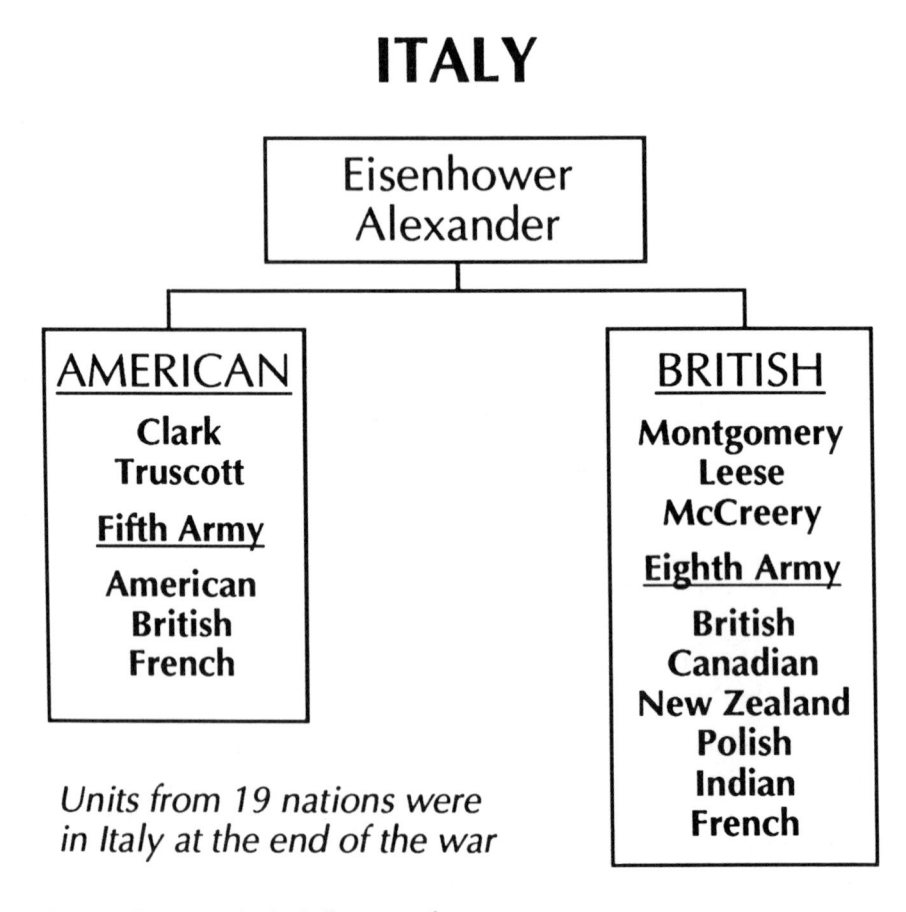

ITALY

Eisenhower
Alexander

AMERICAN

Clark
Truscott

Fifth Army

American
British
French

Units from 19 nations were in Italy at the end of the war

BRITISH

Montgomery
Leese
McCreery

Eighth Army

British
Canadian
New Zealand
Polish
Indian
French

Command structure in the Italian campaign.

some American leaders may now regret your dissent. It is to be admitted that such directions would have taken us over many mountainous areas and probably would have caused even higher casualties than anyone could have anticipated.

I did end up as Governor General of Canada after the war for six years. Just about the length of War II. I was proud when you were elected President of the USA, and we again became friendly neighbors in our postwar adventures.

I'm glad you managed to survive the crusty Montgomery, but I always would have been glad to serve under you as ground commander in Europe. Monty's press was too good and the British public wanted a so-called battlefield hero. Just think of the many times he could have been a greater hero by exploiting Alamein, Italy, Normandy and the flight of the Germans in September, 1944. At that time they were confused, defeated, and fleeing to reorganize defense of the homeland. He certainly would have taken a lot of the pressure off American and French troops if he had thrown caution to the wind and pursued the enemy when he had all of these opportunities.

Of course I ordered the bombing of the Abbey at Cassino on the recommendation of my subordinates. A strange thing has happened over the years — the American Fifth Army commander, Mark Clark, was charged by many, including some British historians, of destroying the Abbey. Actually, bombing was urged over and over by my commanders along with a lot of soldiers on the ground. I did it, and the Americans got the blame.

The huge abbey was like a fatal attraction — a magnet by day and a ghost by night.

Speaking of your old buddy, Clark, he captured Rome all right, and it was the only time we had a serious difference. I wanted to trap the German Armies below Rome. I still think I was right. But Clark knew the world wanted Rome. He struck out and got it. Some historians say he was wrong and even gave me the credit for capturing Rome when it was not in my immediate plan. The mountainous terrain would have made the pincer a difficult one. The Germans were clever defenders, as we found out, and we paid a high price for victory in Italy.

Field Marshal Harold Alexander, Earl of Tunis

Author's note: Nigel Nicolson, British author, described Alex very succinctly: "He not only commanded his men but represented them

. . . His method of command was less by order than by influence and persuasion. His instinct for the higher conduct of war was based on a feminine intuition for what was or was not possible and for what was thought to be possible by those whose duty it was to carry out."[2] "Eisenhower and Alexander were perfectly matched. Alexander was the British Ike and Eisenhower, the American Alex."[3]

All of which is to say he knew his soldiers and his generals from first hand knowledge. He coordinated a great effort under trying conditions.

When Rome fell, Alexander at 53 was promoted to Field Marshal, and it was back dated so he would outrank Montgomery. Alexander was four years younger than Monty and one of Churchill's favorites.

IKE SAYS:

Dear General Alexander,

You were my sort of man and general. You took your job seriously but not yourself or your personal desires as did your countryman, Montgomery, whose ego knew no end. My theme was cooperation. Your theme was cooperation. Together we made a good and effective team to direct the combined arms on the ground — on the sea and in the air, to win the battles of Tunis in North Africa and the conquest of Sicily. Our invasion at Salerno left a lot to be desired, but we didn't have the forces to ensure quick success in that operation. Historians have been cruel in their assessment of the bitter and hard Italian campaign where so many of our men suffered and died — a longer campaign than any other by our forces in Europe.

You were my deputy, and you took direction — a team player who put victory ahead of personal glory. Likewise, my other British deputies in charge of air and sea forces were effective. Together we displayed and practiced Allied unity, which was my first goal in order to have success on the battlefield. You would have been my choice for deputy of the Normandy invasion and head of British-Canadian forces, but our superiors took the hero of the moment, Montgomery, for the role. You were left with the difficult job of directing the Mediterranean effort. You directed the rugged Italian campaign and liberated Rome with American forces before we invaded France. You liberated Greece and then supported our big invasion thrust into southern France. We gave you Gen. Mark Clark and Gen. Jacob Devers. I also left you one other outstanding fighting American general, Lucian K. Truscott. I really wanted him for the Normandy leadership. I did get him briefly for the invasion into southern France, but had to give him back to you for the Fifth Army command after he, with Gen. Alexander Patch's direction and support, had pushed his corps into contact with my forces coming down from the north. You held a steady hand over our forces and gave me the nudge when I needed it. At your insistence, I relieved the American, Maj. Gen. Lloyd Fredendall, after the Kasserine Pass fiasco, and at Salerno I relieved Maj. Gen. E. J. Dawley. I was inclined to hang on to both because they were selections of Gen. Marshall, and I wasn't sure that they were totally responsible for the failures of the green American troops and commanders, in many cases of momentary defeat. But you persisted, and for that I give you thanks. I was new at the game and appreciated your counsel.

At Salerno you supported the ground troops with confidence and more firepower when Clark's forces were in a tough four-day battle to hold the beachhead. You made sure our forces stayed Fortunately, the Mediterranean effort into southern France gave us new supply ports we needed desperately. Historians are inclined to forget this role in the second invasion of France.

You are entitled to a little second-guessing about why I drained your officer corps and troop strength. I never gave much consideration to helping out with a stab-in-the-back attack into Italy near Genoa after my troops were ashore from the French-Italian border to the west.

Our cooperation made my position secure as supreme commander, although many critics were yelling for my scalp after I installed Admiral Jean F. Darlan as French commander in North Africa and again when I failed to strike out and capture Tunis before we bogged down, giving the Germans time to organize defensive positions. At the time, all of us thought Montgomery's Army would drive to the west with more speed and less caution. But you knew Montgomery better than I. Many thought you would get my job as supreme commander because of your combat experience, rank and standing with British leaders. But Marshall supported me when President Roosevelt might have wavered. Also, I have to admit I had an advantage over you and your British commanders: the French would never have fought under your command, but they would under mine. Both Churchill and Roosevelt knew that problem very well. I recognized your talent but also recognized that the French had a role in the decision, though it may have been more negative than positive. At least the climate was favorable for my advancement.

You had a bad habit though, General, for badmouthing our inexperienced American troops. They were green and not always at the training level necessary for combat. And don't forget that the Germans knew this also and took advantage of it at every opportunity. You failed to realize that my army was a young one and had not been in uniform very long. Only eleven months had elapsed since Pearl Harbor when we invaded North Africa. Many of our veterans and early draftees were also serving in the Pacific. We had an untrained, poorly disciplined army until we went into battle. And then I think you finally realized that the American soldier was the equal of yours and courageous enough to win many a battle. He (soldier and general) would attack sooner, harder, faster and in greater numbers than yours in many areas as the war went on — Italy, Normandy, the Bulge. Let no one question the ability or courage of the individual soldier of the British empire. Likewise the same qualities of the American soldier.

When you developed your final battle plan to conquer Tunis with only the British Armies, thereby squeezing out the American II Corps, I took great issue with you and changed your plan. I reminded you that America had given some of its best equipment to your army and that the bulk of the future fighting would be by the American soldier. We were not going to sit idly by while the British grabbed up all the glory in the final conquest of the German Afrika Korps. I went further to remind you and your nation that if the American people felt our troops were not to play a major role in the fight to free Europe, they would have insisted on an Asian-first strategy.[4]

Because of your prejudice about green American troops, you didn't want to give Gen. Patton a major offensive mission after Kasserine Pass, but he made a good showing anyway. He certainly showed up your Montgomery four months later in Sicily.

But Gen. Bradley and I overcame you in the final drive for Tunis. You wanted to attach II Corps to British command and, like Pershing in World War I, we didn't go along. I demanded a mission, separate sector and a battle-worthy objective. We moved the entire unit from south to north and then drove successfully into Bizerte, liberated our sector and captured 40,000 prisoners. How was that for a turnaround? You British, I must finally admit, were still looking down your noses at our combat experience, including mine as a commander. But you saw the light.

Your troops helped us in setting up new training programs to make our men more combat ready. It reminded me of Pershing's experience in World War I when his troops were shipped directly overseas with little or no training. Like the French in World War I, you were heavy on defense. Americans were offense minded. We wanted to win the war, in both cases, and go home. We took your advice but continued to fight both wars in our attack manner. In World War I our boys were better disciplined and more experienced as backwoodsmen, hunters, expert riflemen, people who lived a spartan life. In World War II so many of our city boys were afraid of the dark, didn't know how to read a map having enjoyed an easier life in a prospering America. They had not been trained mentally or physically for the rigors of the battlefield, but they had the right fiber and learned the ways of combat fast.

You found out how good we were in Sicily, again. Patton moved fast and his troops made end runs by sea to beat Montgomery to our final objective, freeing another country. Shortly after the Salerno invasion I turned attention to the Normandy invasion and lined up a new team for the big thrust to end the war. I knew that I was leaving the theater in good hands with you, Clark and Truscott.

After our invasion of France in the north, I then turned to my second thrust into southern France. Your influence was felt when Churchill kept insisting that we forget the operation in favor of your forces driving up the Italian boot to Trieste using some of the forces I needed to destroy the German army in Europe, west of the Rhine.[5] By this time my command was established firmly enough to win. It was a hard pill for you to swallow in Italy, much as it was for Montgomery who kept trying forever to keep me from taking over control of the ground fight in France and the final drive in Germany.

I finally complained in my diary about the British press. It would use the terms "boldness" and "initiative" when you and Montgomery were mentioned but referred to my role as a friendly administrator in charge of Allied teamwork.[6]

When it all was over we both found that our work was not yet done. I returned as Army chief for a while, then became a civilian and President of Columbia University only to be recalled to rejuvenate NATO. Next it was the Presidency for me when I saw my duty to ensure in peace the victory we had won in war. You became a good neighbor as Governor General of Canada. The English-American teamwork continued. Although we had our differences initially, we welded success in a great crusade.

D.D.E

Letter 13

**William Simpson.
U.S. Army photo.**

SIMPSON — ON TO BERLIN!

Dear Ike,

Greetings from your Ninth Army commander:

My credentials?

1. I reached the Elbe River on April 11, 1945 where you held me.
2. I could have captured Berlin at the end of the war if I had been allowed to do it.
3. I was a state-side three-star general whom you didn't particularly want but Gen. Marshall did, and so I got the job.
4. I was well over 6 feet tall with a clean shaved bald head who demanded and got perfection from his commanders and men who gave you success after success.
5. I could get along with that Limey, Montgomery, whereas most of the rest of you seemed to have trouble.
6. Now if you don't remember a late comer to the Normandy team, I would remind you that in your memoirs you said if I ever made a mistake it never was brought to your attention?[1]

Am I qualified now to speak?

Well, how did I get there? After the service in the Mexican Expedition under Gen. Pershing, I went to France in World War I and rose to chief of staff of the 33rd Division. Back home I went to the usual schools and was on the general staff planning group for a while. Steadily I went through division, corps and up to army command. When we got to Normandy I took command of the Ninth Army. We took Brest and headed east to join the big show. It seems I was attached to Montgomery's group quite a lot. Not that I'm complaining. I'll never forget that when Monty bragged about his great endeavors once too often, you grabbed my Army and gave it back to Bradley in a hurry. I probably could have gotten to the Rhine River much earlier if Monty hadn't dragged his feet. He waited until he could get organized for his ill-fated airborne attack. At this time the Germans were in a confused retreat but we didn't move fast enough. What a mistake.

The Ninth Army got a bloody nose at the Huertgen forest along with the First Amy. We worked the northern flank and suffered severe casualties. It was our real baptism of fire and may have better prepared us for the horrors of the Battle of the Bulge. Both conflicts will live long in history, as you know, Ike. At the time of the Bulge I was in the flatlands of the Netherlands. Ninth changed direction and instead of going east we turned south to take over part of the northern lip of the Bulge. Of course Patton attacked the southern lip, and Hodges held the other part of the north lip with hard fighting everywhere — it was our most serious counterattack of the European theater.

After the surprise at Remagen where First Army captured a bridge before it could be destroyed, Monty gave his order to cross the Rhine. Meanwhile, Third army went across. The crossings did not speed up Monty. After a massive supply and troop buildup the Canadians moved before midnight of March 23 and reached the east bank against sporadic opposition.[2] The Ninth went across the next day, and you and I joined the assault forces at midnight. We "mingled and talked with the troops!" You reported in your memoirs the men "were remarkably eager to finish the job"[3]

One of the classic battles I like to recall is the encirclement of the heart of industrial Germany by my Army and Hodges' First. After the Rhine crossing, we maneuvered the two armies on the flanks of the target and forced the surrender of 317,000 prisoners including 30 generals.[4] The Germans were finally trapped into surrender, but German Field Marshal Model could not believe the speed of the envelopment and refused to surrender even though his Chief of Staff and American Maj. Gen. Matt Ridgway tried to persuade him to do so. A brilliant commander on both the east and west fronts during the war, Model wandered into the dense part of the forest near Dusseldorf and shot himself April 21.[5] Actually his positions had been encircled since early in April.

Now the stage was set for Berlin. I was in Gen. Bradley's command, thanks to you, and the end of the war was in sight even though the Germans continued with fierce pockets of resistance.

Unaware of your decision to forego a drive to Berlin, my staff and subordinate commanders deduced that the Ninth Army had drawn the honor of capturing Berlin. Brad said to "be prepared to continue the advance on Berlin or to the northeast."[6]

We got to the Elbe River and the word was flashed to you. You reconsidered your decision not to go to Berlin.[7] You wanted to know how many casualties it might cost to drive on and capture Berlin. Bradley estimated 100,000.[8]

I had a plan to enlarge the Elbe River bridgehead (it did suffer from a counterattack as we were discussing the future plan) to include Potsdam, a suburb of Berlin. On April 15 I flew to Brad to present it. He telephoned you for a decision and on overhearing the conversation, I knew I had the answer. You said no, and we were ordered to clean out Magdeburg and wait for the Russians.

Historians have done a fairly good job of recording the circumstances, but in 1966 I took serious disagreement with two writers, John Toland, *The Last 100 Days*, and Cornelius Ryan, *The Last Battle*. They were both reviewed by Brig. Gen. S.L.A. Marshall for the *New York Times*, and I took severe exceptions to the review and the reports by both authors. The thrust of both volumes indicated my army was strung out with exposed flanks and in bad shape, supply and logistical wise. I wrote strongly that this was not the case and Ninth Army could have led a last victory into Berlin. I reminded all three and the reader that I had three Army Corps and 13 Divisions ready with all the power and supplies I needed to defeat a retreating army. I also pointed out that my bridgehead across the Elbe could easily be expanded and that I was holding a tight leash on my commanders. All signs were go from our viewpoint. Gen. Slam Marshall had written that my statement of how my troops stood when the halt was called was "categorically wrong." He was the one who was wrong. Neither author contained any statement of mine as to how the army's troops stood at the time. I explained in some detail their excellent condition and the positions of my army.

Besides, I wrote, the "German forces had completely lost cohesion and the troops were in the pocket and had nowhere to go." At no time were the operations we had just completed in supply trouble.

Little did my commanders know of the political restraints placed on you. How much you knew about our position and the Russian progress, we didn't know. We do know now that many historians and the Russians claimed Berlin was in their hands late in April but admitted they had to fight house to house, street to street, and building to building to clear the city, at a terrible price of casualties.

Your decision to stop where we were was accepted by all in good grace, albeit with a certain amount of disappointment. How it all might have turned out had we gone on is, of course, a matter of conjecture. "At the time the feeling throughout the Ninth Army was that the Germans knew their collapse was imminent and that they would much prefer to surrender to us than to the Russians. I am convinced that the U.S. Ninth Army could have captured Berlin well ahead of the Russians if it had not been stopped on the Elbe, April 15, 1945."[9]

At least I thought I got the record straight. It was the only time I recorded any extensive report on the misunderstanding.

After the war I soon had to retire because of my physical condition — severe arthritis and heart problems. I did enjoy my association with the Alamo National Bank as a vice president for several years until failing health slowed me down.

I told Saul Pett, of the Associated Press, in an interview in 1954:

"You're only human if you miss it. You train all your life to command. Finally you get an army. You lead troops in battle. You have a personal staff of 150 or 200. You make big decisions. And then suddenly, nothing, you're on your own. You miss the troops most of all. You miss the big staff. You miss being top dog. You're relieved not to have any more heavy responsibilities, but at the same time you miss the big decisions. You're glad to get out from under all the damned regulations but you find yourself missing the bugle calls. You go to Ft. Sam occasionally for retreat. It makes you feel kind of funny. You recall many things."[10]

I sure did miss it. I missed you and even missed Monty. I was growing old.

To say I was proud of the Ninth and what it accomplished would be an understatement. We came into the battle late in the war but we made up for a lot of lost time and ticked off our objectives like clockwork. Steady and never failing.

William H. Simpson.

Author's note: In a handwritten letter to the author on March 27, 1976, Simpson recorded: "Receipt is acknowledged of your letter and the article about Berlin enclosed therein. It was nice to hear from you again." (It was on "Could Ike Have Taken Berlin?")

"It gives me great pleasure to know that you were at Camp Wolters in 1941 when I was in command there. I congratulate you for going from private to major general . . . in 22 years.

"My health is not good now. I have severe arthritis in the lower three vertebrae of my lower spine one of which pinches my sciatic nerve which passes through my right sacroiliac and right hip which is most painful. I also have a slow down in my heart function due to my age — I will be 86 years of age this coming May — 1976 — which causes my heart to fail to pump all of the blood from my lower legs and feet. I take a heart stimulant daily and other medicines.

"You ask several questions about Berlin and some other questions in your interesting article and ask for my comments.

"My dear wife died in 1971 in the 50th year of a very happy marriage. I could not live alone so I sold my house in 1972 and moved into the hotel. (Menger, San Antonio)

"For these reasons — my poor health and change of residence — I shall not try to write comments on your splendid article but refer you to two books in which I think you may find authentic answers to your questions."

The books were, *The Mighty Endeaver,* by Charles B. MacDonald and, *The Last Offensive,* also by MacDonald. He gave the addresses and page numbers to recall what really happened during his leadership of the Ninth. He was mentally alert and obviously his script, while difficult to read, proved his mind was still sharp enough to recall the details of reference materials and also how to get them.

He was asked in the same letter if he had studied postwar books enough to realize how so many British writers were changing many events to prove how green the Americans were and how much better the British could have handled the entire operation. He answered: "I know little of the British rewrite of World War II." He returned the article with "kindest regards and best wishes."

The author was a draftee when he first saw Gen. Simpson at Camp Wolters, Texas. Following a rugged three months of basic training under the Texas sun and a few mesquite trees, a battalion of trainees was assembled for Gen. Simpson to bid them farewell before their shipment to regular units in the army. He looked every part a soldier — ramrod, 6'1" clean-shaven head. After you heard his message — even though you were hoping that your year of training would be over soon and that you would return to civilian life — there was little doubt as he spoke that he knew war was inevitable. He softened the blow partly for what was to come. There must have been a message there also, when the supply sergeant or Uncle Sam's railroads lost all our civilian clothes en route to Camp Leonard Wood in Missouri. In a short time we wouldn't need them any more anyway. That brought the term "tough shitsky" close to its real meaning.

IKE SAYS:

Dear Bill,

Gen. George Marshall sent you to me at a time when I had plenty of generals to promote to army commander, but your experience, stature, knowledge and all-around ability made you the most eligible and deserving in our chief of staff's thinking. And he was right. I once said that if you ever made a mistake, it never came to my attention.

You served with Pershing in Mexico in the days of Pancho Villa and with Marshall in World War I as chief of staff of the 33d Division. You were decorated with the Silver Star. You organized one of our basic training camps when recruits were pouring into the army at a rate of thousands a day. You were known for your grasp of tactics. Besides, you were affable, well-liked and quick-witted.

You joined us after we had broken out at Normandy, and your Ninth Army took over the occupation of the Brittany peninsula. Paris fell on August 25, 1944, and you moved to the fighting front teaming up under Bradley with Courtney Hodges' First Army and Montgomery's British-Canadian troops. You worked well in your relations with both generals. In fact you probably got along with Monty better than any other American general, and that is saying a lot. Your army's first blood bath came when you joined Hodges in reduction of the Huertgen Forest, a

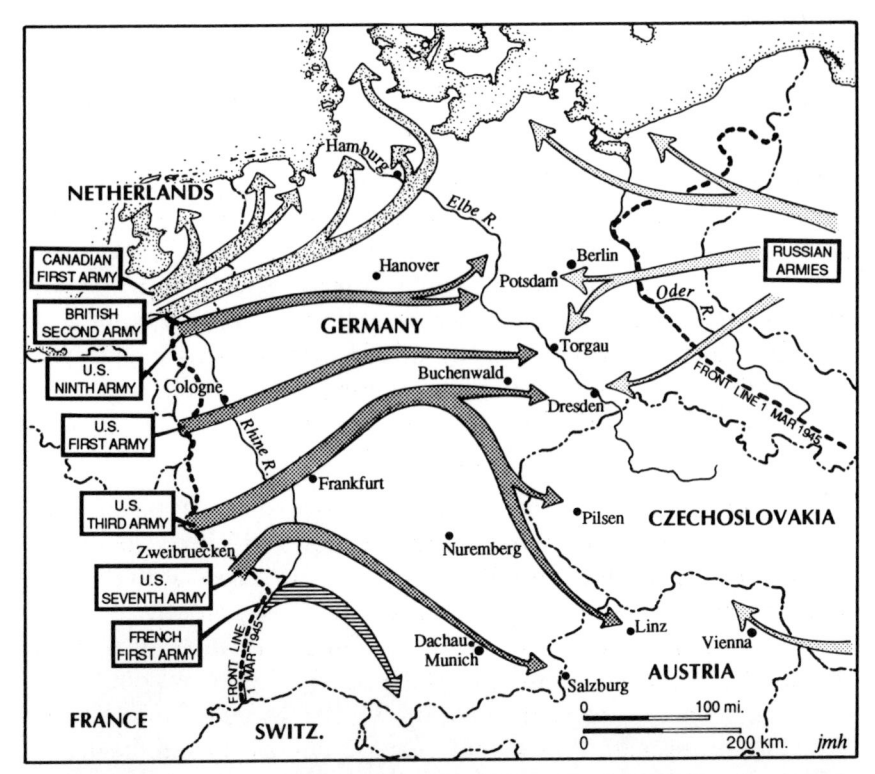

The final push from East and West in World War II. Note how close the Russians were to Berlin on March 1, 1945. It looks easy now but it was hard then after many years of weary warfare.

thankless but important task. Our casualties were high. Some have said we should have sealed it off, but I was determined to destroy the German Army west of the Rhine and we did just that, despite what critics said then and say now.

When the Germans hit us in a massive and costly counteroffensive in the Ardennes, I gave Monty your army and also Hodges'. I told you both that, "I know that you will respond cheerfully and efficiently to every instruction he gives"[11] The story is well-known. Gen. George Patton saved the day and Monty held back his armies until the bulge had been dented enough to stop the German attack. This is not to say that your troops didn't suffer from enemy fire, bitter cold and weeks of treacherous combat as we closed the gap and moved east to cross the Roer River, necessary before we broke the Rhine defenses. Your Operation Grenade was a great success, despite the flooding obstacles created when the Nazis destroyed the dams and canal dikes.

After the operation you were ready to cross the Rhine, but Montgomery said no. He wanted to wait — again — for his set piece assault. The British conveniently forget all of that now. It was surely a frustrating experience for you and for me.

History little records the many deeds accomplished on your unglamorous front, as compared with Patton's winter long fights at Metz, Saabrucken and other places deep into the Rhineland. He had lots of war correspondents with his headquarters. For the record you got to the Roer in late February and by March 2 reached the Rhine. In the Rhineland campaign your army killed 6,000 Germans and captured 30,000. You were almost an instant success. Through it all, I gave you, Patton and Hodges friendly pats on the back and let you fight the battles as you knew how to do so well.[12]

Your drive across the Rhine was almost unopposed and you encircled the northern half of the Ruhr industrial complex with great speed. You headed straight for the Elbe River with an army mass of 13 divisions with 341,000 men. I stopped your army when you urgently requested permission to head for Berlin. It was no longer a military target, and the Russians were closing in at a rapid pace. Besides, it was not to be in our zone of occupation as decided by the Big Three political leaders. When it was estimated we might lose up to 100,000 men in the drive, I repeated my no. I admire you for challenging my decision many years later in the *New York Times* article, but my decision was wise.[13] Besides, we had to worry about a possible final stronghold in the south and, as you know, the enemy continued to resist strongly in many sectors as we drove east in the final days to meet the Russians.

You left the army shortly after the end of the war and didn't get your fourth star until 1954, with 10 other generals who had never received the rank commensurate with their assignments and responsibilities in the final months of the conflict.

You went on in life to a successful civilian post as a bank executive in your beloved, native state of Texas. Though you had many physical ailments you were 92 when you died in 1980. Perhaps some day a historian will search out the records and write a personal account of the accomplishments of Bill Simpson and the gallant Ninth army. You deserve better treatment than the historians have given you, although the official documents are full of your many successes.

Certainly you were famous for being one of the few American generals who could get along with that crusty Montgomery. That was no easy task, I know. After the Bulge, the only accolade you got in his memoirs was a curt: "It has been a great pleasure to work with Hodges and Simpson; both have done very well."[14]

D.D.E.

★ ★ ★ ★ ★

From Howitzer Year Book, West Point Military Academy.

DWIGHT DAVID EISENHOWER
ABILENE, KANSAS

Senatorial Appointee, Kansas
"Ike"

Corporal, Sergeant, Color Sergeant; A.B., B.A., Sharpshooter; Football Squad (3, 2); "A" in Football; Baseball Squad (4); Cheer Leader; Indoor Meet (4, 3).

"Now, fellers, it's just like this. I've been asked to say a few words this evening about this business. Now, me and Walter Camp, we think —"
—*Himself*

This is Señor Dwight David Eisenhower, gentlemen, the terrible Swedish-Jew, as big as life and twice as natural. He claims to have the best authority for the statement that he is the handsomest man in the Corps and is ready to back up his claim at any time. At any rate you'll have to give it to him that he's well-developed abdominally — and more graceful in pushing it around than Charles Calvert Benedit. In common with most fat men, he is an enthusiastic and sonorous devotee of the King of Indoor Sports, and roars homage at the shrine of Morpheus on every possible occasion.

However, the memory of man runneth back to the time when the little Dwight was but a slender lad of some 'steen years, full of joy and energy and craving for life and movement and change. 'Twas then that the romantic appeal of West Point's glamour grabbed him by the scruff of the neck and dragged him to his doom. Three weeks of Beast gave him his fill of life and movement and as all the change was locked up at the Cadet Store out of reach, poor Dwight merely consents to exist until graduation shall set him free.

At one time he threatened to get interested in life and won his "A" by being the most promoising back in Eastern football — but the Tufts game broke his knee and the promise. Now Ike must content himself with tea, tiddledywinks and talk, at all of which he excels. Said prodigy will now lead us in a long, loud yell for — Dare Devil Dwight, the Dauntless Don.

★ ★ ★ ★ ★

Ike was chided for his unscholarly devotion to eating and sleeping in the cadet yearbook. In the academy record, Ike wound up 61st in academic standing among his 164 classmates; in conduct he was 125th, with a whopping total of 211 demerits. By contrast, his classmate, the future General Omar Bradley, was 44th in scholarship and sixth in conduct.

Letter 14

Mark W. Clark. U.S. Army photo.

YOUR NO. 1 MAN UNTIL . . .

Dear Ike,

I was promoted to general before you, but when I saw a star I knew it — you were by far, in my opinion, the diplomat-soldier-planner to lead our forces in Europe. Gen. George Marshall, a man both of us admired, agreed. When I picked you out as No. 1, on a list at Marshall's request, he turned and said, "I'm glad you agree. I've already decided that."[1]

We were the two stars in Marshall's firmament. I was to become your deputy and II Corps commander in charge of training troops in the buildup of our forces in England for the invasion and liberation of Europe. I had already gone through a major overhaul of our techniques in training in the states. Our maneuvers and new ideas, with the 3d Division at Ft. Lewis captured the attention of Gen. Marshall and his deputy, Lt. Gen. Lesley J. McNair, who later was to be killed accidentally by our bombers in the St. Lo breakthrough at Normandy. He wanted to be up front to see the jumpoff and apparently wanted a command in the European theater.

The big maneuvers in Louisiana in 1941 were the payoff. From then on it was one promotion after another. You always wanted a division to command, but you went up so fast you never had the chance. You skipped all the higher command slots except the top — Supreme Allied

Commander. My war planning assignment gave me responsibility of enlarging and training the Army and also the planning for a global war inevitable long before Pearl Harbor.

After the training mission in England, in 1942, it was all out for invasion of North Africa. You sent me in a submarine to negotiate with the Vichy French and I tried to persuade them to lay down their arms and join our fight against the Nazis and drive the Germans from North Africa. (The State Department official, Robert Murphy, earlier had conferred with French Maj. Gen. Charles Mast and five civilians.) The invasion was a success, but politically we had to deal with Admiral Jean Darlan, who was a loyal Vichyite. He was the boss man, unfortunately. Darlan and Gen. Alphonse Juin did get the French to quit fighting in Algiers, Casablanca, and Oran. But we never were able to persuade Darlan to convince the French to turn around and fight the Germans in Tunis rapidly enough to insure an early victory. Free French forces did help us greatly, later, as the British and American troops drove both east and west to liberate North Africa. Because of the recognition of Darlan, the press and political leaders of both Great Britain and America were up in arms over the deal. We had no choice in the matter, really, but we were both severely criticized.

We had no desire to negotiate politically. All we wanted to do was send our troops in to fight. But American lives were at stake and our decision was a wise one.

The heat ended when Darlan was assassinated. But still we didn't have a French leader, and at that time Gen. Charles De Gaulle was hated by Roosevelt and disliked by Churchill. In the meantime, the French Navy destroyed its ships on orders from Vichy, and we lost what could have been a powerful naval force in our continuing fight to control the seas. We had to wait a long time for our leaders to calm down and to recognize De Gaulle as the leader of the Free French in Algiers. We eventually won that fight. You were to enjoy your friendship with the French leader for a long time, even though he and his fellow countrymen kicked you out of France with your NATO headquarters some years after the war, when the Russians started to rattle their sabers.

When you ran into trouble in North Africa at Kasserine Pass you wanted me to take over II Corps. Having already established my Fifth Army, I said no. You took Gen. Patton for the job. It was a good move. Successful too. You said you were not allowed to establish an Army in the II Corps crisis area. When the time came for Sicily, I was in the wings and again wanted to save my Army for the first American landing on the Continent in Italy.[2] You agreed and sent Patton with his Seventh Army and Bradley as the Corps commander. This turned out to be an early victory though difficult at times, because the Montgomery plan put all of our eggs in one basket instead of driving against the enemy in two directions to attack and capture the enemy forces faster. At that time one of our major worries was whether or not the Navy and the Air Corps could support the effort in two landing sites. The problem was to plague us again in the Italian campaign.

Patton and Bradley never much liked me for my influence with you, but I hope I didn't disappoint you. If we had had more troops and air support we could have won a faster victory in Italy and perhaps even gone on to liberate a lot of Eastern Europe. Of course, Stalin, Marshall, and Roosevelt wanted us to invade France both north and south as soon as possible. Churchill was really on the fence. He wanted to attack the soft underbelly of Europe, all right, but he also knew the Germans were still bombing England and were preparing for even more awesome land-based weapons which were to rain so much havoc over his island. The buzz bombs were terribly destructive and also held a psychological mind-trap for the civilian population. An invasion through France and the lowlands of Belgium and Holland would finally silence those weapons, but it took a long time.

So on the last day of 1943 you left me to my fate, and I stayed in Italy. Actually you, FDR, and Marshall gave me a chance to command the Seventh Army in the invasion of Southern France, operation Dragoon, but I stayed with my favorite, the Fifth. Later I was to become 15th Army Group commander in the Mediterranean and picked up a fourth star. My stars shone brightly as I deceived the Germans and sneaked into Rome with a command maneuver that drove straight from the Anzio beachhead into the Catholic Capital of the world. Christians all over the world celebrated the Vatican's liberation from the Nazis. It was a great victory and one we deserved.

Remember that Ultra, the British intelligence system that broke the German code and read many of the signals between Hitler and his generals during the war, had said all along after the Salerno invasions that Hitler planned to pull his troops out of southern Italy and defend the northern part of the boot. In fact, good German troops poured into the Salerno area, battle positions north of Naples, and again at Anzio. At least we kept our promise to Stalin to contain as many German divisions as possible. British historians have challenged the change in direction ever since, but Rome was in my zone and our chances of trapping the German armies between the British Eighth Army front and the Anzio forces were nil. I have always hesitated to tell my gut feeling about the British fighting efforts (not fighting quality) ever since we first arrived in London to plan our large scale invasions of enemy-held territory. To think — the British wanted to make the drive for Rome a joint effort when their forces were many, many miles behind our troops!³

Our final separation in Italy recalled our many pleasant years together. I was a company and battalion commander in World War I and being wounded ended my combat career in France. Afterwards, there came a lot of dull stateside duty — imagine two years as a post exchange officer. But assignments improved. There was much schooling, duty as a National Guard instructor in Indiana, Ft. Benning, War College Command and General Staff school, Ft. Lewis and then the General Staff assignment.

I remember when we got to London that the first driver in the car pool turned us down because she was looking for a three-star general. We didn't qualify then. Your driver turned out to be Kay Summersby and mine was a redhead named Betty. You kept Kay on for the duration, but I decided I didn't need a female along as I inspected and trained the troops. Our relationship had its irritations during the war, but we didn't fall out until after the war when you were President. You became Army Chief of Staff and apparently were determined that Bradley would succeed you. I went off to become the Military Commander and Governor of Austria. There we made a determined stand to fight off any Russian overtures and, with a lot of personal work and persuasion, the voters gave our U.S. team an overwhelming victory in the first postwar vote. It stunned the Russians. From then on they were easier, though not much, to get along with. It was my chance to prove that if you stood up to the Russians you could win. When they harassed our trains, we told them we were ready to fight to use the rails without interference. When they harassed us in our air space we warned them to be ready for a fight. We told them we were ready to shoot to kill on the ground or in the air. The disputes were settled. I didn't win many admirers in Washington, and when I said what I thought, the State Department (Marshall by now was secretary of state) was in a state of confusion. They were not willing to be tough with the Russians but I was. I couldn't help but think that if you and the Allied leaders had agreed with me, we would have gone from Italy to Yugoslavia and other East European countries to prevent the Soviet takeovers and our victory would have been more complete. Our treaties plan with those territories were tossed out when I made sure the Russians were not to prevent the liberation of Austria. For once I won over the State Department.[4]

But back to the war. You stayed with the follow-up invasion of southern France, and I gave you my three finest American divisions just as we were on the verge of winning a bigger victory in Italy and on to the East. I tried to convince you and Marshall that the French divisions under General Juin could handle the invasion alone. I was overruled. I always felt that was a mistake, and it was the beginning of the end of our cordial relations. In my first book *Calculated Risk*, I lamented the fact that I had to give up good troops for the invasion of Southern France instead of driving through Italy and into the Balkans.[5]

"I was bitter that we were going into Southern France for the wrong goal when we should be directing our efforts to the East, across protected bridgeheads over the Adriatic provided by Tito, and through the Ljubljana Gap. I felt then that was the operation to make, and I still feel that it might have changed the post history of World War II, as far as the United States-Russian relations are concerned."[6]

After the war the 36th Division veterans got their backs up over the fiasco at the bloody Rapido River crossing below Cassino in Italy in January, 1944. At that time we were landing without opposition at Anzio to form a pincer move on the Nazis. Without taking advantage of the high ground, initially, and without adequate engineer support the river crossings failed. Earlier, the British had crossed below the American position but I had no follow up to exploit the drive on the high ground to the northeast and the envelopment of the Abbey, the much-feared monastery, which the Germans claimed was never manned but did provide observation sites in the surrounding territory. The land masses extended both east and west of the Abbey. Just imagine the results if we could have followed up the British success with a follow through on the Garigliano with French and American troops. Such allied cooperation at the time didn't exist for such an operation to take place then.[7]

We fought over the Cassino land for weeks and then the British forces demanded we bomb the Abbey into oblivion. While I later got credit for the bombing at the insistence of our Allies, it was my boss, British Gen. Harold Alexander, who actually ordered the strikes to destroy the monastery. Even British historians have failed to hold him responsible for it. The GI, though, wanted it bombed, it also should be recorded.

The Anzio beachhead held against vicious counter attacks. Hitler was determined to eliminate our forces there. We went in without opposition but I had half of the three divisions needed to exploit the landing.

As you know, relations with the British were not easy. In our Italian invasion Montgomery failed to drive north fast enough to help my forces. After the enemy was beaten, repelled, and withdrawn, Monty arrived on the scene to announce the juncture at a press conference. I said at the time, "I never felt the warmth of his hand." When I went to call on him he was conveniently gone from his headquarters. "The British were difficult to get along with, more so than the French or the Poles. They had been fighting a long time, they had lost heavily, they had many battle trained commanders, and most of all, the British had their objectives, and sometimes they interfered with the objectives of my country, and sometimes they required the spilling of more American blood than I could take."[7A]

With Alexander's help we got more troops after the drain for Normandy took place, and launched a massive attack in May, 1944, to drive across the Rapido and up the Liri Valley and at the same time break out of our Anzio beachhead. We tied down and destroyed more Germans on Italian soil. Of course that was the objective all along — force the Germans to send more men to Italy to help take the pressure off the Russians, and to prevent any massing of troops before the invasion at Normandy.

"My objective always was to continue to attack and kill more Germans," thus making your job less difficult. Our role of the Fifth Army in Italy was an unglamorous one which might be compared to the role of the guards and tackles of a football team who are never heralded but do their dirty work in making holes in the line so the fleet-footed backs can run for a touchdown." The holes were made in Hitler's lines, Ike, so you could make your touchdown and, "I know we contributed to that end".[8]

Rome, luckily, fell after the Anzio breakout, and two days later you invaded France. My troops got two days of headlines, and after a long winter's fight deserved them.

You were greatly aided by my troops from the Fifth Army, which led the invasion of the Seventh Army into southern France. It was your idea, and I'm glad you stuck with it. Little does the world know of the pressure you got from Churchill not to make the invasion there. Along with the French, the Seventh Army forces became the 6th Army Group

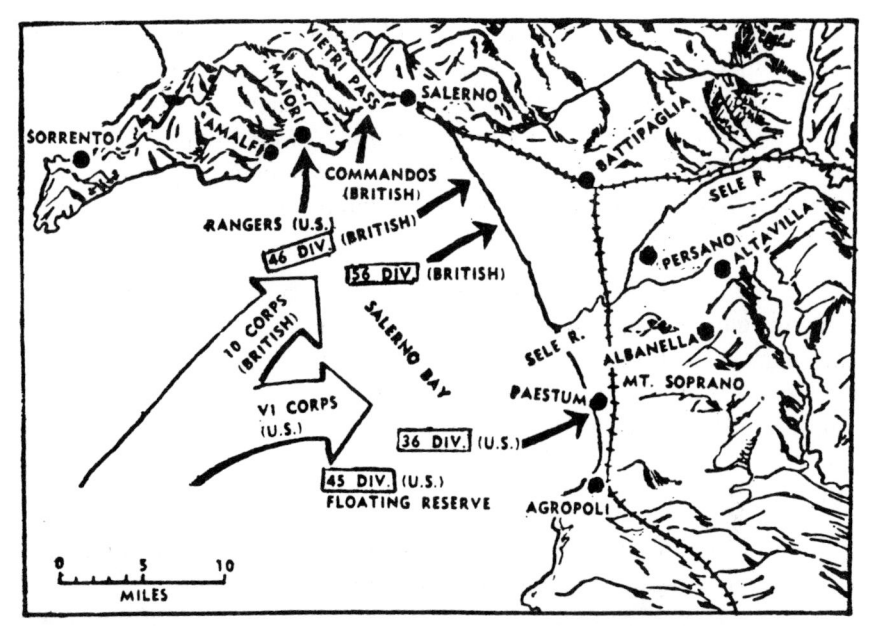

General Mark Clark invaded Salerno, Italy, September 9, 1943. Map from *The Indianapolis News*. (Tom Johnson.)

under Lt. Gen. Jacob Devers. Would I have become an Army group commander earlier if I had taken the Seventh in? Devers' forces joined your men coming down from the north in less than four weeks and by November had driven more than 300 miles.

Except for the counterattack at Mortain in Normandy, the Huertgen Forest, and the horrible Battle of the Bulge, your troops drove across France with skill, bravery, and great maneuverability and virtually destroyed the enemy army west of the Rhine, as you had planned. With the crossing of the river your forces drove east and south and we drove north, and linked up on May 4, 1945, at the Brenner Pass.

After the war we continued our separate ways. I was still playing second fiddle to Bradley, just as I did when you selected him as your deputy for the Normandy invasion. After the surrender, as noted, I moved into Austria and was appointed Allied High Commissioner. Following that assignment it was the Sixth Army in San Francisco and then back to the training command as Army Field Forces Chief. My next assignment was to Korea to succeed Gen. Matt Ridgway, who had replaced MacArthur. When you took off your uniform to run for President, Matt took your place in Europe, and President Truman sent me to the United Nations command in Japan and Korea. After you were elected, you came to Korea and were only interested in seeking enough facts to justify an armistice to end the war. You didn't want to hear my attack plans to drive back to the Yalu River and defeat the Communists. You were to be satisfied with the restoration of the 38th parallel, as was President Truman and the United Nations. My plan, apparently, was similar to MacArthur's which you heard when you got back to the USA. Both were shelved.

I signed the armistice as you directed, against my better judgment, but you again were the boss.[9] After I decided to retire you asked me to stay on for a Washington assignment, but I went to the Citadel Military College as president for 10 years. It isolated me, somewhat, from the youth rebellion of the 1960s but enabled me to be aware of the fears and hopes of young people. The Army experienced this wave of distrust also.

I will give you credit for forcing the Russians to agree at the peace table to the neutrality of Austria as a nation in 1955.

You also gave Marshall the brush-off because he was a Truman man and, by this time in your campaign, you implied the country had gone soft on Communism, corruption and crime. Marshall, the former chief of staff, former Secretary of Defense and Secretary of State, was no longer in your corner. Likewise for yours truly. I guess Marshall and I were both out of the straight arrow mold. Patriotism and loyalty were our cornerstones. Political compromise was hard for us to understand. We faded away. I made a manpower study for you in 1955, and it recommended universal military training, which battle Truman had lost earlier. You didn't agree to my UMT study and never asked me to do another assignment. I did have the privilege of serving as chairman of the American Battlefield Monuments Commission until my death in 1984. We continued to establish many memorials to our war dead, and it was my pleasure to revisit the areas where we both insured many a military victory. I was the last of the great Army commanders to die — at age 87.

Mark Wayne Clark

Author's note: Clark refused to admit the inadequacy of the corps and army engineer troops at the Battle of the Rapido River crossing. Actually, many of the engineers fled in the face of fire. Also tanks could not be used initially and air support was inadequate. If fire support was withheld, we sure didn't surprise the Germans. It was a poorly planned river crossing with many green troops in the area south of Cassino. If

Maj. Gen. Geoffrey Keyes, II Corps commander, had only used a holding force there and committed his mass of troops to the exploitation of the crossing northeast of Cassino through the high ground, the Rapido fiasco might have been avoided. Clark wanted to drive through the Liri Valley with his reserve armor for an early linkup with the Anzio forces. The German forces were too strong for a frontal breakthrough. Of course the mountainous approach might not have provided an early linkup with the invasion forces to the north either.

The entire Anzio-Rapido operation was an ill-conceived idea of Churchill's and his British associates to harass Hitler and possibly delay the big invasion in the north or south of France. He really wanted a breakthrough into the Balkans through Italy. The capture of Rome was a high price to pay in American lives.

Anzio casualities:

4,400 killed in action
18,000 wounded
More than 6,000 POWs.

Clark Pulls Ike's Leg

The biggest maneuver in the pre Pearl Harbor buildup during World War II took place in Louisiana in 1941. Gen. Marshall was the overall boss and Lt. Gen. Lesley J. McNair was his deputy. In turn Gen. Clark was McNair's deputy, having been promoted from lieutenant colonel to brigadier general over 5,000 other officers. This was done along with other promotions to break the old mold of seniority and to emphasize younger commanders or potential commanders. The promotion was a blessing for Clark but a handicap. Ike was still a colonel and chief of staff of the Third Army (Lt. Gen. Walter Krueger), which gained victory over Lt. Gen. Ben (Yoo Hoo) Lear's Second Army in the maneuvers.

At the final critique, Clark ran the show, because McNair was hard of hearing and detested being on the podium. Ike was in the audience, along with most of the future leaders of World War II. Clark was handed a list of promotions of one and two-star generals. He read off the list and "omitted Ike's name on purpose." He could see the "terrible, trigger temper of Ike soaring on his face — red with anger."

"Just a minute," Clark added: "I omitted one name, Dwight D. Eisenhower." What happened next is a bit confusing. Clark, recalled in 1976 that Ike never complained about the trick until after World War II.[10]

"I got a hangover. Does it show?"

The original of this cartoon by Bill Mauldin was given to the author after the artist's visit to Indianapolis for the "500" Festival and 500 Mile race in 1965. Both were veterans of the bloody Italian campaign.

Martin Blumenson reports in his biography of Clark that, "As the gathering broke up, Eisenhower came toward Clark laughing. 'You son of a bitch,' he said. 'I'll get you.' Clark was laughing too as he extended his hand in congratulations."[11]

Clark recalls: "Ike and I never had any operations disagreements. We worked together for many years. In fact when Marshall and McNair wanted a list of the 10 top generals to run the American invasion in Europe I wrote Ike's name with 9 ditto marks afterwards".[12]

Clark obviously enjoyed being in the decision-making rung of generals. When Marshall called him in about his ditto list, Marshall said he agreed. In fact he had already told Ike he was the man to lead the troops in the big show. Marshall obviously knew at that point that Roosevelt would never permit him to leave his side in Washington for the duration. He never publicly said so though.

Why "Yoo Hoo"

Gen. Lear got his nickname, "Yoo Hoo," because some of his 2d Army troops on a motor march yelled "yoo hoo" to the girls on a golf course in Tennessee. Lear was playing the course, heard them and punished them. The action received wide press mention.[13] It is interesting to note that when an old friend of Capt. Harry Butcher (Ike's naval aide), Red Cross man William Fine, came to SHAEF headquarters and complained about a division (36th) being in the line for 133 days without rest in Southern France, Butcher turned him over to General Lear whom Eisenhower had brought to France in an administrative capacity.[14]

A Personal Comment

As a company-grade officer, I lived through 11 months of the Italian campaign of World War II serving in Gen. Mark Clark's Fifth Army before going to southern France. I started out not liking the general and certainly disagreed with a lot of his tactics, but I learned in my studies of the calculated risk in Italy that Clark was not all wrong. I also came to realize that he had a lot of bad orders from topside and that some of his subordinates were not too smart. And, certainly, our Allies were not always giving Clark and his Army a great deal of help.

It was my pleasure over the years to know Mark Clark better than any other top-ranked general in the "Dear Ike" commentary. We fussed and argued about battles and campaigns many times. I did long interviews with him and laid out the battles as I saw them as a company grade officer. While he didn't always agree with me, he certainly would listen and sometimes he would interrupt with, "That's a good point" or . . . "We could have done better at times." I told him, frankly, that he hurt the morale of the troops by always saying "Fifth Army" in press releases instead of identifying units under his command. He replied that if he had to do it over he would have done the same thing. Higher headquarters finally got smart and unit ID became commonplace. Someone thought for a long time that the enemy would not know what unit was where until it captured a prisoner.

We argued over the invasion of Salerno, the taking of high ground before attacking cities and communication areas, outflanking, river crossings, frontal attacks — all phases of modern warfare in the frame of War II. The more you read about Clark the more you admire and respect the man for his bravery: Going in a submarine into enemy territory in North Africa before the invasion, exposing himself (quite a target at 6 ft. 3 in. tall) to enemy fire in a daily routine of inspection, planning and tactical or strategic maneuvering. As the years went on our correspondence increased. To the last days of his life, he had almost total recall.

Clark and I argued about his U.S. tactical Corps commanders. He agreed with me partly on Gens. Ernest J. Dawley and John Lucas. I had escaped with a few others when my battalion (36th Division), pushing out of the beachhead at Salerno, was captured by the Germans on an exposed flank. Gen. Dawley thought the British and 45th Division were in position to support our position without armor, engineers, or air support. Our defense was to stay hidden during the day. When I got back to our lines, my regimental commander could not believe he had lost a battalion although an earlier commissioned messenger (Capt. Theodore Andrews) had given adequate warning several hours before. He asked me to talk on the telephone to the division and then corps commanders and tell them what happened as our battalion of some 800 men was overrun. Maj. Gen. Fred L. Walker, the division commander, took the news calmly and said he had already moved forces to slow the enemy advance and had liaisoned with the 45th division on the ground to take up the slack on the flank. When Gen. Dawley was given the same report he just kept repeating: "I can't believe it," and asked me to say again and explain it over and over. He obviously had lost control of the battle plan and was unaware of the gap. Dawley always said, in his critiques of our training problems, "Don't follow the light and let the lantern go to hell." He lost both the light and the lantern at Salerno and soon afterwards was relieved at the insistence of British Gen. Alexander through Ike, Clark and the division commander, Walker, were not totally convinced of the necessity of the relief move. Give the British credit for that one. Also for offshore naval gunfire support at the beachhead. Walker relates that he was ordered to ride in a jeep with Clark and Dawley on a command look-see in the battle area and on the way back Dawley kept referring to Ike and Clark as "boy scouts." (Obviously because he was so much senior to them.)[15]

Years later it was revealed that mutiny took place on the British front at Salerno when the fighting was at its peak. Some 700 replacements sat on the beach and refused to join their units. Most finally agreed to follow orders with some persuasion but 192 were courtmartialed. A number of Scottish troops were involved and were reluctant to join units other than from their own country.[15A]

Lucas was a pleasant fellow, as I learned at rest camp in Sorrento after his relief at Anzio, but didn't have the drive necessary to sustain the Anzio beachhead. His Corps earlier had sort of staggered up the peninsula from Naples without a lot of planning or direction. Lucas had replaced Dawley. When Lucas took the VI Corps to Anzio, Gen. Keyes replaced him on the Liri Valley front by extending the II Corps. VI Corps had struggled forward without much air support or British push on the eastern portion of the boot after the capture of Naples. Of course the Anzio invasion was short of troops and air support also. All of this has to be kept in mind if you want to second guess Clark's operation.

When Lucas failed to exploit his unopposed landing at Anzio, in January, 1944, with Clark's okay, he was relieved by Maj. Gen. Lucian K. Truscott of the famous 3d Division. Truscott was an excellent battle leader who stabilized the beachhead and later broke out of the Anzio quagmire. In August, 1944, he took his corps into southern France with great imagination and speed. He later returned to Italy to succeed Clark as Fifth Army commander, when Clark moved up to 15th Army Group commander and obtained his fourth star.

The third corps commander whom Clark earlier had defended without question, was Keyes, a task force commander in the North African invasion. Keyes listened to few and tried to bull his way through, only to a get a bloody nose at the Rapido River with the 36th Division. Veterans of the Texas outfit (mine) never forgot or forgave the impossible mission. Clark defended Keyes' planning and also defended his G-3, Brig. Gen. Donald Braun, in the attack plan. When told that they really didn't know what was going on — for instance a completely inadequate engineer support plan for clearing mine fields, bridging the river or tanks in support — Clark shook his head and said, "You have a good point there." He personally didn't like Monday morning quarterbacks, but he was very sympathetic while listening to the stories of battles from comrades who had been there. Clark pointed out that both Dawley and Lucas were assigned by Marshall because of old school ties. He felt he couldn't refuse to take them, and there weren't too many battle-proved generals at the time of the invasion in 1943. Lucas was a fatherly looking type with a corncob pipe while Dawley was a handsome, striking military figure with a riding crop, highly polished boots and pink riding breeches.

Clark never agreed to my assessment of Keyes. During the final days of the war he had promoted him to lieutenant general. Naturally, Clark got the blame for his corps commanders' mistakes and the 36th Division veterans later protested the Rapido fiasco. This probably prevented his appointment as Army Chief of Staff, although Clark would never admit it.

An unnoticed fact is that Gen. Omar Bradley raided and riddled the Keyes II Corps staff which he had in North Africa and Sicily when he became First Army commander. Ike told him to take whomever he wanted. He took 25 officers initially. "In effect, I cannibalized the II Corps staff to form my new Army staff," Bradley recalled.[16]

Clark once told me about the offer to command the Seventh Army in southern France: "I told the high commands that I had survived the near disaster at the Salerno invasion and Anzio had been a fiasco, because I only had half of the three divisions I wanted for the invasions. And in both invasions I had untested corps commanders who could not be decisive in battle, failed to protect their flanks, and were not aggressive. They had been friends and comrades of my superiors, and I could not refuse their assignment." When he saw the statement in cold print he apparently changed his mind and said he had not made so rough a statement.[17] As always, a good commander was willing to take part of the blame for the mistakes of his subordinates. Marshall did the same thing for Brig. Gen. Leonard Gerow during the Congressional hearings on the Pearl Harbor alert message.

After studying the Rapido River fiasco, Gen. J. Lawton Collins, the hard driving and talented VII Corps commander in the First Army drive for Normandy and across France, told Martin Blumenson in 1985 that he had decided that Keyes was responsible for the Rapido diaster. After the war, Collins spent years studying the actions of corps commanders and came to the conclusion that most battle mistakes were by corps leaders.[18] Of course corps commanders were relieved of administrative work so they could spend time on tactical maneuvers in the battle zones. Corps fought divisions, and armies directed the corps.

Clark never gave Gen. Walker much credit for his efforts as commander of the 36th, the first American division to land on defended enemy territory in Italy in September, 1943, against strong and unexpected opposition. The troops on the assault ships had been told of the Italian surrender just hours before debarking but were warned not to expect a friendly walk in. His division held despite many counterattacks by the newly arrived German units. Later the division fought with great success in the Purple Heart Valley after being rested, retrained, and filled up (casualties had been severe at Salerno — one battalion in one day lost more than one half of its 800 men). After fighting at San Pietro, Mt. Maggorie, and Mt. Sammucro (where Ernie Pyle wrote his story of the death of Capt. Henry T. Waskow) the division got even more replacements for crossing the Rapido after again suffering heavy losses. Engineer support was pitiful. Some troops panicked and fled. Tanks could not be used and air support was nil.

But three months later a practically new 36th division with many experienced officers and men was at Velletri, on the Anzio beachhead with another frontal attack in prospect. Then Walker's finest hour occurred. His troops found a hole in the enemy line, with only a cow path available for vehicular support, and sneaked through the gap without preparatory fire of any type. They were in the Alban Hills the next morning which held the key to the city of Rome. But it was hard for Clark to give Walker credit, because he was still smarting over the division massacre at the Rapido. Later he recalled the Velletri by-pass operation with pride — "one good maneuver and a most valuable one to his Army's efforts." After capture of Rome, Gen. Walker was sent back to the States to become commandant of the Infantry School, because he had so much battle experience. Walker made the mistake of having two sons on his staff which met with considerable criticism above and below his level of command. One son was his plans and operations officer, the most vital staff spot in a division, and a younger son was an aide. He was forced to relieve them both during the Italian campaign and also his chief of staff. Higher commanders thought he was too slow to relieve ineffective commanders.[19]

The move of Walker to Benning was a good one for the Army but a sad day for the division. The farewell parade found many men in tears. It was, to many, like losing a father and another battle. His men loved and respected him a great deal. And the division had just had its greatest victory since the Salerno landing with its entry into Rome. A slightly hunch-back scrapper, Maj. Gen. John Dahlquist, replaced Walker and led the division onto even greater victories in the invasion of Southern France (133 days consecutively) and the drive into Germany.

Clark the Man

Outside the formal and dedication-to-duty Clark there was a warmer man. He appreciated a lot of the little things in life and gave of himself to public service as a speaker until he began to wear down, on his fourth pacemaker. He loved to go back to Italy, particularly Positano, along the Amalfi drive, where his troops had gone ashore on the invasions at Salerno as a back door approach to Naples. He was the honorary mayor of Positano, and smiled broadly, with his eyebrows arched, as he reminded one of the honor. When he went to Brazil, for a reunion with his former troops, he was thrilled when the populace swarmed into the streets and yelled: "Markie Clarkie, Markie Clarkie." When he went to Italy for one reunion he shook hands with all men present. Afterwards his associates chided him for shaking hands with the descendants of the unit then aligned with the Communist Party. He said he didn't know about their political affiliation but the unit had been "damm good" fighters in the war.

A man of greatness, he was in touch with greatness most of his life — knowing Churchill, Roosevelt, Marshall, Ike, the King of England and many others. He talked about them as if they were old neighbors and he was recalling backyard conversations.

He always laughed when he recalled President Truman's remark about all generals being squirrel heads and one in particular at Salerno. Truman called Clark to reassure him he was not talking about him.

On our last meeting at a luncheon in Muncie, Indiana, Clark held forth for more than an hour in relating high points in his life. When asked if he wanted a drink before lunch, he replied: "Yes, let's live dangerously." As he talked he held my wife Barbara's hand on his right and mine on his left. Little did we know that he would die of cancer a short time later. He never complained although he was obviously suffering from the pain as I now recall the event. He had declined the offer of a larger public luncheon in Indianapolis.

A Strange Romance

It may have been a dirty trick, but on one of the interviews over the years I pressed hard on Clark about the Ike-Kay affair. Was it real? I threw a curve, I guess, by asking about the Kay-Dick Arnold affair (the colonel she was going to marry after the North African campaign). Clark replied: "You mean the Ike-Summersby romance?"

"Well, not really," I replied: "but since you bring up the next one, what about it?"

Clark said: "It was a strange one to say the least. Actually we had met Kay as Ike's driver in London, and I had a redhead named Betty. She drove me for a while, but I decided it was not correct for a corps commander with troops to have a female driver. (How lowly he made "Corps" sound to an ex-private and ex-lieutenant. "Corps" sounded like heaven to most G.I.s).

With total recall, as always, Clark went on: "So I ditched the redhead. Well, Ike never ditched Kay. She became his constant companion. She was ever by his side — secretary . . . driver." Clark would often pause to take a deep breath and think of his answer to a tricky question.

Question: A companion, then, more like an aide?

Answer: "She could determine Ike's every anticipation. She was constantly by his side. As for the romance, I never questioned him about it. I never wanted to know."

When told that Ike's army aide, Col. Ernie Lee, had said that Ike could have had anyone he wanted in Europe including visiting movie stars, because he was so popular and so charming with great charisma, Clark frowned and shook his head: "I never really discussed Ike's romance with Kay with him. I never felt it was any part of my business."

It was understood that these remarks were not to be used until after Clark's death. At his funeral, his widow, Mary, told the author that I should report what he said when I wrote memoirs of the general. Likewise for some of his comments about the British leaders. She knew of his great loyalty but had witnessed some of the rehash of the war by some not-so-friendly interviewers in their home in Charleston, South Carolina. He had recalled one specifically for the author:

"In fact, British author Alec Nicholson sat in this very room and accused me of not following orders in 1944 to entrap the German armies and ignore the capture of Rome. I told Nicholson that I considered it a personal attack in my own home, and that no where in the records could he prove any such orders existed." He told Nicholson that the interview, which had been going on for three days, was ended.

Wearing his best British manners, Nicholson "humbly apologized for his misstatement." To Clark that was adequate acknowledgment of his rightful decision.

"But authors and historians continue to write what they please," Clark observed. The interviewer could see that this discussion was a very intense one. It bothered the general no end that history is likely to record this misinformation permanently.

IKE SAYS:

Dear Wayne:

You were a resourceful, faithful, methodical, brainy army planner and trainer of troops. I always enjoyed our association. While you were six years younger and got your star first, your cooperation was 100%. Our joint efforts with the British and French in the early days of the war laid the basis for our teamwork-unity-alliance of allied forces for success in the war in Europe. You were brave both in your secret submarine mission into North Africa for negotiations with the French and on the battlefield. At 6-3 you were a good target, as we always kidded you.

We had our differences: You refused to take over II Corps at Kasserine Pass in North Africa, since you wanted to make it a Fifth Army operation. I refused to make it an Army mission. Then you held off on Sicily, because you wanted the army mission for the invasion of Italy. You got your choice, but you gave us a lot of thrills and anxious moments as you hung on by your fingernails for several days. You made plans for a possible evacuation of the beachhead, but the rest of us thought differently. You really never wavered in your determination to stay ashore, and history may have overwritten your alternate plan in case you were forced into another Dunkirk. We have to give Gen. Harold Alexander credit for bringing in additional offshore fire support for the battered British and American forces on the beachhead but not Gen. Montgomery who did not move his Eighth Army north from the Italian toe and heel to help you at Salerno.

You were offered the Seventh Army for the very important invasion of southern France but opted to stay in Italy and get your fourth star sooner probably as the 15th Army Group commander. You saved British general Alexander from a nearly fatal plan. He wanted to fight out of Cassino, in the south, and throw a hook into the Germans below Rome by pushing east across the mountain mass from Anzio. You broke out of Churchill's Anzio beachhead and changed directions to capture Rome two days before the invasion at Normandy. It was an outstanding maneuver. It all came about when the 36th Division found a tiny area of undefended terrain behind Velletri through which troops penetrated the enemy's defenses, and you marched an army across the Alban Hills and the plains of Rome. You could never give Maj. Gen. Fred Walker credit for his success and sidestepped him into the commandant's job at Ft. Benning for a stateside training mission. We never promoted him but the state of Texas did after the war.

You were about the only American who agreed with Churchill, Tito, Alexander and the King of England who wanted us to concentrate our main efforts in Italy and a push into the Balkans. When the British could not keep pace with our advances in Italy, I knew the drive was nearly impossible, requiring troops that I needed for the invasion of France. This was the first Marshall plan for ending the war, by massing our troops on the most direct route to Germany.

You were proud of the 19-nation force under your control in the final victory in Italy. Then you took over in Austria. There you stood up to the Russians and won the war of nerves, telling the Russians off including public damnation for their conduct in the Austrian occupation. The state department and Gen. Marshall got disturbed over your performance on that one, but you did win the disputes with our so-called ally, Russia, with whom we were trying to get along. You lost out on the Army chief of staff job to Bradley for a couple of reasons. One was the fiasco at the Rapido River crossings which the Texas veterans brought up through Congressional hearings after the war. Also, Bradley was a fellow Missourian to whom President Truman had turned to handle the Veterans Administration after V-E day. Of course Brad was my No. 1 man for the biggest invasion of the war at Normandy. His handling of the problems of veterans obviously won him a lot of Brownie points. He succeeded me as chief. After another training mission, you ended up in the shoes of MacArthur shortly after his relief (Ridgway was there at the time and served a short while until I decided to run for President and he took over NATO). You saw many other old friends and comrades take their turns as chief of staff in the postwar years.

I made you sign the armistice with the North Korean forces, backed by China and Russia in 1953, much to your horror. You were in the MacArthur mold and wanted to continue and perhaps seek revenge. I was in agreement with President Truman's plan to establish the 38th peace parallel border and knew full well that the American people were fed up with the Korean war. It was bleeding the nation — both in blood and money. Our victory goal was re-establishment of peace at the 38th parallel.

You came home and retired although I wanted you to continue to serve your country. Just what job was never really discussed. You did a survey on manpower needs, and pulled the old Truman chestnut out by recommending universal military training. I was in agreement with that but knew it could not be sold to the American public at that time — or ever? Lots of people wanted it and the plan would have insured adequate manpower for the armed forces. Unfortunately too many people were against the idea of continuous conscription and I went against you again. I never offered you any other tasks but you did your job as president of the Citadel very well and became a national figure. I got the impression that you were taking up with the right-wingers of the nation and didn't quite understand the changes and social upheavals which were taking place — for better or worse. You lived to be the last surviving army commander of World War II, dying at age 87.

You are right in your description of the mission the British laid out when we first took over the American effort in 1942. We were to take the war to the heart of the enemy and re-establish freedom in Europe by removing the Nazi stranglehold. It was no easy task but we got it done.

D.D.E.

P.S. I have no comment on your remarks about my relationship with Kay Summersby. You played your part in the cover-up for many years.

Author's note: Gen. Clark was proud of the fact that he and Ike had compared notes enough that their writings after the war would not be in disagreement. The success of that agreement could be questioned by the serious student of military history, particularly about the campaign in Italy.

Letter 15

Courtney Hodges.
U.S. Army photo.

HODGES — QUIET BUT GOOD

Dear Ike,

Do you still remember that my Army, the First, was the first to get to and capture Paris in World War II? The liberation of Paris on August 25, 1944, climaxed a brilliant sweep across France with Gen. George Patton alongside. I was the quiet one, busy and hard working, who never wanted a lot of press, and perhaps my press officers did a bad job. We allowed the French and others to take part in the Paris victory parade. I observed the fall as just another phase of the operation to destroy the German Army west of the Rhine River, as you planned. At that time little did I know about Aachen, Huertgen Forest and the Battle of the Bulge.

History has compared me with Gen. Patton. I'll bet I had more tanks under my control than he did. We may have been a bit more methodical — versus Patton's dashing reputation — but the First led the battle parade most of the time.

I joined the 14th Infantry and got my commission after a competitive course, shortly after the rest of my West Point class was graduated. I was on the Mexican border and served in War I with the 5th Division. I came home as a lieutenant colonel wearing the Distinguished Service Cross. I told Saul Pett, of the Associated Press, long after War II that I "was proudest of my DSM in the days when I was throwing hand grenades" at the enemy.[1]

I went back to major and attended the usual Army schools and later became commandant of the Infantry School where the bulk of your major leaders received such good training. I progressed up the ladder until I found myself as deputy of the First Army under Lt. Gen. Omar Bradley at the Normandy invasion. When Brad became 12th Army Group commander on August 1, 1944, I took charge in my long-held rank of lieutenant general (February, 1943). I had the wide front at times and probably covered more ground than any other commander and won more strategic objectives than most. But I never bragged about it.

I still can't believe the number of times my Army was bloodied — Aachen, the Huertgen Forest and the Bulge in the Ardennes. It is amazing how many of us survived.

Aachen was rough going for the troops who were getting battle weary and their casualties mounted daily. We finally leveled the town and the Huertgen Forest loomed ahead. *Life Magazine* said the battle was "Taking place in American military history beside such classic struggles as the Wilderness and the Argonne Forest."[2]

While I agreed with most of your planning, I think we should have sealed off the Forest with a holding force and encircled it on a more concentrated scale. The fight reminded one of the earlier battles of hedgegrows[3] in the Bocage country in France shortly after the landing. By the time we got into the Forest, nonbattle casualties rose at an alarming rate because of the rain, snow, mud and cold which caused severe frostbite and trench foot cases.[4]

Author Russell Weigley reported: "The Huertgen Forest was a worse military tragedy than the Wilderness or the Argonne."[5]

The Battle of the Bulge was even worse. The German counterattack affected the entire forces under your command on the Continent, except for the British who only helped with one division. It was a surprise attack. Our intelligence failed completely and there were rumors, at least, that you might not survive. But survive you did — in fact you got another star just like you did after the fiasco in North Africa at Kasserine Pass. The Germans simply butchered our forces and lines and penetrated 50 miles deep at one point.

The American casualties tell the story:[6]

   8,000 dead
   48,000 wounded
   21,000 prisoners

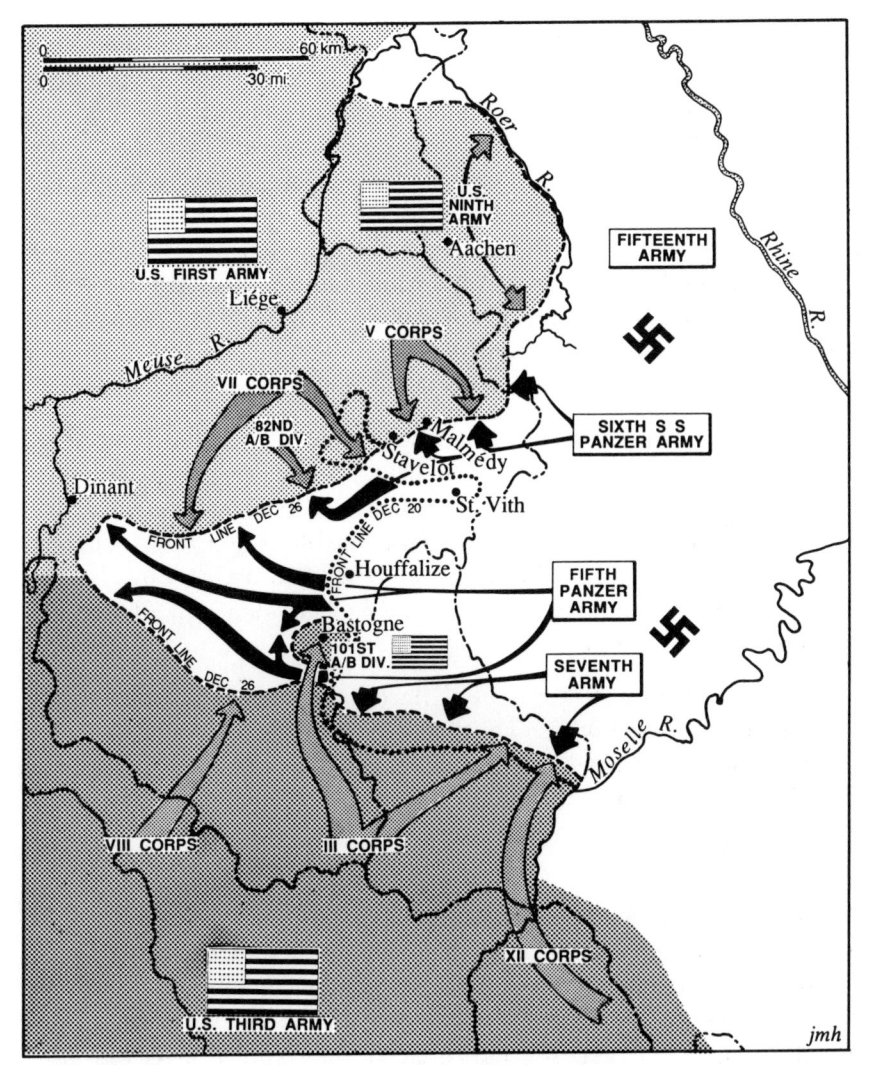

The battle of the Bulge. America's worst defeat in World War II.

In your book, *Crusade In Europe*, you report that the German commanders admitted to a loss of about 90,000 casualties in the Ardennes battle. The enemy also suffered heavy tank, assault guns, motor transport losses and planes. Their record keeping by that time of administrative disorder could only produce estimates.

The other armies came to our aid and we recovered to continue the long winter fighting, but it was slow and tough. My divisions recovered, and we landed a tactical gift from the heavens — a bridge intact over the Rhine River at Remagen, March 7. The Germans had failed to blow it up. The disaster for the Germans infuriated Hitler, and he now set about even harder to try and keep us from penetrating German soil any deeper. But his final jig was up, and with your help and Brad's we pushed everything across we could and wounded the enemy deep in its bowels. Our luck didn't please Montgomery though. He was waiting to launch his crossing with a set battle plan about two weeks later. The crossing didn't hurry him up either. By this time we knew that the war couldn't go on forever and we had success after success as did the other armies. It was good to have Gen. William Simpson on one side and Patton on the other. With the Ninth we encircled the Ruhr and the industrial might of Germany was no more. Victory was with us.

When V-E day came I was preparing to take my beloved First Army to Japan. The surrender ended all of that planning. We finally ended up at Governors Island, N.Y., and I retired in 1949 at 62 to Texas to be near Ft. Sam Houston where I could live a routine life as a citizen. I told Pett (AP) that my four-star retirement pay of $8,800 a year buys "just a fraction" of what I once had as an Army commander with allowances, quarters and a big staff.[7]

But I added: "I was frugal enough in retirement but my motto comes from an old Chinese saying something like: "When you retire you must interest yourself in the small things close around you and remember that the thing from which you retired is past."

Courtney H. Hodges

Author's note: The worst of the Bulge assault came in the middle of the area commanded by Maj. Gen. Troy Middleton's VIII Corps. He has seldom been given credit for holding our forces together until the counterattacks took place by U.S. forces. When panic broke out, it was Middletown who never quit fighting. (Hodges almost made the mistake of ordering a withdrawal from St. Vith, a critical objective for the Germans, but he waited until the 101st Airborne entered the fight.) At nearby Bastogne, during the battle, two German officers came to the front with white flags. They had a request for our surrender. The famous answer was "nuts" by Brig. Gen. Tony McAuliffe and the action sparked the troops and their leaders. Ike had asked for Middleton after the outbreak of War II. He had left the Army between wars to be dean of administration at Louisiana State University, where he returned after the war as president. When Ike made the request for Middleton as a corps commander, Gen. Marshall said he was crippled with arthritis of the knee and under treatment at a hospital. Ike stayed with the request because he thought if Middleton "went to battle in a litter" he was better than anyone else. Ike said he'd rather have a general with weak knees than a weak mind.[8] Middleton recalled for the United Press International, in an interview in 1959, that he just sort of "hopped along," but "you don't notice things like that when somebody's shooting at you."

The knee story has been credited to Marshall also. Bradley, likewise, takes credit for it in his autobiography.

IKE SAYS:

Dear Courtney,

Indeed, you were the quiet commander and ranked most of us in the American military pecking order in the European campaign. You sure had Marshall and Bradley on your side. All of us needed a quiet steadying force at times. Your wisdom paid off but too many correspondents tried to pair you off with Patton, the showman and braggart. Your success on the battlefield almost equalled his. You had one of the prize commanders in France, Maj. Gen. J. Lawton Collins, whose VII Corps stormed across the beaches at Normandy, freed Cherbourg — our needed port — and then spearheaded the drive of First Army across Europe.

You got to the top the hard way after failing at West Point and enlisting as a private. You saw the best and worst of duty — the Mexican Punitive Expedition in 1916-17, then as a major with the 6th Division in World War I plus a couple of tours in the Philippines. Your experience and ability resulted in your rise to the head of the Infantry board at Ft. Benning where Gen. Marshall kept tab on all of us in his little black book. You were a two-star general before many of us ever got a star. I once reported that you "had done more to bring about the victory in Europe than any other army commander."[9]

In fact, once after Gen. Patton had told a British women's group that since the British and Americans would have to rule the world after victory, we should get to know each other better, I was so mad that I decided you could handle the Third Army as well as Patton could.[10]

Actually people forget that we had originally planned a big buildup in Brittany for our supply ports and that Third Army was visualized as the force to free that territory for us to supply and reinforce our drive East. My plan to push Patton through the breakout, conceived by

Bradley, and the landing in southern France shortened the war a great deal. We sometimes thought it would be a two-year fight but victory came 11 months after the invasion at Normandy.

Your army suffered heavy casualties at Aachen, Huertgen Forest and the Ardennes. Your army — with Maj. Gen. Troy Middleton's VIII Corps — was smacked right in the mouth with the German offensive punch in the Ardennes which weakened our forces in the middle of the theater and the Germans, as usual, very wisely hit us at our weakest point.[11] Sensing my misjudgment immediately, I sent two armored divisions from you and Patton to Middleton without delay. My decision to employ the 101st Airborne, in SHAEF reserve, at Bastogne was one of my best tactical moves in the war. With the leadership of Middleton and so many other gallant commanders all down the line, we blunted the forces which were destined for the vital port at Antwerp and a disruption of our entire battle front. It failed to reach Antwerp but it sure played hell with home front morale and our drive to the Rhine. I committed Patton, who volunteered the major effort with a switch of 90 degrees to stab at the heart of the penetration south at Bastogne. Your forces were so strung out by now that I gave your army to Montgomery along with Simpson's Ninth. If any American commander ever forgave me for this, in the name of communication, command and control, it never surfaced in postwar writings.

When Montgomery got your command, a British officer recorded that he strode into your headquarters "Like Christ come to cleanse the temple."[11] And in the midst of all the confusion in the counter punch the weather grounded our planes. We had to fight without our boys flying in the wild blue yonder for support. People forget that. As Patton moved in for the kill, praying for better weather all the way, the skies cleared.

We restored our lines and pushed the Germans back to fight us once more and then you got your big break of the war. Elements of the 9th Armored Division found the Ludendorff bridge across the Rhine intact and away the forces of Uncle Sam went, deep into the heart of Germany. I told Bradley to pour everything over the bridge he could get his hands on. By the time the bridge collapsed a few days later, we had a strong toehold for our last thrust into the enemy's homeland. The Nazis would soon be in a rout. At the time, many were overly concerned about a possible German Alpine stronghold in the native land of so many Nazi and SS organizers, sympathizers, collaborators and fighters. To many American GIs there was little difference between Nazi troops and the German army. They were all fighting us to the bitter end. Under questioning as we drove toward Bavaria, many of the Germans tried to hide their identity on the battlefield and their houses but some broke down and admitted their party affiliation. Hidden in closets and other places were SS arm bands, Swastika medals and plaques, which revealed their true identity. Little wonder that the Holocaust hunters are still uncovering Nazi executioners long after the end of the war.

After your success at Remagen, we knew the war was about over and all of us from the supreme commander on down to the private soldier knew that victory was in our grasp, although the German forces held out in strongholds all over Germany and resisted with great force including V-E day in some areas, and caused us many casualties.[12]

Patton sneaked across the Rhine before Montgomery did in his set-piece massive buildup to again capture many newspaper headlines. Seventh Army and the French joined the drive and from then on it was a race to search out and destroy the Germans. You met the Russians first at Torgau while Simpson was nearing contact with them on the Elbe where he wanted to drive on to Berlin, but I stopped him. We thought it would take another 100,000 casualties to make the conquest. There are reports that the Russians suffered 1,000,000 casualties in their drive for the Nazi capital.

You were the first army commander that Gen. MacArthur was willing to take in the Pacific. The atomic bomb ended that planning and we all returned to peacetime garrisons to train for another war which was only a few years away — in Korea.

D.D.E.

Letter 16

Jacob Devers. U.S. Army photo.

DEVERS — COMMAND AT LAST

Dear Ike,

It took you a long time to give me a real tactical command, although you did put me in charge once, while you took a leave in the Mediterranean in the North African campaign.

My promotions during the two wars were fast. I went to all the right schools, had some good staff assignments, and successfully commanded a variety of peacetime units. I was an early advocate of armor on the battlefield.

I got to England before you for invasion planning and I spent a lot of time in North Africa getting along with the French and British. Both liked me and I worked to earn their respect so we all would make our best efforts in the various theater operations.

When you returned to England in January, 1944, to take command of the Normandy operation, I went to North Africa to take your place, but the British slipped Gen. Sir Henry (Jumbo) Maitland Wilson in as the No. 1 man. But I supported Allied unity 100% and aided Gen. Mark Clark and Gen. Harold Alexander in the Italian campaign. For that service my decoration, the Oak Leaf Cluster to my Distinguished Service Medal said it well: "General Devers' leadership was an important factor in the Italian campaign . . . and the advance to the Gothic Line culminating in the fall of Florence."[1]

My next mission was to support and pull off the invasion on August 15, 1944, in southern France. You and Gen. George Marshall, offered the Seventh Army to Clark but he decided to stay in Italy. He might have feared the invasion would be called off, at Churchill's insistence among other reasons. You gave me Lt. Gen. Alexander Patch for the Seventh. With Marshall's blessing, I was given the 6th Army Group at age 57. Our troops made great advances within a month to join your forces and command in the short period of thirty days. My group became operational on September 15 and we gradually built up the strength of the Seventh Army, French troops, and other supporting elements.

Clark often wondered if he might have received his fourth star sooner if he had taken the Army assignment and then might have received the group instead of me with its four-star rank. That would have given him a level commensurate to Gen. Omar Bradley and Gen. Bernard Montgomery. He later received the 15th Army Group in Italy and his fourth star.

My 6th Army Group command included the U.S. Seventh Army and a large French force. I helped to organize the French resisters within southern France. You would have made an Army commander, George Patton, a four star before me, but the wise old fox of the American Army, Gen. Marshall, prevented that move by you.[2]

You tried to get me to evacuate Strasbourg after the French had just captured their beloved city on the Rhine. Gen. Charles de Gaulle ordered the French to stay there during the Battle of the Bulge fiasco without withdrawing. In fact De Gaulle told you to leave the decision up to me as the field commander. I ordered the French to stay. It would have been crazy if the French had turned around and fought our forces, in order to stay on land they had already captured. We stretched the French and American forces to blunt Hitler's second part of the Bulge counterattack while protecting Patton's flank simultaneously.

I also was proud of the way I reduced the size of my staff. Everytime your headquarters made a plea to find trained, experienced and qualified men and officers for units in the field I probably led your hit parade. A higher headquarters can get top heavy and I knew that and did something about it regularly.[3]

While it was difficult to get along with the French, they were real fighters when they decided to attack. They were masters at finding new local supply sources when they exhausted theirs in that cold and wet winter of 1944-45. Many American GIs said that when the French attacked they often knew of huge chicken and cattle farms in their zone.

We crossed the Rhine. But now we were headed for what the Allied high command feared was the Southern Redoubt, where there might be masses of troops hidden to further delay the war once the northern fronts collapsed and opened the way to Berlin.

We kept them off balance and the German people in the area finally realized that the ball game was over. It was a comfort to have Georgie Patton along in the fight for Hitler's old home lands in Bavaria and Austria.

Along the way the 13th Airborne Division was assigned to my group and the advance was so rapid it became the only American division to enter Europe and never engage in active battle.[4]

I never got around to writing my memoirs. I never got into the right humor.

History will record that under my leadership, the French helped to win the war in southern France. You helped me when I needed it. That is not to leave the impression with you that I couldn't have done more and gone faster with more troops, weapons, ammo, gas, and, especially, more air power.

Vive le France and Bully for England

Jacob (Jakie) Devers

Author's note: Devers was a most pleasant companion during the Patton stamp dedication November 11, 1953 at Ft. Knox. He was the senior officer there and, of course, had been one of the leaders in the development and use of armor over the years. He told me he was organizing his memoirs and asked if I would be interested in helping him. Since I had two jobs at the time - helping to run a metropolitan newspaper and serving in the National Guard spanning the rank of lieutenant colonel to major general, the time was never found. He even sent a message years after the Patton stamp show confirming that he was still trying to write something. I suggested several persons who could have helped him write his story. Unfortunately, history has lost most of the wealth of his rich memory. Likewise, it was impossible for me to find the time to study Col. Ernest Lee's files and memoirs. He was the senior Army aide to Ike and later, a successful Indianapolis banker, who died before he got his input into print. He did have the honor of escorting Ike to the podium at his first major campaign address in Indy in 1952 and turned on his famous smile when Ike was elected. He was there all the way with Ike and commanded the highest respect of the inner family. Kay Summersby, Ike's confidante, wrote: "He resembled a worried blood hound and was incredibly efficient. Tex was the one who ran the office and saw to it that everything worked . . . He never relaxed. He had a big booming voice that used to drive us crazy."[5]

IKE SAYS:

Dear General Devers,

You were another senior member of my team who for sometime outranked me. You were graduated at West Point six years before me and served on the faculty for several years between assignments in Hawaii, the School of Fire (later field artillery school at Ft. Sill) and occupation duty in Europe. After War College you went to the Panama and received your first star in May, 1940.

In the spring of 1943 at 55 you were named commander of the Army in Europe after you got your third star in September, 1942. After I left the Italian operation later in that year to command the Normandy invasion there was no need for you in London, so you moved to the top American command in the Mediterranean theater. Your sphere then included support for the Italian operations. Your glory day came when Seventh Army invaded southern France, in one of my best maneuvers of the war, which Churchill opposed with all his strength. He failed, and we won a great battle in an area we had not even tried to exploit earlier in our strategic thinking. When your forces drove north to join my armies we made the American army and the French into Sixth Army Group with you in command — again another one of Marshall's boys went to the top.

You also had the knack of getting along with the British and French. You understood how necessary their support was in the give-and-take teamwork in our victory crusade in Europe. You were an early arrival in our command structure in Britain and at the end of the war you were arm-in-arm with our French comrades as we drove deep into the heart of Naziland's beloved Bavaria.

You got your fourth star in March as the end neared. You also did the most with the least troop allotment on the continent. General Bradley and I drained off a lot of your talent, because your theater was the only one where we had experienced officers except for a few from the Pacific theater. You often gave us replacements from your headquarters including rifle company commanders. The one leader I wanted was Maj. Gen. Lucian Truscott, the star of the Italian campaign. I had him under my wing for a while when he led the invasion of southern France with the VI Corps and I wanted him for my new Fifteenth Army, but he was needed more as commander of the Fifth Army in Italy so we reluctantly let him go back to take Mark Clark's post when Wayne was moved up to army group commander.

You had Lt. Gen. Alexander Patch to lead your Seventh Army. He was another one of the good selections made by Marshall when he plucked him from the Pacific to join our team. Some historians say our casualties were light in the invasion but what does that trite phrase mean when you know soldiers, sailors and airmen were killed there or maimed for life? Every fighter lost there also reduced our effective battle strength and by the fall of 1944 our drain on manpower was beginning to be a serious problem. The replacements we got were young kids without adequate training, in many instances, and officers were younger. The miracle of it all was that America did produce so many good sailors, soldiers and airmen from its civilian ranks.

The battle at Montelimar was a classic. We crunched the German 19th Army in a hard, swift drive up the Rhone Valley, the river being our only protection on the west. It is hoped that historians will eventually get all of the facts straight in that battle before the veterans have all gone to their just reward with the rest of us. Historians and readers of war battles so often forget that besides the successful battles they are reading about there was always the potential of what the enemy might do against your best efforts. The real fear of the unknown may be known only by the soldier on the lonely field of battle. We learned about the unknown at Kasserine Pass, Anzio, the Bulge and many other places, didn't we?

Your drive north to join Gen. Patton was spectacular. You fought through the famous towns of Dijon, Besancon, St. Die and to the Rhine from Mulhouse to Strasbourg. Your north flank hit Bitche where we later had to make a temporary withdrawal after the Germans hit the Ardennes.

In our drive from the south, the Germans stubbornly held out between the French and U.S. troops to form the Colmar pocket, which we encountered after the winter long drive through the treacherous Vosges mountains. With new green divisions added to your veterans of earlier campaigns, you played a needed — but perhaps thankless role in destroying the German army west of the Rhine as planned.

Since our major efforts were all planned for the north, we didn't exploit your invasion to help Gen. Clark near Genoa. We also could have made a thrust to roll up the Germans along the Rhine Valley from the south, and thus an earlier crossing of the river. Perhaps we were not flexible enough to exploit our successes.

Wasn't it silly to think that our arrogant ally, Gen. Montgomery, had the gall to ask for some of your troops in southern France for his area on the north flank of the Bulge. You not only could not spare them but we had no means of getting them there. I gave him the First and Ninth Armies but he was never satisfied. He always wanted my command on the ground battle. Because you understood the British as well as I did, it is interesting that Monty never came to my headquarters for command conferences. (*Author's note:* Ike's son, John, says he never came but Stephen Ambrose writes that he did once.)

When the Bulge threw us back on our butts, you took up much of the slack on our right flank with speed and tactical wisdom. I wanted the French to pull out of Strasbourg, but Gen. DeGaulle told me to defer to your decision on the ground and I changed my mind. We stayed. It was a short-sighted view I had because losses were so bad that I feared the Germans would move massed forces in your direction as intelligence reports indicated. G-2 failed in the Ardennes and I didn't want to suffer another murderous counterattack within a month. You did give some ground to avoid being chopped up in your extended positions. It was one of the few times we fell back in the war to tighten our lines and play a defensive role.

Obviously, we didn't want our troops to begin fighting one another — the Kraut was more than we could handle at the moment. DeGaulle had control of France, and while he was beholden to us for supplies and equipment, he threatened — and could have carried out — a serious rupture of our communications and French support.

Your battle efforts were excellent and your new port facilities at Marseilles a vital turning point in the winning of the European war.

Your loyalty and cheerful help were always reassuring to me. Your mark in history is well deserved, and the day should come when a biographer will give you the recognition you earned. Your ready smile and optimism helped many a commander along the way to victory. Our

British and French allies also knew of your aggressive spirit and battle worthiness. Thanks.

D.D.E.

Eisenhower poses for a picture with Kay Summersby in North Africa. This and other pictures with them together irritated his wife, Mamie.
Photo courtesy, Dwight D. Eisenhower Library.

Letter 17

Alexander Patch.
National Archives photo.

PATCH: ACTION ON 2 FRONTS

Dear Ike,

I was another one of your quiet commanders as boss of the Seventh Army when it landed in Southern France to strike north and join your forces coming down from the north. Fortunately for me, the Mediterranean command gave me three of the best divisions from Italy, much to Gen. Mark Clark's horror — the 3d, 36th and 45th, all American, along with a strong French Army.

Gen. Marshall and his assistants kept close tab on the records of his colonels and generals and selected most of the Army and Corps commanders. My initial success as a machine gun commander came to Marshall's attention in World War I in France. After the war I was commander of Ft. Washington, attended the War College, and helped to develop the three-regimental concept for an infantry division. When I was sent to the Pacific in World War II, I took many untrained troops and organized and commanded the Americal division, which made the first offensive effort of the Army's war in the Pacific on Guadalcanal. My force then was enlarged into XIV Corps and included Marines.

When I returned to Washington it was announced that we had shot down a Jap plane with Admiral Isoroku Yamamoto aboard. At a luncheon meeting I brightened up when the news was announced and indicated that I had issued the order which resulted in the bombing.

Such revelation indicated that we had broken the Japanese code, which they immediately changed. It was reported that I revealed the fact that we knew an enemy bigwig would be on the plane on a certain route on a certain date. A guest at the luncheon called the Navy Department to complain about my disclosure. In turn Admiral Ernest King, whose relationship with Gen. Marshall was "frosty as ever," wrote to the Army chief and complained that the Army had revealed Navy Department secrets and wanted me reprimanded in no uncertain terms. The crafty Marshall refused to do so on the grounds that such an admission would tell the Japanese we knew more about them than we wanted to acknowledge. I was told of my error, but Marshall kept his faith in me.[1]

I returned to the states as a corps commander and then became Seventh Army commander in Europe. I got the assignment, because Clark had to stay in Italy for the eventual command of the entire Italian operation. Our forces met each other at the end of the war at Brenner pass in May, 1945.

Our landings in southern France were a great success and some historians have written that the operation was a near pushover. They failed to read the casualty lists. I gave 49-year-old Maj. Gen. Lucian King Truscott, my brilliant VI Corps commander who had broken out of the Anzio quagmire to capture Rome, a free hand. I told him to fight his battles and he would have my full support. In his memoirs he seemed to take more credit than he deserved when he described the success of his corps.[2]

He also goes out of his way to criticize the landing of a regiment (142) at an alternate beach near Frejus when the Navy and the division commander approved of it. He seems to forget that we found the area heavily mined and the casualties would have been great. Likewise, another regiment was landed at an alternate site to avoid the water obstacles and mines at the port of Frejus.[3]

But all of that is not to denigrate his most brilliant maneuver, under the command of Brig. Gen. Frederic B. Butler, of a mobile reconnaissance in force by the combined arms with an infantry backbone to scout deep into the enemy territory. In this case it was up the middle sector of the invasion thrust. Another force (36th Division minus elements in Butler Task Force) drove north on the Army right flank at the base of the Alps and captured Gap and Digne; following this Grenoble was taken with the aid of local partisans whose uprisings were very helpful and productive. The 3d and 45th divisions composed the main forces which drove into the German army as it retreated northward with the Rhone river valley for its escape route on the western flank.

It was almost a battle by the book. The Butler Task Force dodged the enemy, captured prisoners, showed up at spots in the enemy's rear and had a field day as the GIs liked to call it. It was almost like a holiday and the troops were jubilant. After all, they had never tasted victory like this since Sicily (3d and 45th), and the 36th (Rome) had been battered with severe casualties three times in the bitter Italian campaign. The French received them with open arms and, at times, almost too much vino. It was strange to find fresh fruit and vegetables, eggs, and chicken in even limited amounts. The French shared their wealth with the GIs and perhaps some of their love.

By the time Butler Task Force got to Montelimar, which was designated for a trap of the withdrawing Nazis, it only had a "recon" element, a rifle company for a concealed lookout point to relay fire orders for the artillery to interdict the German forces in the valley beyond. The 36th Division then closed in on the Montelimar battle. The first regiment failed to establish a block at La Concourde just north of Montelimar. The enemy fire was heavy and all of a sudden the picnic had turned into another cliff hanger as our casualties began to mount for the first time. Meanwhile Truscott's forces were pushing the retreating Army into the very faces of the single division. The division was spread out for many miles and it took several days to get Maj. Gen. John Dahlquist and his entire division in a position to establish an effective roadblock. The forces did not have adequate tank and tank destroyer weapons to reinforce the infantry and the terrain was rugged, ringed with hill masses. Without realizing it Truscott had spread the division over hundreds of miles in three directions. Truscott was about to relieve Dahlquist until he got to Grenoble and found out that he had been very successful in his drive for Grenoble and he could not abandon an exposed position and gather all of his troops together in one battle area in a matter of hours. It was wise that he did not relieve Dahlquist, because he drove his division for 133 days through southern France, a record which was unmatched at the time. And it was with much success. He was a real fighter.[4]

Actually the battle of Montelimar has been incorrectly reported by many so-called experts. Critics have said that the 36th Division failed in their defense efforts to block the Germans. Actually, the fighting was some of the toughest the Seventh Army encountered in France. It was short, intense and costly. As we blocked the Rhone Valley, the Germans repeatedly broke out in different directions to find new escape routes in the rolling and beautiful country side of the Provence-Rhone Valley area. In the end, we fought them hill for hill, road network for road network, building to building, room to room, and man to man. Here we did have a lot of help with all types of artillery and air power to interdict the retreating forces to inflict heavy casualties. Again we seldom had adequate armor. One infantry battalion went into a night attack east of Montelimar with rifles only and infiltrated a German tank unit without firing a shot. In the middle of the night the battalion commander gave an almost unprecedented maneuver of left flank by the numbers and the battalion silently moved east over the mountain back to its original assembly area without any battle casualties.[5]

Truscott, one of the great field commanders of the war, described the Rhone Valley from Montelimar to Loriol: "Road and railroad were lined with tanks, trucks, guns and vehicles of every description. Hundreds of railway cars loaded with guns and equipment, including not less than seven of the long range railway guns like the 'Anzio Express' which had tormented us so much at Anzio. Hundreds of dead horses and dead bodies littered the plain south of Loriol . . . the sight and smell of this section is an experience I have no wish to repeat."

Truscott added that he knew of "No place where more damage was inflicted upon troops in the field," and noted "It was done almost entirely by ground weapons, artillery, tanks, tank destroyers and demolitions." (Air support was difficult because of a lack of forward ground control — this problem was to plague the Seventh Army and many other units throughout the war).

And to those who wrote that our casualties were light in the invasion, let them cast their eyes on these figures: Again Truscott reporting; "Montelimar netted some 5,000 prisoners, destroyed more than 4,000 German vehicles, and eliminated the 338th and 189th German Divisions. In fourteen days, at a cost of 1,331 killed and wounded, the VI Corps encircled Toulon and Marseilles, almost destroyed the German XIX Army east of the Rhone, captured 23,000 prisoners . . . Even if Montelimar had not been a perfect battle we could still view the record with some degree of satisfaction."[6]

Truscott was making me look good as he had done for Gen. Mark Clark in the Fifth Army in Italy. He was to return there later to command American ground troops in Italy and to receive his third star although he wanted to stay in your command.

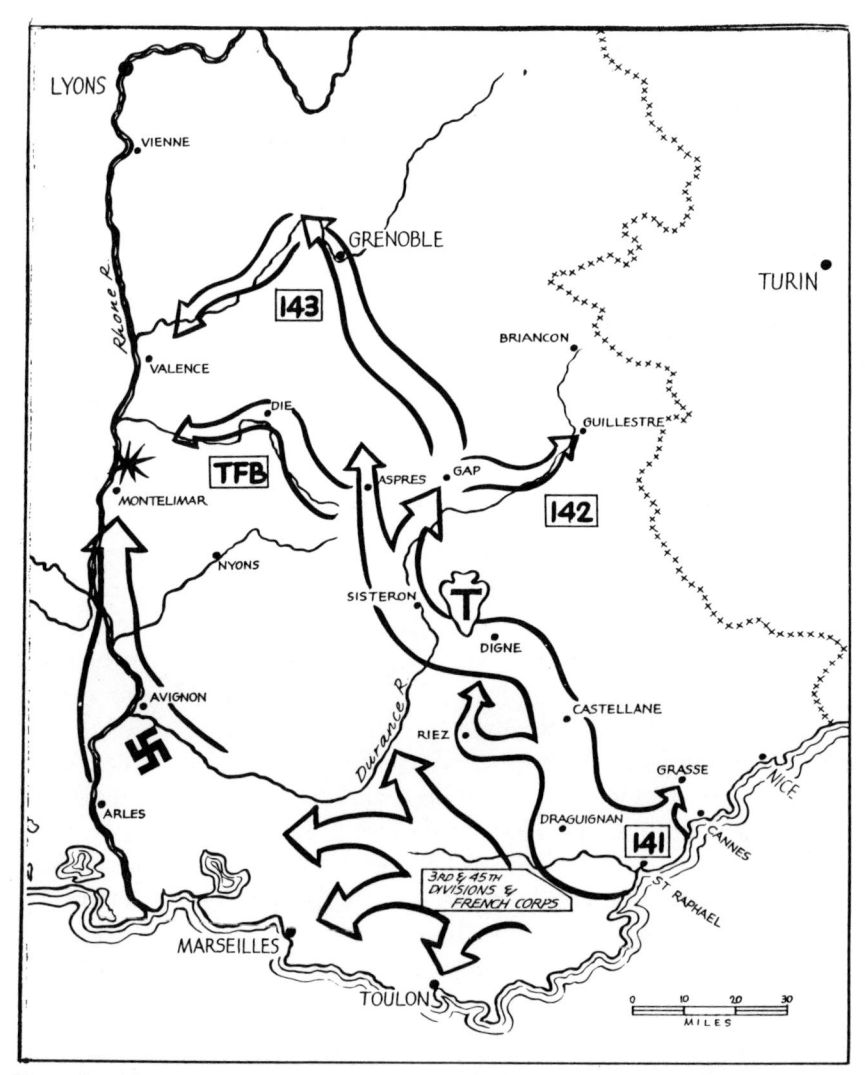

The second front in France operation on the Riviera was one of the most successful operations of World War II. The 36th Division (T patch) drove to Grenoble and Montelimar. The author was a part of a daring sneak maneuver behind the enemy lines (TFB). 36th Division History map.

In the fourteen day period mentioned, my Army had gone more than 100 miles from the beaches and some elements were still another 100 miles farther north. It was probably Seventh Army's finest hour. With the success at Montelimar (Paris was liberated as we won the battle there so you know what the headlines reported), my Army, with the Free French, went on to liberate Lyon where the local population rose up. We won without a fight. But as we drove north to Dijon (mustard capital), Besancon, and Vesoul, the Germans were reorganized and the resistance stiffened. We spent the winter fighting in the miserable, snowy, cold, wet land of the Vosges Mountains and created the Colmar Pocket. We thought we had the Germans trapped there but actually, as it turned out, the Germans just formed a magnet for American commitment and it wasn't until three months later that we smashed it.

We had to wait for the end of the Bulge battle up north to obtain adequate forces to defeat a stubborn and fierce German Army, which never would admit it was already defeated. Only an occasional prisoner would admit to Hitler's downfall. They kept thinking he was going to deliver victory with another secret weapon, so they fought on and on with valor and determination from their miserable position of one retreat after another in the wake of a terrific and overwhelming shellacking from artillery and other ground fire.

One unit went for 30 days without air support and when Gen. Devers found out about it, by personal reconnaissance, he ordered air support. It was effective, but unfortunately some of the fly boys hit our own positions. Thank goodness the troops were partly protected by nearby stone buildings.[7] One can only wonder what would have happened if you had decided to cross the Rhine at the southern tip with the French and American troops that you had at your disposal. A sneak attack might have met misfortune but a successful one would have meant we could have rolled up the Rhine Valley months earlier than we did. Perhaps support would have been the problem. It would have taken airborne troops for a vertical envelopment and equipment which might not have been available, let alone the means of getting them there. Did some leaders still want to downplay the French and the role of Gen. Charles de Gaulle? Makes one wonder, doesn't it?

I could be seen on the battlefields quite often and kept the pressure on to hook up with the Normandy invasion forces where you took command of my Army. I drove one division (36th) for 133 days without rest except for "rehabing" a battalion or regiment occasionally. Seems every time a unit got into a rest or training area, I needed it, on the front again. Later on I gave a Congressional Medal of Honor to one soldier and at the review for him, the troops were in full battle gear and marched off the parade field for the front lines and our final push to the Rhine.

After the Colmar fight, we crossed the Rhine, and again it was a school solution in chasing the enemy. We picked up the fight at Regensburg on the Danube River (it wasn't so blue or beautiful at the time) and captured our prize, Herman Goering, the long time No. 2 Nazi, near Kitzbuhel, Austria (locale of the Grand Hotel a la Barrymore, Garbo and Crawford). Also we liberated a lot of French leaders, including Paul Reynauld, and captured thousands of German prisoners, including dozens of generals who also thought they were going to organize the southern Redoubt as a fighting force. Allied fears were not unfounded as many historians have reported.

But back to Goering. His capture was an example of poor reporting. The American press proclaimed in big headlines that the Americans fed Goering chicken and rice for his first meal in captivity. Hell, that was what everybody ate that day and out of a tin can. My generals, Dahlquist and his assistant, Brig. Gen. Robert C. Stack did not shake hands with the Nazi. They sent him on to my Army headquarters for interrogation. There was no dining and wining of the general. The American press did later issue a retraction and correction on the event, but who remembers that?

The interview by Stack and Dahlquist was an interesting one which needs to be related. Goering asked, through an interpreter if he should wear a pistol or ceremonial dagger when he appeared before you. Stack, who knew he'd never see you, surprised him by speaking German: "Das ist mir ganz wurst." Stack explained that literally the expression meant "that's goose liver bologna to me" but in German slang it meant: "I don't give a damn."[8]

We had our differences with the French, but Gen. Jacob Devers, 6th Army Group commander, kept us all in line — fighting the enemy, instead of our Allies. We covered lots of ground, supported and reorganized the French underground and opened up new supply ports. Because of our drive, the French got to the Rhine River first at Basel before any other Army.

I am sorry I died in November, 1945, at age 55 and never lived to see you go on to even greater heights in the world as President of the USA.

Alexander (Sandy) Patch

P.S. Oh, yes, Ike, my VI Corps commander in France, Gen. Truscott, who also did not see combat in World War I but like you knew his tactics and understood how to fight both small and large units, loved to relate his favorite story about your constant companion, Kay Summersby. In the North African campaign in Tunis he reported this incident: "We left Tebessa late in the afternoon . . . Gen. Eisenhower had directed me to have his sedan come down from Constantine to meet us at dark in order to avoid the long drive back in open bantams which we had used because of the danger of air attack. I told Col. Don Carleton, Chief of Staff, to leave Miss Summersby behind, as I doubted that Gen. Eisenhower would want her in the forward area under the circumstances. I made a mistake. It was the only time in all of our associations that Gen. Eisenhower showed irritation with me. Miss Summersby was the only driver in whom Gen. Eisenhower had complete confidence for black-out driving at night."9

And I should mention that my 36th Division had the famous 442d Infantry attached to it most of the time under Gen. Dahlquist's control. As you know it started out in Italy as the 100th Japanese-American battalion and then was enlarged to a regiment. It fought long and hard in the winter of 1944-45 and finally got the recognition and honors it deserved. I trusted Dahlquist with the unit because he had compassion and could employ four regiments at one time. It was one of the few outfits which had the old square division concept of four regiments which we changed in favor of the triangular division when the Army remodeled its fighting units upon mobilization before the war.

Author's note: Gen. Truscott was one of the great corps commanders of World War II. His brilliant record would stack up against any other general in the Army. He enumerates his battles in one of the best books about the War, *Command Missions.* One of the highlights includes the written suggestion to his Army commander, Gen. Patch, which outlined a plan to seize Belfort Gap on the Rhine and drive north to outflank the entire German effort and perhaps bring a quick end to the war in Europe in the fall of 1944 for which so many hoped. Patch turned down the plan initially and then explained the plan to Eisenhower. Ike likewise turned down the plan because he was deferring to Montgomery (there we go again) who was planning a big drive up north. History records that Monty's plan failed miserably at Arnhem and that Truscott's plan was shelved. History will record that this was a big mistake in both directions. It is a shame that Truscott's plan was not adopted. Perhaps it was another case in which the commander in the field knows more about winning a tactical, and even strategic, battle than the brass in the higher military, semi-political headquarters.

Truscott also had a plan to invade northern Italy near Genoa, to relieve the pressure on the Fifth Army and trap the Germans who held on with stubborn resistance all through the winter of 1944-45. Truscott, who was so successful in his end runs in Sicily, was turned down on two of what might have been great maneuvers in the war.

A short, stocky man, Truscott reminded one of Patton. He was bombastic and daring but caring. He even addressed every officer in the three divisions of his corps before the invasion of southern France. It was an inspiration to be a part of his audience, and he obviously set the stage for one of the most successful invasions of the war.[10]

IKE SAYS:

Dear Sandy,

You were the steady commander. While I had several corps commanders who could have commanded Seventh Army in Europe, our leader and boss, Gen. Marshall, flagged you for a greater command after your success in the Pacific. He knew that Gen. MacArthur already had his lineup of army commanders and you were at a dead end. He also remembered your brillant record in World War I and all of your excellent work in reorganizing the Army structure to make it more combat worthy. You were in his little black book of future commanders, which he had started at Ft. Benning so many years before. What a mind he had, and what a knack for selecting officers!

I perhaps never gave you adequate credit for your victory in southern France, and you were too modest about your accomplishments. I must admit that I was proud of the invasion there because it was my idea. I had to overcome Churchill's opposition. Your press corps was not of great number and obviously our newspapers always looked upon the invasion as a secondary effort not a second front in France which it should have been labeled. You also had a VI Corps commander Maj. Gen. Lucian K. Truscott, who was brilliant on the battlefield in Italy and again in southern France. He managed to grab most of your headlines and receive the ultimate in press coverage when *Life Magazine* gave him a spread. I was glad you mentioned the exploits of Truscott in your letter to me. I think, on reflection, that he downplayed your role, but we all know how much strain and effort it took for you to work with and fight alongside the gallant French Army. They were back home and inclined to do what they liked whenever they liked to do it. Their attacks were sporadic, intensive and sometimes delayed in execution for one reason or the other.

While you had some of the best American outfits, one has to recognize that casualties and replacements over the long haul did affect your sustained fighting index as you struggled through the Colmar Pocket stalement in the long winter months.

Your capture of the supply port at Marseilles was one of the great achievements. It provided our forces with a mass of material and equipment we needed desperately to sustain the battle. It was a staging area for many divisions which were needed all along the front. Little did we realize its potential. As one reflects, an earlier invasion in southern France might have brought an earlier victory. Some have said the campaign had light casualties, the opposition was negligible, and drew few Germans from other fronts. But those people don't know the hurt of casualties, the fierce determination of a retreating German or the horrors of war as you did in War I and in two theaters of fighting in War II.

History gives your army a bad rap concerning how you treated Hermann Goering, Hitler's No. 2 man, when he was captured in southern Germany at the war's end. An erroneous report by a newspaper reporter said that your generals shook hands with him and also fed him a deluxe chicken dinner. The truth is that your generals did not shake hands with him and the chicken came out of a canned ration of the day's issue. He was handled as any other prisoner — through the chain of command, although he thought you would present him to me because of his rank in the Nazi world.

Your Army's history was an early publication and you had the foresight to make sure it was collected. But it is a shame your diary was destroyed before it could be published for the historical record of your brilliant success. Apparently your wife decided to destroy the diary after your untimely death at 55 in 1945. Your experiences and postwar writings and suggestions would have been valuable additions to American history.

I must admit that my deference to Montgomery up north may have resulted in failure to exploit your successes in the south when you reached the Rhine River first. I guess my theory of destroying the German Army west of the Rhine precluded any great thinking about deep drives into Nazi rear areas.

You made me look good in invasion Dragoon even in the eyes of Winston Churchill who fought against my plan for such a long time. After taking a lot of British advice in the early months of war the time had come for me to make the major decisions, and I did. Thanks to you, your troops and our French comrades, we scored SUCCESS. The

French, both fighting and the underground forces, were glad we were liberating the biggest portion of France in a hurry. The German forces in most of Vichy France just disappeared. Thanks.

D.D.E.

Eisenhower as president wearing a hat. AP photo.

EPILOGUE

Quiet Resolve

Age 23 I became a combatant, unwilling as I was (draftee) in World War II — the biggest, most costly, bloodiest and most important war in mankind's history. Through good fortune, luck and sheer survival I continued to serve my country in uniform for more than 21 years. Again through survival and a few smarts I managed to go from private to major general in the American Army. A lot of people helped me along the way and to them I'll always be grateful.

I have always lived my life with the constant memory of those loved ones I lost along the way — comrades who paid the price of death so that I and others might enjoy lives of freedom and to continue the fight for tolerance, love and sharing of those human values that are perpetual but always need protection.

So with that introduction, I offer a few comments about the war and the people involved in the great global conflict that at least gave us peace, with anxiety, during most of my lifetime.

THE RETURN — We came back from victory on the battlefield ready to return to civilian life. Overseas and in uniform we were the majority where we lived. At home and out of uniform we were once again in the minority. We had to tolerate civilians who were still complaining about gas rationing, sugar shortages, etc., but it did not bother us. We were back home with loved ones and a chance to start life all over again. We always remembered those we left behind with their dog tags and a simple cross to mark their burial. There were not any parades for most of us and we didn't want any. We had paraded around in uniform for years. It was a spiritual arousal to leave the front lines, get cleaned up, put on a semi-dress uniform and hold a parade. There we honored those who had excelled on the battlefield with decorations and the rest of us just hoped we'd have the courage to do likewise in the next campaign — and be rewarded.

There were no monuments erected to us and our war but we didn't expect any. Those honoring the heroes and servicemen of previous wars were adequate for us. We had just continued a tradition. Oh, yes, many of us were interviewed by our newspapers and a few on radio (no television in those days). Our best friends who realized what we had been through offered a firmer handshake or bigger hug. Our rewards were few except for the best one of all — a return to our loved ones. We had trouble finding a place to live (without relatives, that is) and a car to purchase although many of us had the ready cash. Clothes were scarce but that really didn't bother us — we had worn old and dirty clothes for years.

OUR MEDALS were few. I had all of five. Nowadays servicemen have row after row of ribbons and many of them have hardly heard a shot fired in anger. Do you realize the small percentage of servicemen who actually go into combat? Damn few. Of course the supply and support forces are necessary. But to hear many of them relate the war now you would think that most of them were on the front line all the time. The same applied to some war correspondents in Europe who showed up, made a few notes and left shortly after a few enemy rounds landed in the area. Ernie Pyle was the exception. There were others like Wick Fowler, *Dallas Morning News*, and a lad named Johnson, of the *Chicago Sun-Times*. Movie Producer John Huston came and lived with front line troops to do a film short on San Pietro. He had planned it to be a big tank-air war — a bombing spectacular — until we told him what war was like in the mountains of southern Italy. We didn't have much air support — we were fighting with old-fashioned small arms. Even tanks were too vulnerable to be effective. As a result of finding out what war was really like Huston produced one of the few films depicting the little, real picture of war. Most newsmen stayed at a higher headquarters and wrote their copy from there. I will refrain from naming three famous American journalists who came to the Rapido River after we had practically lost our ass and scurried back to safer quarters when a little sporadic enemy fire started landing on our positions. I am sure some correspondents did accompany front line troops in other areas but Italy was the poor man's theater. We did not provide good copy, they said, but Pyle thought we did.

War is a life of horror for those who stay in the front lines day after day, week after week, month after month. The attrition rate was high. The draftee replacement was less prepared for battle, seemed to be younger all the time, thinner, less educated and perhaps even less motivated. But once he became a member of the team he learned fast. He learned to fight for his family — be it a squad, platoon, company, battalion or regiment. Competition was keen among squads, companies, etc., even divisions. The GI was proud of his division and his Army's accomplishments but he only lived and experienced the little picture. From his foxhole or defiladed position on the ground he just hoped the generals who paraded around occasionally were really winning the war somehow. He became a master in the study of terrain for his own protection or for a good field of fire, a machine gun or mortar position. Little wonder that many of us had no affinity for the game of golf after being so close to terra firma those many long days and nights. The GI's role seemed mighty insignificant at times but also mighty treacherous.

It is estimated that probably only one in 15 men in uniform saw combat — and many of those for only a short period of time. Of course if you survived you might have had to go through the entire war period from the invasion of North Africa to the occupation of Germany or from Pearl Harbor to Okinawa. Those were heroes of the first order. Many became psychos but most of us lived through it all. A definition of a psycho has always escaped me.

SURVIVAL IS BASED on a lot of things — pride mainly. You don't want to appear afraid in battle or on the front line. While you are scared as hell inside, you have to appear calm and confident on the outside. You can never admit to the possibility of defeat or you are likely to be defeated. Why you survive and the fellow next to you is killed or seriously wonded is another equation I have never solved. Your human dignity has to survive and you have to serve your family well — carry your role and not let your fellow comrades down in a time of need. You fight for one another. The American medic certainly displayed as much heroism in this respect as any others. The front-line soldier, though, never forgot that the medic could spend most of his time in safer surroundings and enjoy a few comforts of life denied to the front liner.

Soldiers in the Second World War had been toughened by the depression of the 1930s — privation and even hunger had been experienced. The family was a close knit group out of necessity. Parents instilled discipline in their children. And children obeyed. Teachers were stern and strict. Most kids knew that the punishment at home would be worse than any inflicted by the teacher if the parents learned of their failings, misbehavior, smart-aleckness. The church was a way of life. Elders and ancestors were honored and revered. They had hope for a better life. They wanted their own families to carry on their family heritage. They wanted to love and be loved. They enjoyed fellowship, comradeship and accomplishment. Many of these traits were reflected on the battlefield when it came time to leave home and family, take up arms and fight to defend their own freedoms and those of others they would never see, meet or know. Their mission was to find something more important to die for than themselves. Little more could be offered or expected from the GIs of World War II. They won the fight, in part because they had allies who had been fighting for freedom and self-preservation long before Pearl Harbor.

OUR BRITISH ALLIES could be irritating at times. The British often had a condescending attitude — this included some of our Canadian friends north of the border. The French were good fighters when they decided to fight. I guess the same thing could be said of the British. Our Russian ally was much admired and we kept situation maps on his progress and prayed for yet another major "Russky" offensive on the eastern front.

Most irritating of all was the British habit of stopping in the afternoon for tea. The battle would stop in their sector and the enemy knew this would happen regularly. The most glaring example I encountered was near the famous Abbey at Cassino, Italy. The British blokes lighted their fires for the daily brew in a semi-exposed position. As darkness descended the German artillery forward observers zeroed in on our positions with all they had. Innocently enough we, as next-door neighbors, suffered just as heavy casualties as did the violators of defensive security. Likewise the Indian troops. They came charging in one night to pass through our units behind Cassino with jeep lights on, smoking cigarettes and making one helluva racket. The enemy fires gave us crippling casualties even though we were in a reserve position. It was an attitude and lack of discipline that we, who had just been fairly well butchered by the enemy at the Rapido River, could not understand.

Then as we finally approached Rome, the British wanted to horn in on the victory glory. Gen. Mark Clark wisely prevented that but even Gen. Clark would not admit that the 36th (Texas) Division was first to Rome, because we had failed to cross the Rapido five months earlier and effect a linkup with the Anzio beachhead forces. I know we were there first because I was in the outskirts of Rome long before Clark had the 88th Division and other forces pass through us for the glory day, June 4, 1944, to free the Holy City, the citadel of Catholicism. He proclaimed victory in the name of his Fifth Army. Gen. Clark learned in our talks that it was hard to forgive him for this lack of identification of a deserving division.

We Americans had our own enemies. The Military Police became an empire in themselves. We could conquer a place and the MPs would put it off limits — another no man's land. Granted some soldiers lost control when we found wine, women (dang few in Italy) and a rest area but, by and large, the MPs became just another enemy. They played a necessary role, but they overplayed it. Some were dressed up so they didn't even look like soldiers.

DISCIPLINE IN WAR is not an easy thing to maintain. Battle usually is not an automatic procedure, though many men did things on the fields of fire without thinking and were heroic without orders. The malingerers had to be dealt with and it was not easy. One can quickly recall the most famous encounter of alleged malingering of the war when in Sicily Gen. George Patton slapped two soldiers in a hospital. The general was an intensive fighter and did not fear death. Most men in battle do. So his reaction was automatic and wrong. That is not to say that men do not have to be manhandled in battle. Some men were inclined to drop their weapons so they would not have to fire them. Some men tried to hide. Some men tried to jump on tanks and trucks in a moving column so they would not have to walk anymore for a while — and literally get lost from their unit as it moved forward. Here manhandling was a necessity. It wasn't anything to be proud of — to shove or push men into battle but if the situation required it that is what you did. You had to constantly reinstill the family feeling, that your next effort was for the good and survival of your outfit. Flag and country seemed a long way off. Daydreaming was out. Concentration on the fire fight, be it big or little, was paramount at the moment. Your existence or position might prevent disaster. Your knowledge of how to fire anything from a pistol to a field artillery gun was essential to success. You never thought of it in that manner. You just knew how to do something or have someone nearby who knew how to do something that might mean the difference between victory or defeat. It was not a pleasant place to be but you were there, and the job of holding the unit together and keeping it ever alert against the enemy was your mission, no matter how big or small.

IN ENDING this book one often wonders why and how so many fought so hard and so long on the battlefield. Some veterans will say they just did it and never really knew why. Great feats of heroism were performed without direction. The author and former Marine, William Manchester, in *Goodby Darkness* wrote a very effective fighting code. He jumped his hospital stay, as so many of us did, to rejoin his unit — his temporary home, his loved ones and the only world — though small it was — he knew.

He recalls: "It was an act of love. Those men on the line were my family, my home. They were closer to me than I can say, closer than any friends had been or ever would be. They had never let me down, and I couldn't do it to them. I had to be with them, rather than let them die and me live with the knowledge that I might have saved them. Men, I now knew, do not fight for flag or country, for the Marine Corps or glory or any other abstraction. They fight for one another. Any man in combat who lacks comrades who will die for him, or for whom he is willing to die, is not a man at all. He is truly damned."

One of the biggest fears in battle was the possibility that you could be shot by your own people. It might be by one of your own people — a weapon fired by a trigger happy, fellow comrade. The same was true of short mortar or artillery rounds or incorrect friendly positions on the firing map. Likewise air power — particularly if they were firing vertically over your position, and not horizontally, where they would encounter extra-heavy fire from the enemy side. Early in the war we learned a new principle of war — if the airplane shoots at you, fire back. While we might not hit anything with our small arms, the pilot seldom returned. One time one did return on the Salerno beachhead. We had damaged his plane and he returned on foot, raising hell because our entire battalion on the side of the hill mass fired back at him when he was on our position near Paestum, Italy.

AFTER LIVING THROUGH World War II one wonders how he ever survived the ordeal. Or the vitamin deficiency (face sores, etc.) frozen feet, even the body odor of the living and the stench of the dead. One reads about the superior German Army — dedicated to Hitler in the military tradition of loyalty and fighting to your death. Surrender was a dishonorable estate. The ruthless Russians had a like attitude. It was nothing for tanks to drive through their own units in quest for victory. A general, defeated in battle, would likely find himself in a private's uniform the next day. The Germans and Russians had professional armies. American fighters in the main were a bunch of freedom-loving civilians, unprofessional at times — and proud of it. We weren't prepared for war and a lot of gallant, bright, strong, brainy young men gave their lives because their comrades were not always professionally skilled in the art of war. Some of their comrades fled when they should have stayed and fought another day. Others surrendered when the going got too tough. But the slackers, deserters and malingerers were few when you remember that the draft drew men from all walks of life.

Some in our society had grown soft by 1941 when the sneaky Japs attacked Pearl Harbor. Many of our youth had left the farms and frontiers of America and moved to the industrial areas to make the big money. The woodsman was disappearing. Young boys, unless they had lived on a farm or had been Boy Scouts or hunters, could not find their way in the dark, sense direction or identify various noises. No one ever made a survey of how many soldiers in invasion waves could swim — a lot of them could not.

Because some of our youths had become soft, many Americans didn't want to take orders. There were a lot of "mamma's boys." There were a lot of boys who didn't obey their fathers who had tried to teach them obedience, loyalty, patriotism and family unity. The best outfits always had family unity. In the end, our youths proved brave, courageous and gung-ho for victory. The American GI had a lot more to live for and to look forward to in life than most of his allied comrades. He made victory possible, and gained praise of friend and foe.

IN THE SPRING of 1945 as victory in Europe seemed closer, despite the enemy's stubborness and our fatigue and battle weariness, new revelations unfurled — what the Holocaust was all about. As we drove into the heart of Naziland we found that human destruction had been going on since Hitler had come to power in 1933. It was an experience never to be forgotten. Many troops uncovered concentration camps, displaced persons with all types of diseases, starvation and mass murders. One of the worst horrors of all was viewing first hand the baking ovens where humans were destroyed and perhaps even more penetrating and haunting were the train boxcar loads of dying, dead, wounded and emanciated bodies — mostly skin and bones — stacked like logs in various positions. The stench was overpowering and the anger one felt in his heart for this Nazi Holocaust was one that would last a lifetime. It was impossible to imagine anything so awful — we had seen death on the battlefield, seen blood and gore in all directions from the front lines to the "MASH" evac hospitals. We had had buddies killed along side, suffered from shell shock (that condition was sometimes termed psycho in World War II) — suffered from running sores and malaria and the other ailments men suffer from in battle. But nothing had been experienced like this massive destruction of the human race that Hitler and his colleagues had been carrying on. Is it any wonder that many are still on the hunt for Nazi war criminals? Of course, the Japanese, such as Tojo and his war lords, were murderers also of all forms of human beings — women, children and soldiers. The infamous Bataan death march has been the most noted but their prison camps were hell holes of misery and starvation. It was an era mankind should never have to relive. Only by forgetting can it happen again.

AFTER 18 MONTHS of combat, I recorded the following thoughts as the day of victory neared:

In the last several months I have felt tired and wilted in several ways — mentally and physically — but most of all I still wanted to do my job daily better than I did it yesterday — do my job better than anyone else could — do my job to help others and aid them in building men strong and brave — united in one purpose — to destroy Nazism and all its evils. Too tired to continue. I added, God, we pray, give us light, give us hope and courage, give us victorious peace.

This was my farewell to my beloved 2d Battalion, 143d Infantry, 36th Division, as the officer who had outlasted all of the others in the battalion:

". . . Years will diminish the memory of towns, cities, villages and houses we have captured and the rivers we have crossed, but the stirring bravery of those gallant soldiers who have lived, fought and died so that we can live as free Americans, will be a shining example of us all forever . . ."

So I dedicate this effort to the men (yes, the grunts and dogfaces in the main) who stayed, fought, and died — who never got home to their families. World War II was a terrible, yet gallant, time in history. Through recall of memories and much research this has been a pleasant experience. It was a time of learning and understanding.

★ ★ ★ ★ ★

God and the Soldier, all men adore
In times of danger and not before.
When the danger is past and all things righted,
God is forgotten and the old soldier slighted.

— From a long forgotten British troop at Gibraltar.

★ ★ ★ ★ ★

IN LOOKING BACK over the study of 40 years of World War II, it is difficult to pinpoint all of the big name heroes. Of course, Winston Churchill emerges as the architect of the war in Europe, who wisely guided his American cousins and allies along the victory path. He may have been the greatest leader of the 20th Century. Americans, though, provided him with the military might and leadership to make victory possible — along with our Russian comrades. But remember, after years of warfare, his people were weary. Winnie was voted out of office shortly after V-E day. He did return as Prime Minister later.

General Clark commented about Churchill in one of our many conversations: "Churchill was a very forceful leader. Once he decided a policy, that was the word for every British subject. This compared to President Roosevelt and other American leaders who debated plans, policies and operations so long that final decisions may have been watered down to become less effective than they could have been. Singleness of nation policy would help in any future American national political-military adventures."

President Franklin D. Roosevelt, who had so much to do with providing Churchill with the tools of war, died on the eve of victory after suffering ill health for several years. The GIs in the field mourned the loss of their commander in chief, though many of their families had never voted for him nor ever wanted to go to war. He was a great one also.

Russian Dictator Marshal Stalin, ruthless killer that he was, deserves credit for rescuing his country from near defeat. His troops counterattacked the Nazi enemy, suffered the most casualties and inflicted the most casualties on the enemy. His forces also engaged the most enemy troops.

GENERAL EISENHOWER comes out as a superb and unmatched leader of combined arms and combined nations. No one had ever achieved what he accomplished — uniting nations and armies in a massive, combined effort. Ike's presidesntial potential showed clearly in his Crusade operation. His dream of an interstate highway system must have come in 1919 when he was part of a convoy that crossed the United States to test equipment and to show the need for better highways. The convoy of 81 vehicles went from Washington to San Francisco in 62 days at an average speed of 6 mph, covering 58 miles on an average per day. Then he saw the magnificient German autobahns in the war and the combination gave us an interstate highway system. Through all of this Eisenhower also managed to have a balanced budget in his Presidential tenure.

Ike's mentor and the American architect of the war in the Pacific and Europe was General George C. Marshall, the Army chief of staff who personally selected most of the army, corps and division leaders of the conflict. FDR would not let him leave Washington to lead the Army in

Europe. Marshall mobilized the country and knew how to handle the U.S. Congress. He also had the ability to persuade the British to join our plan of action and like it. Of course, Patton emerges as the top battle Army field commander.

General MacArthur was the great hero in the Pacific, but Admirals Chester Nimitz and William Halsey deserve equal praise. The real heroes were the infantrymen, marines, pilots and sailors who manned their weapons of war for total victory. They never knew when they were going home — or if home and families, loved ones would be the same.

I've written a lot about the magnitude of World War II. Here are some casualty figures in the greatest conflict in the history of the world:

Total: 50 million — plus????

By country:

Russia:	20 million
China:	3 to 15 million — impossible to estimate because so many civilians were killed over vast areas.
Germany:	4.5 million
Japan:	2 million
France:	500,000
Great Britain:	500,000 plus 120,000 Empire troops
Italy:	500,000
United States:	300,000 (compared with 53,000 KIA in World War I)
Holland and Belgium:	200,000. Heavy considering small populations.
Finland:	82,000

It was estimated that 5.5 million Jews were murdered by the Nazi plus other non-Jewish civilians.

The number of Germans, Poles and others killed by the Russians is unknown.

Yugoslavia lost an estimated 1 million civilians.

Other Eastern European countries: 4 million (estimated).

The United States probably kept the best records — many records were lost during actions — bodies were blown up, people changed areas and names.

In short, it was a terrible time in history.

FINAL NOTE: This book in no way covers the role of the Air Force and the Navy in the Eisenhower operations in Europe. It was simply too big an assignment to integrate all the heroic actions of these forces. Other historians have covered them in the past and will in the future.

Some day history may decide the wisdom of the lack of tactical air support for the immediate aid of ground troops versus the strategic bombing of industrial sites and communication installations, railyards, etc. For example, if the strategic and tactical bombings could have been in more direct support of the invasion targets and the immediate battle areas, it surely would have saved more lives than the scatter-gun manner often employed by the armed forces. The bombing of the Abbey at Cassino, Italy, was done in February, 1944, when the ground troops of all of the allied forces in the area were exhausted and in no position to carry out a follow through attack on the ground. In many cases the German weapons factories were underground and a major bombing might only cut production up to 15%; the damaged areas, airfields, etc., were quickly rebuilt when they were far behind the battle lines. It will be an interesting study when a critical and detailed analysis is made of our employment of air power. Likewise for our Navy forces. Just imagine how effective big aircraft carriers could have been to our assault forces in Italy or the Normandy invasion.

Granted, a lot of air power and naval forces had to be diverted to the Pacific but a two-front war has to be weighed properly for speedy victories. It appears that some of our planning, execution and delivery of men and power may often have been misplaced.

Despite all the obstacles, hazards, misdeeds and enemy stubborness, America won its military victory in World War II. Peace was the goal and it was achieved. Our greatest ally, Great Britain, lost its Empire and suffered severe economic losses after the war and watched as Germany and Japan, our enemies, rose to economic power and positions of great prestige in the world.

Victory was not easy but the American G.I. carried his freedom banner with quiet resolve, determination and with the pride and confidence of his ancestors in mankind's eternal struggle for a better world for all. — The Author.

★ ★ ★ ★ ★

The author, Wendell Crane Phillippi, was born in Zionsville, Indiana, on July 4, 1918. After graduation from Indiana University, he joined the staff of *The Indianapolis News* for a year until he was drafted on June 10, 1941. He returned to *The News* after the war and was managing editor for 22 years until he left in 1984. He served in the 36th Division in North Africa, Italy, France and Germany earning the Silver Star, Combat Infantryman Badge, Bronze Star for Valor and Cluster for Meritorious Service, the Purple Heart in seven campaigns and two invasions. He served in the reserves for 15 years and became commanding general of the 38th (Indiana) National Guard division with two-star rank. In this period, he went on active duty at Ft. Benning, Georgia, during the Korean War. In October, 1962, he was in the Pentagon in Washington awaiting activation orders for the 38th Division in the Cuban crisis when the Russians backed down in the face of an American Blockade and removed missile sites. The division ranked at the bottom at the outbreak of the Korean War but was No. 1 in the Cuban crisis era.

Phillippi has traveled back to World War II battlefields for many years. He has visited the beaches at Paestum, Italy, where his first invasion took place, Persano, the hill masses at Cassino and Purple Heart valley, the Rapido River, Anzio, Velletri, Rome, and Grosseto.

He has returned to the Riviera and the landings areas in Southern France twice, Montelimar three times, Dijon, Colmar, the fields of France north of Paris where the Commonwealth troops fought, Belgium and other parts of Europe in his research for this book.

Phillippi resides in Indianapolis and Brown County, Indiana.

NOTES
Letter 1 (Marshall)

1. Forrest C. Pogue, *George C. Marshall* (Ordeal and Hope), p. 145.

   (Note: Actually there was a lot of bitterness by draftees at the time of being called up in peacetime when friends stayed home, got better jobs, sometimes even married their girl friends and started a family. It was a tough task that Marshall and other Army and Navy leaders faced in those uneasy times of an undeclared war with known enemies — Germany and Japan. The American G.I., including this one, just did not want to admit that he had to give up years of civilian life. The dissension was reflected in Congress. The National Guardsmen and Reservists in organized units, and draftees were told their service would be for a year. This meant the releases could start in October, 1941. The hope of early release spread like wild fire across the nation. Everywhere one could see signs of O-H-I-O on buildings, bulletin boards, PXs, letters, guns, etc. It became a greeting between friends and fellow soldiers. It meant Over the Hill in October — or absence without leave, not desertion since war had not been declared. President Roosevelt and General Marshall faced a mass exodus of draftees and Guardsmen. The draft extension was passed in a miracle vote of 203 to 202. One vote kept an almost feeble and ineffective Army in the ranks to be trained for the great conflict of World War II which was just ahead. The Army took lots of measures to try and improve Army morale. There were more and better movies, service clubs were constructed with libraries filled with best sellers, rations were increased and improved, etc. October came and the mass exodus did not occur. But the grumbling continued until Pearl Harbor when the G.I. realized he was in for the duration. — Author)

2. Pogue, Marshall (1880-1939), p. 256.
3. Ibid., p. 274.
4. Ibid., p. 326.
5. Leonard Moseley, *Marshall Hero of Our Times*, p. 514.
6. Ibid., p. 244.
7. D. Clayton James, *The Years of MacArthur*, 1941-45, p. 596.
8. Ibid., p. 598.
9. Barbara W. Tuchman, *Stilwell*, p. 125.
10. Ibid., p. 124.
11. Lazzio M. Alfoldi, The Hutier Legend, *Parameters*, Vol. 5 (1975), pp. 69-74.

    (Note: General Marshall was a great leader. His deputy, Brig. Gen. Leonard Gerow, chief of the Army war plans division, took responsibility in the Congressional hearings for the failure of Maj. Gen. Walter Short to understand the alert orders for a possible attack at Pearl Harbor some ten days before it occurred. But Gen. Marshall refused to let Gerow take the rap and said while Gerow had direct responsibility he (Marshall) had full responsibility for what or what had not been done. The controversy of adequate alert has gone on for years. If you want first hand information on what happened, read a transcript of the original hearings in Congress. Historians have taken both sides of the issue over the years. The truth is we did not have adequate arms to defend Pearl. The Navy, with its ships lined up like ducks on a target range, and the Army simply did not believe war was imminent. — Author)

Letter 2 (Patton)

1. Ladislas Farago, Patton: *Ordeal and Triumph*, p. 152.
2. Ibid.
3. Ibid., p. 157.
4. Personally heard by author, Camp Edwards, Mass., October, 1942.
5. Martin Blumenson, *The Patton Papers, 1940-45*, p. 721.
6. Ibid.
7. David Irving, *The War Between the Generals*, p. 240.
8. Ibid., p. 392.
9. Ibid., p. 412. (Note: Martin Blumenson told author in 1985 that Jean Gordon was in love with one of Patton's staff officers and when he refused to divorce his wife after the war she decided to end it all.)
10. Ibid., Farago, p. 792.
11. Ibid., Irving, p. 278.
12. Robert S. Allen, *Lucky Forward*, p. 302.
13. Ibid., Irving, pp. 95-96.

Patton Prayer
(To men of Third Army 11-12 December, 1944.)
Almighty and most merciful Father, we humbly beseech Thee, of Thy great goodness, to restrain these immoderate rains with which we have had to contend. Grant us fair weather for battle. Graciously hearken to us as soldiers who call upon Thee that armed with Thy power, we may advance from victory to victory, and crush the oppression and wickedness of our enemies, and establish Thy justice among men and nations. Amen.
(The weather lifted on December 20.)

Letter 3 (Rommel)

1. Charles Douglas-Home. *Rommel*, p. 70.
2. Desmond Young, *The Desert Fox*, p. 19.
   (Note: When Churchill put General Alexander in charge of the Western Desert operation in North Africa, he said: "Rommel, Rommel, Rommel, What else matters but beating him?" British Official History).

Letter 4 (Summersby)

1. Robert H. Ferrell, *The Eisenhower Diaries*, p. 145.
2. Kay Summersby, *Eisenhower Was My Boss*, p. 7.
3. Kay Summersby Morgan, *Past Forgetting*, p. 133.
4. David Irving, *The War Between The Generals*, p. 319.
5. Ibid., Summersby (Boss), p. 94.
6. Ibid., p. 34.
7. Ibid., Summersby (Past Forgetting), p. 263.
8. Ibid., p. 264 (Note: Kay was 37 at time).
9. Ibid., p. 275.
10. Ibid., p. 279.
11. Dwight D. Eisenhower, *Crusade in Europe*, p. 132.
12. Robert S. Allen, *Lucky Forward*, p. 134.
13. James M. Gavin, *On To Berlin*, pp. 141-2.

14. Stephen E. Ambrose, *The Supreme Commander*, p. 246.
15. Ibid., Summersby, (Past Forgetting), p. 269.

(Note: Kay Summersby over the years in her writings has tried to leave the impression that Ike was madly in love with her and in effect their relationship was way beyond hand holding and constant companionship. She says that Ike tried to make love to her without consummation because he could not maintain an erection for mutual satisfaction. He said it was no use because of the age difference. She told him to be patient and the time or age factor was not important (18 years).

After the war Ike could have gone home and stayed if he had wanted to. Europe could have been resettled without him so he could rejoin his wife, Mamie. General Marshall had steadfastly said that Mamie could not be stationed overseas and she would not even agree to fly to a place like Bermuda for a lovers reunion. It left Ike up the creek.

So if Kay did or did not fulfill his sexual life their love story is still a great one.

After his hero's return to America following V-E Day in May, Ike returned to Europe and Kay for a continuation of their relationship and postwar problems. The interesting question that arises is why Ike did not take some form of hormone pills. Testosterone has been around for some time. Certainly a doctor is treated on a personal basis by a commander and rank plays no part in their association normally. So if Ike had needed medical help it was readily available.

Note: As this book went to press, it was learned that testosterone was prescribed for General Eisenhower in Europe during the war. The information came from the papers of Dr. Thomas W. Mattingly in the Dwight D. Eisenhower Library.— Author.

Obviously Ike was under a great deal of stress during the war and that alone as medical authorities will tell you is sufficient reason not to be able to maintain an erection and pursue intercourse on a regular basis. Whether medication would have helped has always been debatable. Many doctors think such pills just have a "psychic" effect and may be more important mentally than physically.

The idea of sleeping with some one other than your long-time bed partner, the fear of pregnancy (which Kay obviously wanted), the scandal (in those days at least) of a married man with a child by another woman — all of these can be deterrents in the sex act for some people. And older men have better erections in the morning as Dr. Ruth Westheimer often points out and Ike was a busy man at the crack of dawn (besides night duty often) and he could not have stayed in the sack if he had wanted to. His whereabouts were guarded and well known by the inner circle which also proved a handicap during the affair. It was only after the war, as Kay points out, that they could have more intimate times together without worrying about being caught in an embrace or relaxation.

Also remember at the end of the war President Truman is supposed to have told Eisenhower that he would do anything in the world for him — whatever he wanted including the Presidency. Obviously after Truman thought that over he changed his mind. But here you have a man trying to have an extra-marital affair and the possibility that a great war hero (remembering Washington, Grant and others — Ike knew his history well) could be President of the United States. He would be commander in chief of all the armed forces — not just commander of a task force for Operation Torch into North Africa or supreme commander of armies in nations in the greatest invasion ever made in the history of man at Normandy.

If this dream of Presidency were to come true he had to remain true to Mamie. Kay had been a pleasant affair as his son John and others realized during most of the war. Ike had flaunted his picture with Kay in front of Mamie in publications around the world. Kay was a driver, aide, secretary (who could not type), receptionist, hostess in the naive days of the 1940s. You might be talked about but you could sure get by with it in those days if you were an international hero. Some of Ike's closest advisors and friends commented to him about the relationship. Others were afraid to. And so many had their own girl friends.

Ike was truly in a dilemma. The body may have wanted one thing but the mind another. All of which is nothing new as doctors can tell you.

It is interesting to note that John Eisenhower, his son, at one time was about to go public with an admission of the Ike-Kay relationship (one wonders if he knew whether it was consummated) but historical colleagues and friends at the Army War College discouraged him from doing so. All of which was part of the big cover up over the years. Who can say if it was right or wrong?

So, dying of cancer in 1973 at 66 why did Kathleen Helen McCarthy-Morrogh Summersby Morgan write the book and mention that their romance was never consummated because of impotency? Very simple in the words of William Congreve:

"Heaven has no rage like love to hatred turned,
Nor hell a fury like a woman scorned."
  or
Colley Cibber: "We shall find no fiend in hell can match the fury of a disappointed woman."
As Ike said, "She is Irish and tragic."

★ ★ ★ ★ ★

Here follows a description by an Irish writer, Dermot Russell, County Cork, about Kay's homeland estate and a native's report on her life:

Innis Beg is an "island" on the estuary of the River Ilen which flows through Skibbereen and on to the Atlantic in Roaring Water Bay. It's quite a sizeable "island" in that it has about twenty houses, including a few holiday homes and also including the manor house which is reported in good condition, is regularly maintained and is looked after by a caretaker who goes into it every now and then. The house is presently unoccupied, but at regular stages down the years has been occupied by people who rent it. The owners of the house are the McCarthy-Morrogh family who were certainly owners back in the last century.

But it is not strictly an "island," rather a section of land which is reached by driving out the main road from Skibbereen to Baltimore and then turning off at the appropriate place, crossing a tiny bridge to reach the "island," on which there are also farms.

So we move to Kay Summersby. Her "line" is as follows. Alex McCarthy (born Cork 1771) of the Drishane McCarthys (near Millstreet) married Eliza Fagan and they had five daughters and seven sons. The third daughter, Helen, married James Morrogh of Hyde Park, Cork and they had three sons, James, Alex and Edward.

Son James married his cousin, Anne Stubbeman, and in these days became known as James McCarthy-Morrogh of Inchibeig. His son became Col. D. McCarthy-Morrogh of Inchibeg and and their daughter was Kathleen McCarthy-Morrogh.

Through her sheltered life on Innis Beg her only troubles were whether rain would spoil the hunting and tennis parties, etc. She had the old fashioned life of ease, largely without her mother who lived mostly in London, and spent time traveling the continent.

Eventually Kathleen went to London, working for some time as a film extra. She married a man named Summersby but it broke up in a short time. She was working as a model when war broke out, joined the Motor Transport Corps and found herself driving American officers . . . including Eisenhower.

That was the start of her association with Ike, and indeed in 1942 she went with him to North Africa after she had met and fallen in love with an American officer named Dick Arnold. Their wedding was set for June but shortly before that he was killed in action.

Later in the war she set about becoming an American citizen but from there on her life cannot be traced here. But in 1949 she did publish a book called "Eisenhower Was My Boss." Apparently the book was extremely popular here in Ireland and was well read up to early 1961, when the old age of the copies forced most of the Irish libraries to take it from circulation.

It is not known if Kay Summersby ever returned to her native Island near Skibbereen . . . but the manor house there is still owned by the McCarthy-Morrogh family, of which she is a member.

Incidentally, Inchibeg and Innis Beg (and Inishbeg) are one and the same place. In olden days it was known as the former, and Innis Beg took over latterly, and is now the name used on the maps here.

16. Ernest N. Harmon, *Combat Commander*, pp. 112-3.
17. Dwight D. Eisenhower, *Letters to Mamie*, Edited by John S. D. Eisenhower., p. 98.
18. Ibid., p. 276.
19. Ibid., pp. 11-12.

Letter 5 (De Gaulle)

1. David Hapgood and David Richardson, *Monte Cassino*, pp. 182-3.

(Note: The Polish Corps of 50,000 men had "emerged from a world of nightmare unimaginable to the Westeners around them." Stalin had ruled over half of Poland in a ruthless manner followed by Hitler's Nazi attack and subsequent treatment of violence and terror. — Author)

2. Bernard Ledwidge, *De Gaulle*, p. 193.
   Russell F. Weigley, *Eisenhower's Lieutenants*, p. 554.
3. H. Montgomery Hyde, *Stalin*, p. 510.
4. Stephen Ambrose, *Eisenhower* (General), pp. 176-7.
5. Ibid., p. 240.
6. A Canadian veteran of the Ortono (Italy) campaign, told the author his unit never moved for three months in the winter of 1943-44. Interview January, 1986, St. Petersburg, Fla.

Letter 6 (Roosevelt)

1. James MacGregor Burns, *Roosevelt*, p. 415.
2. Ibid., 416.
3. Ibid., 485.
4. Ibid.
5. Ibid., 495.
6. The truth of the matter is that the American Army was ill-prepared and equipped for the campaign in North Africa. It was a training ground for men and commanders. Our tanks were inadequate and our anti-tank weapons were almost useless. Our air support was inadequate. Eisenhower could not be blamed for the defeat. — Author.
7. Mark Clark position paper for 60 Minutes. See TV Guide November 11, 1972.
8. Ibid., Burns, p. 501.
9. Ibid., p. 207.
10. Ibid., p. 208.
11. Jim Bishop, *FDR's Last Year*, p. 95.
    Roosevelt's role as commander in chief of America's forces is now surfacing more and more. In the early postwar years the generals and admirals have been given the lion's share of credit. See Eric Larabee's "Commander in Chief" and D. Clayton James' "A Time for Giants." — Author.
12. Washington Post, May 5, 1985.
13. Ibid., Bishop, p. 601.
14. Ibid., Burns, p. 501.
15. William Bragg Ewald, Jr. *Eisenhower the President*, p. 27.
16. Ibid., p. 36.
17. Ibid., p. 37.
18. Ibid., p. 25.
19. Ibid., p. 24.
20. Ibid., Burns, p. 416.
21. Kay Summersby, *Eisenhower Was My Boss*, p. 89.
22. Ibid., p. 94.

(Note: The American nonfraternization policy given to the troops following V-E Day, devised in part by Secretary of Treasury Henry Morgantheau, a Roosevelt confidant, was impossible to enforce. I know I tried to carry it out in good faith. We staged raids, lectured and cajoled — all without success. It just proved that the American GI was a lover of the human race besides being a successful fighter on the battlefield. Once it was over, the troops were willing to forget and forgive. Many of us really did not trust the Germans but we had no other choice but to get along with them. Gen. Patton over the years, along with others, respected the

Germans for their fighting qualities and tended to overlook the killing inflicted on the battlefield and the ruthless deaths caused by the Holocaust. Both sides had worthy points in the nonfraternization policy but the Russians, who refused to cooperate fully in the postwar peace, made us choose up sides again and Germany became our ally. The drive to continue to seek out and prosecute the leaders who allowed the mass murders in the years that have followed is to be greatly admired. — Author)

Letter 7 (Truman)

1. Dwight D. Eisenhower, *Crusade in Europe*, p. 444.
2. Author's interview with Mark W. Clark, February, 1976.
3. Sen. Jenner told the author it was rhetoric, but he was sticking with the accusation. Interview, 1966. I commented that he was wrong, and the senator snorted.
4. Author Robert Ferrell reported that they quickly forgot their differences and enjoyed an animated chat.
5. Merle Miller, *Plain Speaking*, p. 338.
6. Ibid., DDE, p. 444.
7. Omar Bradley-Clay Blair, *General's Life*, p. 445.
8. I. George Blake, *Paul V. McNutt*, pp. 345-7.
9. Stephen Ambrose, *Eisenhower (General)*, p. 443.
10. William Bragg Ewald, Jr. *Eisenhower the President*, p. 32.

(Note: It is interesting that President Harry Truman never thought professional military men should be President. It would be hard to define his qualification but here are the presidents who held varying grades of general officer rank.)

George Washington
Andrew Jackson
William Henry Harrison
A. Zachary Taylor
Franklin Pierce
U.S. Grant
Rutherford B. Hayes
James A. Garfield
Benjamin Harrison
Chester A. Arthur
Dwight D. Eisenhower

Andrew Johnson was appointed military governor of occupied Tennessee and also has been listed as a general by some authorities.

Many others held lesser rank during their lifetimes.

He often used his opinion on the matter to prove that he had not offered Ike his support for the Presidency at the end of World War II. Eisenhower and Gen. Omar Bradley, whom Truman liked and respected very much, both claim he did make the offer. — Author)

Letter 8 (Churchill)

1. Author's interview with Gen. Mark Clark, February, 1976.
2. Bernard Ledwidge, *De Gaulle*, p. 158.
3. Winston Churchill, *Memoirs*, p. 494.
4. Ibid., 495.
5. Ibid., 432.
6. Ibid., 497.
7. Samuel Eliot Morison, *Sicily-Salerno-Anzio*, Vol. IX History of the U.S. Naval Operations in World War II., p. 303.

   (Note: Morison points out that the Iron Duke actually said: "It has been a damned nice thing — the nearest run thing you ever saw in your life . . . By God! I don't think it would have done if I had not been there." Eisenhower might have said the same. Morison also points out that a "large share of credit for the successful conclusion (at Salerno) . . . must be accorded to General Alexander." He was British deputy commander under Ike and above Clark. Clark got a lot of the blame for the near disaster of the operation but personally managed to hold the stage and take credit for its success. — Author)

8. Max Hastings, *Overlord* (D-Day in Normandy), p. 25.
9. Lucian K. Truscott, *Command Missions*, pp. 444-5.
10. Russell F. Weigley, *The American Way of War*, p. 354.
11. Ibid.
12. Ibid., p. 321.
13. William Manchester, *American Caesar*, p. 428.

    (Note: Manchester explains that Stalin secretly joined the anti-Japanese coalition. "In return, in the Far East the Soviet Union would be given certain privileges in Manchuria, the Kuril Islands, and northern Korea, and recognition of Outer Mongolia's autonomy. Except for the Kurils, the Russians were given nothing they couldn't have had for the taking. The Combined Chiefs of Staff had told the President and the prime minister (Churchill) to yield whatever the market demanded. They and their theater commanders, including MacArthur, appeared to have every reason to be pleased, and they were."

    Some historians forget that the American Army was getting a bit weary at this point and our casualties in both theaters had been mounting especially in the final drive to secure bases to invade Japan. Draft quotas were becoming harder to meet. The Russians had paid a high price to get control of much of eastern Europe. The Soviets just kept countries they had conquered with great sacrifices. The American leaders and the average G.I. were not fighting to conquer more territory — just the opposite was true of their Communist ally. — Author)

14. Philip Ziegler, *Mountbatten*, p. 657.
15. The author's battalion headquarters and its regimental headquarters officers pleaded and begged for more engineer crossing equipment for the operation. The actual operation was just like the rehearsal on the Volturno river — all fucked up.
16. *History of the Second World War*, p. 2202.

    (Note: It was little wonder that Churchill and the British nation needed retaliation. Just remember that from September 7, 1940 until November 3, there was an

average of 200 bombers attacking London every night. At the same time other industrial target cities and airfields were being attacked. — Author)
17. Ibid., p. 2203.
18. Ibid., p. 2207.
19. Interview with Tom Moses, a Navy officer on the landing and later president of the Indianapolis Water Co.
20. Ibid., Hastings, p. 197.
21. Alan Moorehead, *Eclipse*, p. 71.
22. Cornelius Ryan, *A Bridge Too Far*, p. 76.
23. Ibid., p. 599. In the nine-day battle casualties totaled 17,000. Enemy losses totaled 3,300. Dutch civilian losses were in the hundreds at Arnhem and Oosterbeek and up to 10,000 for the nine day Market-Garden operation.
24. David Irving, *The War Between the Generals*, p. 265.
25. Ibid., p. 402.

(Note: An excellent article on Churchill's role in the development of the tank is contained in *Armor* magazine (US) September-October, 1947 by Robert A. Vogel.)

Letter 9 (MacArthur)

1. Stephen Ambrose, *Eisenhower (General)*, p. 92.
2. Ibid., p. 97. The average bonus was $1,000 and only half had been paid when the Bonus March occurred in the summer of 1932. Some historians think that MacArthur had the backing of Secretary of War Patrick Hurley when he drove the marchers out of their camp sites.

(Note: Now we would call the bonus marchers lobbyists and give them an office with telephone probably and the Jefferson Memorial ground for an encampment. — Author)

3. D. Clayton James. *The Years of MacArthur 1941-45*, pp. 718-9.
4. Ibid., Ambrose, p. 135.
5. James MacGregory Burns, *Roosevelt*, p. 501.
6. Gen. Walton H. Walker had the 8th Army in Korea (later Gen. Matthew Ridgway) and Lt. Gen. Edward M. Almond commanded the X Corps. MacArthur's greatest defeat came about in part because the command was not unified. The Chinese simply drove down the high ground between the two forces. It was MacArthur's most disastrous defeat and contributed to the reasons for his relief by President Harry S. Truman, his commander in chief. MacArthur tried to run the battle from Tokyo. He never moved to Korea to establish a combat command post — a major violation of the principles of war. — Author)
7. Carol Morris Petillo, *Douglas MacArthur*, p. 151.

(Note: Ted Morgan in his biography of President Roosevelt, relates an interesting comment about MacArthur's Eurasian mistress in Washington. The comment took place when Admiral William D. Leahy, the President's White House chief of staff, accompanied the commander in chief to a meeting in Hawaii with MacArthur. Leahy commented: "He could have won the suit. He was a bachelor at the time. All he had to do was look everybody in the face and say: 'So what? Cunt can make you look awfully silly at times.' " p. 731. — Author)

8. Ibid., pp. 165-6.
9. Ibid., James, p. 661.

10. Burke Davis, *The Billy Mitchell Affair*, p. 327.
11. Ibid., Petillo, p. 139.
12. Ibid., Davis, p. 328.
13. Ibid., Petillo, p. 159.
14. Ibid., p. 211.
15. Ibid., p. 214.

Letter 10 (Bradley)

1. Omar Bradley-Clay Blair, *A General's Life*, pp. 128, 151.
2. Ibid., p. 130.
3. Ibid., p. 281.
4. Ibid., p. 170.
5. Ibid., p. 363.
6. Ibid., p. 200.
7. Ibid., p. 410.
8. Merle Miller, *Plain Speaking*, p. 324.

Letter 11 (Montgomery)

1. Interview Mark Clark, February, 1976. Clark said: "Montgomery was an artist in battle. He did not attack until he had assurance there was no chance of failure — this contrasted sharply with American generals, who are taught to go, go, go."
2. The story goes that Gen. Patton contacted Gen. Montgomery in the sweep across Europe and asked why he was moving so slowly. "Because I'm running short on petrol," explained Monty. The next day a messenger from Patton's staff reported to Montgomery and handed him one gallon of gas, with this note: "At the rate you are moving, this should suffice."
3. Montgomery lost command of the invasion forces in the summer of 1944 because Gen. Marshall and others felt that Eisenhower should take direct control of the battle on the Continent. He did so early and when the story broke, the British complained bitterly about a loss of face for Monty. Actually when Eisenhower agreed to Monty's plan at Arnheim he did not realize it would lead to a major fiasco. Of course Bradley and Patton were bitter when he gave Montgomery control of Hodges' First Army as the Germans drove through the Ardennes. Then Monty failed to counterattack when Patton did and later tried to take credit for saving Eisenhower and the American forces.
4. In 1975 Reserve Brig. Gen. John Eisenhower, son of the general, recalled that his father wrote to Gen. George Marshall, Army Chief of Staff, about the Berlin objective since he was the executive agent of the Joint Chiefs of Staff. John pointed out that Ike critics fail to realize that the Supreme Commander only took orders on strategic matters from Washington. He was against a drive for Berlin but wanted to "make sure he was in tune with Allied political policy," John added. It was by then a political move, not a military move. Roosevelt, of course, was a sick man. It was to be assumed that Marshall, like Ike, knew America still had a massive obstacle in its path to victory still — the defeat of Japan — and the fewer casualties in Europe the better since Ike knew the German army was finally defeated — (Letter to Author, June 20, 1975)
5. Stephen Ambrose, *Eisenhower*, (General), p. 392.
6. Ambrose, *Eisenhower*, (President), p. 228.

7. Ibid., p. 501.
8. Bernard Law Montgomery, *Memoirs*, p. 166. Montgomery also complained that he never saw McNaughton in his many visits to Canada after the war. Montgomery says that the division commander did not want to be bothered with the former commander McNaughton in Sicily.
9. Letter from Gen. Harper to author, November 28, 1974.
10. Ambrose (President), p. 499. See author's article in addenda on "Why Ike Didn't Take Berlin."
11. Ibid., John Eisenhower letter to author.
12. Cornelius Ryan, *A Bridge Too Far*, p. 76 ©Simon & Schuster Inc..
13. *American Heritage*, February, 1976.
14. *New York Times*, April 16, 1976.
15. (Note: Eisenhower always wanted a roundtable with leaders of the Allied nations to debate and record what really happened in some of the famous battles of World War II. The idea never came about. He proposed that the meeting take place at Camp David in Stephen Ambrose's book on the General. Ann Whitman, secretary to Eisenhower during the White House years, remembered that Ike wanted such a roundtable at Camp David in an interview in February, 1987. She said it was one of the things she remembered that her boss talked about on World War II, while President. — Author)

Letter 12 (Alexander)

1. Interview with Mark W. Clark, February, 1976.
2. Nigel Nicolson, *Alex*, pp. 239-40.
3. Ibid., p. 173.
4. Stephen Ambrose, *Eisenhower (General)*, p. 234.
5. Ibid., p. 328.
6. Ibid., p. 299.

Letter 13 (Simpson)

1. Dwight D. Eisenhower, *Crusade in Europe*, p. 376.
2. Charles B. MacDonald, *The Last Offensive*, p. 303.
3. Ibid., p. 305.
4. H. Essame, *The Battle For Germany*, p. 205.
5. Ibid.
6. Ibid., MacDonald, p. 379.
7. Ibid., p. 399.
8. Ibid.
9. *New York Times Magazine*, June 12, 1966, pp. 34-5.
10. Saul Pett, *Atlanta Journal and Constitution*, March 3, 1954.
11. Stephen Ambrose, *Eisenhower* (General), p. 369.
12. Ibid., p. 385.
13. Ibid., p. 533.
14. Bernard Law Montgomery, *Memoirs*, p. 277.

(Note: Besides his frustration in not attacking Berlin, Simpson was ready to cross the Rhine in early March, 1945, long before Montgomery was willing to risk the adventure. See Stephen Ambrose's *The Supreme Commander*, p. 614. — Author)

Letter 14 (Clark)

1. Author's interview with Mark Clark, February, 1976.
2. Ibid.
3. Clark letter to author, April 27, 1982.
4. Mark Clark, *From the Danube to Yalu*, p. 20.
5. Ibid., Clark interview.
6. Ibid.
7. Clark letter February 25, 1976.
7A. Ibid.
8. Ibid.
9. Ibid., Clark (Yalu) pp. 295-6.

   (Note: During his last assignment for Ike on the manpower study Clark, in addition to Universal Military Training, insisted on a summer training program for the nation's youth. He had such a program going on at the Citadel and in effect its mission was to take young men who could not find work into a para military program which the Regular Army had helped to supervise during the depression under the Civilian Conservation Corps. Clark told me he felt that Eisenhower never gave the program any serious thought and was a bit bitter over the outcome of his last assignment from the President. As head of the military Battlefield Commission he was still invited to the White House. Ike's secretary, Ann Whitman, called him a handsome, tall man who towered over the scene and was very impressive. — Author)

10. Ibid., Clark interview.
11. Martin Blumenson, *Mark Clark*, p. 54.
12. Ibid., Clark interview.
13. Forrest C. Pogue, *George C. Marshall*, (1939-42), p. 101.

    (Note: Gen. Lear had been dissatisfied with the training and discipline of the 35th National Guard division and was coming down hard on its commander, Maj. Gen. Ralph Truman (cousin of later President Harry Truman) a veteran of the Spanish-American war and World War I. His units were having too good a time in some local communities and their antics surfaced. When some men of the 35th passed a golf course in Memphis they "proceeded to utter wolf whistles — described as 'yoo-hoos' at several young ladies on the course." One of the golfers in civies happened to be Gen. Lear. He told them to stop whistling. They told him to shut up. When he got back to his headquarters he "ordered these men to be brought back from their home station at Ft. Robinson, Arkansas, and required to walk back part of the 45 miles to their post." It resulted in a 15-mile march followed by a 15-mile ride which was fairly severe for those days. — Author)

14. Harry C. Butcher, *My Three Years with Eisenhower*, p. 758.
    Fine was a personal friend of many of us in the 36th Division. He was capable, respected and admired by GIs and Generals alike.
15. Fred L. Walker, *From Texas to Rome*, p. 258.
15A. Carlo D'Este, World War II in the Mediterranean. p. 112.
16. Omar Bradley with Clay Blair, *A General's Life*, p. 207.
17. Clark letter, February 25, 1976.
18. Blumenson to author, April 11, 1985.

In a letter to the author, Indiana University Journalism Professor Ralph Holsinger remembers Maj. Gen. John Lucas well at Anzio. He was a private first class in the code room of VI Corps Headquarters in 1944:

"As a code clerk in Corps with the 57th Signal Battalion I handled a great many classified messages with Army and the divisions. I do recall that after we hunkered down, Corps kept asking Army for more men and material. Finally, during one of those times in February when the Germans were pushing at us pretty hard, Mark Clark fired back a message, personal to Lucas. I deciphered it. It said in effect that Army had given Corps all the men and material it reasonably could. Clark also told Lucas that if he didn't get the Corps moving toward Rome, and doing so pretty quickly, 'I'll come up there and show you how to do it.' Because the message was top secret, the rules required me to double seal it and deliver it personally to the general. I found him in bed — it was sometime toward midnight — in another wine cellar off the main square at Nettuno. It was deeper than the one corps HQ was in. He didn't like being waked up, but he took it. Well, as you know, we didn't move, although I am sure a lot of men died trying. Anyway, Clark came up a few days later, removed Lucas and replaced him with Truscott (Lucian, major general, 3d Division commander). The rest is history.

"When Clark's book came out after the war he said he relieved Lucas because of illness, I wrote Clark with the brashness of a young reporter to remind him that he was distorting history. I got a long letter from him, which I cannot find, conceding that he had indeed messaged Lucas as above, but saying he wanted to spare the family embarrassment. With all respect to you of the officer corps I have always thought on the basis of my distant exposure, that Lucas was more chickenshit than commander of troops in battle."

19. Blumenson to author, April 12, 1986.

Letter 15 (Hodges)

1. Saul Pett, Associates Press story, *Atlanta Journal* and *Constitution*, March 28, 1954.
2. Russell F. Weigley, *Eisenhower's Lieutenants*, p. 364.
3. Hedgerows as defined by Martin Blumenson in *History of World War II:*
"The hedgerow, a fence half earth and half hedge, 3 to 15 feet high — a direct wall several feet thick, topped by bramble, hawthorn, vines, and trees. Enclosing plots of arable land to protect crops and cattle from ocean winds, breaking the ground into tiny walled enclosures, the hedgerows provided the Germans — who dug into the base, where they were concealed by the vegetation — with made-to-order defenses." p. 1840.
4. Both winters of the war in Europe were cold, wet, and miserable. We all carried an extra pair of socks, but once your boots and socks were soaked you just kept wearing them throughout the day. At night or in a quiet, no fire time you could change. Hopefully your other pair would dry out. You slept on them, exposed them to air or put them on a warm motor hood if one was available. Trench foot was a serious problem throughout the winter months. Your feet were cold, turned blue and white. If you were in the front lines constantly you might have to go to a hospital for treatment. The feet of many never responded properly and veterans have had cold feet ever since with pain in extreme temperatures, wet shoes or

other exposure. It was not a pleasant physical ailment to bring back from the war for a lifetime of recurring pain. — Author.
5. Ibid., Weigley, p. 433.
6. Dwight D. Eisenhower, *Crusade in Europe*, p. 365.
   By comparison with Normandy invasion casualties (June 6 to July 24, 1944):
   16,293 dead
   43,221 wounded
   5,087 prisoners.
   Total World War II deaths: 281,557 battle deaths
   113,842 other deaths
7. Ibid. Atlanta Journal and Constitution.
8. Stephen Ambrose, *The Supreme Commander*, p. 621.
9. Stephen Ambrose, *Eisenhower (General)*, p. 298.
10. Ibid., p. 365.
11. Ibid., p. 369.
12. Line units were in constant contact with the enemy up to and including V-E Day while higher echelons were living it up. George Seldes in his book "Witness to a Century" quotes *Time Magazine*, May 28, 1945, on casualties on the final day of war: "In World War I, 215 soldiers were killed and 1,114 wounded on Armistice Day. In World War II on V.E. Day in Europe, one was killed, 12 wounded." Nothing was more feared than a sniper bullet or an undetected mine if the war was supposed to be over. Howard S. Wilcox, of Indianapolis, a major in the 63rd Infantry division recalls: "We were still playing cops and robbers with German armored units when we received word in the vicinity of Landsberg that the war was over."

    Wilcox also tells a good story about the time he received the British Military Cross:

    "About a month after the war was over, I was a major commanding a battalion and received a message from His Majesty, the King of England, to be present at a specified time in a town about 100 miles from our location to receive the BMC from General Montgomery. My jeep driver and I left about 5 a.m. When we found the huge stadium where the ceremonies were to take place, they refused to let my jeep driver enter. That helped put me in a good mood.

    "There were 18 Americans to be decorated. We stood at attention for nearly an hour while all the brass were introduced and moved into position. I thought that every damn ant in Germany had crawled down my back. With 'W' being the end of the alphabet, I moved some 75 feet to the front and saluted Montgomery and General Bradley. Bradley returned the salute. I'm not sure Montgomery did. All I cam remember is him asking me how old I was. I replied, 25, sir. He then looked up at Bradley, who was about a foot taller, and said " 'You Americans do the damnest things.' " My inner reaction was to tell him what he could do with his medal.

    "I met Bradley years later. I asked him if he remembered the incident to which he replied: " 'I felt like bashing the little guy.' " He explained that the British rarely promote anyone to field grade until they are 40 or near."

Letter 16 (Devers)

1. Martin Blumenson and James L. Stokesbury, *Masters of the Art of Command*, p. 178.

   (Note: Devers was an expert in the training and development of armor techniques and organization.)
2. Author's interviews with Jacob L. Devers, Ft. Knox, Ky, November, 1953.
3. Ibid.
4. Ibid., Dwight D. Eisenhower, *Crusade in Europe*, p. 417.
5. Kay Summersby, *Past Forgetting*, p. 47.

Letter 17 (Patch)

1. Leonard Mosley, *Marshall Hero of Our Times*, pp. 256-9.
2. Lucian K. Truscott, *Command Missions*, pp. 421-3.

   (Note: Truscott reminded one of Gen. George Patton — short, bombastic and successful. He got three of the top divisions in the war with the most combat experience — 3d, 36th, 45th. The division commanders never have received the praise and honors they deserved. Two, John E. Dahlquist and John W. (Iron Mike) O'Daniel, did get four stars in later service. — Author)
3. Ibid., Truscott, p. 414.

   (Note: The Navy and the division officers made the wise decision of not entering the port of Frejus until it was cleared. The original plan was to go ahead on into the mined areas. The city was flanked which meant fewer casualties and the invasion was more successful than most of the men ever hoped for. Truscott again, while critical of the change, later admitted the maneuver saved lives. — Author)
4. Gen. Dahlquist was a real fighter. A bit hump-shouldered, the University of Minnesota ROTC graduate looked a little like a bulldog ready for a fight. He drove the division relentlessly and gave it new confidence after the Rapido disaster, the hairy invasion at Salerno and the hard battles in the Purple Heart Valley before Cassino. He had a doubly hard job because when Gen. Mark Clark relieved the 36th commander, Fred L. Walker, he made a lot of men and officers, who almost cried at his farewell parade, furious. The relief took place after the successful breakout at Valletri on the Anzio beachhead and the capture of Rome. — Author.
5. The battalion was the 2d, 143d Infantry, the author's outfit. When I found during a night attack that we had infiltrated the enemy tank area without adequate weapons to fight them, a word-of-mouth relay message got through to headquarters and we very quietly made a left flank move of an entire battalion to return over a hill mass to our original position. — Author.
6. Ibid., Truscott, p. 433.

   (Note: Montelimar was a real head-on military engagement. We had sneaked large forces behind the Germans and one division was pushing them south in the Rhone Valley and two were pushing them north into our position. It was a gallant, hill-by-hill, house-by-house, room-by-room struggle. The main battle occurred in a short period of time and the Germans had been roundly defeated. Historians have failed to give the battle its proper credit because Paris was liberated at the same time — and that's where the headlines went. — Author)

7. The location was Riquewihr in the Voges Mountains and the author experienced the attack — his second since landing in southern France.
8. 36th Division quarterly Vol. V. No. 1, spring, 1985, p. 10. Brig. Gen. Robert Stack was a likeable guy and amazingly enough he looked in build very much like Goering, long time designated heir to Hitler. In fact Stack's fat appearance made him look like anything but a general. More like a buffoon and some commanders and GIs felt that way about him at times. But he was brave and appeared on the battle scene at the most unexpected times. While nornally his role was to fight the infantry forces with his commander worrying about the combined arms, Dahlquist was such an on-the-ground fighter that he often overshadowed Stack and all of his other infantry commanders in the battle to close with the enemy. Stack did lead various task forces and often served as a useful buffer when Dahlquist and other higher commanders showed impatience when an attack was progressing slowly or got bogged down. Actually, of course, the assistant division commander had no troops to control while the other assistant division commander (also a BG) for artillery had under his control the weapons with the most explosive fire power in a division. — Author.
9. Ibid., Truscott, p. 170.
10. Ibid., Truscott, p. 441. The author was present at one of the pep talks. We were herded into an area like cattle but it was an effective rally for success. Truscott actually had great talent and wanted to invade Italy in the north where Mussolini had stabbed the French in the back when Hitler invaded to the West in 1940. He was lucky in the fact that Hitler refused to send reinforcements to aid the defending forces in the south of France and could not move troops in the southwest area across the Rhone River in time to be effective.

Addenda A

QUESTIONNAIRES

The following are responses to questionnaires the author mailed in 1959-60 to some of Gen. Dwight Eisenhower's commanders in World War II. I know of no such report anywhere else. Since Gen. George Patton died at the end of the war in 1945, Gen. Paul Harkins has kindly answered his questionnaire.

General Collins Answers

Gen. J. Lawton Collins, was one of Bradley's outstanding corps commanders — perhaps the best. Here are his answers.

What was your best decision? (And how did you make it?)

"I'm at a loss to answer your first question, except perhaps to combine it with the answer to your second question reference the hardest decision. This latter was unquestionably the decision to counter-attack on Christmas morning of 1944 with the 2d Armored Division against the leading elements of the 2d Panzer Division near Celles, Belgium at the height of the Battle of the Bulge. There is a first-rate article on this decision in the May 1947 issue of the INFANTRY JOURNAL, written by Hanson W. Baldwin.

"The hardest battle in many respects was the fighting in the Huertgen Forest near Aachen during the winter of 1944-45.

"As a result of the defeat of the Germany Armies in the Battle of the Bulge, our crossing of the Rhine and the drive from the Rhine to the Elbe was much easier than we had originally anticipated.

"My happiest moment was on the evening of June 17th when we broke through the German positions at the base of the Cherbourg Peninsula and I knew that we had Cherbourg in the bag.

"It is difficult to choose among the great division commanders who served in the VII Corps. Matt Eddy, Ralph Huebner, Max Taylor and Matt Ridgway and a number of others were topflight division commanders. These men all rose to higher commands in which they also distinguished themselves. Considering the time that he and his 3d Armored Division served in the VII Corps, his great personal gallantry, tremendous drive, and natural qualities of leadership, I will say that Major General Maurice Rose was the top division commander in the business until he was killed at the head of his division near Paderborn.

"I could not possibly make a choice as to the "best unit" of among the 20 divisions that saw service in the VII Corps. I will say that the 1st, 4th, 9th and 104th Infantry Divisions, the 2d and 3d Armored Divisions, the 82d, and 101st Airborne Divisions were the cream of the crop and that the 3d Armored Division made the greatest contribution to the success of the VII Corps from the time of the breakthrough in Normandy to the Elbe.

"The IX Tactical Air Command, under Major General Elwood R. Quesada, furnished excellent close support to the VII Corps from Normandy to the Elbe. We could not have possibly made the rapid progress we did without this support. In addition, the VII Corps also was supported by some 1,500 heavy bombers and hundreds of medium and fighter bombers in the massive aerial bombardment preceding Operation Cobra which lead to the breakthrough near St. Lo in July, 1944."

April 1960

General Middleton Answers

Lt. Gen. Troy Middleton was a veteran of two World Wars and President of Louisiana State University. When he was regimental commander of the 142d Infantry, 36th Division, prior to the war he was one of the most liked and respected commanders I've ever heard of by both enlisted men and officers. He took the 45th Division into Sicily and Italy where he again proved his battle worthiness. He did tire in 1943 and had an absence from the battlefield for several months but took VIII Corps into Normandy and was most successful in holding together the various fragments of units in the Battle of the Bulge.

What was your best decision? (And how did you make it?)
"To hold Bastogne during the battle of the Bulge. After a careful study of the situation."

What was your hardest decision?
"To hold Bastogne in the face of great odds."

What was your hardest battle?
"Argonne Forest in World War I"

Were any of your battles easy, although you had anticipated them being hard?

"Yes, capture of the Britany Penn. up to Brest in World War II."

What was your happiest moment?
"The Armistice in World War I."

Who was your best subordinate in battle?
"Colonel, later, Brigadier General C. M. Ancorn."

Your best unit?
"157th Infantry, 45th Infantry Division and 101st Airborne Division."

Did the Army Air Corps support you at all times?
"The Air Force did a good job."

December 1959.

Gen. William Simpson, Ninth Army Commander wrote

What was your best decision? (And how did you make it?)
"My best decision was to postpone an attack by my Ninth Army which involved crossing the Roer River, because that river was flooded by the Germans when they blew up the penstocks of several dams above the crossing sites. This flood would have cut off the troops who crossed first from the remainder of the army."

What was your hardest decision?
"The above, in connection with the crossing of the Roer Rover."

What was your hardest battle?
"I believe the hardest battle my Ninth Army fought was the attack that I made in November 1944 through the mud to close the Roer River. This resulted in one of the biggest and hardest battles of the war."

Were any of your battles easy, although you had anticipated them being hard?
"Yes, the battle which involved crossing the Roer River after the floods had subsided and in which the objective was the Rhine River. My plan of battle made the fight easier than I had anticipated."

What was your happiest moment?
"When my Ninth Army became operational on August 25, 1944."

Who was your best subordinate in battle?
"There was little choice between my three Army Corps Commanders (A.C. Gillem, Jr., J.B. Anderson, R.S. McClain.) and at least

three of my Division Commanders were outstanding and all were top flight commanders."

Your best unit?

"The Second Armored Division was the best armored division and the Thirtieth Infantry Division was probably the best infantry division although the Eighty Third Infantry Division was a close second."

October 1960

Gen. Jacob Devers Answers

Gen. Jacob Devers after commands in England and North Africa became Sixth Army Group commander in France after the invasion of southern France.

"Sorry that I am unable to answer your questions at the present time. I have been away for several months — a fact which has prevented me from accomplishing what had been my intention.

"Your questions, of course, as you know, are not easy to answer. All battles were hard; all decisions are difficult to make; and as to the best subordinate in battle — there was no single one — there are always two, and if you cite two, you wonder whether there weren't three.

"Without elaborating, I believe that the Army should now have control of its own air force. The Army Air Corps did support me at all times at the local-level with what they had.

"We must always have civilian control at the head of the Department of Defense, but there is one thing sure — civilian control should be cut to one-tenth of what it now is, without changing the three services. The staffs of the three services must be cut — and cut sharply — in order to enable them to accomplish things quickly and efficiently.

"You can see from the above that I am generalizing to some extent. Actually, if I had this problem to solve, I would start by cutting a tremendous number of civilian secretaries and assistants, etc., from the Pentagon Building — and at the same time reducing all staffs materially — and then I would go on from there."

October 1960.

Gen. Clark's Interview With Author

What was your best decision (And how did you make it?)

The decision to take Rome. I took a chance and captured the

eternal city just two days before the invasion at Normandy. If I had followed the British plan we would have tried, in a fruitless effort, to trap the German armies south of Rome. My immediate superior, Field Marshal Alexander, desired a joint liberation with 5th Army and the British Eighth Army.

What was your hardest decision?
To cross the Rapido River below Cassino in order to launch a major attack in conjunction with the invasion to the north at Anzio and thereby trap the enemy forces.

Were any of your battles easy, although you had anticipated them being hard?
All of my battles were hard — nothing came easy in Italy although the drive from Rome to Florence was a relatively easy push.

What was your hardest battle?
The invasion at Salerno. It was touch and go for four days.

What was your happiest moment?
The capture of Rome.

Who was your best subordinate in battle?
Lt. Gen. Lucian K. Truscott. He was 3d Division commander following the Salerno landing in the Volturno — Purple Heart Valley campaigns and then at Anzio where he was made a Corps commander. I brought him back from Southern France to succeed me as Fifth Army commander. A two-star jump within 10 months.

Your best unit?
My three divisions I gave to the Southern France invasion: 3d Infantry, 36th Infantry, 45th Infantry.

If I had to reduce it to one it would have been the 3d probably, my alma mater. It accomplished many miracles including the break out of the Anzio beachhead. It also had the nation's top medal winner, Audie Murphy.

February 1976

Harkins for Patton

Gen. Paul Harkins, a staff officer and probably the closest Patton confidante in Third Army, was theater commander in Vietnam during the Kennedy administration.

Here are the answers to the author:

"I have noted your conclusions regarding General Patton and I hesitate to agree or disagree specifically but will make some broad comments.

"Best decision. Though the decision to attack on the south flank of the Bulge with only three divisions was a good one, I think General Patton's decision to 'attack, attack, attack' at all times was far more reaching.

"Hardest decision. All decisions reference combat seemed to come easy to him, but as he told me once 'Why shouldn't they. I have studied war for forty-two years and I think I know a lot about it.' He felt like a surgeon who had practiced his profession for some length of time and knew exactly what veins and arteries to clip and what muscles to incise during an operation. Some people have criticized him for making quick decisions but he never considered that criticism justified.

"Hardest battle. I think all battles are hard, depending on where you are in the chain of command. A Private sitting in a cold, frozen foxhole suffering only intermittent shelling might think it was just as hard a battle as another man engaged in the attack on a fortified position. Some battles are tougher than others but it would be difficult to say which was really the hardest.

"Easiest battle. Certainly the Rhine crossing was easy for Third Army. As a matter of fact it wasn't a battle at all. The battle for the crossing had been won when Third Army broke though the Siegfried line.

"Happiest moment. I think he was happy all the time when his armies were on the move. I never got the opinion that he was really competing with other commanders. He was fighting a battle in his army to the utmost of his ability and, although he knew what was going on on the other side of his army boundaries, it didn't seem to bother him too much.

"Best Subordinates. I think it would be difficult to single out his best subordinates. All Corps and Divisions he commanded did a wonderful job, and I believe in checking the record you will find that he relieved no senior commander for cause in combat unless the cause was sickness or circumstances over which he had no control.

"Best unit. The 4th Armored Division was a crack outfit and engaged in many spectacular operations. Again, I think it would be unfair to say it was the best unit as all were good and you must remember General Patton commanded forty-two divisions in the Third Army alone, not counting those that he commanded in Africa and Sicily." October 1960.

Addenda B

Why Ike Didn't Take Berlin

Reprinted from *The Indianapolis News*, April 29, 1982.
By Wendell Phillippi

In April, 1945, Berlin fell to the Russians as World War II came to an end in Europe. As the years grow more distant from the end of World War II, some veterans seem to be more and more agitated that U.S. forces failed to capture Berlin before the Russians.

Such a feeling raises these questions:

Could we have taken Berlin first? If we could, why didn't we? And yet another interesting question: Since the Russians were within 40 miles of Berlin in February 1945, why didn't the Red Armies capture the German citadel and end the war sooner?

There are three considerations:

1. Gen. Dwight D. Eisenhower, the supreme commander of Canadian, British, American and French forces, deployed his troops on a broad front in late 1944 in order to destroy the German army west of the Rhine River. This was done for two reasons: The river was a major obstacle and Ike wanted to avoid many bloody battles on the Siegfried Line which, while not impregnable, was an armed fortress or could be made one and a fight there would have caused heavy casualties. He also didn't have enough airborne forces to effectively jump over the Siegfried Line. His plan no longer included Berlin as a military objective.

2. The British wanted to take Berlin to make Field Marshal Montgomery (its biggest hero) the one and only hero of the Allied forces in World War II. This was a worthy but immodest goal. Actually, Monty was still smarting because American Gen. George Patton, Jr. had made a monkey of him in the Sicilian campaign in 1943. (Monty was the first major hero of the Allies at El Alamein in North Africa where he finally defeated the much feared German Field Marshal Erwin Rommel).

3. The Russians seemed to be even more confused than the Americans and British in the pursuit of Berlin. In February, 1945, while the Americans were recovering from the severe losses from the Battle of the Bulge, the Russians were only about 40 miles from Berlin. Some

Russian generals wanted to head straight for Berlin and end the war. Marshal Vassili Chuikov, an Army commander, wanted to take Berlin at once. He claims that during a conference of Army commanders, Stalin called up and told the leaders to forget the Berlin plan and head north for Pomerania to destroy Adolf Hitler's famous "Vistula Army Group." Otherwise the Berlin assault would have a highly vulnerable northern flank of hundreds of miles. This did not worry Chuikov because he reasoned that once Berlin was captured the war was over. At the same time, other Russian forces were busy with a drive from Hungary and Austria, a thrust to make sure the American forces didn't beat them to Czechoslovakia.

Which Was Right?

Marshall Giorgi Zhukov denies the telephone call took place. He says the operation was not as simple as Chuikov thought and that the Soviet troops would be overextended in the Berlin drive. He agreed with the Stalin order to consolidate on the Oder River. Stalin, of course, always had in mind that the Red Army drive against Warsaw in 1920 — was defeated; because its flanks were not secured. If it had been a success, Poland would have become part of the new Russia after World War I and a great buffer against Germany.

An interesting sidelight in the 1945 spring drive across Poland is the fact that the Russians moved 220 miles in 14 days. Considering the weather, supply and terrain, this was no easy accomplishment. Of course the Russians fought differently than the Allies. If a two-star Russian division general was not successful he often found himself reduced to private the next day. And if a general disobeyed orders, the firing squad was his next obstacle.

Why didn't the Americans disregard agreements and strike for Berlin as so many veteran and second guessers now claim the U.S. should have done? Three reasons:

1. It was estimated that America would suffer 100,000 casualties. After the Bulge massacre and still facing the conquest of Japan, few American leaders or soldiers were eager to capture Berlin for the historical record.

2. The Southern Redoubt in Bavaria was widely rumored to be a new stronghold for the German forces. A new fortress might be a trap for the American leaders who still remembered the Bulge. The possibility for a massive battle in Bavaria and the mountains of the Alps loomed large

in April 1945. Historians may laugh about the myth now, but it was real in the minds of the doughfeet in the field. The area was in front of the American 7th Army and the Free French Army and both units had fought for eight months in constant battle without great resources of supply. Elements of the 7th Army had gone 30 days in one period of operations without air support in the drive through the Vosges Mountains. Ike knew he could not count on the forces in Italy because the British held a large portion of the front and they were slow fighters in the Italian campaign.

3. The Big Three, Churchill, Stalin and Roosevelt, at Teheran had already agreed to the partition of Germany in November 1943, and Berlin was to be under joint control in the Russian area of occupation. (Just why America didn't have guaranteed land access to Berlin may never be known and such a predicament led to the famous Cold War airlift to Berlin of 1948-49.)

All this second guessing about Berlin raises another interesting point:

If Germany as its generals and some historians claim (the Russians agree) wanted the United States forces in Berlin before Russia, why didn't Hitler just give up? Actually the Germans fought Americans with great ferocity. With the newly recruited troops of old men and young boys the Germans inflicted severe casualties on the American forces. All of this made a deep impression on Ike. Our quick and successful drive to the Elbe — from where we would have taken off for Berlin — met fierce resistance. Road blocks, mines, panzer-fausts (anti-tank weapons), rear-guard units, and nebelwerfers (automatic multimortar), the still effective and dreaded 88, buzz bombs and the new jet airplanes all combined to slow the drive although at times, the Allies did make tremendous gains.

The End At The Elbe

American forces got two bridgeheads across the Elbe in April but part of one by the 2nd Armored Division was actually driven back across the river. It was a remarkable feat for the decimated enemy army.

At many a postwar division reunion, the comrades of the 83rd U.S. Infantry Division have lamented that Berlin was within its grasp when it was told to stop short of the German objective. In April 1945, a division combat commander, Brig. Gen. Sidney Hinds, was shocked into insubordination and told Gen. Simpson, "That's not right. We're going to Berlin." Needless to say, Gen. Simpson did stop his troops and its veterans have been criticizing higher headquarters including the State Department and the White House ever since.

Hitler was awaiting death in a bunker in Berlin but still he commanded an amazing amount of respect from his generals and admirals who felt some miracle would still bring victory for the Fuehrer's adopted country. (He was born in Austria.)

A message from Eisenhower to Stalin in March 1945 has become a great controversy as the years have not mellowed the dispute over the capture of Berlin. The message informed Stalin that the objective of his drive would be the Leipzig-Dresden area rather than Berlin. Stalin, ever distrustful, surmised that Ik was up to dirty tricks and immediately told commanders of his two army groups that the Allies were trying to beat the Red Army to Berlin. Army commanders needed no more direction. Their mission was to capture Berlin. Actually Stalin placed Konev and Zhukov in competition to capture the last objective in Europe.

Reserve Brig. Gen. John Eisenhower, son of the general, recalls that his father wrote to Gen. George Marshall, Army Chief of Staff, about the Berlin objective since he was the executive agent for the Joint Chiefs of Staff. John points out that Ike critics fail to realize that the supreme commander only took orders on strategic matters from Washington. He was against a drive for Berlin but wanted to "make sure he was in tune with Allied political policy," John says. It was by then a political move, not a military move. Roosevelt, of course, was sick man.

In October 1944, Monty had agreed with Ike that Berlin was not a good objective. But as he neared with the encirclement of the Ruhr (thanks to American 1st and 9th Armies) Monty's mind was changed — probably by Churchill. Monty in late March had informed the British chiefs of staff his axis would be Wesel-Munster-Herford-Hanover and "thence via the autobahn to Berlin, I hope." This infuriated Ike. And the British were mad as hell over the change of plans. Such disharmony on the brink of victory.

Monty Loses Forces

To make sure he knew what the British were going to do, Ike took the U.S. 9th Army away from Monty. The British were perfectly willing for the Americans to make the drive and then Monty would take the credit. Casualties, so long as they were not from the Empire, didn't worry them. Monty's forces would be busy capturing the key ports of the Baltic Sea.

The British even claimed that the message to Stalin was used an an excuse to transfer the 9th Army back to American control. In other words, to use Stalin indirectly to control Monty. It points up the bitterness between Ike and Monty which really never surfaced during the war.

Ike never complained about Monty during the war and his correspondence after the war never mentioned any such bitterness. Monty's bragging after the war must have really hurt Ike.

The only American general who went along with Monty was Gen. William Simpson, 9th Army Commander. In a letter to the *New York Times* in 1966, Simpson concluded he could have taken Berlin. He then complained that Gen. George Marshall, the American Army chief of staff, didn't know he had troops only 53 miles from Berlin. He says he had eight divisions or about 150,000 troops, for the operation on April 16. Meanwhile, the Russians had massed more than 1 million assault troops for the drive to Berlin. The Russians reached Berlin six days after Simpson claims he was ready for the assault and the Russians met his forces on the Elbe three days later.

Eisenhower knew his troops well. He knew they were tired. His was basically a civilian army which still faced another major enemy — Japan.

He also knew Monty's troops well, especially in Normandy where their D-Day objective, Caen, was not captured for six weeks.

So why didn't we take Berlin before the Russians? Ike was under tremendous pressure from Washington officials and the American public (even the lowly GI) to end the war in Europe with the minimum of casualties and to head for Japan. The critics then, and the conservatives later, didn't know what front-line action was all about. How many four-star generals and how many conservative writers ever spent a night with a front-line rifle company or a battalion headquarters?

The Berlin Prize

The GIs had spent months and years getting there. If the Russians wanted the Berlin prize with all its casualties, then let them have it. Ike also had to avoid a major military engagement with the Russians. He knew about the various times our own units had ended up mistakenly striking each other. How the Air Force had bombed or strafed friendly forces on the ground. He also knew his military history well enough to recall that some of his generals, including Gen. Patton, wanted to punch the Russians in the nose to let them know who was superior. Also, many Germans thought America would join forces with their defeated armies to attack east and run the Russians out of German territory.

Ike knew he must have a natural barrier between the forces of the two nations. The Elbe River was such a place where the forces halted to eventually exchange handshakes instead of crossfire which was always a possibility as the supreme commander knew.

The question remains: Could we have captured Berlin before the Russians? Probably so, but at a high price. But by the time some of our commanders decided we could get there it was too late. The Russians were already on the way.

With the capture of Berlin, World War II was near the end although many a GI who had fought for years didn't believe it until he was safe at home and the Japanese had surrendered a few months later. Hitler ended his part on the 30th of April by suicide — a shot in the mouth — to silence the strongest voice in German history.

On May 2, 1945, Berlin surrendered to the Russians. The war in Europe ended officially May 8.

Addenda C

DRAFTEE TO STARS

Dear Ike,

I was a member of your crusade on a rather lowly level in World War II. In fact, when I was a private I yearned for private first-class or corporal stripes. It seemed like such a step up in the military pecking order. We lowly privates almost worshipped those ranks. The idea of becoming a sergeant or more would have felt like going from driving a Ford Fliver to a Lincoln Zephyr. It was a rank-conscious army and I guess it is still so now.

Time in grade made me a pfc but the unit had to promote me to corporal to be eligible for officer candidate school. I had gone through basic and advanced training like so many other college graduates who were drafted before Pearl Harbor. We thought it was one year and back home.

The Marshall plan was for the Army to train officers within its own ranks instead of giving direct commissions, as the Navy and Air Force often did — even though privates had the same qualifications as friends who went up fast because of civilian education and occupational experience. But that is another story.

When I barely got through the 90-day boy wonder course because most lieutenants and captains, who were running the programs, deemed many people who were not of great soldierly appearance or attitude (read publication as PM newspaper and Nation magazine) did not suit their thinking. Besides the reserve officer who had worked for a long time for a commission actually resented the rapid advancement of civilians who had come into service for a variety of reasons.

Wearing the bars of a lieutenant was great but when one looked around there were so many of us the insignia was almost commonplace hardware. The double bars of a captain were the goal. Finally to first lieutenant overseas, while many of our OCS friends advanced much faster in new units formed at home training bases because of lack of officers and rapid expansion of the Army.

But, lo and behold, the promotion to captain came and one looked around to see the woods full of captains. The rank of major then appealed (many captains hated majors who often gave them orders willy-nilly and often didn't know what they were talking about or hadn't had the experience of a first-class lieutenant in combat). The rank game continued. But a majority came along and, gracious me, there were more majors around than ever dreamed about. As the years went on, the desire to change the color of the leaf from gold to white occurred. It all came, but there were lots of those also.

The rank of colonel loomed and there weren't too many of them. But with the end of the Korean War, colonels were in abundance. With stars in my eyes (although I dearly loved to wear the spread of a colonel's eagles on my collar or dress uniform) promotion to brigadier general came, as the years in the National Guard rolled by. But on the horizon appeared many other BGs, who likewise were weekend warriors in charge of large units. And besides the Air Force has always promoted faster (including movie actor, Jimmy Stewart, whose drill time was always in question). So many units called for BGs.

And about this time, and with the end of World War II, many states could appoint almost anyone with a little experience and rank to the rank of general as adjutant general or some other staff duty. For most civilians there was only one rank left and it did prove to be an exclusive society — the two-star rank of major general. There you looked around to find a friend. It was the ultimate, though at times a lonely rank, when you were avoided by some of your old friends and fellow officers.

Furthermore, with two-star rank the three- and four-star generals treated you with a great deal more respect. A few civilians reached three-star rank, but they were so few and far between they didn't rankle you.

As the years went on we encountered the Vietnam War, forced retirement, and proliferation of command jobs, plus career management (manglement we called it). In the computer age of specialties, four-star generals became as common as colonels in your early days in the Army.

The rank business was a funny thing in World War II. Many top promotions and the rank of many others came about primarily because the British kept promoting and outranking American leaders. The unification act only added to a diversity in rank and diffusion of command. And through it all, America promoted its officers because Congress would not give adequate compensation to military leaders equal to civilian pay. Many did get more money from civilian pursuits than in the military — although not as many fringe benefits.

Regardless of the adage that rank has its privileges please accept the author's, thoughts, comments and complaints about World War II in "Dear Ike,".

W.C.P.

CREDITS

My thanks to the many people who helped in the writing and publication of this book. The list is endless but I will attempt to cite the people who endured the most in my labors. When people asked me how long I had been writing the book I got used to saying 40 years or almost half of my lifetime.

Robert H. Ferrell, distinguished history professor at Indiana University. Without his help, inspiration, guidance, criticism and editing, this book would not have been produced.

My wife, Barbara Caniff Howden Phillippi, who helped to edit and correct the copy. She was invaluable in making sure a nonmilitary person could understand the letters.

Brig. Gen. John S. D. Eisenhower, who wrote answers to my many inquiries about his father and provided material for the book.

Gen. Mark Clark, who consented to many interviews and wrote long letters offering his position on my battle areas and wartime problems.

Clark's second wife, Mary, a dear friend over the years, gave me permission at the general's funeral to reveal any information Mark had shared with me in private conversations. He had many "gut feelings" about the war which he preferred not to express during his lifetime.

B. Clayton Jr., author, and his wife Marjorie, for their inspiration and patience.

Other members of my family: The late Georgiana Pittman Phillippi, my wartime bride, who tolerated 22 years of active and reserve military duty. Son Frank Phillippi who suggested changes, and daughter, Ann Perry, for her help.

Martin Blumenson, author.

Colleagues at *The Indianapolis News* over the years: Eugene S. Pulliam, publisher, the late Louis C. Hiner Jr., Washington Correspondent; the late Herbert P. Kenney Jr., book editor, Wayne Fuson, Wendell Trogdon, Bill Pittman, Bill (Moose) Roberts, who said to write and "tell it like it was," Tom Johnson, Jim Johnson, and my secretaries, Corinne Baker, Monty Green, Ruth McIntire, Pat Purcell, Patty Espich.

Lloyd Shearer, editor, *Parade Magazine*.

Dr. Ottis N. Olvey.

John M. Hollingsworth, cartographer, Indiana University.
Carol Roberts Howden, Ike cover page sketch.
Robert Doeppers, photographer.
Dwight D. Eisenhower Library and former director John E. Wickman, and present director, Daniel D. Holt.
Ann Whitman, secretary to Eisenhower in the White House years.
David A. Holt, librarian, Patton Museum, Ft. Knox, Ky.
Col. Richard L. Gruenther, Ret., and the Association of Graduates, United States Military Academy.
Col. Ernest Lee, Eisenhower's Army aide in World War II, who shared his thoughts and ideas for an Ike book many years ago.
Wes Gallagher and Hal Buell, The Associated Press.
United Press International
Librarians at *The Indianapolis News:* Sandy Fitzgerald, Cathy Hess, also a former secretary, and Charlesetta Means.
Librarians at Hussey-Mayfield Library (Zionsville) Helen Mills, Lou Ramsey.
Helen Steinmetz, former Brown County librarian.
Brig. Gen. Theodore H. Andrews, wartime commander.
Maj. Gen. Joseph (Bud) Harper.
Maj. Gen. Alfred Ahner.
Maj. Gen. Howard Wilcox.
Maj. Gen. Robert Moorhead.
Sandy and Cyril O'Driscoll, Cork County Ireland.
Dermot Russell, Cork Examiner.
Robert Haiman, Poynter Institute.
Robert Donovan, author.
Joe Herrington, New York Times.
Professor Ralph Holsinger, Indiana University.
Hal Woodard, lawyer.
Michal Howden, teacher, author, consultant.
William Bauer, author.
Vona Lauman, Willi Townsend, Bert Carter, Graphics LTD.
The Bar Bumpers at the Columbia Club, with whom I refought many military battles at lunch and the bar over the years. Those would include Tom Moses, David Cleveland, Clay Collier, Al Zimmermann, William Chambers, Jack Otto, David Brewer, Robert Shumaker, Bill Cohrs, Allen Sharp, Frank Bonavito and the rest of the gang.

Bibliography

Alfoldi, Lazzio M. *The Hutier Legend*, Parameters, Vol. 5, 1975.

Allen, Robert S. *Lucky Forward*. New York. The Vanguard Press and MacFadden-Bartell. 1947 and 1965.

Ambrose, Stephen E. *Eisenhower* (Soldier, General of the Army, President-elect 1952). New York, Simon and Schuster, 1983.

— *The President*. New York. Simon and Schuster, 1984.

— *The Supreme Commander*. New York. Doubleday & Co. 1970.

Army Almanac, Stackpole. Harrisburg, Pa. 1959.

Atlas, *The Magazine Of The World Press*. New York. Aspen Publishing Co. May 1966.

Bauer, William B. *Operation Torch:* The Allied Gamble to Invade North Africa. New York. St. Martin's Press, 1986.

Bishop, Jim. *FDR's Last Year*. New York. William Morrow & Co. 1974.

Blake, I. George. *Paul V. McNutt*. Indianapolis, Central Publishing Co., 1966.

Blumenson, Martin. *The Patton Papers* 1940-1945. Boston. Houghton Mifflin Co. 1974.

Mark Clark. New York. Congdon & Weed, Inc. 1984

— *St. Lo:* Battle of the Hedgerows, chapter in History of the Second World War. Hicksville, New York. 1966.

— *Masters of the Art of Command*. with James L. Stokesbury. Boston. Houghton Mifflin Co. 1975.

— *Bloody River*, Boston. Houghton Mifflin Company, 1970.

Bradley, Omar N. *A. Soldier's Story*. New York. Henry Holt and Co., 1951.

— *A General's Life* (with Clay Blair) New York. Simon and Schuster. 1983.

Butcher, Capt. Harry C. USNR. *My Three Years With Eisenhower*. New York. Simon and Schuster. 1946.

Burns, James MacGregor. *Roosevelt*. New York. Harcourt Brace Jovanovich, 1970.

Churchill, Winston S. *Memoirs of the Second World War*. Boston. Houghton Mifflin Company. 1959.

Clark, Mark. *Calculated Risk*. New York. Harper & Brothers, 1950.

— *From the Danube to the Yalu*, New York. Harper, 1954.

Collins, J. Lawton. *Lightning Joe*. Baton Rouge. Louisiana State University Press. 1979.

Colville, John. *The Fringes of Power* (10 Downing Street Diaries 1939-55). W. W. Norton & Company. New York, London, 1985.

Davidson, Eugene. *The Trial of the Germans*. New York. Collier Books, 1966.

Davis, Burke. *The Billy Mitchell Affair*. New York. Random House, 1967.

Douglas-Home, Charles. *Rommel*. New York. Saturday Review Press, 1973.

Eisenhower, David. *Eisenhower: At War (1943-45)*. New York. Random House, 1986.

Eisenhower, Dwight D. *Crusade in Europe*. Garden City, New York. Doubleday & Co., Inc. 1948.

— *At Ease* (Stories I tell to Friends). Garden City, New York. Doubleday, 1967.

Eisenhower, John S. D. *The Bitter Woods*. New York. G. P. Putnam's Sons. 1969.

— *Strictly Personal*. Garden City, New York. Doubleday, 1974.

— *Letters to Mamie by Dwight D. Eisenhower*. Garden City, New York. 1978

Esposito, Col. Vincent J. *The West Point Atlas of American Wars*. Vol. II, Frederick A. Praeger. New York. 1959.

Essame, H. *The Battle For Germany*. New York. Bonanza Books. 1969.

Ewald, William Bragg, Jr. *Eisenhower The President*. Englewood Cliffs, New York. 1981.

Farago, Ladislas. *Patton: Ordeal and Triumph*. New York. Dell Publishing Co., 1970.

Ferrell, Robert H. *The Eisenhower Diaries*. New York, London, W. W. Norton & Co. 1981.

Frye, William. *Marshall Citizen Soldier*. Indianapolis, New York. Bobbs Merrill Co. 1947.

Gavin, James M. *On To Berlin*. New York. The Viking Press, 1978.

Hapgood, David. David Richardson. *Monte Cassino*, New York. Congdon & Weed, Inc. 1984.

Harmon, Ernest. *Combat Commander*. Englewood Cliffs, New Jersey. Prentice-Hall, Inc. 1970.

Hastings, Max. *Overlord*. New York. Simon and Schuster. 1984.

History of the Second World War. Printed in USA. BPC Publishing Ltd. 1966.

Howitzer Year Books, The West Point Military Academy.

Illustrated Encyclopedia of Military Vehicles. Englewood Cliffs, New Jersey. Prentice-Hall, Inc. 1980.

Hyde, H. Montgomery. *Stalin*. Farrar, Straus and Giroux. 1972.

Irving, David. *The War Between the Generals*. New York. Congdon & Weed, Inc. 1981.

James, D. Clayton. *The Years of MacArthur*, 1941-45. Boston. Houghton Mifflin Co., 1975.
Ledwidge, Bernard. *De Gaulle,* New York. St. Martin's Press, 1982.
Lewin, Ronald. *Rommel.* New York. Ballantine Books, 1970.
Lockhart, Vincent M. *T-Patch to Victory.* Canyon, Texas. Staked Plains Press. 1981.
Lyon, Peter. *Eisenhower.* Portrait of the Hero. Boston-Toronto. Little, Grown and Company. 1974.
MacDonald, Charles B. *The Last Offensive.* Washington, United States Army. 1973.
Manchester, William. *The Last Lion.* Winston Spencer Churchill 198. 1874-1932. Boston. Little, Brown and Company. 1983.
— *American Caesar,* Douglas MacArthur. 1880-1964. Boston. Little Brown and Company. 1978.
— *Goodbye, Darkness.* Boston. Little, Brown and Co. 1979-80.
Marshall, George C. The Winning of the War in Europe and the Pacific. Biennial report of the Chief of Staff, U.S. Army, July 1, 1943-45. Published for the War Department in cooperation with the Council on Books in Wartime by Simon and Schuster.
The Merck Manual. Rahway, N. J. Merck Sharp & Dohme Research Laboratories. 1982.
Miller, Merle. *Plain Speaking* (an oral biography of Harry S. Truman). Berkley Publishing Corp. New York. 1973-4.
Montgomery, Bernard Law. *Memoirs.* New York. World Publishing Co. 1958.
Moorehead, Alan. *Eclipse.* Hamilton Ltd. London. 1945.
Morgan, Ted. *FDR.* Simon and Schuster. New York. 1985.
Morison, Samuel Eliot. *Sicily-Salerno-Anzio.* Vol. IX History of The U.S. Naval Operations in World War II. Little, Brown and Company. Boston. 1954.
Moseley, Leonard. *Marshall Hero of Our Times.* New York. Hearst Books. 1982.
New York Times. *Churchill.* New York. Bantam Book. 1965.
Nicolson, Nigel. *Alex* The Life of Field Marshal Earl Alexander of Tunis. New York. Atheneum. 1973.
Patton, George S., Jr. *War As I Knew It.* Boston. Houghton Mifflin Company. 1947.
Petillo, Carol Morris. *Douglas MacArthur,* The Philippine Years. Indiana University Press, Bloomington, 1981.
Pogue, Forrest C. *George C. Marshall: Ordeal and Hope.* 1939-42. New York. Viking Press. 1966.

— *George C. Marshall: Organizer of Victory, 1943-45*. New York. Viking Press. 1973.

— *The Supreme Commander.* Washington: U.S. Department of the Army. 1954.

Ryan, Cornelius. *A Bridge Too Far.* New York. Simon and Schuster. 1974.

Summersby, Kay. *Eisenhower Was My Boss*. New York. Prentice-Hall, Inc. 1948.

— *Past Forgetting:* My Love Affair with Dwight D. Eisenhower. (under name Kay Summersby Morgan) New York. Simon and Schuster. 1976.

Truscott, Lucian K. *Command Missons*. New York. E. P. Dutton and Co. 1954.

Tuchman, Barbara W. *Stilwell and the American Experience in China*. 1911-45. New York. The MacMillan Co. 1970.

Walker, Fred L. *From Texas to Rome*. Taylor Publishing Co. Dallas. 1969.

Webster's American Military Biographies. Springfield, Mass. G & C. Merriam Company. 1978.

Weigley, Russell F. *Eisenhower's Lieutenants*. Bloomington. Indiana University Press. 1981.

— *The American Way of War*. New York. MacMillan Publishing Co., Inc. 1973.

Winterbotham, F. W. *The Ultra Secret*. New York. Harper & Row. 1974.

Young, Desmond. *Rommel, The Desert Fox*. New York. Harper & Bros. 1950.

Young, Peter. *World War II Almanac*, New York. Bison Books. 1981.

Ziegler, Philip. *Mountbatten*. New York. Alfred A. Knopf. 1985.

INDEX

A

Aachen 95,193,194,198
Africa Korps 35,37,90,106,160
Alexander, Harold 27,94,97
    104,106,107,128,138,139,145,147,148
    and Eisenhower 153-61
    Con't 177,184,190,191,201
Andrews, Theodore 184
Anders, Wladyslaw 58
Anzio 61,90,91
    97-99,106,108,155,175-178,181
    185-187,191,205,210,212
Ardennes 19,30,36
    67,109,149,169,194,195,206
Arnhem 29,92,105
    108,135,139,144,149
Arnold, Richard 49,189

B

Bastogne 20,30,31
    149,196,198
Blumenson, Martin 32,47,183,186
Bradley, Omar 7,8,14
    20,26-28,33,35,39,43
    44,76,79,80,91,92
    94,104,106,107,109,123
    and Eisenhower 125-136
Bradley (con't) 137-140,143
    148-150,153,154,156,160
    164,165,175,176,179,186
    191,194,196-198,202,204
Brooke, Alan 14,43,74
    94,103,110

C

Caen 28,127,133
    139,141,143
Calais 19,28,36,108,143
Casablanca 26,60,147,174
Cassino 58,61,90
    91,97,98,106,157
    177,180,181

Chennault, Claire 9,66
Churchill, Winston 2,6,9
    14,29,43,57-60,65,67,74
    and Eisenhower 83-111
    Con't 133,139,140,149
    156,159,161,174,175,178
    181,188,202,204,217,218
Clark Field 68,115,120
Clark, Mark 7,8,21
    27-29,31,47,51,67
    76,77,84,90,91,97
    104,106,107,114,118
    120,128,133,139,142
    147,148,154,156-158,161
    and Eisenhower 173-192
    Con't 201,202,205
    206,209,210-212
Clay, Lucius 46,55,124
Collins, J. Lawton 7,31,43
    91,143,186,197
Corregidor 114,115

D

Dahlquist, John 188,211,215,216
Dakar 9,88
Daniel, Margaret Truman 8,45
Darlan, Adm. Jean 60,88,159,174
Dawley, E.J. 4,76,154,159,184-186
DeGaulle, Charles 15,16,50
    57-63,68,73,88,103,174,202,206,214
Devers, Jacob 20,29,58
    104,125,133,150,158,179
    and Eisenhower 201-207
    Con't 214,215
Dewey, Thomas 71,81,117
Dieppe Raid 97,105
Dunkirk 60,154,190

E

Eichelberger, Robert 115

271

Eisenhower, Dwight D.
  and Marshall 1-17
  Patton 19-33
  Rommel 35-39
  Summersby 41-55
  DeGaulle 57-63
  FDR 65-74
  Truman 75-82
  Churchill 83-111
  MacArthur 113-124
  Bradley 125-136
  Montgomery 137-151
  Alexander 153-161
  Simpson 163-171
  Clark 173-192
  Hodges 193-199
  Devers 201-207
  Patch 209-219
Eisenhower, John 41,53,144,206
Eisenhower, Mamie 8,45,47
              50,52-54,78,110,124
Eisenhower, Milton 82
El Alamein 15,38,87
          137,141,142,147,153,157

F
Ferrell, Robert H 41
Fredendall, Lloyd ... 27,35,39,154,159
Free French 20,73,88,213

G
Garigilano River 97,98,177
Gavin, James 7,52,92
Goering, Hermann 215,218
Gordon, Jean 23,33,47

H
Harding, Warren G 5,46,78
Harmon, Ernest 7,35,53,91
Harper, Joseph 143
Hitler, Adolf 12,25,29
            32,35-37,58,59,63,65
            84-86,88-91,93,99
        102-104,108,125,127,134
        147,154,175,177,178,181
          196,202,203,214,218

Hodges, Courtney 19,28,29
         31,43,91,92,95,107,109
        126,128,130,148,150,164
              168,170,171
  and Eisenhower 193-199
Hoover, Herbert 5,114,120
Hopkins, Harry 5,67
Huertgen Forest 95,125,164
            168,193,194,198

J
Jenner, William 76,82
Juin, Alphonse 58,61,174,177

K
Kasserine Pass 12,13,19
         21,25,26,32,35,39,67
          106,128,132,154
      159,160,174,190,194,205
Kennedy, John F. 47,77,80
Kesselring 36,147
Keyes, Geoffrey 98,181,185,186
Kreuger, Walter 2,114,120,181

L
Leahy, William D. 60,67,70,88,89
Lear, Ben 181,183
Lee, Ernest 50,53,189,203
Lucas, John 184-186
Ludendorff Bridge ... 109,125,135,198

Mac-Mc
MacArthur, Douglas 2,4,8
            9,11,20,22,32,66
        68-71,76,77,79,80,103
  and Eisenhower 113-124
  Con't 126,132,135,179,180,191
              192,199,217
McAuliffe, Tony 143,196
McCarthy, Joseph 76,82
McNair, Lesley G. . 2,114,173,181,183

M
Marshall, George
  and Eisenhower 1-17

Con't 19,45,46,55
65-69,71,74,76,77
80-82,84,87,91,95
97,99,104-107,110
114,115,118,120,123,127
132,140,149,154,159,163,165,168
173,175-177,180,181,183
186,191,196,197,202,204
209,210,217
Metz 20,29,170
Middleton, Troy 7,26,91
126,134,196-198
Mitchell, Billy 119,122
Model, Walther 36,194
Montelimar 205,211-213
Montgomery, Bernard 13-15,19
26-31,38,43,76,90-92
94,95,105-109,120
126,128,130,133-135
and Eisenhower 137-151
Montgomery, Bernard, (con't) . 153-161
163,164,168-170,175,178,190,196
198,199,202,206,216,218
Mulberry Seaport 101,102
Mussollini, Benito 13,29,90

N

NATO 75,145
Normandy 12,14,36
38,39,65,70,95,99
107,108,111,115,125,126
128,132,133,135,138,139,141
148-150,157-160,163,164
168,173,178,179,194,197,201,204,214

O

Operation Torch 105,133

P

Patch, Alexander 20,29,63
133,150,205
and Eisenhower 209-219
Patton, George, ... 13
and Eisenhower 19-33

Con't 35,36,39,44,47,52,58
67,91,92,94,95,97
104,106,107,109,110,119
126-128,130-132,134,135,137-140
147-150,153-155,160,161
164,170,174,175,193,196-198
199,202,203,205,217
Pearl Harbor 3,11,66
68,87,114,115,120,160,174,186
Pershing, John J. 2,4,11
127,136,146,160,164,168
Pyle, Ernie 129,130,159,187,202

Q

Quezon 69,115,121

R

Rapido River 58,90,97
98,106,155,177,178,180
181,185-187,191
Remagen 95,109,125
135,150,164,195,199
Rhine River 58,61,63
68,92,95,99,109,125
130,133,141,150,161,164
169,170,179,193,195,198
202,203,205,206,214-216,218
Ridgway, Matt 92,122,144
149,164,179,191
Rommel, Erwin 3,26
and Eisenhower 35-39
Con't 108,132,138,147,153
Roosevelt, Eleanor 46,69,70
Roosevelt, Franklin D. 2,5,9
27,46,57-60
and Eisenhower 65-74
Con't 77,81,84
87,88,95,103,114,121
132,159,174,175,188
Ruhr 125,135,140,150,170,196
Ryan, Cornelius 28,105,165
Rutherfurd, Lucy Mercer . 46,69,70,78

S

Salerno 13,76,106
107,141,142,154,156,158
159,161,175,184-188

Sardinia 13,106,107
Seigfried Line 31,125
Simpson, William 31,43,91
　　　　　　　109,128,131,140,148,150
　and Eisenhower 163-171
　Con't 196,198,199
Smith, Walter Bedell 43,104,130
Stack, Robert C. 215
Stalin, Josef 16,58,59
　　　　　　　65,66,72,78,84,95,110,175
Stilwell, Joseph 9,10,66
Summersby, Gordon 42
Summersby, Kay 6,8,33
　and Eisenhower 41-55
　Con't 69,74,78,96
　　　　　　　110,118,124,128,130,148
　　　　　　　176,189,192,204,215,216

T

Taft, Robert 47,117
Telegraph Cottage 43
Tito 156,191
Truman, Harry 4,5,45,48,72
　and Eisenhower 75-82
　Con't 107,117,122,130
　　　　　　　132,135,179,180,188,191,192
Truscott, Lucian 35,104,133
　　　　　　　158,161,185,205,210-212,215-217

U

Ultra 96,175

V

Van Fleet, James 5,91,122
Von Arnim, Juergen 36,38

W

Walker, Fred L. 184-188,191
Walker, Walton 122
Waskow, Henry T. 187
West Point 4,42,113,193,197,204
Whitman, Ann 1

XYZ

Zhukov, Georgi K.I 16,45,72,140